HOME
MOUNTAIN

**This Large Print Book carries the
Seal of Approval of N.A.V.H.**

HOME MOUNTAIN

Jeanne Williams

Thorndike Press • Thorndike, Maine

LP

Library of Congress Cataloging in Publication Data:

Williams, Jeanne, 1930-
  Home mountain / Jeanne Williams.
    p. cm.
  ISBN 1-56054-167-9 (alk. paper : lg. print)
  1. Large type books. I. Title.
[PS3573.I44933H6   1991]   91-12284
813'.54—dc20   CIP

Thorndike Press Large Print edition published in 1991
by arrangement with St. Martin's Press, Inc.

Cover design by Michael Anderson.

The tree indicium is a trademark of Thorndike Press.

This book is printed on acid-free, high opacity paper.

For Sally and Spoff
Who love the Chiricahuas and have done
so much to protect them

I

Could there be water in a haunch of the crouching mountains that ringed this plain like massive beasts, slate gray, purple, and ash, the more distant a blue only a hint more solid than the sky? This immense, flat plain was eternity, Katie MacLeod thought, and it seemed eternity since they'd left the burned cabin and their parents' graves by the Nueces River in Texas. Pa had reckoned it about seven hundred miles to his dreamed-of watered canyons of Arizona Territory's Chiricahua Mountains. Katie, with her younger brother and sisters, had been traveling ten weeks, since the middle of March, making only about ten miles a day because of the cows, hobbling a horse each night to round up the grazing stock in the morning.

Now, without water, each expanse seemed to last forever: lava-strewn flats; brilliant short-stemmed golden poppies so velvet-leafed and lovely it seemed they couldn't grow in this harsh land; thickets of catclaw and mesquite, which at the end of May were achingly, softly green against bleached clumps of grasses high as Katie's waist, showing only a faint tinge of fresh growth.

Water. They had to find it soon. Katie's tongue, numb and swollen, hadn't been able to moisten her cracked lips since yesterday. Thank goodness that the baby, little Rose, had stopped crying. She'd had the last of the water from the kettles that morning, she and ten-year-old Jed. Melissa, just turned thirteen, croaked that she wasn't thirsty, and trudged now on the other side of the horses, walking, like Katie, in order to spare the horses their weight. Jed's tow head bobbed behind the cows he was urging along. Rosie traveled in a box cushioned and secured by their bedding. If there could just be water when she roused!

Katie stumbled as she glanced toward the water keg that had betrayed them yesterday, one of its iron bands jarring loose enough to let all the water seep out. In spite of the wide-brimmed sunbonnet that gave some protection from the sun, though it plastered her hair to her scalp and the back of her neck, her eyes burned from the glare and fine dust plowed up in small spurts by the horses and cattle who dragged their hoofs rather than lifting them. Only Shiloh, the blood bay yearling stallion, had any spring to his gait, though he'd given up his customary exuberant circling and stayed close to his mother, Jenny. In order to spare the horses as much as possible, Katie changed teams after the noon rest, letting the golden sorrels, Honeybunch and Babe, take turns pulling with Chili, a bright chestnut with a red mane and tail, and Jenny, who, like her colt, Shiloh, was a rich dark red.

Poor creatures! They had nothing to say about where they went or what happened to them. Katie silently promised them that, if they survived this journey, they'd always have the best grass and feed she could contrive.

Only where were those grassy canyons Pa had seen on his way back from California nearly thirty years ago? Where were the sparkling creeks shaded by giant sycamores and oaks that had kept him dreaming of moving out here to establish a ranch? The family had been almost ready to start the journey when the cabin caught fire. . . . Katie shut out that memory. It was yesterday morning when the horses and six pale brown spotted Guernsey cows had sucked up silty water from a dip in what, from Pa's rough map, must have been the Animas Playa, more sand and mud than water. From the map, Katie had counted on finding water in the San Simon River. It ran through Cochise County, formed just that January of 1881, the southeast corner of Arizona Territory, bounded by New Mexico Territory on the east and Old Mexico to the south. When, this morning, they'd reached a watercourse that she was sure had to be the river, it was dry sand in both directions.

Unable to believe it, she'd followed the parched bed both ways. Not a trace of water. The river was dry. Rather than follow it in the hope of finding at least a seep, she made the agonized decision to keep going west. Somewhere among those marching mountains was Fort Bowie, guarding Apache Pass, and farther on, Tombstone. The largest town in the Territory, it was the county seat and a mining center renowned as much for its wickedness as for its silver.

Across New Mexico, they'd stayed in sight of the Southern Pacific Railroad tracks. At both the dusty little towns of Deming and Lordsburg, they'd been warned to watch out for Apaches. The great Victorio and most of his men had been killed the autumn before down in Mexico, but his aged uncle, Nana, had in January raided the mining camp of Chloride, killed some travelers along the road to Silver City, and vanished again into Mexico. There was no telling when and where he'd strike again. Katie had watched for Indians all the way from El Paso, this news deepening her worries.

From Lordsburg, they struck southwesterly on a rutted way ground by freighters and by the first ranchers daring to move into the region since the Chiricahua Apaches had been forced onto a reservation several years ago. The Chiricahuas were, like Nana's Mimbres or Warm Springs band, another of the various groups of Apaches. No settler knew when a raiding party might break away, killing and running off horses and cattle on an escape to Mexico. Katie hadn't seen Apaches, or anyone, since leaving Lordsburg, making for the Chiricahuas, the distant mountains Pa had remembered as paradise.

To Katie, they looked more like hell's lava boiled over and frozen. Despairingly, she studied the rents in the mountains. Which had water? What if none of them did? The animals and children might have the endurance to struggle up one canyon, but if they found no water — oh, she had been a fool, a wicked fool, to bring her brother and sisters out here to die!

Rosie made a plaintive mewling sound, not her usual lusty wail. All of a sudden, Katie's legs gave way. She collapsed rather than sat, and since she was guiding the team by Jenny's halter lines, they stopped, too. If it hadn't been for the children and the animals, Katie would have just stayed there — rested — gone to sleep. But Rosie's feeble protests reached through the haze, compelled Katie to think.

Pa once told of how, in the California desert, he'd opened a vein in his horse's neck and sipped blood, which kept him alive till he reached water. Katie was afraid of killing a horse or cow, though it might come to that, very soon. Dragging herself up, Katie took the baby, put her against her shoulder, and patted her sweaty little bare back.

Rosie's body felt dangerously light to Katie, as if her bones were filled with air. When they'd left the small hardscrabble Nueces ranch, Flossie had been giving milk, but she'd gone completely dry about a week ago. In Lordsburg, three days ago, they'd spent their last coins on beans, cornmeal, and, since there was no canned milk, a big jug of milk for the baby. Wrapped in a wet sheet, it had fed Rosie till yesterday evening when Jed drank the last souring drops.

That was when they discovered the leaking keg. All the water they had left was in the teakettle. Katie took a scant mouthful last night and one this morning, and Melissa drank only half a cup each time. About midmorning, Rosie got the last of the water in a thin cornmeal gruel. Now the sun dazzled giddily halfway to the western peaks, and Katie wondered fearfully how long a three-month-old could live without anything to drink.

Jed's eyes were sunken, and his face had a frightening pallor beneath its tan. Melissa, without a sound, curled up beneath the wagon, faded gingham dress so stained and torn that it was hard to guess it had once been blue. A thick yellow plait spilled from the sunbonnet that had been her pride because of the ruffles Mama had sewn around the brim. Ordinarily Mama had no time for such niceties, but in the last months she'd carried Rosie, she'd gotten so heavy on her feet that she'd had to leave most of the active tasks to Katie and Melissa while she sewed and mended. Katie's eyes were too dry for tears, but they stung, and her throat ached as she realized that these clothes they were wearing were the last Mary MacLeod would make for her children — the children Katie had brought to this terrible place.

The railroad stretched to the north, but Katie doubted if they could make it that far, and *if* they did, how long would it be before a train came along, and *if* it did, would someone see the MacLeods and stop? No, they simply had to move on, make for one of the canyons, and pray for water. She'd leave it to the cows and horses. They were supposed to be able to scent water a long way off.

"Melissa." Katie touched the hot, dry cheek. She spoke with difficulty, tongue a dry sponge. "Get in the wagon, honey, and hold the baby."

"I — I'll walk —"

Katie loved this brave little sister with her eyes, too weary to hug her. "M'liss, your weight won't matter now." The canyon the animals chose would have water, or it wouldn't. "Climb up and try to keep Rosie quiet."

After one blue glance that held all the questions and fears they both were feeling, Melissa clambered onto the bedding and cradled the baby, whose fine dark hair was just starting to curl. Rosie took after Pa's side of the family, with dark hair and eyes. Jed and Melissa favored Mama, and Katie didn't look like either one, with her green eyes and brown hair streaked with dull flame where the sun reached it. When he was in a good mood, Pa teased her about it being too bad she wasn't like a sorrel horse since they didn't fade in the sun.

Rosie, blessedly not crying, squirmed till her knees were beneath her and her head nestled on Melissa's shoulder. Melissa's eyes were already shut. They reminded Katie irresistibly of that song, "Poor Babes in the Wood," which had always brought her to tears in spite of its being so lugubrious. On the whole, she thought starving in the woods might be easier than dying of thirst. When she could think at all.

Was there anything she could discard to lighten the load? They'd started that morning, as always, as soon as it was light enough to see, and she had left behind the big iron kettle used to boil clothes, make soap, and render lard; the table; and a bench. Now, from the back, she wrestled out her mother's carved oak rocking chair and hesitated, panting, leaning on the wagon as she considered the plow, the churn, the saddle, Pa's shotgun, and the small harp, wrapped in blankets to protect it from heat and dust.

With shovel, mattock, and hoe, she could scratch up enough earth to plant corn and a garden. The share and handles stuck on everything, but she finally worked the heavy implement to the edge and let it drop. She buried her face against the saddle for a moment before letting it fall beside the plow. She wasn't sure that she had loved Pa, but he was the only one they'd had, and apart from its usefulness, the saddle should have been Jed's.

The harp, though, brought over from South Uist, one of the Hebrides, by her mother's mother, when the landlords had cleared their people from the Western Isles of Scotland to make room for sheep — the harp was too dear to leave behind.

Dragging herself to the horses, Katie encouraged them with pats and rasping endearments. The reins were looped back and fastened to the wagon seat. The horses were gentle and too tired to bolt. Katie took Jenny's halter line, and the weary team responded, tugging the wagon into motion. Jenny was named for her grandmother, the famous Denton mare raced by the notorious Texas outlaw Sam Bass, who turned to robbing trains and stagecoaches, was shot from ambush, and had a song made about him. All the mares had Steel Dust blood and all would foal that summer — if they, and the tiny colts growing inside them, lived.

"I'll keep the best colts," Pa had said in one of the scarce moments he let his family glimpse his dreams. A dour man, Pa, with lips pressed together in a tight crease and the lines of his face hardened into a disappointed, suspicious look that relaxed only when he thought of what he'd do in Arizona. "That's brand new country for ranchers, and they'll need good cow horses. I'm goin' to breed the kind that can work cows, pull loads, and plow six days a week and race on the seventh. Some grin at a quarter horse's big jaws and hindquarters, but they start like a jackrabbit, they're strong, and they're biddable."

That last counted with Pa; certainly none of his children dared talk back to him, nor Mama, so far as Katie could remember. She couldn't recall her folks saying anything to each other except about the most practical,

16

everyday matters. Mama must have gotten terribly lonesome, Katie thought, far from any neighbors in that little cabin on the Nueces River of West Texas. At least Mary MacLeod had her harp, and no matter how hard-worked she was that day, she'd usually played a little while with her children around her after Pa had gone to bed — on the front stoop when it was warm enough, in front of the fireplace during winter. She'd turned Gaelic songs into English and could pick out the tune of any air she heard.

That sweet, true voice in the gloaming . . . Katie's shoulders heaved with a dry sob. Oh, she needed Mama and she always would, and how could she raise the children, even if they lived through this?

As she plodded on, her mind felt as if it were unraveling, as if she could keep it with her body only by keeping hold of Jenny's halter and concentrating on something other than this extremity. She pondered her parents, as she had ever since she started growing out of childhood when parents simply *were* and you speculated about them no more than about earth beneath your feet or sky overhead.

Why had a girl almost her own age, and surely very pretty — for Mama had been that, even worn from hard labor in and out of childbed — why had she, arriving at Hays, Kansas, on one of the first trains, married a man old enough to be her father, a freighter hauling provisions down to Camp Supply in Indian Territory, especially when Mary had kept working, washing and cooking for the railroad hands? "I put in every bit as much as your Pa toward buying our cows and horses," Mama had said. "He owns stock in some mining companies but he'll never part with them." It was the stock certificates Pa had run back into the blazing cabin to rescue, those and some hoarded greenback money hidden in a carved-out chink in the logs behind the bed. The fire had caught while he was off getting the wagon wheels repaired for the journey. He drove up like a madman and ran into the inferno. Mary, if she'd even thought of them, hadn't known where the stocks and money were, though she and the children had managed to get out most of their possessions. Katie had helped her mother drag James Mac-Leod outside, but he'd died of his burns next day while his wife writhed with a baby coming too early.

Whatever the reason they had joined their lives, they had ended them together and were buried beneath a live oak on a high bank overlooking the river. Pa had already been getting ready to leave for Arizona, so Katie went ahead. They had no relations close enough to matter and lived a day's ride from any neighbor. No one would even know they were gone till some rider chanced by, saw the charred ruins and two graves, and wondered what had happened to the young 'uns, but more especially where those Steel Dust horses had gone and those fine Guernsey cows.

When they crossed the Pecos, Katie had spelled out the words scratched on a piece of board fastened to a cottonwood tree: LOOK OUT, YOU SINNERS, YOU ARE HEADED FOR HELL! She had laughed at it then, but —

She blinked. Had that memory conjured up the sign she must have been staring at without really seeing? No, it was real, and so was the tent beside it and the big, broad man spraddled in such shade as there was, a rifle on his lap. It didn't take Katie long to spell out this sign, fastened to a barbed-wire fence surrounding a well and a trough hollowed out of a giant cottonwood that must have been hauled from some canyon.

WATER — TWO BITS A HEAD

The track merged here with a wider, deeper one that cut from the eastern rim of the mountains toward where Fort Bowie must be. Far off in that direction, a spread-out wagon train crept west.

Katie almost fainted with relief. They hadn't seen a human being since turning off at Lordsburg, so even this man, whose red face barely showed through bushy gray whiskers, was a welcome sight. She couldn't quite believe the sign. A nickel a head was the most she'd seen charged at any private well, but it didn't matter. She'd spent their last coins in Lordsburg. The man could see the animals had to drink. He couldn't refuse them.

Scenting water, the cows jostled forward. The horses raised their drooping heads and broke into a trot. The man pushed up from the crate he sat on and shut a long wire gate, blocking the way and pointing his Winchester at Flossie, the lead cow.

"Eleven head of stock," the whiskery man said, grudgingly, as if he'd like to charge for his words, too. "Two-seventy-five for them." He peered past Katie into the wagon. "Four of you, less'n you got someone hid in the beddin'. Three-seventy-five all told."

Sound caught in Katie's windpipe, abraded her throat. "We — don't have — money."

"Or any sense, neither! What's a passel of kids doin' out here?" He spat tobacco viciously. "Reckon I have to give you snotnoses a drink, but that stock don't water unless you got jewelry or somethin' like that to pay. They can't be too bad off. You must have watered 'em at the river."

"The river was dry."

"Dry? You must be lyin', gal, or out of your head. The San Simon gets mighty low this time of year before the rains. Runs underground for a spell sometimes. But it's never plumb dry till you get on the far side of the cienega."

"It is now. Like powder."

He shrugged. "Don't signify."

Mama's plain wedding band was buried with her, and that was the only jewelry the MacLeods had ever had. Desperately, Katie said, "Keep one of the cows."

"What do I want with a cow?" For the first time, the man studied the horses. "But these nags look like they might do to ride. Leave me the golden sorrels, and you can water the rest and be on your way."

Two Steel Dust horses for water that if he'd had any decency he'd have given away? That water meant life, but outrage gave Katie strength as well as a reckless notion she didn't even try to weigh. She just knew she wasn't turning over those mares, not while she breathed, but the horses, cows, and children were going to have their drink.

"Mister," she said, wishing her voice weren't so choked and raspy, "my pa had a real good double-barreled shotgun, almost new. Let us drink and you can have it."

It was a trade she'd have gone through with, had she thought of it before he tried to take the horses; now she meant to give it to him in quite another way if he made it necessary.

"Guess I'll have a look."

Leaning the Winchester against the gate, he slouched toward the wagon. Katie went around to the back and lifted the weapon out from under the bedding. It was loaded; had they been jumped by Indians or robbers, there might not have been time to shove in the cartridges.

The man had followed so close that Katie sickened at his reek of sweat, whiskey, filth, and tobacco. Summoning all her courage, she faced about, planting the double barrel in the belly pouching over greasy striped pants.

His jaw dropped. Tobacco juice spilled down his chin. "Whoa now, sis!" he began, pupils of his mud-colored eyes constricting. "You shorely cain't —"

"Move and you're dead."

Sweat beaded in the thickety eyebrows, ran down the edges. "Now, sis!"

"Hush!" She had acted in rage and desperation, but she didn't want to kill him. Unless she did, or wounded him, how could she get the children and animals safely away?

One thing at a time. It was terrifying to

think that a squeeze of her finger could end this man's life, but the thought also filled her with power, all the more intoxicating after being so utterly helpless. "Melissa!" she called, never taking her eyes off the corpulent water-hog. "Open the gate, honey, and let the cows in to drink. Unhitch the horses, but don't let them founder. Jed! Draw up a pail of water. You drink, and M'liss, give Rosie some, and then bring me a cup."

How she was going to drink without giving the man a split second's opening, she couldn't guess. She just knew she could die blissfully if her mouth and throat were wet. Rosie was whimpering, but soon she could drink.

"Sis," wheedled the florid man. "I was just funnin' you. S'posin' you ease down that gun and have a cup of coffee, friendly-like. Reckon I've even got some canned milk if'n you need some for that babe."

"Was I fillin' your moccasins, lady," came a voice from beyond the wagon, "I'd perforate old Missou and plumb help myself! Two bits a head for water! Missou, you mangy devil, it's a marvel some of those bull-whackers haven't snugged you up in that bobwire and left you to feed any buzzard that'd stomach you."

"Don't listen to Lord Bill, sis," whined the entrepreneur. "He's an outlaw, and so'll you be if'n you heed him."

"Oh, I have a little trouble readin' brands now and then," said the newcomer sunnily. "But I'd never sink so low as to charge any livin' thing for the water God put in the desert." He had reined his big gray gelding to where Katie could see him and drew a Colt .44 from one of the twin gunbelts that crossed his slim waist. Wavy black hair showed beneath a dove-gray Stetson, and his dusty black boots were fancily stitched. He looked the way most cowboys wanted to but didn't. Katie thought he wasn't a cowboy, quite.

Blue-gray eyes, brilliant in his sun-browned face, studied her, laughing at first, then puzzled. "I guess you're not a growed-up lady," he said with some regret. "But you must be a right pretty kid, when you're not so frazzled. Get your drink, little honey, and see to those young 'uns and critters. I'll keep an eye on old Missou. He's more whiskers than anything, but he bears watching."

She trusted him as she did the light. Too near collapse to argue that she wasn't a kid, that plenty of sixteen-year-olds were married and mothers, she hurried to help lead the horses inside, and closed her eyes as she filled her mouth with water from the dipper Jed held out.

Cooling, wet, wonderful, though her cracked

lips stung. It felt as if the sips were instantly absorbed by her tongue and the membranes of her mouth, but a little trickled down her throat like cool, sparkling liquid crystal. Melissa had taken her cup to the wagon and drank while spooning water into Rosie's mouth. Katie wanted to go on drinking but knew they'd get sick if they drank too much, too fast.

Cautioning Jed and Melissa to wait a while for their next swallows, she mixed gruel thin enough to go through the rubber nipple of a nursing bottle. They had several of these because Mama's breasts had caked when Jed was little, and he'd been raised on a bottle. Holding the baby while she sucked thirstily, Katie watched the tall stranger from the corner of her eye.

How had he gotten a name like Lord Bill? He'd picked up the Winchester, pulled a .44 out of Missou's belt, and now he thrust these deep into the wagon under the spade, ax, and other gear.

"Missou's sorry he was so inhospitable," Lord Bill grinned, strolling over to the wagon but keeping his gun pointed in Missou's general direction. "He laid in a big stock at Willcox last week, and he sure hopes you'll accept some of Mr. Borden's canned cow and some canned peaches." His gaze went over the horses and cows, lingered on Jed and Melissa, who were drinking again, blissfully but with admirable restraint. Smile fading, his eyes held Katie's. "What in the world are you doing out here, kid, and why didn't you fill your water containers at the San Simon?"

"It was dry."

"Dry?" He was as incredulous as Missou. "Sure about that?"

"Don't we look it, mister?"

Frowning, he said, "Guess I'll have to have a look after we get you set to rights. I'm still waiting to know what you young 'uns are doing out here."

She'd cry if she really tried to explain. "Our folks died while we were fixing to start west. Pa remembered these mountains and wanted to take up land. So that's what we're going to do."

"Just you kids??"

Over Rosie's sweat-damp ringlets, Katie looked at him defiantly. "We don't have anybody but us. And I'm the age my mother was when I was born."

"More's the pity." His tone roughened. "Nothin' wears a woman to an early grave than marryin' young and havin' a kid a year till her teeth and bones are ruined. If you've got any sense — which I kind of doubt or you wouldn't be out here like this — you

26

won't figger ropin' a husband is the way to get help with close herding these young 'uns. You'd just wind up with more kids and more work."

"It's not your lookout, mister, what happens to me." Katie tried to sound cold and haughty, though she was mad to the bone. "I have to thank you for helping us out, but we can manage fine now if you'll just tell us where's the nearest canyon with good water."

He gave a slow, soft whistle, sent her a searching glance, and threw back his head and laughed. "I'd forgot heifers grow their horns early in Texas."

"Don't you be calling me a heifer!"

"Ma'am — lady, miss, I sure meant no offense." Lord Bill looked humble, but the edges of his long, straight mouth twitched. "What do you want me to call you?"

"I'm Katie MacLeod. Melissa's over there with Jed, and our baby's name is Rosie."

He swept off his hat and bowed with an elaborate gravity that made her yearn to kick him. "Honored to make your acquaintance, Miss Kate. I'm Bill Radnor."

"Missou called you Lord Bill."

"That's because folks are always saying to me, 'Lord, Bill!' " he said with a twinkle so that she couldn't tell if he joked or not. "Here, Missou, give me one of those Borden cans."

27

Missou had come out of his tent with an armload of tinned peaches and milk. Bill Radnor used his pocket knife to punch holes in the top. "Try this on the baby. Not a yearlin' yet, is he?"

"*She* is three months old." Katie mixed milk into the thin gruel, and Rosie enthusiastically approved, cheeks dimpling as she tugged harder. "Now, sir, if you know the country, would you suggest a place we could settle?"

Radnor frowned and sighed. "Best thing, since you've come too far to go back, is push on to Willcox. They've got a big old adobe church Colonel Hooker built for 'em to hold meetings of all brands of religions, and I hear they're startin' a school. It's a freightin' center for supplies bound for Tombstone, the forts, and the reservation at San Carlos, but there's women and kids and you could likely get work at a store or hotel."

"That's not why we came seven hundred miles! Can't you see those are good horses? The blood bay mare is a granddaughter of Sam Bass's Denton mare. They all descend from Steel Dust and are bred to a Steel Dust stallion. And those are milk cows. When they come fresh, we'll have milk and butter to sell. We're going to have a ranch!"

"Those horses are going to draw thieves, red, white, and polka dot."

"There were thieves in Texas, too, and no law close enough to matter."

"Who's going to do the man's work on this ranch of yours?"

"We'll manage. I helped Pa with all the outside work. Melissa's strong and Jed's growing."

"And I reckon," he said sarcastically, "that this infant can look after herself till she's old enough to herd cows and break horses."

"That's none of your concern, Mister Radnor. If you won't tell us which canyon to head for, we'll just make for that one where some hills trail out on the flats."

"If you're bound and determined —" His gaze fixed beyond her, and Katie looked to see the swaddlings had fallen from the harp. "Can you play that?"

"Of course, but —"

"That deals us a whole new hand." He pointed at a broad opening, almost a valley, running between smaller mountains toward a long irregular stretch of them. "Turkey Creek's yonder and the grass is good. Mining camp called Galeyville tucked away in there on a hill. Couple hundred people live there steady, and must be another hundred comes and goes. You could sell your dairy stuff there."

"I don't want to live in a mining camp."

"Won't have to. Spread out in the grasslands two–three miles away. But if you'll make some music in the camp for a couple of days, you can get your corral built, and your cabin, too."

"How?"

He took off his hat, and the wind tousled his thick hair that glinted black as a raven's wing. "Well, Miss Kate, miners mine ten hours a day six days a week and don't hanker for more work when they're off. The other men, ones like me who come and go when the fancy takes 'em, most took to cowboyin' to get away from a farm and diggin' postholes and such."

"And then they quit cowboyin' to get away from work," growled Missou, plopping down on the crate.

"Why, you old razorback!" said Radnor with no visible rancor. "At least none of us ever set up next to a waterhole and charged sufferin' brutes and humans for a drink. I heard you were up to this game, but reckoned it was too low even for a shorthorn run out of Galeyville for dealin' from a cold deck."

"It's not like I was the onliest one," grumbled Missou. "But this beats cards all hollow! Twenty-wagon outfits pay fifty dollars, and most days there's three to five of 'em."

"Is that the truth?" said Radnor, and before turning again to Katie, he studied Missou in a way that made the heavy-bellied man squirm. "You couldn't hire the boys to work for you, Miss Kate, but if you'll make them some music, they'll take care of whatever you need done — and lettin' them get to know you would be the best way to keep them from runnin' off with your Steel Dust horses." He flicked a practiced eye over the cows. "Needn't worry about those critters unless some Apaches bust loose and crave a big feed. Cattle that get stolen around here have to be able to travel fast and far."

"You ought to know," Missou grunted. He added righteously, "Galeyville's where them as is too wild for Tombstone hangs out, girl. Best skedaddle for Willcox."

In spite of her brave words and the fact that she was strong for her size, Katie knew that the kind of cabin, corral, and other structures she could raise with the children's help would be pretty makeshift. How wonderful it would be to have everything done all at once and built to last! Wistfully, she considered, but finally shook her head.

"Galeyville doesn't sound like a fit place for children."

"In the usual run of things, maybe not," Radnor conceded. "But there's a mighty nice lady runs a boardinghouse. You could stay with her. Besides, right now there's two preachers camped there, a Baptist and a Methodist, wagin' war for the strayed sheep, though I reckon there's more goats." His tone went softly coaxing, and she knew he'd be mightily hard to refuse if he set his mind on something. "What could you want more 'n two preachers for chaperones?"

"If they're already contesting for listeners, I shouldn't think they'd want me drawing away people."

"Oh, they're not feudin' for an audience, Miss Kate. Weekdays and Sundays, the Reverends Thomas and Daggett been combin' the brush and arroyos for prospects, and on Saturday — bar business is too good on Sunday to close up then — they hold forth in the biggest, best saloon in Galeyville. Thomas starts exhortin' around nine in the morning, and when he runs out of steam, the Reverend Daggett pitches in. It's mostly the same bunch sits there kind of humble — though maybe they're sleepin'. If you'd play in between the sermons, I bet you'd lure in a whole new batch of sinners. You could play Saturday, and I'd guess Babcock would close the bar an hour or two on Sunday. By then you'd ought to have your tree fellers, teamsters, cabin raisers, and post-hole diggers. We could use milled lumber from the sawmill across the mountain, but logs'll hold up longer and keep you warmer in winter and a sight cooler in summer."

"But how will I ask —"

"Leave it to me." Radnor chuckled. "And if it's your plow and kettle and furniture litterin' the trail, and that Texas saddle with the big ox-bow stirrups, I'll borrow a wagon and team and go back for it all tomorrow. Bride Malone'll be ticked to have you and the kids till your cabin's built."

"I don't have any money."

"Got a harp, don't you? Bride would let you stay for a song, but don't worry, I'll make it right with her."

"And how," blurted Katie, "am I going to make it right with you?" She stiffened with suspicion. After all, Missou had all but accused him of stealing livestock and Radnor hadn't denied it. "I'll give you a cow, Mister Radnor, but not a horse."

His eyes chilled like a norther bearing snow. "Don't recall asking. I'll fix that water keg of yours, fill it, and soon as your horses rest, we'll trail out of here. Goin' to be dark before we make Galeyville, but the moon'll help us in."

"What about my Winchester and .44?" yelped Missou, upsetting the crate in his hurry to rise.

"See that first little pointy hill? There's sort

33

of a cave washed out on its north side. We'll leave your play-toys there."

"But that must be nigh onto eight miles!"

"More like nine," Radnor agreed. "And you're going to have to hoof it on account of I'm unhobbling that spavined old broom-tail of yours and shooin' him off the premises."

"You're leavin' me out here afoot and without a weapon, Lord Bill? What if Apaches trot through here? Or a bunch of outlaws?"

"You old fraud, you're sweatin' over the poor emigrants you won't get to fleece. You're lucky I don't take that big pouch of gold cartwheels and 'dobe dollars you likely have in your bedroll, and scatter it 'mongst the poor."

"Lord, Bill! You won't do that!"

"Nope. Even a centipede needs a stake when he wiggles off to a new range."

Missou went red, then pale. "If you think I'm quittin' the easiest money I ever made —"

Taking a hammer and pounding the slipped band back in place on the water keg, Radnor shrugged. "Suit yourself, but when I get some leisure, I'm comin' back with some of the boys."

"You wouldn't run a man off his property!"

"Certain not. Won't touch a strand of your dadgummed bobwire, though I purely hate the stuff. But there's got to be more water around

34

here, and we'll just dig till we make another well."

Missou's eyes bulged, and the veins in his neck and forehead swelled. "Why, of all the sneakin', dirty, low-down tricks! You aims to cut the price to a dime — maybe a nickel!"

Radnor beamed. "It's goin' to be free, Missou. Free like God gave it. So after you collect your guns and horse, you might as well look for a new hand. This one's busted as a flush with four diamonds and one heart."

He reached the well in a few long, easy strides and opened a can of peaches for the children before he pulled up the bucket. Katie felt a pang of misgiving as Jed and Melissa watched him with worshipful eyes. What could come of a man like this being their hero? She should take his first advice and turn the wagon toward the town called Willcox, the one that sounded a lot more decent than any mining camp could be.

Where she'd be lucky to find some slaving work that would pay enough to feed and house herself and the children? Where there'd be no place to keep the cows and Steel Dust horses?

No. Katie took a deep breath and gazed toward the mountains. The MacLeods were going to have that ranch.

II

For a moment when she opened her eyes, Katie thought she was in the Texas cabin. But that had burned, and the wall she stared at now was made of rough boards. Yesterday rushed back in an overwhelming welter of images — the desperate thirst, Missou's hoarded water, and — a feeling of warmth glowed all through her — Bill Radnor.

As they splashed across Turkey Creek last night and the cows and horses drank deep, he'd ridden up the hill toward the yellow lights and considerable racket of the camp. Returning while the team labored up the hill, he said cheerily, "Couple of miners are moving in together so you can have a room. Bride's getting it ready. Your horses and cows'll be safe in Babcock's corral."

What a relief to have everything arranged! She would almost have given him a horse. Her cheeks burned as she remembered how cool he'd gotten when she'd accused him of expecting such a payment. He'd still been a little stiff when he carried a sleeping Jed into Mrs. Malone's last night after leaving the wagon in back. He'd brought up the harp and the sack that held clothes a little cleaner than what they had on. She had to get their things washed, along with the bedding, soiled from the journey. They all needed baths and their hair washed. Mrs. Malone was a long-boned, diamond-faced woman with kind dark eyes and black hair streaked at the temples with white. She brought a basin and kettle of hot water last night along with the first store soap they'd ever seen, white and good-smelling, not yellow and harsh like that Katie had helped Mary make with lye leached from wood ashes and carefully saved scraps of fat.

Even Jed shouldn't mind a good scrubbing with nice soap like that, Katie thought. Katie looked forward to the sheer bliss of getting clean, really clean, from hair to toenails. Last night, she'd just washed Jed's face, neck, and hands before letting him curl up on a pallet on the floor. Rosie got a sponge bath and clean diaper improvised by Mrs. Malone from a worn-out sheet torn into squares, tiding Rosie over till the accumulated diapers could be thoroughly scrubbed, rinsed, and sunned white. How much a person could do with water besides drink it! And how wonderful it was to know it was in that pitcher, and that there was plenty for everything — drinking, baths, animals, laundry — in that creek below the town!

Never again would she be far from water

if she could help it, Katie decided, and the land they settled on must absolutely be watered by a year-round stream. Rosie made a soft noise and snuggled closer to Katie's back.

Tucked between her older sisters on a spot protected by a towel-covered oilcloth, Rosie had slept soundly till now. Except for a touch of wind, she was apparently none the worse for their journey. The experimental stretches of her arms and legs began to grow emphatic.

Hastily, before a howl could wake Melissa, slumbering with her sunburned face nestled in the pillow, Katie changed the baby and then dressed quickly in her best and only other dress, black calico brightened with tiny colored flowers. Setting her teeth, she hastily yanked a comb through her hair a few times, and caught Rosie up as she opened her mouth in a hungry wail.

Guided by the aroma of coffee, Katie hurried downstairs to the kitchen where miners daubed up the last vestiges of molasses with their final pancakes, emptied their enamel cups, and departed, picking up lunch buckets from a shelf, each selecting his hat from the array of small-brimmed rounded felt ones hung on pegs. These hats were a wonderment to Katie, so stiff with what smelled like pine resin that they were veritable helmets.

The men ducked their heads politely as they

marched past Katie, some muttering a shy " 'Mornin', miss," while others grinned at Rosie, calling her variously a "bonnie lass," a "fine colleen," *"eines schönes Mädchen,"* and "a pretty little sweetheart." The dozen men wore baggy trousers or bib overalls stuffed into boots or ankle-high brogans, and heavy shirts over undershirts. Long-handled drawers, once white, showed through holes in several pairs of trousers. Most were bearded, and all had long moustaches except for two strapping fair-haired young men, obviously twins, with infectious grins and dancing blue eyes. Three short black-haired, green-eyed miners were built so much alike, with massive chests and arms sprouting ludicrously from spindly hips and legs, that she wondered if they, too, were brothers.

Rosie had been diverted by them as they clumped up the street fronted by more saloons than stores and one big dance hall, with per-haps a score of small adobes and shacks of metal or rough lumber scattered behind. But then the baby whimpered and began to suck at her fist.

"Don't fret, *macushla,* your milk's warm and ready." Bride moved with surprising grace for a large woman and had a strong, low-pitched, gentle voice. Her eyes lit with pleasure as she held out her arms, and Rosie

39

allowed herself to be taken and cuddled against a rather spare bosom. "Maybe she'll let me feed her while you have breakfast, dear," said Bride. "There's pancakes warm on the griddle and oatmeal in the kettle. Help yourself, do." She scrutinized Katie closely. "After you eat, why don't you sleep some more? You still look frazzled."

"Oh, Bride, there's so much I have to do! My hair's dirty and our clothes, and —"

Bride laughed, and that softened her austere face, made her look pretty and ten years younger. "Well, soon's you eat, you can set about getting all clean and righteous! Water's heating out back so you can do your washing, and now the lads are out of the way till evening — may the Lord preserve them in that dark hole — you can have your baths here in the kitchen and not have to lug buckets up the stairs."

After warming milk for Rosie, she settled in a chair with the baby while Katie poured molasses and milk over a bowl of oatmeal. "No need to roust out your brother and sister, Katie. Let them sleep and get on with what you need to do. I'll enjoy minding the baby. Never had one of my own." Radnor had said that Bride had lost her husband two years ago in a mine explosion in Tombstone, had supported herself there by washing and packing lunches, and had finally saved enough to set up her boardinghouse. She hadn't wanted to stay in Tombstone because she was constantly reminded of her husband, Michael.

Knowing this, that life hadn't been easy for this woman who still had a merry laugh and kind eyes, Katie said, "I can't thank you enough, Bride. Mr. Radnor must have told you we don't have any money, but I'll make it up to you. When the cows come fresh, I'll supply you with butter and milk."

"You will, at a proper price. Wheesht, Katie, what are we here for if not to help each other?" Before Katie could argue, Bride went on, "Besides, Lord Bill promised you'd give me a song. My grandfather was a notable harper in the old country, but sure he had to leave his harp behind and so I never heard him." She added wistfully, "You wouldn't know some songs in the Gaelic?"

"I would," laughed Katie, joyful at being able to do something to please this warm-hearted new friend. "But tell me, why do you call him Lord Bill? So did Missou but Mr. Radnor made a joke of it."

"He would," Bride nodded, "But he could have been a lord and had a big estate in England, too, had he been willing to go over there and live. Seems his daddy was what they call a younger son of some duke or earl or suchlike, but his elder brother died without children a few years back, leaving Bill next in line. He'd have no part of it, though, when the fancy lawyer who'd traveled over to explain it told him that he'd have to go over there and live on the estate in order to inherit — live there for always. Bill said he was his mother's son as much as his dad's, and the English family hadn't thought she was good enough for his dad to marry. Moreover, he was too used to going where he wanted when he wanted, to settle like a gravestone." She added pridefully, with perhaps a touch of wistfulness, "There's not enough gold in the world to hold Lord Bill where he doesn't care to be."

It was as romantic a story as Katie could have wished. Dreamily, she pictured Radnor as she had first seen him on his big gray horse, head thrown back, blue eyes dancing, darkened with that changeable gray undercast that made it hard to be sure about their color. Bride's sigh called her back to the moment.

"Gaelic was the tongue of my grandfather. I don't understand more than a bit, but to hear it makes me happy deep inside. Like holding this little one."

The baby, making soft, bubbly cooings, reached for a tendril of black hair escaped from pins that drew Bride's hair into a coiled mass at the back of her head. Katie, feeling as if part of an unbearable load had been eased from her shoulders, leaving her able to carry the rest, sipped her coffee. Rich with evaporated milk, it strengthened her, and when the last of it was gone, she went more eagerly to her washing than ever she had before. After weeks of washing in muddy creeks or scant pails of water, it was close to a delight to have tubs, a scrub board, a big copper boiler, and plenty of soap. There was, she decided with a wry chuckle, nothing like a really terrible journey to make a person appreciate what they took for granted.

Never, never again, would she waste a drop of water.

While sheets and other whites simmered in the big copper boiler supported on an iron grate over a fire in the backyard, Katie went to visit the horses and cows, pausing on the way to spell out the signs on the businesses lining the long single street nestled under big live oaks, facing the creek and flats beyond. Babcock's saloon and big corral sat alone on one side of the street. Katie's first glimpse that morning had been of what seemed a row of saloons, but now she counted to find there were only thirteen of them scattered amidst six general stores, one bearing a post office sign; four restaurants; a bakery; several butcher shops; a barber's, and a boot shop. *The Galeyville Bulletin* had to be a newspaper. The Cosmopolitan Hotel was little more than a sprawling shack, and none of the buildings, mostly erected from rough-milled unpainted lumber, provoked admiration, but to Katie it seemed an impressive town, and she hoped to have enough money before winter to shop in the stores, buy shoes for all of them, and perhaps even some dress material and — she put a tight rein on her dreaming. This winter, they'd do well to afford shoes for Jed and Melissa. But next year — well, with hard work and good luck, she could walk into those stores with the proud confidence that she had cash money to spend.

Babcock's corral was made of long upright slabs rived from logs and weathered silver-gray. Set close together, they were joined with wire, and there was a wire and post gate. Letting herself inside, Katie was sure the animals must think they'd died and gone to heaven. A water tank, fed from a stream, was shaded by big oak trees. Underneath the boughs, the animals were munching hay. The journey had made them gaunt, but by the time the cows calved in a few weeks, they should be fully recovered, able to feed their young, and, Katie hoped, produce enough extra milk to pay Bride.

There was also Bill Radnor to settle with. He must be paying the corral owner for letting the animals stay there, and the hay wouldn't be free. She'd give him one of the Steel Dust colts, maybe even the yearling, when the colt was old enough to ride, but that would be another year, and she didn't like being beholden to him that long. Of course, short of saving his life, there was no way she could repay him, but maybe she could sell enough butter and milk to at least return the cash money he'd spent on the MacLeods' account.

The horses had been curried and their manes and tails brushed. Had Radnor done that? She caressed them all, feeling guilty over the way their bones thrust against their hides, and rubbed each cow between the ears before returning to her task.

By noon, colored garments and Rosie's things and sheets, beautifully white, dried on what Bride called "manzanitas," bushes with tiny, faintly reddening berries surrounded by bright tough green leaves growing from burnished red-brown limbs. "Thank goodness, it has no thorns," said Bride. "The berries are mostly seed, but crushed and steeped in water, they make a nice drink."

While Rosie slept in her box, Katie helped Bride with the dishes before luxuriating in a bath and getting her hair so clean it squeaked. After Melissa and Jed devoured their fill of pancakes almost afloat in molasses, they bathed. Katie inspected Jed's ears and neck and made sure that his tow head and Melissa's yellow one were washed and rinsed to brightness.

Bride had bathed Rosie, so the MacLeods were fit to face the world. After a noon meal of hearty stew and golden biscuits, Jed rushed off to explore the camp while his sisters helped Bride make the beds and tidy the rooms shared by two to four miners, who thought their lodgings well worth a dollar a day of their three-and-a-half dollar wages. Because she didn't want to cook and make lunches around the clock, Bride only boarded men on the day shift.

"When I hear the charges go off, I know it's time to put the coffee on and set the table," she explained, rolling out pie crusts while Melissa lulled Rosie in the big oak rocker and Katie peeled potatoes. "You see, girls, when a shift's nearly over, the blaster makes up paper cartridges filled with powder, and the miners drive these into holes and tamp them with damp clay. Then the blaster yells, 'Fire in the hole!' and lights the fuses while the men get out as quick as they can without stumbling or bumping into something. The next men start their shift by mucking out the ore left by the blast. You can bet I'm always glad to count all the lads coming in even if they are so dirty their mothers wouldn't know them and their poor stomachs are too puckered with fumes and rock dust to relish my best cooking. Spicy, salty stuff's what they crave, the kind that's sold in saloons or served free to give the men a thirst — sardines, oysters, pickles, anchovies, sausage, pig's snout, smoked tongue — all that truck that just aggravates their innards the more!"

This was clearly a source of indignation to Bride, who expertly crimped the crusts together and set six pies in the oven, three dried apple and three dried peach, each filling simmered with raisins, molasses, and spice. There was still a mound of pie dough, and she made this into balls and swiftly rolled them out.

"Pasties for tomorrow's lunch," she explained. "Stuffed with onions and chopped leftover meat and vegetables, they make a fine meal. My three Cousin Jacks — Cornishmen — the black-haired ones with funny little legs that don't look stout enough to carry those great large chests — feel like they've got to have them, but the other lads relish them. Love their saffron buns, too, do Hal Trego, Jerry Polfax, and Tim Penrose. Even it weren't for their tiny legs and big chests, you can tell Cousin Jacks by their names. 'By Tre-, Pol-, Pen-, and O-, You the Cornishman shall know.' "

Chopping meat for the pasties recalled her earlier grievance with the purveyors of unwholesome viands. "I tell my lads they can go to the saloon after supper if they're fool enough, but any that stop on the way from work to fill up on that junk don't need to darken my door except to get their plunder." She grumbled on about the trials of trying to tempt dyspeptics, especially those with no better sense than to embalm their livers in whiskey, but Katie scarcely heard.

Where was Bill Radnor? she wondered for the hundredth time that day. Even if he had gone after the abandoned MacLeod possessions as he'd promised, she'd expected him at least to come by first to see how they were. Maybe — she burned at the thought — maybe he'd been kind because he was sorry for them but didn't want to be bothered any more than was necessary. If that were so, she'd certainly take no more favors from him. Her lips trembled and she pressed them tight together, blinking back tears.

He'd seen her yesterday when she was grimy, bedraggled, and about to drop from exhaustion. It wasn't fair that he didn't stop to see her now when her well-brushed hair glinted with coppery lights and she was clean and had on her only respectable dress! True, her face was windburned and her lips chapped, but Bride had given her a green velvet ribbon, tying back Katie's hair with gentle hands in a way that flooded Katie with longing for the cherishing she'd never had. Mama had never touched her more than necessary. Katie had tried to convince herself that it was because she was the eldest and her mother had so much work to do, but when Mary had given Jed a quick hug or braided Melissa's hair, Katie achingly wondered why, just once, she couldn't get the hug, feel her mother's hand rest on her cheek or head.

Bride brought her back to the present by saying, "This ribbon's just the color of your eyes, dear, deep green with gold behind so they're always changing, just like the seas of Ireland my grandfather sang about though he'd left his harp."

Katie flushed with pleasure but couldn't help but wish Bill Radnor had said that. "Have you ever seen a big lot of water, Bride, like the ocean?"

"Bless you, child, I was born in Nebraska and raised in Kansas. Most water I ever saw was when the Arkansas River went on a rampage — and that was plenty for me." Her brisk voice turned dreamy as she stoked the big woodstove, washed her hands, and began to punch down the pungent sourdough bread from its first rising. "I dream about Ireland, though, especially when it's hot and parched — a green, green island in soft mists with the sea racing up to it in great green waves with the crests like manes and the seabirds crying, white like the foam." She smiled a bit sadly and began to shape the glossy dough into loaves. "Oh, in my dreams I've seen it though never with these eyes of my body."

"My mother had a song almost like what you said," Katie remembered. "I haven't turned the Gaelic into English yet, but I can tell you what it means without trying to make it rhyme."

"Could you get your harp and play it now?" asked Bride. "That's all the potatoes we need to put around the roast, so there's nothing to do for half an hour. I'll brew us a nice pot of tea."

Upstairs, Katie unwrapped the harp. Passed down through generations of her family, it was, according to her mother, much smaller than most Celtic harps, with only twenty-two strings, but its soundboard of black willow wood had a deep, mellow resonance. The arch and pedestal were inlaid with crystals and brass tooled into fantastic birds and beasts that grew out of twining plants.

" 'The Lowland sheep took our land,' " Mary had told her children, repeating her own father's bitter-triumphant words. " 'But they couldn't steal our songs.' "

As if handling a loved person, Katie used her petticoat to polish the wood and get all the dust out from between the mountings that held the wires. The brass harp key was fastened to the notch of the pedestal by a leather thong. Katie tuned the strings, wondering as she tested them if the harp had really belonged to Mary MacLeod, a renowned ancestress of the seventeenth century. That famous Mary of long ago had made songs against English rule and for that was commanded not to compose her poetry either inside or outside the house. She'd gotten around that by standing on the threshold while she made up her songs. Katie knew one of them and was playing with the Gaelic in her head, hoping to devise an English version before her performance tomorrow between Methodist and Baptist sermons.

Back in the kitchen, she rested the harp on her knees. "I'm out of practice," she apologized. "I haven't played since — since we left home."

"Sure, to me it'll sound sweet," Bride promised, pouring tea from a fat, wildly flowered pot and setting cups near Katie and Melissa.

With a sigh of content, she sank down in a chair, but she also reached for a basket of mending and threaded a needle.

Katie played a few short airs to limber her fingers and then hummed till the tune came to her fingers and the Gaelic words to her lips, which she sang first before turning them into English.

I would go, I would go with you, across the Irish
sea,
Where billows rise, where whales and monsters
war
While the while ship ploughs the proud waves
that eddy
round the stern — Oh, I would go, I would go
with you . . .

Next, she sang her favorite song, a lullaby she often crooned to Rosie.

I searched the hill from end to end,
From noon to night and night till dawn,
I searched down to the water's edge,
I could not find my cubhrachan.

I found the track of the otter brown.
I could not find my cubhrachan.
I found the track of the spotted red fawn,
I could not find my cubhrachan . . .

"That's mighty pretty," came a voice from the door. "But what in the world is a *cubhrachan?* Sort of a cub?"

Heart leaping, Katie turned to look up at Bill Radnor. Freshly shaved, he smelled astringently spicy and wore a clean deep blue shirt with a white silk neckerchief knotted loosely at his muscular brown throat.

"I suppose you could call a baby a cub," said Katie, laughing. "*Cubhrachan* means 'little fragrant one.' "

"Speaking of fragrant ones, you sure are, Bill," teased Bride. "Doused in bay rum, mane clipped, cheeks scraped, and boots shined! You've been to the barber."

"Have to help keep old Jake in business." Radnor grinned. "By the time I got back from fetching Miss Kate's gear and stowing it back in her wagon, I was dusty as a prairie dog diggin' a new hole in a drouth." Turning his attention to Katie, he narrowed his eyes and his brow furrowed. "You sure look different, Miss Kate. Close to grown-up." He rubbed his ear. "Maybe you hadn't better play at Babcock's tomorrow."

From being nervous of Bill's plan, Katie had come to see it as the quickest way to get a ranch going. It was her turn to scowl. "Did you ask the preachers and the saloon owner?"

"Sure. They were tickled pink. Soon as

Brother Daggett gets through exhorting around ten o'clock, you can play till Brother Thomas sails into the heathen at eleven, and then in the afternoon till you get tired or the crowd's so thirsty the bar has to open." His tone was reproachful. "Seemed like a good idea yesterday, but now —"

"You mean I looked so awful that you couldn't imagine there'd be any problem with my entertaining." Katie bit off the words. "You figured on everyone feeling sorry for the poor little waif! Well, I don't want them feeling sorry. I want them to enjoy my songs enough to think they're worth something! And if preachers can hold services in a saloon, I reckon it's all right for me to sing there."

Retreating before her onslaught, Radnor cast a dazed appeal at Bride. "You tell her, Bride!"

"It's a marvel of a notion," she beamed at him. "And I'm proud of you for thinking it up." When he groaned, she said bracingly, "Don't be a daftie, Lord Bill! Won't I be going with her and bringing her safe home? Won't you be standin' in the back with your .44s?" With a sound that was more than a sniff and less than a snort, she picked up another sock. "Katie, darling, give us another song."

In spite of her determination and bold

words, Katie had a hollow feeling in her stomach next morning as a grim-mouthed Radnor, harp hoisted on his shoulder, escorted her and Bride across the street to Babcock's saloon. A sound of hammering came from the blacksmith's at the end of the camp, but otherwise everyone who wasn't down in the mine seemed to be making for the saloon. There were only two other women. Bride paused to introduce Katie to Myra Firbank, the buxom proprietor of a restaurant, whose sharp, dark eyes raked Katie and lingered on Radnor; and Sarah Metzger, kindly of manner, gray of eyes and hair, who ran the largest general store with her husband.

Nearly all the men, whether garbed as miner or cowboy, greeted Radnor with jokes about the harp while they appraised Katie as well as they could without staring. Radnor gave them an all-inclusive "Howdy, boys," stowed the harp behind the bar, and kept close to Bride and Katie.

Tables had been pushed to the sides of the big room, and the floor was crowded with what looked like every chair in town, including Bride's. A black-moustached, balding man hastily finished shrouding a large painting above what Katie surmised was the bar — it, too, was draped with sheets — but she caught a glimpse that made her blush.

That painting! It was of a lady with not a stitch to her pink hide, sprawling in some bushes with a bunch of grapes in her hand! If she'd tried that in this country, she'd have been too busy pulling thorns out of her backside to loll around eating grapes!

Some women sat together in the back of the room, nicely dressed and quite ordinary-looking except for lips and cheeks a bit redder than was natural. These, thought Katie, stealing fascinated glances, must be whores and harlots. Only they didn't look the way they should, weren't glittering with diamonds and rubies, or posing in filmy lace to display maddeningly beautiful bodies. They weren't beautiful, in fact, just average.

Disillusioned, Katie turned to see the black-moustached man place a box on a small table in front of the decorously hidden bar. "There you are, Brother Thomas," he said, wiping his brow and smoothing another sheet over the improvised stand. "That whiskey carton'll make a good place to put your Bible."

"Thanks, Brother Babcock." The Reverend Thomas had a booming voice that reverberated like the blasting charges in the mine. Made to look even taller and more cadaverous by a black linen duster worn over black trousers and a white shirt with black string tie, he had a bushy black beard and hair peppered with gray. His piercing dark eyes noted each face in the assembling crowd with a strange mixture of excitement and disgust. "Brands for the burning," he whispered as if to himself and swung to Radnor in a stance as challenging as if he'd raised his fists. "Welcome, Brother Radnor. I'm glad the Lord has moved you to seek truth and mercy and get yourself a new hand."

Katie thought Radnor stiffened the slightest fraction, but his smile was genial. "Don't stick your iron in the fire for me yet, Reverend. I'm escorting the ladies. I reckon you've stuck your feet under Mrs. Malone's table a few times so you know her, but Miss Kate Mac-Leod just got to Galeyville night before last."

"Hah, the young lady with the harp, King David's instrument!" Black eyes drove into hers with physical impact. She was close enough to see thready little broken veins in his nose and the large, coarse pores of his skin. A sour, disappointed smell rose from the black duster. Katie wished she could step back, but there wasn't enough room. "Are you saved, Sister Kate?"

Pa had intoned long graces over their meals, and once, years ago, a preacher on his way west had stayed all night and read his Bible and prayed with the family, but that was Katie's total religious education. Puzzled, she said, "I'm not lost. We never were, really, just caught without water in the desert."

Bride's laughter pealed, Radnor's lip twitched, Mr. Babcock snickered, and the minister reddened. "Would you joke about your soul's salvation or are you that ignorant?"

Katie flushed, hurt and bewildered. "I didn't know you were talking about my soul, Reverend Thomas. But I guess, yes, I am pretty ignorant. Mama taught us to read and cipher and write a little, but there wasn't a school close enough for us to go."

Shamefaced under Radnor's cold stare, Reverend Thomas said, "Never mind, child, I see you're an innocent. But that innocence could be your destruction so you listen careful to the sermon."

Stepping behind the improvised pulpit, the preacher thumped his Bible down and raised his arms. "Rise up on your hind laigs, brothers and sisters, bow your heads, and join me in prayer." A hush fell as the minister's voice resounded. "Our Father, Thou art the Great Dealer and knowest all our hands and what we need to fill 'em. We know, Oh Lord, Thou wouldn't cold-card us though our mortal minds cain't figger why some are dealt aces full while others get a pair of deuces or wind up with busted straights and flushes. We believe, Lord, that Thou only expects us to play our hands the best we can without poor-mouthin' or blaming Thee for not givin' us better cards. We know we can't bluff that final hand, that Thou wilt call every bet and we better have what we claimed we did. Lord, Thou didst hang around with barkeeps and sinners so Thou shouldst be right at home here. Set Thy charges in these stony hearts, Father, that hanker overmuch for the riches of this world, and blast out the gold and silver of the spirit! Amen."

Lifting his head amid the scuffling of people taking seats or, failing that, some comfortable perch or leaning-place, Reverend Thomas scanned the crowd and took a deck of cards out of his vest. He splayed them out, flinging them to the floor and grinding them under his boot. "I preach in the language of cards so you'll understand better, my dear brothers and sisters, but cards are evil. They turn your minds from the things of God, they cause cheating and swearing and killing, and they lure you into swilling the devil's juice. Yes, verily, wine is a mocker; strong drink is raging! There's a rattler coiled at the bottom of every glass! Whosoever looketh upon it is not only not wise, he's dumber 'n the tinhorn that draws four cards when there's aces showing."

His heel and the rough plank floor mutilated the cards, and in utter repudiation, he trampled them underfoot. Katie expected Mr. Babcock to jump up and protest the condemnation of his business, but the saloon owner placidly shifted his tobacco to his other cheek and settled more comfortably in his chair as Reverend Thomas opened his Bible.

"Dearly beloved, all the gospels tell us the soldiers cast lots for Jesus' garments, but John tells us why. His robe was woven without a seam from top to bottom — we'd reckon His mother made it for Him, wouldn't we, just like your mothers made you the nicest clothes they could. So after the soldiers split up His other garments, there was this dandy robe left, and rather then ruin it by dividing, they gambled for it."

He paused sorrowfully. "Yes, right there, they flocked like a bunch of buzzards and shot craps for Jesus' robe. All of you that's been through a mesquite thicket know what thorns feel like. How'd you like to have a wreath of them jammed down over your forehead? How'd you like to drag your cross up a rocky, bare hill like those we got out toward the flats and then be hung up betwixt two cow-thieves —"

There was a shuffling of boots, but the Methodist thundered on. "Yes, Jesus was put to death with a rapscallion on either hand, and one mocked Him, but the other, who must've had some good in his heart, told his pard to lay off and asked Jesus to remember him when He came into His Kingdom. Now even in His pain, brothers and sisters, even in His sweat and blood, with flies swarmin' and so thirsty He must have just croaked the words, Jesus pitied that thief and said, 'Today Thou shalt be with Me in Paradise.' And we can believe that rustler didn't hurt so bad then and died with the promise of salvation. But those soldiers, those blind prideful Romans all stuck up from conquerin' the world, the four hunkerin' down at the foot of the cross — you can bet they damned themselves that day. They're burning in hell right now for that one little game, tormented forever in that lake of fire that's a sight worse than any desert you've ever panted across. Won't be no waterhole for them, not even alkali water. They been in hell nigh two thousand years, and that's the wink of an eye in eternity. Eternity never ends, beloved. Not a one of us can know when it's going to start for us! This is the best chance you'll ever have to toss away your cards and whiskey!"

He stretched out his arms as his fiery gaze ranged from face to face. "You gamblers and winebibbers and cowboys who know more 'n you should about back trails to Mexico — you folks who look decent as white-washed tombstones while within your breasts your hearts are deceitful above all things and desperately wicked — you women livin' where the lights are red and the carpets soft — I say to you, come forward and confess your sins and the Lord will be merciful to you just like He was to that thief."

Some of the men glanced sideways at each other, swallowed, or moved uneasily, but no one accepted the invitation. Katie had never thought before about Jesus' really suffering. She hurt to think about it and burned with indignation at the callous soldiers and those who'd sent Him to such a slow, nasty death, but if He'd die like that for people, would He condemn them to torment forever and ever?

She couldn't believe that; neither could she think of any big sins except being ready to kill Missou if he wouldn't let the animals drink. She wasn't sorry for that, so she sat tight while Reverend Thomas exhorted, pacing up and down.

At last, a lanky red-headed man with a drooping moustache and cowboy garb stood up at the back of the room. "Brother Thomas, that was a mighty good sermon for a Methodist one, but it looks like no one wants to get sprinkled. Could be they crave baptism like the Lord got from John the Baptist, the kind that's plumb complete so they'll know they've been saved. Anyhow, there's a young lady supposed to play a harp in between you and me. Ain't fair for you to use up the whole mornin'."

Thomas glared, but several of the crowd called, "That's right!" and someone yelled, "I came to hear that gal play her harp! Don't mind givin' you parsons a chance to rope me, but you oughta be fair!"

"Fair!" rumbled Thomas. "Shame, Brother Daggett! Lo, I've plowed deep, harrowed up the rocky soil, and now you'll plant your seed and reap the harvest."

Daggett went so red his freckles disappeared, and his hand dropped to where a holster would have hung had he worn one. "I'll forgive that slander, brother, since you're upset over not stampedin' a herd into the Methodist corral. Tell you what let's do. I won't ask anyone to get saved today — though if they want to foller me down to the creek afterward I'll sure baptize them, hoof to horn, total, entire, whole hog, and thorough, and you can do the same for any as can't wait to get sprinkled." He cocked his head and set his hands on his narrow hips. "Here's my proposition, Brother Thomas. Next Saturday, you dally your rope first, brand all the prime stock you can in an hour, and I'll see what

I can do with the drags and the dogies."

For a moment, light blue eyes contended with smoldering black ones, but the congregation was nodding approval and Mr. Babcock got out his pocketwatch. "Sounds like a fair shuffle to me, Reverends, but if it don't suit you, Brother Thomas, we'd be obliged if you'd go outside to argufy on account of it's past time for the lady to sing."

Thomas closed his Bible and stepped back from the disguised whiskey crate. "I'll call you, Brother Daggett! I'm withdrawin' to commune with the Lord, but I'll be back in time to make sure you don't go gatherin' up my sheaves!"

He stumped out. Brother Daggett unfolded himself onto a stool, and Katie noticed that one of his scuffed, split-leather boots had a knife sheathed inside it. He grinned at Katie, and she blushed for it suddenly seemed that all eyes were fixed on her.

Her mouth felt drier than when she'd been traveling across the flats, and her palms were clammy. How could she play in front of all these people? How could she sing? Why had she let Radnor talk her into it?

Springing up, she started to bolt for the door. Radnor was in front of her, slipping his strong lean fingers beneath her elbow, gently but firmly steering her toward the front.

Babcock brought a chair for her, and Radnor fetched the harp, blue-gray eyes serious though he was smiling as he turned.

"Folks, most of your families and some of you came from over the sea like this harp and Miss Kate MacLeod's grandmother. Miss Kate ran into hard luck and had to lighten the wagon. She tossed out a plow and big kettle and furniture — just about everything but her little sisters and brother, but she hung onto the harp, and the songs and tunes, well, they were carried safe in her heart. This is special music, friends, and Miss Kate's a special young lady."

He led the applause. It flowed through Katie like a hot toddy Mama had fixed her once when she was chilling with ague. Katie balanced the harp, and the feel of the wood strengthened her as if her hands, inherited from generations of those who had used the harp, inherited also their skill and sureness.

Smiling at the faces, eager and waiting, she was filled with power and joy. *I'll give you songs,* she thought, drawing a sweet, clear ripple of sound from the strings. *And you will build my house.*

"Are any of you Scots?" she asked. "You'll know this song, then, about the soldier who's going to be executed while his friend is released to return home. The doomed man, though, says he'll reach Scotland first for he'll take the low road traveled by spirits."

At the second chorus, many voices joined in and by the time she finished "My Cubhrachan," there were tears in the eyes of men as well as women. She played a foot-tapping strathspey, a song for the milking, one for spinning, and one for the harvest; for Islanders, men and woman both, had songs for all their work. Then she played a magical, haunting air, about a seal who took human form to win a maid who'd bear his child.

Oh, I am a man upon the land
And I am a selkie in the sea . . .

There was a jingle of spurs outside. A massive-shouldered dark shape appeared above the swinging half-doors, resolving, as he came farther inside, into merely a large man.

Casting a startled glance at Katie and the harp, he doffed his battered cream-colored hat and inclined his head to her. He had thick, springy gray hair and smoky eyes the color of charcoal. Not as tall as he seemed, he was powerfully built, chest and shoulders almost top-heavy above the narrow cord-muscled hips of a rider.

"Sorry to bust in, ma'am," he said to Katie.

Unlike Radnor, he had no trouble in deciding how to address her. His eyes, almost unwillingly, rested on her face a moment before he turned to survey the crowd. "I've got just one question. Did any of you blow up my dam or do you know who did?"

III

Radnor, lounging against the wall, raised a black eyebrow. "The dam on the San Simon? Well, Ed, I'm plumb sorry and surprised to hear you put it there. In a dry year like this, what're other folks supposed to do for water?"

"There's no other folks in the end of the valley." The newcomer chewed off each word and spat it out. "And there's not goin' to be."

"How about those passin' through?"

"That's their look-out. Besides, there'd be spillover from the dam most of the year."

"Except when it's driest," said Bill softly. "Like it is right now. Like it was a few days ago when four kids and their livestock near died."

The newcomer's square jaw clamped. His sunburned face went even ruddier. "You blew up that dam, Radnor!"

"Reckon I did."

"I thought we had an understanding."

"Still do — as long as you don't dam the river."

"I got a right to see my cows have water."

"Certain sure you do. Dig tanks to catch rain. Make holes wherever there's a seep. Channel some of the flow into a pond."

68

Radnor straightened. "Just don't stop the river, Larrimore."

"What's it to you?"

Radnor smiled. "I just happen to think rivers ought to flow free and natural-like."

Muscles ridged in Ed Larrimore's cheek. "I can post guards on the next dam I build."

"Sure. We could have us a hot little war though I doubt we could fan it into as big a one as they had in Lincoln County." Radnor shrugged, meeting the other man's eyes. "What's the sense of it, Ed? No one's crowdin' onto your range, stealing your cattle, or botherin' you."

"And I haven't bothered you, Bill," the rancher said meaningfully.

"So why don't we leave it like that? Settle down for the music and preaching, Ed. When the bar opens, I'll buy you a drink."

"I want one now."

Babcock hastened to get it, rummaging beneath the sheets on the bar. Larrimore's gaze came again to Katie, reluctantly softened. "Go on with your singin', ma'am."

He sat down, arms crossed. Katie knew a fight had been narrowly missed, maybe a killing. Her throat was tight when she started the ballad again, and she struck a few false notes, but Larrimore was such an intent and clearly appreciative listener that her nerves calmed. Hoping to avert further clashes, she scarcely paused between one song and the next till Reverend Daggett began to fidget and she knew her time was up.

Sipping his drink, Larrimore never took his eyes off her. When she finished with a trilling medley of bird songs and was overwhelmed by applause, she didn't know where to look. Blushing, she caught up the harp and fled outside, leaning against the wall, breathless as if she'd been running, full of wonderment.

They loved her songs! Miners, cowboys, business people, harlots, a rancher, even a Baptist preacher and a Methodist one! A heady sensation made her feel light and free, a glow of — yes, it must be power, for hadn't she possessed these minds, swayed these hearts?

From inside, she heard Radnor saying, "Well, folks, wouldn't it be fine to have Miss Kate play for our buryings and marryings and sometimes just for frolic? She needs a cabin built, good corrals, and outbuildings. She'll be playing here the next two afternoons. Meanwhile, those of you who want to help get her and little family settled, you talk to me."

Into the uproar of volunteering and suggestions, Reverend Daggett shouted: "Brothers and sisters! I'm tickled to see Bill Radnor up to something except orneriness, but I got to edge my sermon in here before Brother Babcock yanks those sheets off the bar. Stand up and stretch, stomp a little, and then hunker down. I won't preach long, I promise. Savin' up for next week."

Amid the scrape of chairs and scuffle of feet, a few people escaped. One was Ed Larrimore. Unlike the others, he didn't hurry to one of the saloons that was serving, but halted in front of Katie. He radiated a ruthless, driving force that made her feel trapped between him and the wall.

"Miss Kate," he said, with an obvious but not very successful attempt at speaking softly. "I'm Ed Larrimore. I've got a ranch in the San Simon Valley and an eight-year-old daughter whose mam is dead. Bride says you've got a kid brother and two sisters, one just a baby. I need someone to raise Hallie, and there's room for all of you in my house. You could run it to suit you long as you leave me my pipe and whiskey and keep out of my office. You wouldn't have to do any rough work. Chapita and her daughter, Maria, do the cooking and housework. I'd pay a good wage you could save since your livin' would be free. Why not try it for a while?"

"You're generous, sir, and I thank you." Katie hugged the harp as if it might shield her from the rancher's persuasiveness. His

71

nose was almost flat, and that made his face look even squarer. In spite of that and deep grooves at the edges of his eyes and mouth, he was — an interesting-looking man, Katie decided, though a bit frightening. "We came out here, though, to start our own place. We've got milk cows and five Steel Dust horses —"

"Those in Babcock's corral? I'll buy the horses at more 'n they're worth. The cows, too, though, I'll slaughter 'em for beef. Milk cows are no good in this country."

"You won't slaughter my cows, Mr. Larrimore!"

"All right. The hands can fence them a little pasture."

She shook her head, dismayed by his persistence. "Mr. Larrimore, you — you don't seem to have heard. You're kind and I thank you, but we want our own place."

"That's crazy, girl! Even if there weren't forever Apaches breaking off the reservation, the riffraff of Texas and California have sure swarmed into Arizona. A few kids — and those Steel Dust horses — will be easy pickin's."

"We made it across a dry river." She couldn't resist the jab. "I guess we can manage."

His eyes looked suddenly hard as the lava the MacLeods trudged across. "Don't count on Bill Radnor to look out for you, Miss Kate. He could get hanged or shot any day. Plenty of men both sides of the Mexican border, both sides of the law, who'd give their right hands to do it."

The cadence of Reverend Daggett's adjurations poured out more loudly as the doors swung open. Radnor paused beside Katie, and her uncomfortable sensation of being under siege immediately vanished — not because Radnor was a hand taller than the rancher, but because she knew instinctively that if he were around no one could hurt her without killing him first; and Bill Radnor would not kill easily.

"When it comes to being unpopular, Ed," he said genially, "I reckon you're way ahead of me. I'm kind of surprised you'd ride into Galeyville alone. Couple of the miners and a few cowboys figger you ran them off land that wasn't any more yours than theirs." Radnor's glance flickered toward some horses hitched in front of a saloon signed EVILSIZER'S at the edge of town. "But then I guess you didn't come alone. Looks like your brand on those horses yonder."

"You didn't bother to cover your tracks, Bill. That's why I figgered it had to be you. I'm not a complete damn fool to ride into your hangout alone." His eyes narrowed to probing slits. "Are we goin' to be able to git along like we always have?"

"Don't see why not." Bill's teeth flashed in a careless grin. He put his hand on Larrimore's shoulder. "Come on down to Evilsizer's. I'm settin' up drinks for the house."

Larrimore's eyes swept over Katie's face. "Miss Kate, my offer's open if you change your mind." With a nod, he jerked his hat down over his eyes, and the two men strolled off together, truce struck for the moment though something in the way they carried themselves, a certain wary stiffness in their legs, reminded Katie of two male wolves she'd once seen sniffing each other before launching into a battle.

What kind of understanding did they have? It must be to Larrimore's advantage or he wouldn't have gone along with Radnor's insistence that there be no dam. The pair disappeared into the saloon. Too euphoric at her music's reception to worry long about anything else and much too wound up to sit quietly through Brother Daggett's ringing homily, Katie held her harp in her arms and crossed over to Bride's place.

Radnor poked his head into the kitchen early next morning, while Katie and Melissa were making their way through stacks of dishes, Rosie slumbered in her box, and Bride kneaded a mound of delicious-smelling sourdough.

"Miss Kate, there's a bunch of the boys rarin' to build your house. Some went up the mountain this morning to start felling logs, so we better be deciding where you want to live. Bride, reckon you and Melissa here can close-herd Jed and Rosie while I show Miss Kate some likely places?"

"Sounds like it's time." Bride glanced longingly at the baby. "Katie, I'd love to have you all stay with me or at least build here in town."

Rinsing the last pan, Katie gave Bride a grateful smile. "In a way, I guess we'd all love to — you've been so good to us. But we came a long way to start our own place, and we can't raise horses and have a dairy in town."

"Sure, love, I'm understanding." Wiping doughy hands, Bride gave her a hug. "Go along with Lord Bill but be back by supper because, remember, you're playing about seven o'clock for the miners on day shift."

Slipping off her apron, Katie noticed that Melissa's head was bent as she fiercely polished the tin forks. Poor child, she was bearing too much responsibility for the younger children. With a twinge of guilt, Katie put an arm around thin, stiff shoulders. "I'm sorry to go off, honey, but just think! It won't be long till we have our own house, our own land!"

Mouth twisted, gentian-blue eyes glinting with tears, Melissa blurted, "It'll be your house — your land! You're deciding all by yourself just like you were our mother!"

Stricken, Katie stared at her sister for a moment before anger blazed through her hurt. "If you think it's fun worrying about the rest of you, trying to take care of you — well, Melissa MacLeod, you've got another thing coming! I wish — oh, I wish —" She broke off, unable to put into words how alone she felt, how weighed down with the care of the children — and how sorry she was that Melissa, too, was overburdened.

Melissa's lips trembled, but her small pointed chin thrust out with the stubbornness that had kept her walking beside the wagon instead of adding to the horses' load. Radnor's tanned fingers dropped to her shoulder.

"Sweetheart, your sister has to take the part of your folks. You must know it's tough. She couldn't get along without your helpin'. Why don't we do this? Your sis and I'll pick out a place and then I'll take you to see it. If you plumb don't like it, we'll hunt for something else."

Melissa, sniffing, rubbed her sleeve across

her eyes. *"Will* you, Katie?"

Vexed at Radnor for making promises on her behalf, but grateful that he was willing to go to so much trouble, Katie managed a peace-making smile. "This place will belong to all of us, M'liss. Of course I don't want to settle somewhere you don't like. If Mr. Radnor doesn't mind taking you to see it while I look after Rosie and Jed —"

She ended in a squeal as Melissa, laughing through tears, squeezed her so tight it hurt. "Katie, I — I'm sure I'll like it fine! It's just that — well, it still seems funny for you to be boss over us. And — and everybody treats you like a grown-up, You go off to play the harp and ride with Mr. Radnor while I watch the baby —"

Holding her sister close, and, indeed, Melissa was only a few inches shorter than Katie's five-three and close to her hundred and ten pounds, Katie said, "Well, now you'll get a nice ride with Mr. Radnor while I look after the baby, and when we have butter and milk, you'll probably bring them to town a lot oftener than I will." *And you'll probably have beaus and get married while I'm still raising the little ones.* Now where did that startling thought come from? Giving Melissa a swift kiss, Katie took off her apron and ran upstairs for her sunbonnet.

The MacLeods' old saddle was cinched on a sleek black mare with a blazed face and four white stockings. "After that journey, your mares need to rest and fatten up before they foal," said Radnor, helping her mount and tactfully studying the front of Babcock's saloon while she battled her skirts into as decent an arrangement as possible. "Sweet Alice likes to pretend every rustle of grass is a rattler, but if you keep a firm hand, she'll behave."

Waving to Jed, who was playing with a dog in front of Metzger's store, Katie drew a deep, exhilarating breath as they rode past the last shacks. By the time they returned, she should know where her home would be, where she might live the rest of her life. That was an exciting prospect, but after the exhausting trip, it was marvelous simply to go on a day's excursion, carefree, almost as if she didn't have three young ones depending on her. She needn't even feel guilty about Melissa as Radnor had promised her an outing, too.

The air sparkled like the waters of Turkey Creek as they splashed across it, and the sky, without a wisp of cloud, was the most dazzling blue she'd ever seen. It would be hot later, but at five thousand feet, the night cool lingered among the white-trunked sycamores shading the creek and the oaks, ashes, and junipers beyond. Most of all, in͏̵ infuriating way of considering her than adult, it was bliss and joy to with Bill Radnor on such a splendid ͏one — no one in the whole world — ͏d be as handsome or strong or daring.

Maybe too daring? She thought uneasily of Ed Larrimore, and, to banish that chill, lifted her voice above the sound of the horses' hoofs. "Did you see Missou when you fetched our belongings?"

"Didn't see hair, hide, horn, nor hoof-mark of the ornery skunk," chuckled Radnor. "Out of puredee meanness, he'd filled in the waterhole, but I dug it out pretty good."

Katie spoke her thoughts aloud. "So travelers can water now at the San Simon and the waterhole. You've surely saved some lives."

"Just riles me to see someone hog water in a desert." He slanted her a lazy smile. "I reckon you could say I don't put much stock in any kind of rights that'll let a man starve other folks or keep them from drinking water." He shrugged. "But there's some that'd put a brand on air and sunlight if they could, and keep them to themselves."

She laughed at the wild notion, then sobered. "Ed Larrimore would, I'll bet."

"You'd get no takers on that wager."

The grimness beneath his chuckle made her

ickly, "I don't want to settle on land e takes for his."

Radnor hooted. "Lord love you, Miss Kate, all Ed wants is his land and that next to it. But don't fret. His cattle range the whole San Simon Valley from the east side of the Chiricahuas to the Peloncillos over in New Mexico. They wander up Cave Creek now and again to the aggravation of Stephen Reed, who brought his family in to settle a few years ago. But Pitchfork hands generally keep the cows well east and north of here." At her questioning look, Radnor said, "Larrimore doesn't mind plaguing a few settlers — and they are few — but even if he did bring some of his boys to town the other day, he doesn't want war with Galeyville any more than he wants to keep us in free beef."

Leaving the wooded hills, they rode among rolling slopes where flowers that she knew from West Texas bloomed: Indian blanket, with its deep red-orange center and golden leaves, big white prickly poppies on their spiny stalks, dainty wild mustard, sunny desert marigolds, and clumps of dreamy violet desert verbena. A roadrunner scurried past them, intent on a lizard. Burrowing owls blinked sleepily at them from the earthen ledge above their home. Fortunately, Katie's mare, Sweet Alice, didn't shy at the half-grown rabbits they frightened into bounding away. From a distance, through a veil of grass, a coyote watched them, ears pricked. Farther along, a curve-billed thrasher perched on a cholla, regarding them saucily from its yellow eyes.

"He knows that cholla's a pretty safe place to be," said Radnor. "Trouble is, snakes shimmy right up and rob their nests. But snakes have to eat, too, I guess. And that eagle out there circling may be planning to have a tender young snakelet for breakfast."

Katie followed his nod to the bird just as it suddenly plunged earthward in a flash that for a second struck gold from the dark plumage. She winced. Radnor said, "They miss a lot, you know. But if they didn't keep down rabbits and mice and such, the little critters would plumb overrun us."

The eagle's good luck was his prey's bad, for the raptor stayed on the ground out there on the broad plain rimmed by mountains that, depending on distance and how the sun struck them, were luminous rose, peach, or purple. Katie shivered, thinking that wild creatures weren't the only things to perish in the desert. Her family and animals had been near death. And if the man beside her hadn't chanced along, she might have killed Missou out there.

Never again, if she could help it, would she

cross that vast expanse. But from here, drenched with light, it was awesomely beautiful, only a few isolated peaks thrusting up improbably from the surrounding flats.

With this vista on their right, and to their left, defiles and washes leading into the mountains, they were riding toward a chain of barren mountains ending in one shaped like a haystack with serried rock for its peak. Motioning at them, Katie said, "I don't want to locate on the other side of those." She couldn't explain it, but though she didn't want to live in the camp, neither did she want to feel too far away from Radnor.

He reined his horse westerly in the direction of a funny little hill that looked like a teepee with poles of rock divided at the top. "Good grass through here," he said. "Whitetail Creek runs out of the canyon through the valley, and this bunch of hills that end with Blue Mountain and Haystack cut off lots of that rampagin' north wind."

His gaze swept from that barrier and the yucca-studded grasslands to the hazy blue-green of a long ridge on the skyline above wooded peaks and gray or rusty pink cliffs. He said — wistfully, Katie thought — "If I were stakin' out a claim, this would be it."

"Why don't you?"

He cast her a startled glance. "Guess I'm

not the kind to stay in one place."

Katie's heart sank. For a moment, she couldn't speak. Swallowing hard, she asked in a small voice, "You mean you — you won't be staying in Galeyville the rest of your life?"

He laughed. "I could stay the rest of my life, Miss Kate, but not be there much longer." At her protesting cry, he looked instantly contrite. "I like Galeyville a sight better than Tombstone, Miss Kate, and either one a sight better than any place east of New Mexico. But when the country settles up" — he lifted an eloquent shoulder — "I'll move along."

"You'll run out of wild places."

"There's always Mexico. And just last year, there was a big gold strike in Alaska."

No use to argue, and of course if she'd really stopped to think, she'd have realized that if he'd wanted to ranch or farm, he'd be doing that instead of — what was it that he did? She was afraid to ask and distraught to know that sooner or later he'd vanish from her life as suddenly as he'd entered it.

A *woman* might keep him here. A *woman* might make him think it wasn't boring to sink down roots.

Suddenly remembering Larrimore's smoky gaze on her, she wondered indignantly why he, of an age to be her father, had seen her as a woman when Radnor didn't. The rancher had asked her to look after his daughter, but inexperienced though she was, Katie had sensed his avid male hunger. The men who'd listened to her music yesterday had watched her admiringly, longingly, and this morning as she helped serve the miners breakfast, they stole glances at her and blushed if she spoke to them. It was just Bill Radnor who treated her as if she were no older than Melissa!

Setting her jaw, she determined not to let that bother her. She'd raise Melissa and Jed and Rosie, breed that line of Steel Dust horses, and have a dairy famed for its butter and cream and milk in a country where no one dreamed of milking range cows. That would take hard, steady work, all her time, and by the day Rosie was old enough to marry or look after herself, she, Katie, would be thirty-two or thirty-three.

Taking melancholy satisfaction in contemplating martyred spinsterdom, which she intended to offset by considerable success with the ranch, Katie consoled herself with the likelihood that Radnor would be around for a long time and there was no use borrowing grief. She looked with renewed interest at the oaks and junipers strayed into the open like scouts for the vast ranks of forests behind them. On sandy knolls above the creek, big yellow-centered blooms of evening primrose looked incredibly white and fragile amid pointed gray-green leaves.

As they crossed the creek, a handsome white-fronted bird with white-blazoned black wings and back gripped a tree trunk and regarded them from spectacled eyes that, along with its jaunty crimson cap, gave it a clown look. "Acorn woodpecker," Radnor said. "They peck little holes in dead trees and hide acorns in them for winter feeding because they're one of the birds that stay year round. Cheery they look, when the snow's on and lots of the bright-feathered birds have headed south."

"You seem to know a lot about birds and flowers and things."

"I just watch. Hear those scrub jays screechin' at us? They're real sociable, always in a small group. There's another bigger kind with a dark crest that we may see up on the mountain. It can make a call just like a hawk."

She didn't need to ask about the panic that would cause in small birds. The broad mouth of the canyon began to narrow, the northern side of the mountain on their left much more densely forested than the rockier south-facing cliffs to their right, where wind had scoured away soil and vegetation from the stone skeleton. Tenacious shrubs and stunted trees gripped every niche that held enough earth for a roothold. Again, as in Galeyville, Katie was amazed at how the world created by the watered protection of the canyon differed from the hillocks and plain, though century plants and yucca still daggered their way through the lower growths of manzanita, mountain mahogany with its curly tassels, squawbush buckthorn, and chokecherry. Wild grapevines coiled sinuously on trees along the creek. She cried out in delight at yellow, long-spurred columbines dipping over the stream.

"Those trees with the bark sort of grooved into squares and oblongs is mountain cedar," Radnor said, nodding at a giant trunk that forked into one side all broken and dead while the other part lofted above, luxuriant blue-green. "Looks like lightning blasted part of this one, but they sure hang on."

The dark trunks and deep green needles of pines made the sycamores gleam the whiter, but Katie saw that many of the sycamores, often growing in a number of trunks from one base, had olive gray bark on their lower parts. This bark seemed to flake off continually, leaving greenish blotches that gradually turned to white. Though most of the walnut trees were smaller, a few reared fifty feet high and were as broad-trunked as many sycamores, perhaps four feet thick, though sycamores and pines were the trees that towered above all others.

Warned by a heralding clatter of jays, a herd of whitetail deer bounded from a glade, the upheld back of their tails a flag of danger. Radnor had his rifle in the scabbard at his knee, but made no move for it and Katie was glad. On this day, so rare and joyous for her, she didn't want anything to die.

Where the way was wide enough for two, they talked, Radnor answering her questions willingly enough though without much detail. He'd been born in Missouri, but when the border, several years before the Civil War, became a battleground disputed between pro-slavery men and Kansas Free-Staters, his father hadn't been over from England long enough to work up enthusiasm for either side and had none at all for being pillaged by both. The family moved to Colorado, where William Radnor died of consumption. Fourteen-year-old Bill worked in a livery stable while his mother took in boarders, too proud to appeal to her husband's family, who'd disapproved of his marriage.

"She was still mighty pretty," Radnor said. "Married a mine superintendent who gave her three babies in four years. Ruined her health. When she got pneumonia, she couldn't fight it off. I was long gone by then. Freighted, worked in the mines, broke horses, rode for the Pony Express till the railroad put it out of business. The Express liked to hire orphans, and I came close enough. Drifted down to Texas, then, and drove longhorns up to Abilene and Newton and Dodge. Got my own team and wagon and freighted till I got tired of it. Worked for Jess Chisum in New Mexico and now I'm here."

"You've done a lot of things."

"Oh, those were just my main jobs. I drove a mail stage, scouted for the army, was a blaster in the mines, and even was a deputy sheriff for a couple of months in Dodge."

Katie sighed.

He raised a dark eyebrow. "Guess it sounds fiddle-footed, Miss Kate, but it's sure not out of the ordinary."

"There's one thing you didn't try."

"Robbing trains?"

"Homesteading. Taking up land."

He stared at her, aghast. "Why would a man do that unless he was loco in love with some filly who broke him to double harness and hitched him to a plow?"

"Lots of men do."

"Look, Miss Kate," he said patiently, "no man under forty in his right mind, of his own choosin', would plant and plow and fight drouth and grasshoppers. But nature fixes it so girls get a bloom and shine on them that tangles up a man like a bee mired down in pollen when what he wants is nectar. The poor benighted fella gets drunk with all that sweetness, and by the time he sobers up, he's got a family to support."

"My gracious goodness, Mr. Radnor!" began Katie, between laughter and indignation. "You —"

"And one thing's sure as Gospel. It's in men to wander, at least till their bones start to creak, but it's woman's born nature to nest. That's one reason I came out here. It's depressin' to see wide open country chopped into little squares all planted and plowed and fenced. When they talk about breaking land, it means a lot more than they mean it to."

"Yet you're helping us find land."

"Don't see I can do much else."

He said it so resignedly that Katie's temper rose. "If you feel that way, go right back to Galeyville. I'll find a place by myself."

"Miss Kate, there's no need to go pitchin' and buckin' because I told you the plain truthful facts."

"Facts! Sounded like your own crazy notions to me." She gave him a withering stare. "I thought you felt sorry for women, talking the way you did about them marrying too young and wearing themselves out having babies."

"I am sorry for them — and the men, too. Neither one's to blame. Nature's got her plans

— and snares and delusions — to carry on the race."

"But so far you haven't got snared or deluded!"

He laughed. "Plenty of times. But I always shied away when the gal strolled up to me holdin' sugar in one hand but with the other hidin' a bridle behind her."

"I suppose," Katie sniffed, "that when you turn forty and your bones creak and you're not worth powder to shoot you, then you'll hunt for a warm fireplace and a woman to coddle you."

"Sure, if I live that long. But no woman's going to be that much of a fool."

I would be, she thought. *If I loved a man, I'd marry him no matter how broken down or staved up he was.* "When will you turn forty?" she asked and blushed hotly.

"In about eleven years. Miss Kate —"

"I wish you wouldn't call me that. It sounds like Mistake or Miss Skate or — or —"

"Miscreant? But Miss MacLeod seems pretty cold."

"Bride calls me Katie. I don't see why you can't."

"Be pleased to, Katie, if you'll stop 'Mr. Radnoring' me."

From the start, she had thought of him as Bill, making the name a caress, but it was strange and delightful to speak it aloud. "All right, Bill."

The way narrowed as they made the long, gradual ascent from the canyon and the source of the creek to the ridge she had seen from far back in the valley. Bill took the lead in a silence somehow warmer and more companionable because of their argument. At a saddle or dip on the top, they gazed down at forests that seemed to sweep endlessly away to distant blue ranges.

"The other side of the mountain." Bill's smile had a wry twist. "You always think you're going to see something different, something special, but after the climb, it's generally just more of the same."

"The same is pretty wonderful. You're spoiled, Bill Radnor."

"Reckon so. Yonder's Pinery Canyon. A Mormon named Morse has a sawmill on Turkey Creek in Morse Canyon where freighters get wood for Tombstone and Fort Bowie, and pretty close by, B. F. Smith sells them whiskey. There's another sawmill in there someplace, and a family named Stafford has a home in Bonita Canyon. Once Tom Jeffords had his Indian agency down there in Pinery."

"I thought it was at Fort Bowie." Even in Texas, people had heard of Tom Jeffords, whose friendship had persuaded Cochise to endeavor, for the most part, to get his Chiricahuas to dwell in peace with white men.

Bill laughed. "That agency moved around, Katie. It was at the San Simon Cienega for a while, too, because Cochise moved around over all his reservation, and Jeffords moved right with him. Take a look behind you."

Turning Sweet Alice, Katie gasped at a gray summit she hadn't even seen from below. The serried, weather-sculpted cliffs formed the massive profile of a reclining giant — forehead, bold nose, jutting lips and chin.

"Some poetical folks have taken to calling it Cochise Head." Bill waited till she had looked her fill before turning his horse to the left and starting along and up the crest of the ridge. "Reckon he might not be too flattered, but it's a way of keeping his name on the country."

"His name," echoed Katie with a rush of guilt, for how could the Apaches not have loved this land?

"Cochise is sleepin' in his stronghold over in the Dragoons," Radnor said with a north-westerly jerk of his head. "Though I've heard that Nana, an old Mimbres who doesn't lie, says that this winter he saw the spirits of Cochise, of Mangas Coloradas, and Victorio, rise from the ground at the prayer of a shaman called the Dreamer."

"Do — do you believe that?"

"I don't *not* believe it." Bill stared at the giant profile. "Anyhow, when Cochise died about seven years ago, no one else was strong enough to control his band. There's no way Apaches can run loose with whites coming in and no way a reservation would work this close to Mexico, because U.S. soldiers aren't supposed to pursue hostiles across the line, and all they have to do is scoot to the Sierra Madre where no army can root 'em out. Even when Cochise lived, the Apaches just kept raiding into Mexico like they've done for several hundred years, killing and running off stock. They depended on that plunder like town folks provision at a store. At San Carlos, a hundred miles farther north, raiding parties still break off the reservation and hightail it across the border. They don't pass up any easy pickin's on the way."

In Lordsburg and Deming, Katie had heard horrifying stories of torture, murder, and babies impaled on meat hooks. She didn't want anything like that to happen to her and the children. But still, gazing out across this wild, savagely beautiful country, she felt a pang for those who, except as fugitives, would never stand on this high ground again.

IV

From the saddle, they could see in both directions, but as they ascended, the going was easier on the left slope and they picked their way along it, through scrub that caught at legs and clothing and rocks washed down from the crags. Much too often for Katie's peace, the slip of one hoof on a loose rock — and it seemed they all were loose — would have meant a plunge to the gorge below, but Sweet Alice planted her hoofs neat as a dancer, and in spite of her reputation for conjuring rattlesnakes from rustling leaves, she didn't mince or fidget when Bill's horse precipitated driblets of gravel. Trying not to look down, Katie fixed her eyes on the easy sway of Bill's shoulders, glad that he couldn't see how tense hers were.

If we ever get down, she thought. If we ever, ever get down in one piece —

After dipping perhaps a hundred feet below the top, they had climbed steadily and now came out at the end of the mountain, able to see in all directions. Behind and to the right, canyons and mountains faded at last into the sky. On the left, flanked by a cone-shaped peak stretched into a greatly elongated tip,

Cochise Head dominated the whole canyon. Far below, through foliage that had been their roof little more than an hour ago, the creek glittered like a crystalline serpent twisting from the rocky springs that birthed it till it vanished far out in the muted, shimmering purple and gold of the plain.

"High, wide, and handsome." Bill swung down and helped her to alight. As unsteady from his touch as from hours in the saddle, she gripped the horn till she was sure of her legs. He took off his hat. The crisp breeze stirred his hair, tangling it over his forehead. Katie longed to touch it, smooth the thick black waves. He spoke softly. "From here you can see forever."

"Or farther." The view in every direction was breathtaking, but she was fascinated by this hawk's view of the way they had come, of the straggling line of naked hills spearing into the desert as if guarding the precious water as long as they could. How different the landmarks looked from up here! "That must be the Nippers," she murmured. "And Blue Mountain. Haystack."

"Straight in front, that peak setting away out on the plain by itself, that's Harris Mountain. Named for a family that was killed by Apaches eight years ago, at least the parents and two kids were. A girl about your age was carried off to Mexico. Some U.S. soldiers who were down there chasing Apaches found her a few years ago and brought her back. She showed where her family had been murdered, and the bones were gathered up and buried."

Katie repressed a shudder. "What happened to her afterward?" Katie didn't want to know what had happened in Mexico.

"She wasn't happy with the whites. I think after a while the army let her join the Apaches at San Carlos. Most likely she had a baby." He hesitated. "To maybe ease your mind on one thing, Katie, Apaches will kill a woman, torture or mutilate her, but they very seldom ravish. Think it's bad medicine. Of course, they do take captives to wife, and I guess not many women would object because that'd be a sight better than being a slave. Apaches don't scalp, either, except now and again for a dance trophy."

But they did set fires under men lashed to their own wagon wheels or hang them upside down over slow green wood that boiled their brains. . . . "Hey, that's not why we came up here." Bill seemed to read her thoughts. "I want you to see all the possibilities, get a clear notion of where the creek runs, because most of all, you'll need water. You think it over and we'll have lunch."

He hobbled the horses, who moved around

cropping grass. Untying a slicker from behind his saddle, Bill produced a bundle wrapped in old newspapers that he smoothed for a table-cloth. From the look of it, he'd raided all the stores for delicacies — smoked halibut, oysters, French sardines, butter crackers, several kinds of imported cheese, and things she'd never seen or heard of before, almonds, dates, and figs.

"It's so good!" She nibbled a cracker and a wedge of the Edam cheese he told her was from Holland, across the ocean. "May I save some of mine for Jed and Melissa?"

"I left them a bag of goodies, so you eat up, my girl." He heaped a blue enamel plate and handed it to her with an admonishing grin. "It's fine to have a conscience and look out for the young 'uns, but it's not plumb wicked and depraved to enjoy yourself sometimes. Here, have some sarsaparilla. This overlook is worth champagne, but we don't want you lightheaded when we ease along that ridge."

The sarsaparilla, Katie's first, was sparkling and delicious. So was everything. At this height, the breeze was just cool enough to temper the sunlight. So far from the world below that she felt free of it, Katie savored the air, sure that it was sweeter and far more intoxicating than the champagne she had never tasted.

She listened, enchanted, to the melodious rise and fall of a vireo's song, the staccato of a hairy woodpecker on a blasted pine, the low-pitched *chuck* of a warbler with a yellow-rump — all these birds she had known in Texas and recognized with a thrill of pleasure. Like winged petals, butterflies clung to scarlet paintbrush and a bee hummed approval of the lupines. Colors vibrated, an infinitude of shades and hues in crumbling rocks, earth, and the shadings of green in trees, bushes, and plants, varied from nearly black to feathery almost yellow.

To see and hear and breathe and feel — how blessed to be alive on such a day even if Bill hadn't been there! But he was, he had brought her here, and there could never be a time or place more perfect than these they shared.

Leaning against a ledge, Bill sipped from his tin cup. "Know what this reminds me of?" he asked lazily. "When Jesus was fasting in the wilderness, the devil took him to a place so high they could see all the wonders of the world, promised to give him all of it if Jesus would fall down and worship him. But I don't think they had this fine a view."

"Neither do I." Unable to contain her joy, Katie unpinned the thick coil at the back of her neck, threw back her head, and let the wind lift and riffle her hair. "Oh, Bill! If I died this minute, I'd think being up here had made my life worth living, that I couldn't ask for more."

He laughed with tenderness that was close to pity. "Honey, there's so much you haven't done! So many good and sweet and wonderful things."

His voice changed. From the immense and dazzling plain, she looked toward him, caught in her breath at the luminance of his eyes, which in this light shone with the brilliance of the sky. His smile faded. A muscle knotted in the gash of his cheek beneath the high plane of bone. His gaze searched her as if he was seeing her for the first time. He straightened and half-turned his back, staring across the light and shadow.

"I guess I've never felt happier, either." He spoke softly, as if to himself before rising to his feet. "Got to be going if you're going to play your harp this afternoon." He spread his hand, offering her all that world below them. "What do you think, Katie? What will you choose?"

Hard to believe it was true when only a few days ago, out on that plain, fearing death for her family and animals, she had desperately searched the mountains for a hint of water. Even if she had killed Missou so they could drink, there was no certainty, in this dry season, that they'd have turned up a watered canyon. Bill had saved them. There was no way she could ever repay him.

"Bill, you can have your pick of the Steel Dust mares, and keep the colt, too."

"Now what brought that on?" He furrowed his brow in amusement. "Hang onto those mares, Katie. If I'm still around when one of the foals gets big enough to ride, I'll let you make me a real good deal on it." He swept his arm out over the canyon. "Right now, you'd better be deciding on your place."

"I love the trees," mused Katie, "but I don't want to be in the thick of them, and there's better grazing in the rolling land between the canyon and the desert." Studying the region below, she finally said, "What do you think about building on the north side of the creek where it bends after leaving the canyon? There's grass and scattered trees; that ridge cuts off the north wind; and when it's hottest, the horses and cattle can range up the canyon."

"Couldn't have picked better myself." Bill wrapped the cans and dishes in the newspaper and rolled them up in the slicker, which he tied behind his saddle. "Let's hustle down and see how it looks from the ground. That's where you'll be living, after all."

Of course. A person couldn't live up here,

miles from water, where storms blew fiercest and snow packed deep in winter, where there was little grass and the earth too stony and rugged for a garden and fruit trees.

No, she thought regretfully, getting to her feet. You couldn't live here. But she would still come up sometimes, to wonder and admire. And dream of this time with Bill. He helped her into the saddle as quickly as he could without dropping her, but the feel of his hands lingered, warm and thrilling.

He rode ahead, shoulders rigid, and she had to follow, confused by her own feelings.

"It's a beautiful place," she told Melissa and Bride as she hurriedly tidied herself for her performance. "There's a slope above the creek with plenty of big oaks and junipers. Good grass for the cows and horses, and that line of mountains to the north will keep them from drifting that way. I think you'll like it, M'liss, but if you don't, then find a site Mr. Radnor says is all right."

Melissa scrunched her freckled nose and gave a toss of her head that bounced her long yellow braid with the blue ribbon Bride had found for her. Her monthly flow had started last fall, but something must have happened during the trip when Katie had been too tired and worried to notice. When they left the

Nueces, Melissa was flat as a stave, but now, undeniably, her chest was starting to curve like twin halves of small, firm apples. Growing up, no mistake about that.

How will I manage? thought Katie with a surge of anxiety. *I'm not all that much older than she is. If she doesn't want to mind, I won't be able to make her.* Till now, Melissa had always looked up to her and tried to imitate her, but Katie suspected that was about to change.

"I suppose," said Melissa snippily, "that if I don't like the place you picked, you'll have to go look at the one I choose — and if you don't like it, you'll decide on another spot and it could go on till Jed's old enough to have a say-so!"

"Gracious, I hope not!" Katie giggled at the prophecy but quickly sobered. "Where is Jed?"

Melissa sucked in her breath and glanced hopefully at Bride, who shook her head. "He was pulling grass for old Ignacio's burro when I went to the store right after dinner but I haven't seen him in several hours." She said soothingly to Katie, "He must be visiting with somebody, dear. No need to get in a tizzy."

"But I've told him not to go inside anywhere without coming back to say where he'll be." Heedless of her uncombed hair, Katie was already making for the door. "If he went to the mine or smelter —"

Bride caught up Rosie and hurried out behind the sisters, who started different directions along the single street, calling Jed's name. Before there was time to panic, Jed pushed through Babcock's swinging doors, obviously urged along by an elegant man in striped pants, gleaming half-boots, and a black coat with velvet lapels that opened to reveal a vest of silver brocade worn over a starched white shirt with — yes — ruffles! And the cuffs extending below the coat sleeves were ruffled, too, and fastened with gems that shot many-colored fire, as did the large stone in his ring. A black silk tie was tied in an artfully careless bow in front of the stiff collar.

"Ladies," he said, and bowed.

Dazed by his splendiferous garb, it was only as he straightened that Katie looked into eyes such a light gray that they could have been ice. The skeletal look of his thin face was emphasized by being clean-shaven except for perfectly trimmed sideburns. Dark silver hair waved the slightest bit and, though rather long, was barbered to contour the head. He had a complexion that could almost have been called ivory, and his hands, smooth and supple with impeccably trimmed nails, made Katie ashamed of her own cuticle-torn rough ones.

Katie's stunned silence brought a twinkle to the cold eyes. "I trust I am addressing Miss Katherine MacLeod, madam. Having been away on business, I returned to find praises of your music on every lip. I greatly anticipate the pleasure of hearing you very shortly." One of those slender, pale hands rested on Jed's shoulder. "Your brother chanced in, running an errand for Jake Trimble, our worthy barber. He was so interested in watching the play that I thought it no great harm if he came back after delivering Jake's finger-steadier. I am, at your service, John Diamond."

Katie had never seen a man who lived completely off gambling. In fact the idea had always struck her as incredible, but she suspected that she was looking at one now. If there was anything Pa had inveighed against more than whiskey and harlots, it was gamblers. That this one was so courteous and charming proved him oiled with the devil's grease, but what terrified Katie was the way Jed gazed up worshipfully at the man. With no father or older brother to show him how to behave, he was all too likely, Katie feared, to idolize someone like this.

"Jed," she said sharply, "go fill Mrs. Malone's kindling box. That's your job, remember?"

Jed's lower lip thrust forward. "Aw, Katie! Let me watch just one more hand. Mr. Diamond turns this big ring around, see, and it's just like a little mirror that shows the cards he's dealing —"

The gambler's frosted eyebrows shot up, and the graceful hand tightened on Jed's shoulder. "You noticed that, my boy? Indeed, you've a gifted eye, a natural —" At Katie's glare, he coughed. "I must ask you to keep that under your hat, or rather, beneath that curly thatch. Run along now, son, and do what your sister bids."

With a glance of adulation, Jed went. Was it too late? Was he already infected? "Encouraging my brother to watch you gamble is bad enough, sir." Katie's voice shook and she swallowed hard. "But teaching him how to cheat —"

Diamond had already recovered. "My dear young lady, that kind of refinement is collecting information, not cheating, and I use it only when playing, as I am now, with other professionals who have their own little tricks."

"That's so," Bride interposed. "Jack never deals from a stacked deck or palms cards or keeps them up his sleeve."

He bowed again. "Thank you, Bride." His eyes were cold again as he looked at Katie. "I'm sorry to have upset you, Miss MacLeod. It didn't occur to me that a lad with the run of Galeyville could be corrupted by my com-

105

pany. Since you think so, I'll send him away if he peeps in."

Back stiff and straight under the handsome coat, polished boots clicking, he strode inside, but he controlled the swinging doors so that they didn't flap back and forth. Bride slipped an arm around Katie, leading her across the street.

"Katie girl, it's not the end of the world because Jed watched a card game. He was bound to sooner or later, just like he'll try whiskey someday and see whether or not he likes it."

"It's not just the cards!" Katie wailed. "Jed thinks that — that card-sharp is the grandest man in the world!"

Bride's arm stiffened and withdrew. "He's not the worst, by a long shot, and he's not a card-sharp. He won't play with greenhorns, and many a time, when someone's cleaned out, he's given them money to live on. When a collection's taken up for a killed or hurt miner, he puts in as much as Lord Bill. Jed could look up to a lot worse men than Jack Diamond."

"I still don't want my brother to be a gambler!" Stung by the rebuke, Katie averted her face and hurried upstairs to finish getting ready to perform.

She'd had such a wonderful time with Bill

106

that she'd scarcely given her brother and sisters a thought! She didn't deserve to be trusted with them, but she was all they had. What this proved was that the sooner she got the family, especially Jed, out of Galeyville, the better.

Holding the door for Katie, who was carrying the harp, Bride gasped as she looked across at Babcock's. "Heavens to Betsey, they're swarming like bees to a queen! The parsons sure never drew such a crowd! We'd better go around by the back."

Katie blanched at the jostling throng of miners, cowboys, and businessmen who made way for Mrs. Firbank and Mrs. Metzger. "Bride! There's no preaching today! They — they've come to hear me."

"To be sure, *mavourneen.*" Bride gave her arm an impatient tug. "Come along, let's get you playing before somebody tramples on some other body's toe and a fight starts."

"I — I don't think I can —" Katie's knees actually knocked together. She felt as if her insides had turned to water and she was going to collapse any minute.

"You certainly *can't* not! Disappoint all those folks and make a fool out of Lord Bill? There's more to you than that, Katie."

Bill loomed behind them, fresh-shaved and

wearing a clean blue shirt. "Let me carry that harp," he offered, and gave a soft whistle as he looked across the street. "Say, Katie, I'll bet you could make a living with your harp and not have to ranch at all."

"I'm going to ranch," she said, and suddenly her ribs took shape again with her heart where it belonged and energy filled her. Those were the men who were going to build her house, her barn and corrals. Of course she'd play for them. Even the sight of Ed Larrimore riding up the street didn't paralyze her.

"Let's go." She marched between Bill and Bride as if going forth to battle.

Two hours later, amid applause that thundered in her heart and ears, Katie escaped out the back. Playing for the family had never been like this. What flowed between listeners and a singer that banished weariness and time, wove a magic closeness? At first she hadn't dared look at her audience, but after a while, it had been easy, even with Ed Larrimore somehow established on the front row and John Diamond at the back, surrounded by — women, Katie decided. *Harlot* was an ugly word, and she didn't feel like applying it to anyone in that group with whom she'd shared her music and felt such closeness.

Bride came out, smiling. "What a voice you

have, Katie, and the way you bring tunes out of that harp! How my grandfather would have loved it! Lord Bill's in there now getting the work shared out so's your house can get started. He was mobbed — everyone was that eager to help."

"It doesn't seem right, Bride. A few hours of music for a house and a corral." Katie halted. "Are you sure they don't just feel sorry for us?"

"Of course they want to help, and what's wrong with that?" demanded Bride, shooing her along. "Gives them something to do besides drink and gamble, something they can feel good about. Besides, you'll come back and play for us sometimes, won't you? It would sound so pretty at a wedding."

Wedding? Bride's? None of your business, Katie told herself. "I'd like to come and play now and then," she said.

"Good. To my mind, we need music, something different from what they pound out on the saloon pianos, a sight more than preaching. We'd better hustle, love. My lads will be in, hungry enough to eat a bear. Could you make the biscuits while I do the gravy?"

There was, thought Katie wryly, not much chance of getting the big-head with miners to cook for.

Melissa, shining-faced, rode off with Bill

next morning, and though it was more than time that she had a day of pleasure and respite from looking after the younger children, Katie felt a pang as she waved them off, and the smile on her lips went stiff and painful.

As she watched the fair head gleaming alongside Bill, heard the rippling of Melissa's laughter, Katie hoped that he wouldn't take Melissa up the mountain. Let her go later, with somebody else! Katie knew that was probably the closest, sweetest time she would ever share with him; if he took Melissa, too, it would show that to him it hadn't been that special.

The riders were still in sight when the sound of hoofs, jingling of harness, and a rumbling of wheels and creaking of wagons came from the wagon yard by the smelter. "There they go for your logs," said Bride. "They'll cut them up White Tail Canyon, and, provided Melissa likes the place you chose, the logs can be hauled right to the site, trimmed and peeled and notched and laid up. That's Barney Sykes with the big mules. He's a mason and will put in a good rock foundation before the sills and floor beams are laid. They'll need to be cedar to keep from rotting that close to the ground, but pine'll do for the rest. Of course green logs are going to shrink, and you'll have to keep chinking cracks till they're good and cured."

She called a greeting to Ignacio Flores, weathered dark as a tree trunk and as wrinkled. Mounted on his burro, he looked wispy beside a big man with a bushy cinnamon beard who was almost as large as his own ambling burro. The two reined in, doffing their hats. "I'm Hod Carson, Miss MacLeod." The mountainous one was missing a side front tooth, but it didn't dim his smile. "Nacho and me are goin' to fetch in the best walnut we can find and get it to curing in the kiln so's when you figger out what furniture you need, we can get right to buildin' it."

"But Mr. Carson, I can't pay you!" Katie protested.

"You already have, miss, with your singin'. If I die and go to heaven, I hope the angels sound as sweet." Planting a shapeless black hat firmly on his crinkled hair, he clucked to his burro and rode on with Nacho.

"Hod made all my furniture," said Bride. "He does such nice work that folks from Tombstone lots of times order from him. He makes the handsomest coffins you ever did see."

Tears sprang to Katie's eyes. "It — it's too much, Bride. I can't let them do all that for us!"

"You can't stop them," Bride said. "They held a meeting yesterday while you were gone

— got everything organized. It's not costing money, love, just sweat and know-how. Galeyville's adopted your family. Not much you can do about it short of hurting folks."

"I should at least go over and cook while they're building."

"Every man jack of them can cook, and it's sure easier on Rosie to stay here till the cabin's ready. What we can do is fix a scrumptious dinner to celebrate when the building's done," Bride placed her fingers admonishingly over Katie's opening mouth. "If you're going to stew about the cost of the food, *mavourneen,* we'll keep track and you can pay for it later in milk and butter. But for now, we'd better be after changing sheets and getting the washing started."

Stirring soapy sheets in the boiler, dipping them out, steaming, into the washtub, where they had to be scrubbed on the corrugated board, wringing them out and rinsing them twice, wringing them each time, and finally spreading them on the manzanitas — Katie gave thanks that Bride only changed half her boarders' beds at a time. Katie's old green dress stayed splashed in front and sweated between the shoulders. Rosie slept in her box under the oaks shading the house, and when she fretted, Bride often got to her faster than

Katie, to change, feed, cuddle, or do all three. Jed heaped up a pile of firewood, pulled grass for the horses and cows in the corral, and helped Katie carry the rinse water to Bride's hollyhocks and valiant roses. By then it was time for a quick meal. He wolfed down bread and sausage, then gave Katie a look halfway between belligerence and appeal.

"I can go play now, can't I, Katie?"

"Of course you can, dear. But be home before supper. And don't you even think about peeking inside Babcock's saloon!"

Checked halfway on his joyous dash to the door, Jed turned slowly. "Aw, Katie!" His blue eyes glinted with rebellion in the child's face with its snubbed nose and rounded, dimpled chin. "The men there give me nickels to run errands. I'm saving up for a pair of boots. Katie, listen, I'll give you half —"

"Why, Jedediah MacLeod, the very idea! The less you have to do with that kind of person, the better! Now promise to keep away from there, or you'll have to stay in the yard."

His mouth quivered. "All right!" He rubbed his arm across his eyes and whirled away. "But you — you were a whole lot nicer, Katie, before you started acting like our mother!"

Katie took an involuntary step after him, stopped as the door banged, and clenched her

hands in frustration. "Why can't he understand? I certainly don't like scolding, telling
him he can't do things!" A tear slid along
the side of her nose. "Bride, how will I ever
get him and Melissa raised? Rosie's different.
She won't remember our folks. But the other
two —"

Bride put an arm around her and patted
her shoulder. "Take it a day at a time, dear.
Sometimes an hour or a minute's all a body
can manage! Melissa and Jed have good hearts,
and neither one's scared of work. You'll do
fine once you get settled." Someone knocked
at the back. Glancing through the window,
Bride said, "It's Wing Lee from over Tombstone way. He and some other Chinese raise
the best vegetables you ever tasted. Sell them
to the camps. I order a load every week because
I don't want my lads to get scurvy."

Wing was unloading a slatted crate from a
dainty-hoofed, black-eared little burro that
looked half asleep. Inside the crate was a damp
gunnysack and lining it was a smaller one.
A slim young man in ordinary clothing, Wing
Lee had a long pigtail hanging down his back,
broad, flat cheekbones, and soft, dark eyes.
Smiling at Bride, he carefully shook his wares
into an empty tub.

"Nice carrots today, Missy Malone." His
r's sounded rather like l's. "Radishes. New

114

potatoes. Peas. Onions. Spinach. Ten dollar."

Crisp and tempting as the vegetables looked, that sounded like robbery, but Bride only nodded and stepped inside for the tea can where she kept her operating money. The rest was placed with a Mr. Turner who served as Galeyville's banker though he had no official institution. After a paid and thanked Wing Lee departed, fortified with coffee and a piece of Bride's peach pie, Katie asked how Chinese happened to be in Cochise County.

"Most were part of railroad-building crews or drifted here from other mining camps. They're hard workers at whatever they take up, but lots of people don't like them because they'll work for a lot less. Bisbee's not the only camp where they're not allowed to stay the night. Part of the trouble is that they often start laundries or boarding houses, and those are the two main ways that miners' widows make their livings." Bride didn't say that she was one of these. Carrying the tub into the kitchen, she gloated over the contents. "We'll have spinach for supper and new potatoes creamed with peas. The other things will keep. Thank goodness, there's enough potatoes for most of the week. The sheets should be dry, Katie. We'd best get the beds made and those rooms cleaned."

"It just seems so far from their own country," Katie mused. "Living must be terribly hard in China for them to come here."

"It's starving sends most folks here like the potato famine did the Irish almost forty years ago." Bride shook her head, sighing. "It was about that same evil time that the Cornwall mines began closing. Between them, Cousin Jacks and Irishmen did most of the mining in this country till only a few years ago. Cornishmen are proud, mind — they're Celts like the Irish and Highlanders, though for the most part they be shouting Methodists. When Cornwall copper crashed in 'sixty-six, rather than go on the parish as paupers, thousands of miners came to America. Hal Trego and Tim Penrose were just lads then." Bride's lip curled. "They can talk all they want about religion, and sure, 'tis grand to follow your own without being hounded, but in the main, it was empty bellies brought folk to this country, and the chance of doing better."

Carrying Rosie from room to room, they made beds, shook rag rugs out the windows, swept, and dusted. Besides beds, each room had a washstand with an embroidered cloth behind to catch the splash from the basin, a chest of drawers with an oil lamp in the middle of a crocheted doily, and two straight chairs. Though simple and sturdy, the furniture was sanded smooth and buffed to a mellow sheen.

Katie asked how much Bride had paid for each piece and sighed as she estimated how much butter and milk it would take to pay Hod Carson for what the family would need. It would be much nicer than anything they'd ever had, though. Just as she was wondering how the cutting and hauling of logs was going, there was a pelting of steps up the stairs and Melissa burst in.

"Mr. Radnor showed me the whole canyon!" she exulted. "I love it, Katie, that creek running through forests and out to the plain! I think you chose just right. Can our bedroom window face the canyon?"

Relieved at Melissa's enthusiasm, Katie had to dampen it. "Honey, we'll only have one room."

"Two." Bill appeared in the doorway, tousled hair falling across his forehead. "Because of log lengths, we're going to build two cabins with a dogtrot between, each about twenty by fifteen feet. You girls will have a bedroom and Jed will have a loft above the kitchen. We'll dig you a well, put up a milking shed for the cows, and you'll be all set."

The cabin on the Nueces had had only one room with a sleeping loft for the children; Katie had never heard of such luxury. Shaking her head, she said helplessly, "I don't see how I can ever pay them back for all of this!"

"Why, you're giving a lot of these fellas the first chance they've had to be proud of themselves since they came west," said Bill, grinning. "Make music for the town once in a while, and we'll all swear we won the hand." He broke into a chuckle. "Speaking of winning, did you know there's big bets being placed on which parson's going to corral the most sinners this Saturday?"

Katie was too scandalized to speak, but Bride burst into peals of laughter. "They'll bet on that, will they, the devils? Wouldn't put it past them to get dunked or sprinkled in order to chalk up one more for the side they're backing. And after Brother Thomas preached against gambling! Poor man, I hope he doesn't find out about this."

"Oh, it might sort of tickle him," said Bill. "After all, before he got religion, he was one of the best gamblers on the Mississippi. Must still be a little sporting blood in him. Hope to be back in time for that show. Me, I'm betting on the Baptists."

"For shame!" sniffed Bride. "And where are you off to that can't wait for a bite of dinner?"

"Can't talk the rest of the boys into work and not do some myself. Katie, do you want to ride over about day after tomorrow and see where you want the windows and doors, or do you think you can trust us?"

She wanted to go, not because she didn't trust his judgment, but because she was so excited about the house. It wouldn't be fair, though, to foist the baby off on Melissa for such a reason.

"I'll trust you," she said.

After he was gone, one question roweled her. Had he taken Melissa up on the mountain? Craft was not in Katie's nature, but she now amazed herself by thinking up questions that soon established that Bill had taken Melissa to only the beginning of the canyon.

Vastly relieved, and ashamed of that relief, Katie picked up Rosie's box and went downstairs. While they shelled peas and scrubbed potatoes, Melissa chattered happily about her wonderful day and seemed intent on recounting everything Bill had said or done.

Katie thought forlornly that to Bill there probably wasn't that much difference between her and Melissa. At twenty-nine, three years must not seem important. But it was, for a girl. Even one year could shade her from child into woman. It seemed to Katie, pushed over the line too fast by her parents' death, that she was to have the responsibilities with none of the pleasures.

What? Appalled at her self-pity she gave herself a silent lashing. *She was alive when she might well have been dead of thirst, the children with her. The cows and horses had survived, their means of livelihood. Bride had been so kind to them, and right now half the town was over in the mouth of Whitetail Canyon building them a wonderful home!*

It was downright wicked and ungrateful to whine. As for Bill Radnor, she owed him her life. She was lucky to know him, to see him now and then. Yet the thought of a world without him was like imagining a place without sunlight or music.

V

The Irish and Cornish were at their customary zestful bickering during supper Friday evening one week and one day since the MacLeods came to Galeyville. "Sure, there'd be no ore loaded if 'twas left to you cousins." Pat Shaughnessy's blue eyes glinted with devilment as he speared a saffron bun from under Hal Trego's nose. "Shift bosses ye must be, or at the least, blasters. Which flies in the face of what God clear intended for ye with those great barrel chests and shoulders like hams!"

"Cornishmen were miners before the days of Julius Caesar, old son," retorted Trego, whose black hair was streaked with gray. "Ee should be grateful to be pushing a wheelbarrow since she teached you to stand on your hind legs! Now do ee crave an H'irish shifter or un as knows the work?"

"Strut, ye little banty!" growled Pat. "Are ye stuck up that your ancestors grubbed in the dirt like moles whilst the Irish breathed God's good air under the open sky?"

"And starved!" thrust Jerry Polfax, youngest of the Cornishmen and reputedly the mine's most skillful blaster.

"Ye cousins weren't gobblin' your kiddley

broth and figgy hobbin back in the forties when me own poor mither came over from Skye," jabbed Tam O'Neal. "But on account of ye bein' already used to the infernal mines, ye got the cushy jobs — and keep 'em still."

"Oh, aye!" shrugged Trego. "That's because ee got no stomach for the mines longer 'n it takes ee to find somethin' that's more talk than work! Into politics ye've tumbled like Gadarene swine to swill!" He shook his finger beneath Tam's long nose. "Truth, old son! How many times did ee vote in the last election?"

"And ye, did ye vote at all?" Tam curled a disgusted lip. "Ye cousins don't vote, nor will ye stand up against the owners when they try to grind us down."

"We do our work," said Trego, reddening. "Ee robbin' H'irish, ee not only 'ave two votes in elections, but ee votes ten years after ee be dead and buried!"

"What be use of voting when the president sends the Territory whatever pal un's a mind to — like yon Fremont?" shrugged Polfax. "No more, when Cochise County was organized, did we get to elect the sheriff."

"But Fremont, even bein' Republican and with Tombstone a Republican hotbed, still appointed Johnny Behan, a good Democrat. Pima County deputy sheriff in Tombstone he was, notwithstandin' Wyatt Earp. He's a deputy U.S. marshal and was slaverin' after the job." Tam gave a short laugh. "Pays about forty thousand dollars a year, does the sheriff's work, bein' as how he gets a share of fines and is tax assessor with a claim on part of what he collects."

"If 'un collects," grunted Trego.

"Doubt he'll ever try to collect out here," chuckled Pat. "A sheriff's health could decline a whole lot whilst he was ridin' the sixty miles from Tombstone."

A distant rumble swelled into clanking, creaking, jangling of harness, the rattle of wheels, shouts of teamsters, and the sound of many hoofs. "If they don't have your house built, Miss Katie, sounds like they're anyhow through haulin' logs for it," said Liam Shaughnessy, Pat's twin, who had the same fair, curly hair and blue eyes. "As many of them as there were, it shouldn't take long." He grinned broadly. "Who'd have thought to see the cowboys pile into that kind of work? Johnny Ringo, Zwing Hunt, Russian Bill, the whole shebang!"

Bride opened to a knock and a tall, well-built man with a fluffy moustache and gray eyes stepped in and took off his hat to reveal reddish-blond hair. "Good evening, Mrs. Malone," he said in a deep, pleasant voice.

123

"I have a message from Bill for Miss Mac-
Leod."

Katie stepped forward. He inclined his
head. "A pleasure, ma'am. I'm Johnny Ringo.
I've been wanting to say how greatly I enjoyed
your music, never heard sweeter anywhere.
Bill said to tell you the cabin's done and he
and some of the boys stayed over to finish
up the well. We brought up the wagons since
we're through with them, but we'll go back
next week and put up the corral and shed."
Perhaps he read the disappointment in Katie's
eyes, for he added, "Bill counts on getting
here in the morning in time for the preachers'
showdown."

Bride sniffed. "No, none of you want to
miss that since you've all got money on it."

He only laughed, bowed, and went out.
Katie and Melissa were doing dishes when
Hod Carson stopped by to sketch the dimen-
sions of the cabin and ask what furniture they
wanted, scoffing when Katie said that some
beds, a table, and perhaps even a chest of
drawers would be nice and that they should
be able to contrive shelves and benches themselves.

"Cupboards you'll have, Miss MacLeod,
with good tight doors to keep out mice and
other critters. You'll have a chair apiece, with
a high one for the baby, and she'll need a

crib. When she's big enough, I'll make her a bed like the ones I'm makin' the rest of you. To store blankets and such, you'll need a big chest made out of juniper so's moths won't eat 'em, and I'll make a chest for your brother to have up in the loft. One really big one should do you girls. You'll need a stand for the water bucket and washbasin. The overmantels are good and wide, and so are the windowsills, but I'll put up a few extra shelves." The big man stroked his cinnamon beard. "Can you think of anything else?"

Katie knew there was no use protesting. She'd just have to make it up to Hod and hoped he liked butter and milk. "You've thought of everything," she said, dazed.

That night she was so eager to see the house that she scarcely slept at all.

Bride proposed to feed her boarders and hold a feast for the cabinraisers at the same time that Saturday evening. The oven had been kept going from dawn to night Friday, baking pies, cakes, roast beef, and turkeys, and Saturday morning Bride and Katie missed all but the windup of Reverend Thomas's sermon in order to bake all the biscuits thirty hungry men could devour. Since Katie would play that night, she wasn't entertaining earlier, so she carried Rosie in order that Melissa, too, could witness this duel of the parsons.

As the sisters followed Bride out the door, there was a drumming of hoofs, uproarious shouts, and in a flurry of dust, six horses flashed by and were reined in by their riders at the hitching rail in front of Babcock's. Laughing and joking, the horsemen swung from their saddles, loosened the cinches and hitched their mounts.

Sweeping off their hats, they stood back to let the womenfolk enter the building first. Five of the men were young, and one with sandy hair, blue eyes, freckles, and a big grin, was little more than a boy. The eldest, whose shaggy white hair, beard, and moustache revealed only a little leathery skin, stared at Bride with shrewd dark eyes in which unwilling admiration mixed with the amusement that resounded in his voice.

"Howdy, Mrs. Malone."

Urging Katie and Melissa in front of her, Bride said frostily, "Good day, Mr. Clanton."

The old man chortled. "Well, boys," he said without lowering his voice, "did you ever see ladies in such a rush to get inside a saloon?"

"In case you don't know it, there's preaching going on," Bride flung over her shoulder. "You can't get a drink till afternoon, sir, so you'd best take your thirst down to Evil-sizer's."

"Why, ma'am, the boys and me rode in to hear the parsons," said Clanton piously. "Here, Ike, Billy, hold the doors so Mrs. Malone and the gals won't get smacked by 'em when they swing back. Saloon doors are plumb treacherous 'less you're used to 'em. Why, in Tombstone, ma'am, there's so many swingin' doors that ladies walk in the street and leave the boardwalk to men and dogs who don't mind gettin' knocked down."

Reverend Thomas glared at them. Bride, flushing, escaped toward the rear, though to Katie it was no escape. John Diamond, with a cool smile, rose lazily from the piano bench. The three of them managed to sit on it, Katie in the middle, but Rosie, who'd been peaceable enough while being carried, though she'd been roused from sleep, took a dislike to the situation, doubled her knees against Katie's chest, knotted dimpled fists, and howled.

Katie sprang up, attempting to flee, but Rosie broke off in mid-wail. With a kind of interested sounding hiccough, she squirmed in Katie's arms, peering at someone behind them.

"May I?" came a whisper in Katie's ear. Before she could respond, Rosie was lifted away. When Katie turned, Diamond's light gray eyes quizzically gazed down at her past the baby's head, which he very capably supported with one of those elegant hands while Rosie explored the silver watch chain draped across his vest, gurgled, and gripped a handful of sideburn.

Smothering a yelp, he didn't, to Katie's surprise, force open the tiny fingers. He produced his engraved silver watch and lured Rosie into releasing his hair and grabbing it. She would have mouthed it, as she did everything she could hold, but he diverted her by flipping it open. He knew how to handle a baby, and he couldn't turn a three-month-old into a gambler, so Katie turned to hear Reverend Thomas's last fervent expostulation.

"Beloved friends, we brand our calves early, don't we?" His dark eyes blazed in his gaunt face, boring into his listeners. "We don't wait till they're full-grown and mavericked off by some rascal. That's why Methodists believe in baptizing babies, so that from the start that child starts ripenin' for Jesus, and the old devil, that cunnin' rustler of immortal souls, has a lot more trouble enticin' it up some box canyon that looks green and pleasant and turns into hell." The minister's voice sank hypnotically. "Beloved, that soul may fall from grace but it's had a blessin' right from the start. I leave it to you if that don't make sense. Now you're not infants, but all you hearin' me today, dear sisters and brothers, you can be born again, you can be infants in Christ, your souls as clean and pure as any babe's. Let God work mightily in your hearts, and after you've heard from our Baptist brother, if what I've said makes sense to you, come forward and I'll baptize you so that when your Maker calls, you can yell 'Keno!' and win that celestial pot!"

To loud applause, he sank down on the bench Reverend Daggett vacated. The lanky, red-headed preacher, knife jutting from his boot, looked from face to face.

"Folks," he said in a conversational tone, "Our Methodist brother has used up his time and mine, too, but that's all right. Won't take long to put it to you straight why you'd better head for the Baptist corral before Death's pale rider throws his rope on you. Baptists wait till a person's old enough to know what they're doin' when they get baptized — and when we do it, you know you've had your sins washed away, hoof to horn. What good's a little sprinkle? No use a'tall in the desert of sin! When you're really baptized, when the Great Stockman marks you for his own, folks, you don't fall from grace the way Methodists do, you're branded for good. You don't have to fret about back-slidin' and goin' back for a dinky little wettin' down. I've dug out a hole in the creek deep enough to dunk the biggest of you. You'll never have a better chance — and you may not get another chance. Jump out of the devil's pasture, brother man, sister woman, and follow me to the water!"

He strode toward the door. No one moved. Beaming, Reverend Thomas rose and held wide his arms. "I've got a pitcher of water right here, beloved. No need to drown yourself to get a new hand."

Nobody stirred. As the minister's face reddened, Sarah Metzger called, "Bless you, Brother Thomas, your preachin's so good I wish I could come to the mourners' bench, but I've been a Methodist twenty years, feet dug down and resting on the solid rock of Gospel!"

"We be Methodists, Reverend," said a Cornish miner whose companions nodded. "Amen, that we be!"

"And I've been a Baptist since I attained the age of reason," declared Myra Firbank.

"She must have 'tained it and loped right into unreasonableness," whispered a cowboy. "Ever try askin' her for credit?"

The youngest of the five men who'd ridden in with the white-haired Clanton had been lounging against the wall with the others. Now he straightened. "Somebody's got to get baptized by someone." His blue eyes sparkled, and his snub nose wrinkled in a grin as he drew his pearl-handled revolver. "You fellas there on the front row, if you're that keen on hearin' the preachers, you'd ought to be ready to get sprinkled or dipped."

Myra Firbank screeched more loudly than the saloon girls. Men sort of melted out of their seats, Diamond placed Rosie in Katie's arms. "Stay put," he commanded softly and started toward the young man, who swiveled his gun toward the gambler. Johnny Ringo had his hand on his holster when the door shadowed.

"Billy." Radnor's voice was mild. "This is same as a church whilst there's preachin' going on, and I know you'd never pull a gun in a church. You bet a bundle on this contest?"

"We all did." Billy Clanton stared at Radnor; after a moment, he shrugged and holstered the gun. "Shucks, Lord Bill, we heard you put a hundred dollars on the Baptist parson."

Radnor's ears went pink. "You heard right and I've got a proposition to put to all of you. The reverends have put in well nigh a month combing the draws and thickets from here to the Peloncillos and well nigh to Mexico, and they've preached to us three Sundays. It's not their fault most of us know we couldn't stay on the straight trail now if we took it. I reckon we ought to thank them for worrying about us, and right now I'm putting my hundred on the pulpit here and invitin' you to do the same — whatever it is you bet. My notion is to split it between Brother Thomas and Brother Daggett so they can maybe start churches where the ground's not so stony, or use it to help widows and orphans."

Even covered by a sheet, the whiskey crate resounded with the jangle of a spilled-out bag of silver dollars. In an instant, Ringo tossed down a handful of gold pieces. "More where this came from," grinned Billy Clanton, and added a heap of big Mexican pesos. John Diamond's greenbacks were quickly buried by more coins while Mr. Babcock, bald head glistening, sorted the array into two equal piles. Katie stared, mesmerized. She hadn't known even banks had that much money. It looked a fortune.

"Two thousand, nine hundred, and seventy dollars," called Babcock. "I'll round it off to three thousand — that's fifteen hundred apiece." He stepped around the bar and, producing two sacks, began to fill them.

The room, so full of explosive tension minutes ago, buzzed with laughter, ministers vying with their audience to thank each other. "Katie," whispered Bride. "Let me hold Rosie and you fetch your harp. This would be a

132

good time to sing 'Amazing Grace.' "

The saloon rang with that and half a dozen other songs before the ministers jogged off together, Thomas on a mule, Daggett on a claybank gelding, while all of Galeyville waved and cheered them out of sight, whereupon most of Galeyville repaired to drink at the undraped bar.

"Sure, it's a good thing you came when you did, Lord Bill," said Bride to Radnor as he carried the harp across the street. "Those Clantons and MacLowerys! Why don't they kick up their rumpuses in Tombstone instead of coming here?"

"Oh, they're in Tombstone maybe more than's real smart what with bad blood between them and the Earp clan," said Radnor. "Billy hadn't been drinking. He wouldn't have shot anyone unless he was pushed."

"He drew his gun," Bride retorted. "Jack Diamond was heading for him, and Ringo would have drawn in another second."

"It all blew over," Bill soothed, and chuckled. "Both the reverends aim to build churches now. Think they'll do it in the same town?"

"They might." Bride relaxed and giggled. "I think they enjoy fighting each other almost as much as they relish shouting at the devil. You come on in and have a bite to eat, Lord

133

Bill. Won't be much because we're having that big feed tonight."

Giving Rosie to Melissa while preparing some milk for the baby, Katie sighed blissfully and swept a fleeting glance at Bill. She couldn't look at him too long; that did strange things to her blood and breath.

"I just can't wait to see the house." Her throat swelled and she had to swallow. "I — I guess I won't really believe it till I touch the walls and make sure they won't melt away."

"That'll get you smeared with pitch." Bill poured coffee for all of them, including half a cup for Jed, who grinned delightedly and added canned milk. "You'll believe in those walls, Katie, by the time you get through chinking them as they shrink. The floors should be okay. We found enough dead trees that were solid enough to whipsaw into boards, and we used the same cured wood to make doors and window frames."

A knock came at the door. In response to Bride's "Come in!" Mr. Babcock entered. A stocky, wide-shouldered man in his early thirties stepped after him, removing his hat with a genial smile though Katie was sure that nothing escaped his keen blue eyes.

"Mrs. Malone, excuse us for bustin' in on your dinner," said Babcock, "This here is William Breakenridge, deputy sheriff of

Cochise County. He wants to talk with Lord Bill." The saloon owner hurried out as if making it clear he had nothing to do with the officer beyond introducing him.

"Mrs. Malone, delighted to meet you, ma'am," nodded the deputy.

Radnor said pleasantly, showing no surprise, "Is this a private kind of a talk, Mr. Breakenridge?"

The lawman shook his head. "Don't see why it should be. Sheriff Behan figgers it's time folks in the east part of the county started paying taxes. He's sent me over to assess and collect them."

The pupils of Bill's eyes contracted, but his tone was easy. "Sounds like a right interesting job."

"I hoped you'd think so. I'd like to hire you as deputy assessor to ride along and help me."

Radnor's eyebrows climbed toward the tangling curls of his black hair. "Well, deputy, I sure do admire your sense of humor, but —"

"I'm not joking, Radnor. I've already done a pretty good job of collecting in the Sulphur Springs Valley, and I'll do my best around here, but that best will be a whole lot better if you'll back me." His smile was winningly frank. "I also reckon that's my only chance of getting back to Tombstone alive."

Radnor gazed at him for a long, weighing moment. "But you'd go alone." Shaking his head, he burst into laughter. "Doggoned if I won't do it! Be the most fun I've had in a coon's age. Some of the boys will be here tonight for a big supper. We can take care of them on the spot. I know pretty much to a cow how many head they've got." He frowned, remembering. "I can't ride out with you for a couple of days, though, Breakenridge. Got to finish building a milking shed and a corral."

The deputy's eyes flashed a startled question. "Not for my stock," Radnor chuckled. "For this young lady, Miss Katie MacLeod, and Melissa and Jed here. They've just come into the country, and as deputy assessor, it's my opinion that they shouldn't be taxed till next year, when they've had a chance to get on their feet."

"Sounds reasonable," said Breakenridge with a warm smile. "Welcome to Cochise County, Miss MacLeod, Melissa, Jed." He turned to Radnor. "Why don't I assess Galeyville businesses and property today and then go along and help with that building?"

Beaming at him, Bride said, "Pull up a chair and eat with us, Mr. Breakenridge." She added with a bit of challenge, "I doubt if a soul in town has title to the land they've built on, no more than the ranchers do to what they've claimed. I think, sir, that you'll be assessing mostly personal property."

"I'm sure of it, ma'am," he replied with soft courtesy. "With Galeyville and San Simon the only towns on this side of the county, I'm depending on taxing cows more than anything."

"Great day in the morning!" chuckled Bill. "I'm looking forward to that! Tell you what, soon as we eat, let's go over to Babcock's and collect from the Clantons and MacLowerys before they leave town."

No sounds of battle came from across the street. As they prepared for the supper, Bride, Melissa, and Katie occasionally glanced out the door or window and reported, if they saw him, on the deputy's whereabouts.

"He's coming out of Evilsizer's," Bride said in a tone of amazement. "Well, if he can collect there, he shouldn't have trouble anyplace else in town." She frowned and shook her head. "Good grief, there's Lord Bill a-following him! It was mighty smart of that deputy to think of just bald-faced asking Bill to help him, but I hope Bill won't get hurt with this shenanigan." Looking out again, she heaved a sigh of relief. "There go the Clantons and MacLowerys. I'm glad to see the backs of them. No real harm in the young men, just wild, but that old man gets them into devilment."

Devilment there would have been that morning, and possibly killing, had Bill not intervened. John Diamond might have faced young Billy Clanton down, or killed him, but Katie couldn't imagine anyone except Radnor turning thwarted gamblers into cheerful givers. He was the force behind the building of her house. Now he was, for a lark, proposing to help a lawman collect taxes from the most dangerous men in Arizona.

He was playing, even when his impulsive decisions could well prove fatal. What made him treat life like a tremendous joke? She was afraid he would die, without having really lived his life, die in the midst of his laughter.

Bride's miners trooped in, having washed and changed as usual in a big shed near the mine. The men who'd worked on the MacLeod place, relaxing in various saloons, took that for the signal and swarmed toward the boardinghouse. For that matter, most of the town did, the Firbanks and Metzgers, Mr. Babcock, and most of the other businessmen. Bride must have decided to turn it into a community party, Katie decided, getting more rolls out of the oven and refilling a coffee pot that was already empty as the parade filled plates, most of them borrowed from saloons, filing past the heavily laden table and the stove where kettles of spicy beans and rice simmered while crusty breads exuded delicious smells from the open warming oven. Everyone was there, from the mine superintendent to Ignacio and the saloon girls, except for John Diamond.

By the time the last served joined the overflow in the back yard, the first in line were back for second helpings or hovered over the pies and cakes ranged on the sideboard, usually taking small pieces of several kinds.

Horrified at the quantities of food being consumed, Katie whispered, "Oh, Bride! This cost a fortune! You shouldn't —"

"I didn't," Bride said with a reassuring pat. "The stores gave all the fancy canned meats and fruit and ham. The butcher shops contributed. My lads chipped in, and so did the other miners." She glanced around. "Still plenty of everything, and those who want more coffee can pour it themselves. Come on, dear, let's eat, too."

Earlier, they had filled a tub of soapy water on the outdoor laundry fireplace and heated it and the boiler full of clear water so that as people finished, they could scrape their plates in a pail beside it, which would later be emptied for the camp dogs, and then drop the plates and cutlery in the tub. To Katie's amazement, Bill Radnor began washing the dishes and dropping them in the boiler from which Johnny Ringo and Breakenridge extracted them and wiped them with flour sack towels, passing them to cowboys who accumulated a pile and then carried it to the kitchen. When Katie and Bride tried to take over the task, Bill refused to budge.

"You get the leftovers and dishes put up," he said. "We've got this running smooth as good whiskey. And Katie, be sure to sing that song about the high road and low road."

As she started playing, the full moon rose over the mountains and was near the middle of the sky when her voice and fingers could do no more. When the wild applause finally ebbed, Mr. Babcock stood up.

"Not all of us could work on your house, Miss Katie," he said. "But we wanted to have a part in it. Boys, roll those carts over here and let's fill up that wagon."

Even with the plough, rocker, and other items Bill had salvaged, the MacLeod wagon had considerable room, but by the time Mr. Babcock and the others finished packing in gifts, there was scarcely space for Rosie's box to fit behind the seat.

"A bushel of flour from the Firbanks," Babcock called. "Also two pounds of Arbuckle's and a jug of molasses! From the Metzgers, ten pounds of beans, half a bushel of corn-meal, and a pound of salt. Tea and spices and cough syrup from Rynerson. Bein' as how these young 'uns shouldn't be samplin' our wares, my fellow saloonkeepers, our — er, employees, and me chipped in and bought a good Saltillo serape for each bed, for pretty now, later for warm." The tally went on, everything from a rag doll for Rosie to horse liniment and a rope plaited by Ignacio out of rawhide.

Hod Carson announced that he'd deliver the furniture in about three weeks and could bring any additional presents then. Holding Rosie while Jed and Melissa, awed, stood on either side of her, Katie blinked back tears. Till now, she had managed to hope that some-how, someday, she could pay back what they were being given, but she saw now that that was impossible and would even in a way be an insult.

"There just aren't any words —"

"Your music was thanks." Radnor stepped up beside her so close that, though he didn't touch her, she felt protected. "It's time we went home, folks, and let Mrs. Malone and her boarders get to sleep. But first, let me remind those of you who haven't paid your taxes yet that you can catch Breck across the street at the saloon and save us all some trouble."

Amid groans and good-natured catcalls, someone yelled, "You paid taxes on that herd you got up holed up on the mountain, Lord Bill?"

"I was just fixing to, Jeff," returned Bill serenely. "Come on over to Babcock's and shell out for that forty head you have tucked away over in Horseshoe Canyon."

With Breakenridge beside him, he strode around the boardinghouse toward the street. With shouted good nights and good wishes, the crowd followed. Katie, still holding the baby, went into Bride's arms and wept.

Exhausted as she was by the busy and exciting day, Katie turned restlessly long after Melissa and Rosie were asleep. The people of Galeyville, most of whom had probably had hard times of their own, were determined to get the MacLeods off to a good start, and indeed, without renewed provisions, Katie knew she'd have been forced to sell a cow or a horse. What was a careless frolic for Bill was for her little family the difference between bare survival, if that, and comfort beyond anything they'd known. Now it was up to them to make a go of the ranch, and, most of all, it was up to Katie to take care of her sisters and brother.

The mares and heifers were getting near their time. What a sight that would be, four new colts and five calves frisking on the slopes! There might even be a pair of twins. Yes, she countered, trying not to let her hopes swell too high, there might be twins; but foals and calves could die if something went wrong, and so could a mare or a cow.

Don't count your foals till they're dropped, she thought drowsily, and came awake to the sound of the door opening downstairs. The miners were all in bed, Katie was sure.

A thief? Someone bent on doing harm? No one in Galeyville locked doors. The cowboys might be careless about brands, but there had been only a couple of shootings since the beginning of the town and those were in the light of day. Galeyville men might be lawless, but they weren't sneaky. Still, there could be a drifter. Maybe even Apaches — though it was said they wouldn't attack at night.

All this went through Katie's mind in a second. Then she heard Bride's soft glad greeting, and a quiet masculine laugh that, muffled though it was, Katie, with a stabbed, dying feeling, recognized as Bill's.

The walls weren't thick; in fact, at night it was possible to see lamplight glow through the cracks between boards when there was no light in one's own room. The voices went on and on, punctuated by frequent, intimate laughter. They were just behaving with discretion to protect Bride's reputation. Katie knew this, but it felt like betrayal, it hurt like deceit.

After what seemed forever, the complaining door closed again. Long after boots crunched off down the street, Katie lay huddled in a half ball as if to protect her vitals. She wanted out of this room, out of this house, far away from Bride. It did no good to tell herself that they had only talked down in the kitchen. He had come late, while the town slept. Surely only a lover would do that.

VI

Katie came downstairs next morning with heavy eyes and a dull, throbbing head. Horsemen were trotting by, and as she passed the door, she winced as she caught a glimpse of Bill on Shadow, joking with Johnny Ringer, who rode a dancing strawberry roan.

It was always a rush to get breakfast on the table for the men, and there was little chance to talk. Katie kept her back to Bride as much as possible. Only after the miners had collected their lunch pails and tramped out, some whistling, some surly, did Bride look full at Katie.

"What's the matter, dear?" Bride had a glow on her that morning, but now it dimmed and she drew straight black eyebrows together. "Don't you feel all right?"

Katie blushed guiltily. A lot of good it did for Bride to act sympathetic when — when — Harshly, turning away, Katie said, "I'm fine. Just fine!"

"Sure, and you must be frazzled with all the excitement," said Bride with infuriating understanding. "But if it's your time of month, love, a hot pad might help and some nice ginger tea."

145

"I tell you, there's nothing wrong!" Katie bolted with the water buckets.

Fortunately, it was one of Bride's frequent wash days. The exertion of scrubbing on the washboard and heat of the boiler made Katie's face so hot that she was sure it masked any telltale color when she had to look at Bride, and hard work exorcised much of her pent-up feelings. By the time they sat down to a meal of leftovers, Katie could face Bride without a wave of something terrifyingly like hatred. But when Bride laughed, as she did more often than usual, when she threw back her head and Katie saw the pulse in her long, white, slender throat, then indeed Katie tasted blood. She couldn't, simply *couldn't,* stay under Bride's roof an hour longer than necessary.

She opened her mouth to say that she was eager to see the house and get settled, that she was leaving as soon as she could get their things together and hitch up the team, but then she remembered.

Bill would be there. It would be even harder to be around him, without giving away her feelings, than to stay with Bride. After all, it would only be a few more days. Full of minutes that seemed like hours and hours that seemed like weeks . . .

Stop it! she told herself. *If you could journey all the way from Texas, you can certainly behave*

146

with Bride, who's been so wonderful to you.

That made it worse. If it killed her, though, Katie resolved to act as if she hadn't heard last night. The best way was to stay busy. She volunteered to put the sheets back on the beds they'd stripped that morning, and clean those rooms, since Bride had baking to do. Melissa looked after Rosie and helped Bride. After their noon meal, Jed filled the woodbox and, as usual, disappeared.

What a relief it would be to get him out to the ranch! When asked where he'd been, he virtuously detailed errands he'd run for different storekeepers, but it was the time in between those errands that Katie worried about.

Bride had supper cooking when Katie finished upstairs, and Melissa was setting the table. "Why don't you go out for a breath of air, Katie, now it's cooled off?" Bride gave her a concerned scrutiny. "You look as if you were sickening to come down with something."

"I'm fine," Katie assured her, but gratefully escaped. How was it possible to love Bride and at the same time be furious at her? Stopping at Babcock's corral, Katie gave each horse and cow a handful of grass gleaned from outside the fence, smoothed their bulging sides, and implored them not to have their young till they got to their new home.

"You'll be so proud of your baby," she told each one, except for Shiloh and Flossie, the one cow that wasn't heavy with calf. "And so will I. You're going to be famous all over Cochise County. We'll have the best dairy and the fastest, most beautiful horses in the whole territory!"

Trying to think about this rather than last night, Katie wandered down the hill to the creek. There had to be a nest in that giant, many-trunked sycamore for a red-tailed chicken hawk was flying into it with some hapless little creature in its talons, while jays shrilled and vituperated. Two kinds of orioles, old Texas friends, flashed brightly in the leaves, one with a brilliant orange hood that spread down the sides and broadened to cover the underbody while a sort of black bib ran from beneath the eyes down the breast. The other had a black head and shoulders and white-banded wings, but its body was buttercup yellow.

Hoof tracks cut and ridged the mud of the crossing, but away from the passage, damp loam captured a bewilderment of tracks, some she knew like deer, raccoon, and skunk. Others, like fox, coyote, and wolf, she could try to differentiate only from size. There were many more, some blurring others, a page she supposed an Apache could read with much more ease than she could spell out a newspaper column.

Debris tangled in tree roots and bushes showed where the water had run at its highest. It now ran a good four feet below its bank, sparkling over rounded stones that were white and black and every shade of pink, orange, gray, blue-green, and brown, such a glistening course that it was hard to believe they were the same as the dull, blanched rocks the stream had abandoned. A flicker of motion drew Katie's eyes. She looked upstream to see Jed with — heavens, that was John Diamond without his coat and fancy vest, trousers rolled up, bare feet planted on a boulder jutting into the water. He held a fishing rod, as did Jed.

"Sis!" the boy called, high, sweet voice blended with the lilt of the water. "We've caught two nice trout! Uncle Jack's going to cook them for us right here on the bank so I won't need any supper!" His attention fixed again on the line, but Diamond leaned his rod against a tree.

Trousers still rolled, feet white and naked, he winced his way over the rocks to conversational distance. "I hope you don't mind my borrowing Jed, Miss MacLeod. There are few pursuits as enjoyable as going fishing with a boy about his age."

Upset over Jed's calling the gambler "uncle" and even more by the realization that Jed had no man in the family to look up to, not even a brother, that he was in between one sister old enough to boss him and one too small to be a playfellow, Katie felt inadequate and reproached.

"You seem so fond of boys, sir, that I'm surprised you haven't married so you'd have one of your own. Didn't it occur to you to tell me where you were taking my brother?"

The gray eyes chilled. "I saw him down here trying to fish with string and a stick, Miss MacLeod. You being so careful about where he spends his time, I assumed you knew his whereabouts. I merely got my rod and borrowed one for him." His gaze bored into her. "I thought it was the saloon and cards you objected to, but perhaps it was me."

In spite of his sardonic smile, there was hurt in his eyes. Katie remembered how only yesterday he'd soothed Rosie during the preaching, how he'd moved forward to keep Billy Clanton from terrorizing people. She looked now at his bare feet and suddenly burst out laughing. It was impossible to make a villain out of a man when you could see that he had skinny ankles and hair on his toes.

"I'm sorry, Mr. Diamond," she finally

gasped. "I don't want Jed getting interested in cards, but it was nice of you to show him how to fish. Pa never had time."

"I didn't, either," he said beneath his breath. Before she could ask what he meant, he picked his route back to Jed. Sobering, Katie moved up the hill toward town.

John Diamond could fish all he wanted, but he was still a gambler, dangerous. She couldn't keep Jed from meeting such men, but Diamond was one more reason it would be good to get to their ranch.

How was that going to work, though? On the journey, she hadn't thought beyond finding a place to settle in one of Pa's grassy canyons. That was the dream with which she'd encouraged Jed and Melissa. On their own, it would have taken them most of the summer to erect some kind of habitation, shelter for the animals, and a corral, but that struggle would have bound them together while they grew used to living without their parents, while Katie, of necessity, was in charge. Could she hold them together, Melissa so close in age, Jed so starved for a father?

Beside that formidable yearslong-yet-daily challenge, the goal of breeding fine horses and establishing a dairy seemed only a matter of persistence, hard work, applying the knowledge she had, and learning more. Neither that nor the prospect of raiding Apaches or rustlers daunted her as much as knowing she was responsible, she alone, for raising Jed, Melissa, and Rosie. She wasn't old or wise or patient or kind enough, but somehow, she must learn.

Three mornings later, Bill Radnor and Johnny Ringo rode in to escort the MacLeods to their home. "The other boys are waiting out there," Bill explained, swinging one long leg over the saddle horn. "They were all for being an honor guard, but I told them they'd scare your cows and horses clean out of the country. Ready to go?"

It was the first time Katie had seen him since — since that night. Bile rose in Katie's throat. She had to swallow it before she could speak. "The wagon's packed except for a few things we've needed."

"Fine. I'll hook up the team, and then Johnny and I can bring along the other stock."

"You two just climb out of your saddles a minute and have coffee and some pie," commanded Bride. "Katie, darlin', I wish I could go with you and see your place. I will someday when I can find someone to cook for the lads. Now, let's see, I want to send your supper. There's pasties and apple cake, and I'll put these leftover creamed potatoes in a syrup can."

As Katie hurriedly collected their belongings, stripped their beds, and put on clean sheets, she felt a wave of something like fear. In the two weeks they'd been here, Bride's kindness had made it seem like home. It would be so much easier to stay in Galeyville, where they had been made welcome, work for Bride or in one of the restaurants or stores —

No! They hadn't come all the way out here to do ordinary jobs in town. The MacLeods were going to amount to something, claim land, live on and by it. Besides, how could she stay in Galeyville, where even if she weren't in the boardinghouse, she'd know that just a little way along the street, Radnor went late to Bride's house. With the MacLeods gone, they might not just stay in the kitchen.

Galeyville turned out to see the little procession off, Hod Carson promising the furniture in a few weeks; Barney Sykes, the mason, saying mysteriously that he hoped Katie would like something special he'd done; Mr. Babcock urging Katie to play in his saloon anytime she was in town and to be sure to come for the Fourth of July. Myra Firbank said her restaurant customers would relish fresh butter, and Sarah Metzger said she could sell all the milk and butter the MacLeods could send her.

The barber, Jake Trimble, a wizened little man with frizzy brown hair and whiskers, raised a warning finger. "If your stock raises a commotion in the night, be sure your door's barred and a firearm's handy. It's bound to be either 'Paches, or a mountain lion or bear."

Katie held the lines, Melissa and Jed on the board seat beside her, Rosie in her box packed so tightly behind the seat that it couldn't move. John Diamond strolled from the saloon, perfectly attired, though Katie would never forget his bare white feet. Taking off his hat to her, he nodded, and moved up by Jed. "So long, boy."

"There's a creek by our house." Jed's tone was so hopeful it was nearer to imploring than Katie liked. "Maybe you could come over and go fishing, Uncle Jack."

"Maybe I will." Diamond took a small, grubby hand in his graceful one and shook it as solemnly as if, Katie thought with spite, he were bidding farewell to the governor of the Territory. He stepped back, then, and gave her an ironic smile. "Safe journey to you, Clan MacLeod. May you thrive in your home between the canyon and the plain."

Bride clasped her hand a final time, bent to drop a kiss on Rosie's cheek, and stepped away. Shiloh, joyful at ranging free, though the field adjacent to Babcock's corral had been a large one, whickered at his mother and the other horses as if to ask what they were doing hauling a wagon when it was so much fun to dash away. He outdistanced the ungainly cows and rocketed past Ringo and Bill, though he had to slow going down the hill.

Katie's heart echoed the beat of the yearling stallion's hoofs as, after drinking at the creek, he skimmed along the slope, black mane and tail flying as the sun struck sparks from his dark red coat. It would be hard to give him to Radnor when he was riding age, but no other gift in her power to bestow was fit to give the man who had probably saved their lives and certainly prepared a place for them.

From years ago, she remembered words read from the Bible by a traveling minister — Presbyterian, she dimly recollected. "In my Father's house are many mansions. . . . I go to prepare a place for you." It didn't seem at all sacrilegious to think that Bill had done that.

Mountains to the left, the wide plain on their right, beckoned by what Katie already thought of as the Home Mountain considerably west of Haystack and Blue, they passed Harris Mountain and topped a slope. Home Mountain, with its miter of stone, reared some distance north of the flat claimed by a huge corral, several outbuildings and an impressive double cabin.

Heart leaping high, Katie stopped the team. "Look, Jed, Melissa. There — there's Home Mountain Ranch." It could have no other name, not after that burned cabin in Texas, the long, hard traveling.

"Rather be in Galeyville," Jed muttered, but Melissa cried, "It's *big,* Katie! We won't be all scrunched into one room!" She quieted, caught at Katie's arm, and glanced around. "But there's not another house in sight. We'll be out here all by ourselves."

"We're a whole lot closer to town and friends than we were in Texas," Katie retorted, ruffled at having her joy dampened by the others.

"Yes," said Melissa. "But Mama and Pa were there."

That was unanswerable. Katie clucked to the team, but nothing, that day, could long shadow her delight. Eagerly, she strained to see details that gradually came into view. The house had a rock chimney on either end of each cabin. Men were carrying wood and stacking it along the roofed walkway or dog-trot leading between the two. A big corral enclosed a number of oaks as well as a small building that must be the milking shed. Not far from it was a small square structure that had to be a privy. Katie simply couldn't believe that they had such a splendid place without turning a hand beyond playing the harp. A brilliant flash caught her eye and she stared in amazement.

The windows weren't just open oblongs to be covered that winter with oiled, thin-scraped hide. They were glass. Really, truly glass! Bill had pulled Shadow in and she cried to him, "The windows! I'll pay for them just as soon as —"

"They're from the miners who live at Bride's," Bill said with a grin. "Since they work in the dark except for candles, they appreciate light more than most folks, I guess. They wanted you to have three in the kitchen and two in the bedroom, but we rigged up stout inside shutters that you can close and bar if —" He hesitated. "You can fort up real tight if Indians come, but I'd call that unlikely. When they break off the reservation, they generally head for Mexico *muy pronto*, through the San Simon Valley that's easier traveling. But if a couple of strays get over this way, you just let them take the stock and stay inside. Your shotgun's fine for short range, and I'll leave a Winchester. We left a couple of firing holes in each room that are chinked with wooden plugs. You can pull them out if you need to."

"I can shoot," boasted Jed. "But I have to

rest the barrel on something, that old gun's so heavy."

"I'll learn," said Melissa.

"You all need to be able to load and shoot. Chances are you won't need to, but it's sure better to be prepared." He reined aside to keep one of the heifers from heading up a draw where desert willow and mesquite offered enticing shade. Cinders, so named because her brown spots had sooty hairs mixed in them, had more initiative than the other cows. She and indolent, dainty Lady Jane were Flossie's twins, and Flossie was a sister of Queenie. These two five-year-olds had the aristocratic faces and fine bones of Jerseys, which were close kin to Guernseys, both Channel Island breeds. Ribbon got her name from bowlike splotches on her throat. For her and Betsy, whose spots were the color of thickened cream, both bred to a prize Guernsey bull, Pa had traded a Steel Dust colt last year.

Katie wondered where she'd find a bull. She didn't want to cross the Guernseys with range stock and risk filling milk pails with blue-john instead of creamy rich milk that made delicious butter. Surely there were dairy cows around Tucson. At least it wasn't an immediate worry. Strange to have to take charge of the animals' breeding. That had been Pa's concern. Mama stayed inside, and kept the girls in, too, when a neighbor brought his "cow brute," as Mama delicately termed him, to mount the cows, and of course it was Pa who'd made two trips, riding one mare and leading another, to a rancher with a Steel Dust stallion. Katie could no longer pretend the ignorance of such matters expected from a woman. It would be a good many years before Jed could manage that aspect of the ranch.

Home Mountain Ranch. She tasted the sweetness, the comfort, of that name. Bill and Ringo let the cows water at the creek and then urged them up the bank to the corral. Wagons and horses had beaten a track across the ford, pounding down silt and mud till it was firm. Little water splashed on the MacLeods. The creek wasn't more than knee-high in the deepest places, and like Turkey Creek, channels of bleached white, rose, and yellow stones stretched between stream and bank.

The wagon groaned up the slope as Katie encouraged the horses. Shiloh nickered at the cowboys' horses, who were hobbled outside the corral, and several whinnied back. Ringo opened the corral gate while Bill choused the cows in and rode around to the barn, where Katie stopped the team.

Trailing Shadow's reins so the horse would stand, Bill took the lines from Katie and helped her down. The grip of his hand filled her with radiant warmth. Did he feel it, too? He released her abruptly and swung Melissa down as the men congregated outside the corral.

"Here you are!" Bill said, eyes alight. "Welcome to your ranch! Go look inside. I'll take care of the horses."

It would sound strange if she said she'd like to enter her home with him beside her. Blessedly, Ringo stepped up. "I'll see to the horses, Bill. You'd better steer Miss Katie through that bunch or she'll never get to the house."

Flashing a grateful smile at the man so handsome with his red-gold hair, Katie lifted the baby from her box and started to the gate. Hammering and the resinous smell of pine logs came from the small barn, more of a shed, really, with room for hay and one stall for milking, open on three sides. A husky, dark-haired young man flourished a hammer. "Just about finished, Miss Katie. Still got to put up a pole to hold saddles and hooks for bridles and such."

"That's Joe Hill," said Radnor. "Claims to ranch over in the San Simon Valley though I've never caught him at it."

Hill chuckled. "Well, Bill, you claim to ranch in the Animas Valley — that's on the other side of the Peloncillos, Miss Katie, just across the New Mexico line — but I bet your cows don't see you from one branding to the next."

"All they need to," responded Bill tranquilly.

As they started for the house, Bill told her, "The wood piled on the dog trot is left over from the dead trees used for flooring and doors and windows, so it's ready to use. By the time it's gone, you can start on the leavings from the wall logs in that pile yonder."

"It looks like enough to last a year," Katie said. She wasn't very good at chopping wood and looked forward to the day when Jed would be strong enough to take over that chore. Remembering that Barney Sykes had told her to watch for a surprise, she glanced around hastily, but the whole establishment was such a surprise that she supposed she'd have to search later for whatever it was he'd meant.

Tall, short, stocky, or thin, the men clustering by the door had three things in common. They were all young; all browned from the sun; and all wore boots, Levi's, and broad-brimmed hats that they now held in their hands. They were also so intent on studying their toes that Katie was emboldened.

"This is Hi Phillips." Bill indicated a fair-haired, willowy boy who didn't look as if a razor had yet touched his smooth cheek.

"Hank Snow's hid behind that big black handlebar moustache. This sawed-off kid with freckles and baby blue eyes is Charlie Snow. And — shucks, you'll never keep them straight meeting them all in a bunch like this." He raised a hand to check the men who were crowding forward. "Listen, boys, you just wait your chance to introduce yourselves. Meanwhile, how about unloading the wagon?"

They wanted to meet *her*. Amazed but with her first thrill of the delicious power of being a pretty girl — no, woman! Katie smiled at the eager faces. "I do want to meet you and thank you all. This is so wonderful I think I'm dreaming."

"I want to thank you, too," said Melissa in her sweet, clear voice and a smile that made a number of the cowboys study her more closely.

Too young, their disappointed eyes said, but Katie thought that in three or four years, men would flock to Melissa, and how would she, Katie, be wise enough to protect her? Jed was gazing raptly at the men, especially Ringo. If only I weren't the oldest! Katie thought. Or if the children were young enough to see me as their mother! But they know I'm just their sister, especially Melissa.

No time to worry about that, though. Bill

162

opened the kitchen door to tantalizing odors, and Jed, who'd gradually been coming out of his sulk at leaving Galeyville, bolted in. Katie slipped her free arm around Melissa and followed, stopped in front of the fireplace. A pot simmered on a hook, several Dutch ovens nestled in coals, and a huge coffeepot sat steaming at the edge. "The boys thought it'd be nice to have your dinner cooked," said Bill. "Of course, we're going to help eat it. Now you're here, Slim'll do the biscuits."

Slim was indeed that, also flaming of hair and moustache. Deftly cutting out biscuits with a tin cup on a floured crate, he blushed, muttered something lost in his drooping moustache, and began to fit the biscuits into another Dutch oven. "It all smells lovely," Katie said. Before her eyes, the place changed from an empty room to a home as Hi Phillips placed the rocking chair, in which Mama had successively lullabied her children, between fireplace and window. Ringo unwrapped the harp and stood it in a corner, and Charlie Hughes and Hank Snow improvised a cupboard from the crates filled with groceries and other housewarming gifts from Galeyville, and stowed what would fit, though kegs, jugs, and large tin containers were pushed against the wall. The lamp was placed on the table Bill had salvaged after

Katie had discarded it on that terrible day of thirst. Another crate held washbasin and water bucket with dipper, and burly Joe Hill, apparently finished with the stall, appeared with a bouquet of scarlet and yellow Indian blanket thrust into a tomato can, which he placed, with great care, beside the lamp.

Jed streaked up a ladder to the loft that extended over half the kitchen. "I'm going to live up here!" he called gleefully. "There's a little window where I can watch out for Apaches and bandits, and you girls can't come up without my say-so."

"Look at the fireplace!" Melissa breathed, setting down Rosie's box and going to caress the stones, which had obviously been chosen for beauty, many of them glittering with crystals. Those, and the brilliant blue-green ones, couldn't have come from the creek or they'd have been ground off, but the polished rounded ones did, black streaked with white, dark green, pale green, and every shade of rose and yellow.

"Barney Sykes laid that up like he was makin' a picture," Slim said, rearranging Dutch ovens to accommodate another one of biscuits. "Had us on the watch for good rocks. The fireplace in the bedroom's all that streaked black and white rock. Don't know which one's purtier."

The serapes, tossed on the mattresses, were gray, black, and white with brownish-yellow, so they matched the fireplace beautifully. The main thing about a house was that it be sturdy and have a roof that turned water, but this one — it would be pretty and comfortable as well as shelter.

The fragrance of juniper and pine filled the air. Katie took a deep breath that flooded her whole body with the fresh, bracing pungency. How sweet it would be to sleep in this room! How wonderful, after the burning of the cabin, their parents' deaths, and grueling journey, to have a home again!

Why was Bill watching her with such a strange look, as if he had just noticed something peculiar? And how long, she thought with a painful twinge, would it be before she could look at him without remembering his laughter mingling with Bride's in the night? How long till she could keep from imagining him and Bride loving each other?

She had to stop thinking about that! They had been so good to her, both of them, such friends when she'd had no claim on them, that no matter what they did, she had to accept it and give them her devotion. Her face had stiffened, but she forced a smile. Returning to the kitchen, cuddling Rosie against her shoulder, she looked at each eager young face, calling the names of those she knew, nodding as the others said who they were.

"Melissa and Jed and me — Rosie, too, we thank you all so kindly. It's — it's the most wonderful house in the whole world! And it'll have to be lucky for us because you built it out of goodness. That's chinked into the walls and mortared in the fireplaces and smoothed into every board. We can't walk on the floors or look out the windows or pass through the doors without remembering you." Tears filled her eyes and brimmed over. Ducking her face against Rosie's soft dark ringlets, she swallowed several times before she could go on. "We'll pray for you every night, pray that you'll be as happy as you've made us. And we'll be so glad, so grateful, if we can ever help any of you —"

Some blushed, some looked at the floor as if they'd done something they were shamed by, and others fidgeted. "It was Bill's idea," said Ringo gruffly. "Don't feel beholden, Miss Katie. It's the most fun we've had since Bill rigged the election at San Simon."

At Bill's indignant sputter, Ringo coughed and broke off, but Slim finished. "We saved a mort of cash, Miss Katie, Ma'am, since we weren't boozin' or playin' cards. Maybe when we ride this way you can give us some cold buttermilk and a bite to eat, play us a tune on your harp. Which maybe you'll oblige us with after we eat. But for now, folks, we better get at them biscuits afore they burn."

In the hungry commotion, Katie slipped out, hoping she had indeed seen a privy from the distance. She almost ran into her younger sister, who grasped her arm. "Katie! You'll never, ever guess!" She pointed toward a small square structure of log ends, shingled like the other buildings with overlapping split juniper shakes. "Come see!"

She tugged Katie toward the very thing she'd needed. Floored, aromatic of juniper, two oval holes smoothed till there were no awkward edges. There were even old newspapers. They'd had a rough plank outhouse in Texas, but this —

"It's — elegant!" breathed Katie. "Now run on up to the house, and don't forget to wash your hands before you eat."

The sun was only a handsbreadth above the mountains when the men reluctantly loaded their gear behind their saddles and mounted up. "Breck and I will light out early in the morning on our tax collecting," Bill said. "Probably be gone a couple of weeks, but somebody'll drop by now and then and see how you're getting along."

"For sure you'll come in on the Fourth

of July," implored Hi Phillips.

"The mares should foal in the next few weeks," said Katie. "We won't want to ride into a big celebration with three foals trailing us. Besides the cows will calve soon, and they'll need milking morning and night."

"I can walk, Katie!" Jed caught her arm pleadingly.

"I can, too," begged Melissa. "It can't be more than six miles."

"We'll figger something out," said Bill.

"You hirin' out to milk them cows, Lord Bill?" teased Slim.

"I milked so many onery old bossies before I ran off from home that I reckon I could still do it in my sleep," Bill said. "Anyhow, you kids just count on being on hand for the big doin's. If need be, I'll fetch you in a buckboard and get you home by milking time."

You kids! That stung, but of course he hadn't meant it slightingly, hadn't even dreamed of separating Katie from the children. With a flourish of hats that made some of the horses pitch and crow-hop a little just to see if their riders were paying attention, the cavalcade turned to wave from the other side of the creek before they moved off at an easy canter, most of the horses full of vinegar from not being ridden while their owners indulged in a baffling activity that couldn't be done from a saddle.

Watching them out of sight, Melissa whispered, "Don't they look — glorious? Like something out of a story? Lord Bill runs this part of the Territory, everybody says so, but he and his friends built us our place."

Jed's sigh was longing mixed with hope. "I'm not milking cows when I grow up," he said. "I'm going to —" At Katie's frown, he finished in a defiant mumble. "I'm going to do something else."

"Why, you ungrateful brat!" He stared at her with wide blue eyes that made Katie remember how different he had looked, prostrated and close to death, when they came upon Missou's water hole. They were of the same blood. They had made that journey. Now, as eldest, she had to do her best to raise the others. If she wanted their respect, she couldn't flare up like a child.

"What you do when you're grown is up to you, Jed." She tried to laugh and dropped a hand on Jed's shoulder. "But you heard how much Slim is looking forward to cold buttermilk. Maybe you will, too, when you're his age."

Jed squirmed from her fingers. "I'm going to fix up my loft!" He dashed ahead.

Melissa cast a last look over her shoulder, but the riders had vanished. "Jed's such a

169

baby!" she said in superior way.

I guess we all are, thought Katie, for after the joyful excitement, after the hushed way the men gathered round to hear her play, after being with Bride and other people long enough to get used to company and bustle, Home Mountain Ranch, wonderful as it was, suddenly seemed lonely — away out by itself.

The sun now rested on the rim of the dark ridge to the west. It plunged. In that twinkling, the valley changed from brightness to subdued light, though Harris Mountain glowed amethyst and rose, and the distant plain's hazy gold faded into the soft blue of the eastern ranges.

"We won't need to cook supper," she said, quelling a shiver. "But we've got a lot of straightening up to do, and we'll need to water the horses and cows before we put them back in the corral. We'd better not let them run loose at night till they've got used to being here."

"Rosie's crying," said Melissa. "I'll bet she's hungry — and wet, too."

They hurried to the house. After Rosie's needs were tended to, they left her on a serape, playing with her toes, while they haltered the horses and led them to the creek. The cows could be driven to and from water. After the mares, Shiloh and the heifers were shut in the

170

corral. Katie followed Melissa and Jed to the house, brought in wood and kindling to start the fire next morning, and barred the doors. The windows, so welcome by day, now gave her a nervous feeling as twilight deepened. It was as if all kinds of things, hidden in the night, could peer in at them.

Poking up the fire, Katie ignited a long splinter and lit the lamp with it, turning the wick as high as it would go without smoking the glass chimney. Early to bed they'd be tonight, just as soon as they could eat, do the dishes — and give thanks for their home and the men who'd raised it.

Remembering them warmed Katie, steadied her nerves. Picking up a fretting Rosie, she settled into the rocker. *"I found the track of the swimming swan; I could not find my* cubhrachan. . . ."

Soothed by her own voice, the lamplight, fire, and Rosie's sweet little body, Katie fought down her jitters, but she did resolve that there were going to be curtains on those windows just as fast as she could sew them.

Jed made ready to ascend to his loft — was he perhaps a little frightened, too? He hadn't for months kissed his sisters good-night, except for Rosie, but tonight he did, and seemed to linger in Katie's hug before he went up the ladder.

Rosie had her last feed and was snuggled into her box, which would soon be too short for her. Katie banked the fire, blew out the lamp, and undressed in the dark to her shimmy. Lying down beside Melissa, she listened to the shrilling of coyotes, a song familiar from Texas and all the way along the journey. She'd have to be watchful when the cows calved. Coyotes were no threat to a healthy cow, but weakened animals or newborns offered a banquet, and there were also wolves.

Still, she could scarcely wait to see the colts and calves frisking on the slopes. Smiling, hugging herself, she thought of that and then of Bill on his big gray horse, the way she'd first seen him. This house was his doing, the roof above her head, protecting walls, the solid floor. No matter whom he visited at night, no matter where he roved, he was here, he was her shelter.

Hugging that thought along with her pillow, she thought, *Bless our home, bless Bill,* and then was asleep.

VII

Joy. A melodious worship of the rising sun. Never had Katie heard such a dawn chorus. For a few drowsily blissful moments, she let the songs permeate her: a towhee's *drink-your-tea!* descending in a long trill; the warbling of a house finch; the cactus wren's low-pitched monotony, and the loud, slurred whistle of a cardinal or its lookalike, a pyrrhuloxia. These could be best told from the female cardinal, grayish with only a hint of her mate's scarlet on crest and wings, by comparing the cardinal's red beak to the more somber bird's yellow one. There were other songs Katie didn't know, but surely that rippling, oft-repeated arrangement of notes must come from that clever, familiar mimic, the mockingbird.

In her box between Katie and the wall, Rosie made soft little noises and stirrings that gradually moved from amiability to a notification that she was hungry, undoubtedly in need of a change and a cuddle, and if these matters weren't attended to, she'd increase her volume till they were. The ruler, for now, was graciously giving her subjects a chance to fulfill their duties, but if they lagged —

With a luxurious stretch that sent energy radiating through her body, Katie moved her littlest sister to the mattress and changed her diaper and gown before dressing herself. Leaving the baby beside Melissa, who had burrowed deeper into her pillow, Katie went through the dogtrot to the kitchen, stirred up the coals, and blew them into flame that she fed twigs and sticks.

Even though she still had nightmares of the Nueces cabin blazing, of Pa charred black and bleeding, building a fire was still a marvel to Katie, watching it transform dead wood into living, dancing flame, giver of warmth, comfort, the center of a home. Katie arranged the fuel from small to large in a private ceremony. Warm our home but don't devour it. Cook our food. Give us your friendly, courteous light. Were those burnt offerings the preachers talked about made to God or to the fire itself?

Breaking from her reverie, she called, "Jed! Go let the horses and cows out." Then she raised her voice to carry to the bedroom cabin. "Melissa! Either feed the baby or get the mush started."

Right after breakfast, they deposited Rosie in her box beneath the gnarled oak tree that shaded the west end of the house as well as the laundry's grated fireplace. "We've got to get our garden planted as quick as we can," said Katie, "and we'll have to fence it to keep out animals. By putting it back of the house, we'll have one wall already made. A rock wall would keep out animals and wouldn't cost anything."

"Except breakin' our backs," grumbled her brother. "I want to go up the canyon and see if there's a hole where I can swim or fish."

"Jed! We've got a lot to do! You can just be grateful that we don't have to try to put up some kind of shack and barn and build a corral and all the rest of it!" His lower lip thrust out, and his blue eyes were mutinous. Katie restrained an urge to shake him. "People have given us a wonderful start, but now we've all got to work hard to get the ranch going —"

"Ranch!" sneered Jed. "An old dairy!"

"We'll raise horses, too. It's our chance to amount to something, Jed MacLeod!"

"Soon as I'm big enough, I'm going to hire on at a real ranch."

Wrangling in the old brother-sister way would undermine the authority she had to establish, but it took all of Katie's willpower to control herself. She was silent so long that Jed darted a sheepish look at her.

"When you're old enough, if you'd rather chase somebody else's cattle than milk ours and if you'd rather ride a rough string instead of Steel Dust horses, that'll be up to you," she said at last. "Till then, you've got to do your share."

"Don't be such a baby, Jed!" scolded Melissa. "You don't have to take care of Rosie if she cries in the night. I looked after her and helped Bride while you just played around!"

"I took grass to the cows and horses! I carried in wood and picked up kindling!"

Melissa sniffed. "You certainly didn't strain yourself!"

"I wish I had a brother!" His mouth quivered. "You old girls want to boss me around — you'll never let me have any fun! And Rosie — even she's a girl!"

"That's all the more reason we need you," flattered Katie, and descended lower, to bribery. "Let's work real hard till dinner, and then you two can go swim or do whatever you want during the hottest part of the day. About the middle of the afternoon we'll start again and work till twilight."

In a lightning change of mood, Jed cried, "I'll go cut grass and toss it into the corral so the critters won't graze it down to the roots while we're shutting them up nights."

"That's a good idea," Katie applauded. "If you get tired of that, you can change off and carry rocks for the garden wall."

"I guess that's going to be my job," sighed Melissa.

"It will unless you'd rather plow the garden and corn patch."

Melissa pondered and brightened. "After you're through plowing, maybe I can harness a team to the wagon and haul up rocks from the creek."

"That would go a lot faster, but for now, would you two clear the rocks away from where I need to plow? Please help, Jed, before you start cutting grass."

Katie showed them the area she intended to plow, the corn patch extending from the garden down the east side of the house, where it, too, would have one ready-made wall and would share the garden's. "Just move the rocks far enough away so I can plow," she said, and grimaced. "I'll bet there are plenty of rocks under the ground, too."

There were. It took all of Katie's strength to drive the edge of the plowshare into the ground, but once Jenny got it moving, Katie's main problem was keeping the share from jumping out of the furrow when it struck a big rock. The soil, thank goodness, was sandy from the overflowing of the creek, not clay or baked caliche. Once the rocks were out, and the roots of the scattered grass clumps chopped and blended in, plants should grow well.

Barefooted, skirt kilted to the knee, Katie stopped, panting, both for the mare's sake and for her own, when they'd completed a furrow from the bedroom window curving around the house past the front porch. She was leaving the length of the kitchen for Rosie to have a safe play yard. Maybe a few fruit trees could be planted there for shade. Turning the plow was the hardest part, aside from getting started to begin with, but four or five inches beneath its dry crust, the earth was refreshingly moist and cool, resilient and alive to her feet.

Jed and Melissa hurried to move the stones thrown to the side of the furrow. Rolling an especially large rock out of the way, Melissa laughed. "At this rate, we won't need to haul many rocks! You can just plow them up!"

"I'm not plowing a bit more than I have to," Katie retorted, but she was glad to see the younger ones work cheerfully. It was as if they were set an example by Katie's taking over what had been Pa's job.

Next year, they'd try to double the size of the garden. Except for trading butter and vegetables for necessities, Katie was determined to use what the family didn't need to pay back the value of what the stores and Bride had given them; even the saloonkeepers could set out fresh butter and green onions with their array of food. There was no way to truly repay such kindness, but the MacLeods would do their best.

It took almost two hours to break the small area. To rest her aching shoulders, Katie unharnessed Jenny and rubbed her down before taking her to water. "This is the last work you'll have to do for a long time." Katie told the mare, patting her sweat-damp shoulder and seeing the foal move inside the mare's swollen body. "See, Melissa's hitching up Babe and Honeybunch to haul rocks. You can just loaf around the corral and eat the grass Jed cuts for you."

Jenny nuzzled her, and Katie stroked the mare's neck and murmured with a glance at Shiloh, who had escorted his mother, "You'll be glad to have a pretty little foal, won't you? Eleven months! Does it seem as long to you as nine months to a woman?"

"When you want a change," said Katie to Jed who was cutting grass with a sickle, "you might load the driest manure in the wheelbarrow — I guess Mr. Carson must have left it for us — and bring it over to the garden. I'm going to break up clods with the fork and then spade in manure."

"What can I do when I get tired of that?" Jed's impudence was tempered with a grin.

"Cut grass or pick up rocks," Katie shrugged, laughing. The tined spading fork leaned with hoe, spade and rake in a corner of the intended haymow. Katie left them by the newly turned earth and went to change and feed Rosie, who was just working from tentative complaint to real protest. "Tired of your box, honey? I guess there's still enough shade from the barn to spread a blanket next to it."

Placed on her stomach, Rosie pushed up on her hands and moved her head around, staring curiously, pointed chin outthrust so that she reminded Katie of a turtle. She clutched an oak leaf, studied it for a while, located a ball of fuzz, and when its charm dulled, set out in a wriggling squirm for far vistas. Twice she reached the edge of the blanket. Twice Katie thrust the fork into the clods and scooped the baby up, cuddling and kissing her before putting her next to the barn wall. In mid-squirm, small rear perkily elevated, Rosie drowsed off in her third journey toward the frontier.

Melissa, unloading rocks, went over to smile at the baby and give her a pat on the rump. "She's such a darling, isn't she, Katie? Won't it be fun when she starts to walk?"

"I can wait." Katie paused to lean on the fork and rest. The night chill had vanished, but the breeze, mercifully, still had a refreshing edge though it couldn't keep the back of her dress from clinging wetly between her shoulderblades.

Melissa's eyes sparkled suddenly and she rubbed her arm across them. "Do — do you think Rosie'll miss Mama too much?"

Katie ached as if struck on a half-healed wound, less from losing her mother than because of the closeness there had never been and now could never be. *Why?* Why had Mama been different with her than with the others, never touched her more than she had to, never watched her in the proud, tender way she regarded Jed and Melissa?

It's as if she hated to look at me, Katie thought, staring blindly at the broken sod. As if she were ashamed. I'll never be able to change that. I'll never even know why.

Grief welled up in Katie, and the pain was worse than it had ever been for she had to realize that the part of her life shared with her mother was ended. There was nothing, ever, that she could do to change it, hope that her mother would love her. It was like the moment Katie had stared into the grave hacked and dug so painfully from the rocky soil, the moment she pushed in the first earth on the blanket shrouds that held her mother and father. *Done. Finished. All there was to it.*

Katie said to her dead mother, *I'll try to be better to your children than you were to me. And Rosie will love me the way she would have loved you.*

Shocked at her bitter sense of triumph, Katie went over to embrace Melissa, smooth her yellow hair. It was snarled. Katie would help brush it out really thoroughly tonight. During the journey, they had all wept sometimes, but from her own rush of smothered feelings, Katie suspected that now they had a home, before it could truly be one, they would have to mourn the loss of the old one, the loss of both parents within a few days. At the time, it had been such a stunning disaster that Katie, almost as if her father were commanding her, had continued with his plans, started on the long trail because it was unthinkable to stay there.

The wayfaring, the seeking, settling with the Guernseys and Steel Dust horses had been the last of Pa's orders. He was gone, with all his dour reliability. Katie feared more than loved him, couldn't mourn him, and indeed refused to be remorseful for that. If parents wanted to be loved, they needed to be loving. The plain, sad, bad truth was that Pa had cherished his livestock — and that dreadful, hoarded money he'd died for — a good deal more than he had his family. But Mama —

oh, that was different and a cruel bleeding. Mama had loved the others.

"Rosie will have both of us, M'liss, and Jed, too," Katie assured her sister. "I'm older than Mama was when she had me, and I've had practice looking after you and Jed. Rosie can't miss Mama since she can't ever know her."

"I miss her! Oh, Katie! It's wicked but I wish she'd just let Pa burn with his old money!" Melissa threw herself into Katie's arms and sobbed wildly. "He — he died anyway, and trying to help killed her, I know it did!"

Caressing her sister's bright hair, Katie admitted, "I've thought the same thing."

"You have?" Melissa looked up, startled.

"I certainly have. But, M'liss, it wouldn't have been like Mama to let him die."

Mama would do her duty. She always had, even by the eldest daughter she couldn't love, even without the swift hugs and kisses bestowed to Melissa and Jed. Melissa sobbed a little longer, but then, scrubbing away her tears, she slipped out of Katie's embrace and hunkered down, crooning, to offer Rosie her finger.

Katie went back to the fork. When blisters began to form on her palms, she put on shoes and switched to the spade, where her foot and back did most of the work, beginning with earth already cultivated with the fork. Because the cowboys had been here two weeks with their horses, Jed had easily collected several loads of dry manure, and she dug these odorless clumps into the soil, breaking them up along with the last stubborn bits of clod.

She was beginning to feel, in new places, the burn that meant a shaping blister, and the muscles of her back were cramping when she heard the sound of hoofs. A shadow preceded horse and rider. Reining in a handsome black gelding, John Diamond's accustomed mask dissolved in angry shock.

"That's no work for a woman!"

"It is if she's the biggest person around."

"Well, I'm the biggest now." Recovering his aplomb, he swung from the saddle, keeping a grip on something inside his handsomely tailored coat, something that thrust a small muzzle and long, spotted ears from beneath the gambler's arm, just as Jed came streaking from the corral.

"Uncle Jack!" Seeing the puppy, the boy stopped in his tracks, eyes growing even larger. "Is he for us?"

"I didn't bring him along just for the ride," chuckled Diamond. The pup, not much longer than the man's hand, was solid white except for the spots on his ears and one surrounding his right eye. When Jed took the mite in his arms, it ecstatically licked his ear as if knowing this was his boy.

"Does he have a name?" Jed asked breathlessly, happier than Katie could remember ever seeing him. Pa hadn't liked dogs, so they'd never had one, and he'd never had time to pay attention to Jed beyond belting him if he got into mischief or failed to do his chores properly. Why did it have to be a gambler who took it into his head to befriend the boy?

"Reckoned you should name your own dog." The gambler dusted a few white hairs off his black coat. "He's part hound, like his mama, Hod Carson's dog, but there's not much clue to the father."

"I'll call him Ace," Jed decided, " 'cause that's the highest card in the deck, better 'n the king."

"Sounds good," nodded the man, casting a mirthful side glance at Katie.

"I'll bet he's thirsty," exclaimed Jed. "I'll take him to the creek and let him get a drink. And I bet he's hungry!"

Just let Diamond show up, thought Katie, and Jed uses *bet* in every sentence. But her brother was so pleased with the puppy, and the pup so pleased with him, that she could only say, "He might like some mush."

"With milk?" Jed pleaded.

Evaporated milk cost money. Katie was

determined to keep out of debt, but Jed's eyes were so eager that she heard herself saying, "Well — just a little of what I mixed for Rosie this morning."

Diamond said, "I got some trimmings and bones from the butchers and some scraps from Bride. When anyone rides this way, they can bring you a new supply." He opened a saddlebag and handed Jed a parcel.

With rapturous thanks, Jed put the parcel in the shade and bore the pup down to the creek, where he lapped thirstily before bounding back to the house with his new master. Diamond finished untying a burlap-wrapped object and uncovered a rosebush with a ball of earth around its roots. Though trimmed for replanting, it had several white buds.

"Ohhh!" breathed Katie.

"Got it in Tombstone," said the gambler. "It's a type that does well there, so it should be fine as long as you give it a good deep watering every week unless it rains. Figure out where you want it, and I'll dig the hole."

"Right by the kitchen door." Katie gently touched one of the velvety buds. "Won't it be lovely if it grows tall enough to climb along the walkway roof?"

"It should. It's a climbing rose." Reaching inside his coat, he produced a small gilt box, which he handed to Melissa. "This was in

Shotwell's Store. Seemed to me it was meant for a girl named Melissa. That's Greek for 'bee,' you know."

Eyes shining, Melissa's fingers trembled as she took the top off the little box. "Why, it *is* a bee!" she cried. "Look, Katie! It's just found this flower with red petals!"

The insect was gold with glittering green eyes and the red flower was made of what Katie supposed was ruby glass. It was an expensive gift, the kind neither girl had ever dreamed of getting, but Katie saw no way of refusing it without devastating Melissa. Because Melissa was so young, Katie forbore to chide her when she threw her arms around the gambler and gave him a hug.

"Thank you, Mr. Diamond! It's the — the beautifulest thing in the world, and I'll keep it my whole life long!"

"Wear it in health and happiness, Melissa." While she was fastening the pin to her faded calico, he raised a silver eyebrow at Katie. "I wonder if a gift would ever stir you to such enthusiasm, Miss MacLeod?"

She blushed. Avoiding his cool gaze, she said to her sister, "You'd better not wear the pin around home. It might get lost."

"Oh, can't I? Just for a little while?"

"Well — maybe till after dinner." The man made Katie uncomfortable, but it was unheard of not to invite a visitor to have a meal. "Won't you have dinner with us, sir? I'll fix us a bite just as soon as I finish spading."

"As soon as I finish, you mean." He took off his coat, folded it neatly, and gave it into Melissa's waiting hands. He unsaddled, took off the black gelding's bridle, and let him roll before putting on hobbles. "Don't want you luring that yearling bay into a race," he told his horse as if it could understand him. "Too hot for that nonsense, Raven."

The black nuzzled his vest, got a small hunk of hard brown sugar, and nickered to the horses, who answered and approached. Slowed by the hobbles, he made his way gradually toward them and they greeted each other before they set to grazing.

Rolling up the sleeves of his finely tucked white shirt, Diamond started across the plowed ground. "Your boots!" Katie cried in dismay, for they were polished mirror-bright. "Your clothes!"

"Want to see if I remember how to do this," he said. "I was raised on a Missouri farm where the ground was just about as rocky."

"Uncle Jack, can we go fishing after dinner?" Jed importuned while Ace gnawed at a bone as big as he was. "Katie said if we worked real hard this morning, M'liss and me can do whatever we want till the middle of the afternoon." He sighed and pushed back his sweat-plastered hair. "Then we have to go back to work."

Blood heated Katie's face. She sounded like a slave driver! "We have a lot to do," she said with defensive sharpness. "If you're set on spading, Mr. Diamond, I'll help Melissa get rocks for the wall."

"You're building a wall?" asked Diamond.

"We've got to keep animals out of the garden or there won't be any use planting."

"Well, now, isn't it lucky Nacho's coming!"

"Nacho? Here?"

"I took the liberty to suggest that you might board him in return for some help around the place. You see, Nacho has a drinking problem — needs to get out of Galeyville. He can still sell wood there, but he won't be so tempted to drink if he's living out of town with a family."

Having Nacho around would certainly make Katie feel less alone and ease her burden of total responsibility for the younger children, but she was irked at Diamond's taking such a high hand in MacLeod affairs. Before she could do more than frown, the gambler gave his head a pitying shake. "Nacho lost his whole family — wife and three kids — in the sort of continual fighting that goes on between the Yaquis and the

Mexican government. He drifted to Tucson before the Civil War. After the nuns of St. Joseph of Carondolet opened their school in eighteen seventy, he worked for them till he got tired of town life. Learned mighty good English from them, though I'm probably the only one in Galeyville who knows that. He's never married again, more's the shame, because he sure likes kids."

There was nothing Katie could say except, "We'll be glad to have him."

"You certainly will." Diamond looked smug. "Nacho can lay up the best stone wall you ever saw."

"We can't pay him, not for a long time."

"You can feed him and give him a home. Don't worry. Nacho can earn all he's a mind to by cutting and selling wood. In fact, he probably has more money saved up than most miners in town." Diamond grinned at Jed. "And he likes to fish."

Thus reminded, Jed glanced up from playing with his dog. "Can *we* go fishing this afternoon, Uncle Jack?"

"If we work hard enough that your sister'll let us," twinkled the silver-haired man. He pulled heavy leather gloves — new ones, Katie noted — over his elegant hands. "Show me where you want your rosebush and then I'll get to the garden."

190

★ ★ ★

By noon, Diamond had finished digging manure into the garden. Jed had heaps dumped over the corn patch. Ace's short little legs had given out, and he slumbered by Rosie's box. Katie finished unloading their last haul of rocks, while Melissa tended Rosie and Jed unhitched the mares, rubbed them down, and turned them loose.

How heavenly cool it was inside where Melissa was feeding and rocking the baby! What bliss to rest! Katie's muscles ached, but it was a good ache. They'd made a mighty fine start on all there was to do. Thank goodness — and Bride — they could make a nice dinner of the food not eaten last night, the pasties, creamed potatoes, and apple cake.

Instructing Jed to set the table, Katie got out the food, sliced some cheese, and set out mustard, preserves, and pickles, before she took Rosie, settled her over her shoulder, and sat down. She gave Diamond a defiant look as she bowed her head. "Thank You for our food," she said. "Thank You for our home."

There was no mockery in Diamond's eyes. "Nothing like what my father called 'honest work' to whet the appetite," he said, layering cheese on a pasty with pickles and mustard. "Maybe we'll get lucky, Jed, and catch some fish for supper."

Katie took that to mean he wasn't impressed with the fare, but Melissa and Jed were, relishing each bite. Fair hair damply tendriled around faces flushed from exertion, they were handsome children. No doubt at all that they were brother and sister! Katie pushed the thought away, eating with one hand while she supported Rosie with the other. After a morning in her box or on the blanket, Rosie wanted to be held.

A raucous sound startled Katie into almost dropping her fork. "That's Nacho's burro, Chica." Diamond rose and went to the door. "You're just in time to eat, *amigo*."

Barking with a ferocity that shook his small, furry body, Ace defended the house till Jed scooped him up and greeted the old man he'd gotten to know in town. "Come on in, Nacho! You can sit on my box. I'm through eating."

"A dog *muy bravo*," chuckled the wood-cutter, scratching the puppy behind floppy ears. He doffed a battered hat of indistinguishable hue. "It is permitted, *señorita*, that I live here?"

She had often seen Nacho in Galeyville, of course, but she had never looked at him closely. His hair was still more black than gray, dark skin was stretched tight over ridged cheekbones, and his black eyes were set in deep sockets. His faded clothing was neatly patched. His weathered face put Katie in mind of a carving etched by lightning in the trunk of an ancient tree, and his thin, wiry body added to the impression that he had been honed by life and the elements till he was more bone than flesh, more spirit than substance. She liked and trusted him.

"You are welcome, Señor Flores. Please come in and eat."

"First, with permission, I will unload my Chica. And, *señorita,* I am Nacho, not *señor.*"

Katie had been taught never to call older people by their first names, but formality would be strange if he was to live with them. "You're Nacho if I'm Katie," she smiled.

He flashed white teeth. "Katie." His eyes rested in turn on the other children as if to absorb their faces into his being. "Jed. Melissa." His hand, gnarled and tough-sinewed as a root, brushed the baby's cheek. She grasped one finger and cooed in triumph. "So this is Rosie. I will call her Rosamunda, Rose of the world."

"You can sleep in my loft," Jed offered, amazingly inviting someone into his domain.

"Thousand thanks, *niño,* but I have my tent."

"Maybe you'd like to set it up by the big oak," Katie suggested. She hoped that by winter Nacho would consent to move inside,

193

but she could understand his wish for his own dwelling. She opened sardines and cut more cheese while Nacho, with Jed's eager help, unburdened Chica.

"Yes," she heard the old man saying. "Her hoofs are very small. Thus she finds footing where a horse would stumble and fall. The dark cross on her back and shoulders, that is a sign that Our Lord rode one of her ancestors into Jerusalem. You may graze now, *burrita*, but do not stray off."

He ate with appetite, praising the food. For dessert, Katie shared out the spicy apple cake. When the last sweet taste was savored, Jed sighed blissfully and turned to Nacho. "Uncle Jack and I are going fishing. Want to come?"

"Sometime I will show you how to catch fish by tickling their bellies," Nacho said. "But I see many rocks by the broken ground. You desire a wall, Katie?" He made it sound *Kay-tee*.

"Yes, but you don't need to work in the heat of the day."

"I will search along the creek for the best mortar clay. Then I will sort rocks in my head and pick those I'll use first." He chuckled. "But I will not lift them, Katie, till the sun drops halfway to the mountains. I have lived in this old body long enough to know what I can ask of it, just as I know within a pound

194

what Chica will carry without balking."

When Diamond said he had enough fishing line and hooks and an infinite choice of dry sotol stalks from which to fashion poles for three, Jed somewhat grudgingly allowed Melissa to join the expedition. Tagged by Ace, they set off on foot toward the green canyon. Nacho explored the banks of the creek. Katie did the dishes, grateful that she didn't have to build a fire to start a pot of beans. Even if there were no fish for supper, there were beans left from last night that could heat while the biscuits baked that evening.

Now for curtains. She'd be much less nervous with Nacho there, and Ace, who would, she hoped, grow into a good watchdog. All the same, those bare windows with the impenetrable dark outside made her feel exposed. But sacrifice one of their sheets?

The canvas wagon cover! It was sun-streaked and soiled, so heavy that it would be hard to cut and sew, but that heaviness would make it impossible to see through and would help seal off chill from the windows that winter. She could curtain all five downstairs windows and Jed's small one in the loft and have a bit left over.

Before Melissa hauled rocks, she'd taken the frame and covering off the wagon, and the canvas was sprawled over the wood stacked along the walkway. Katie measured the windows with her arm, marked the fabric with charcoal, and as she cut into it, she thought that she could dye it a pretty soft green by boiling it with leaves.

Delight in their home welled up in her. She'd been right to bring the family here. They wouldn't own the huge ranch Pa had dreamed of, but they'd have their own place by the Home Mountain. She glanced pridefully at the cattle and Steel Dust horses resting in the shade. Soon there'd be calves and colts frolicking along the valley, and one day —

Her dream shattered as the imaginary horses she pictured ranging the slopes across the creek were replaced by three very real and solid horsemen. In quick alarm, she shaded her eyes, let out a sigh.

At least, they weren't Apaches! Sun glinted off holstered revolvers and the barrels of shotguns resting across the front of each man's saddle. There were, of course, rifles in their scabbards. What upset Katie most of all, though, was that the man who rode slightly in the lead on a big claybank was Ed Larrimore.

VIII

Katie didn't go to meet the riders. Scissors still in her hand, she waited in the shade of the house and hoped she didn't look as apprehensive as she felt. Reining up, the rancher took off his hat. His men followed his example, though their eyes made her uncomfortable.

"Howdy, Miss Kate." Larrimore jerked his head toward the heavy red-faced man with a moustache like frayed rope, bald except for a bleached fringe above the ears. "This is my foreman, Shell Brown. Stringbean on my left's Beau Murphree, my top hand." Murphree hadn't filled in his gangly height. Hair, skin, and eyes were the same light brown. As if to make up for this, he wore a red shirt and blue scarf.

Both men nodded as Larrimore named them, and Murphree smiled shyly. Neither spoke. Katie had the feeling no one in his employ talked much around Larrimore without his asking. Her own mouth felt dry and stiff.

"What brings you this way, Mr. Larrimore?" She didn't try to smile. This was the man who'd almost caused their deaths by hogging the river, the man who seemed to think he owned the whole valley. Something about him conveyed menace even though his smoky eyes watched her with indulgence — in fact, that indulgence was itself a threat.

"I hear you've got some Steel Dust mares. I'll meet your price for them."

She gasped. "I didn't bring them all the way from Texas to sell, Mr. Larrimore."

"You could part with one."

"I won't."

The pulses beat in his temples near the thick mass of steel gray hair. After a moment, he said, "We've had a long ride. Aren't you going to ask us in?"

Instinctively, she didn't want him in her house. "The baby's sleeping. If you're thirsty, I'll bring out the water pail and cups."

"If it won't strain you," he said bitingly, and swung from the saddle. Murphree and Brown did the same.

Nacho appeared, the spade in his hand though she didn't think he was using it in his wall building. *"Señores,"* he greeted the men. He looked at Katie as if awaiting orders. With a rush of gratitude, she knew he was showing the men that she wasn't alone and also giving her a chance to ask if she needed his presence or help. "It's all right, Nacho," she said. "I'm just getting these gentlemen a drink of water."

"*Sí, señorita.*" He wasn't going to call her by her first name in front of them, it seemed, nor was he showing his fine command of English. He moved back around the house, but Katie felt better, knowing he was there.

Putting down her scissors — it seemed ridiculous to hold them like a weapon — she went inside and returned with water, cups, and the gourd dipper. The men drank thirstily, nodding thanks each time she refilled their cups. She thought Beau Murphree was probably nice, but Shell Brown's pale green eyes chilled her.

Glancing from corral to outbuildings and plowed ground, Larrimore grunted. "Looks like that gang of Galeyville outlaws fixed you a right nice place. Take my advice, Miss Kate. Don't let 'em use it for a hideout or you'll have big trouble."

"The men who built for us are welcome any time," she said. "They're our friends."

"Damn poor friends for a bunch of kids!" Larrimore's gaze drilled into her. "Miss Kate, show sense! Think about your sisters and brother if you don't care about yourself. Even if 'Paches don't wipe you out or carry you all down to Mexico, your reputation will be ruined if those Galeyville cowboys hang around. First thing you know, they'll be leaving stolen cattle here."

"Stolen cattle?" echoed Katie, heart convulsing as if grasped in crushing talons. She'd had her suspicions, of course, but she hadn't wanted to know. Except for miners and business people, the men drifting in and out of Galeyville had plenty of money but no work.

"Didn't you know, girl?" Larrimore's disbelief changed to amazement as he stared at her. "Outside of mining, dealing in stolen cattle is the biggest trade in the county. The San Carlos agency alone buys millions of pounds of beef on the hoof each year. You can bet the quartermaster doesn't much worry about where it came from. The Clantons sort of control the business in the San Pedro Valley, and the MacLowerys oversee the flow through the Sulphur Springs Valley, but Bill Radnor's kingpin over the whole bunch."

Forced to believe him, Katie tried not to betray her shock. "I heard you say you and Mr. Radnor have an understanding. Could it be you're stocking your ranch with Mexican cattle?"

Larrimore shrugged. "I've bought a few head off Radnor. He gives me a bill of sale and the critters wear his brand. Long as he don't run my cattle south, we'll get along. But that don't make him a fit companion for a girl your age with no daddy or older brother to look out for you."

"Mr. Radnor looks out for us, sir. If he hadn't, we might have died after you dammed the river."

His craggy face reddened. "Anyone crossing the flats ought to be carrying plenty of water."

"They ought to be able to drink at the river and water their stock, too."

"I don't want anybody gettin' ideas and tryin' to settle on the river."

"Are we far enough away?" she challenged.

He glanced scornfully toward the corral. "Reckon a few milk cows and horses won't use enough grass and water to count. It's the principle of the thing."

"The principle?"

"Sure. Emigrants passin' through see you all snug and settin' pretty, they're likely to figger they can squat, too."

"We're not squatting anymore than you are, Mr. Larrimore, or anyone else around here."

"Difference is, missy, I can hold my land — and anything else I take a notion to." He jerked his head toward the corral. "Like I could take those horses."

"The law —"

"There's not enough law in Cochise County — or the whole damn Territory — to stop me."

"Bill Radnor might have something to say about that."

"Ridin' in dangerous places the way he does, there's lots of ways he could get killed. Why, it wasn't long ago he got shot through the hips down in Mexico. Rode two hundred miles to get patched up by the doc in Lordsburg. He's been lucky, but that can change, can't it, Shell?"

"Any time," drawled the foreman. He hadn't taken his cold eyes off her.

"If you think you can scare me —" Katie burst out.

The rancher moved his large head in a deliberate shake. "Not trying to scare you, Miss Kate. Just statin' facts, leadin' up to a proposition that'd be good for us both." He glanced toward his men, who left their horses ground-hitched and sauntered off toward the corral.

By now, Katie's mouth had grown so dry that she had to swallow to speak. "I'm afraid that whatever's good for you, sir, can't possibly favor us."

He raised a placating hand. "Listen. I'll pay you twice what these buildin's are worth. You can put the money in the Safford Hudson Bank in Tombstone where it'll be drawin' interest. Won't cost you a cent to live at my place. You can pasture your cows and horses free, have your own brand. I'll treat your brother and sisters like they was my own kids."

Heart thudding, she stared at him in silence.

Something burned deep in his eyes. The power, the force of him, beat against her. "All you have to do is help with my daughter. Make us a home."

Moved in spite of herself, Katie hardened her heart. "Get yourself a wife, Mr. Larrimore."

"I'm not that desperate," he said with a harsh little laugh. "But the favor wouldn't be all on one side, young lady. I could give your brother somebody to look up to besides cow thieves and gamblers. And you'd be safer from bandits and 'Paches at the Pitchfork than anywhere in the Territory outside of Tucson or Tombstone or Prescott."

"We'd rather take our chances on our place, Mr. Larrimore."

He set his hands behind him as if to keep from reaching for her. She went cold to the bone, fearing him, sensing a threat to more than the ranch. The black center of his eyes spread almost to the rims. "You sure about that?"

"Yes!"

Muscles constricted in his square jaw. "If you've taken a shine to one of those outlaws, God help you, girl."

"I'm none of your concern." She picked up the scissors. "Excuse me, sir, but I have work to do."

His face crimsoned, blanched pale. He took a long stride forward, checked, gazed at her with baffled anger and a kind of raw hunger that bothered Katie more. "If you get some sense in that curly head, let me know. Till then, study on this. You let those so-called cowboys hang around here, and decent folks will reckon you're pardners with them."

"Decent folks in Galeyville know better," Katie retorted. "And I don't care about anyone else."

"You will if the sheriff jails you for harboring stolen cattle."

"It sounds like you're the one running changed brands. I won't do that."

Appraising her through narrowed eyes, Larrimore said gruffly, "I reckon you'd do whatever Bill Radnor asks, girl. He pulled you out of that tight with Missou and kind of got Galeyville to adopt you, so you think he's Jesus Christ. He's a sight closer to the devil."

"Don't you dare stand on my property and talk about him that way! He — he's my best friend in the whole world. Nothing's going to change that." Not even thinking that he spent nights with Bride. To be honest, that troubled Katie more than Larrimore's accusations, though she was unhappily compelled to believe them. She couldn't, however, see much difference between those who stole cattle and the respectable ranchers and business-men who bought them.

"What will change it," said Larrimore, "is when he hangs or gets shot."

"If he does," breathed Katie, trembling, "and if you have anything to do with it, I — I'll do my best to kill you!"

Larrimore recoiled. "Damned if he don't have you talkin' like an outlaw, a nice, sweet, innocent kid! You bein' a minor and all, I got half a mind to see if the court in Tombstone won't give me custody of your brother and sisters. It's plumb outrageous the way Radnor and that Galeyville bunch are twistin' your minds!"

Fingers curving into claws, Katie had to use every bit of self-restraint to keep from attacking him. That would only justify his self-righteous thinking. It was all too possible that a wealthy, influential man could sway a court to do his bidding. The prospect of her family being made Larrimore's wards terrified her more than anything ever had, even her parents' deaths. She *had* to act sane and responsible, not give him any further excuse to pursue such an appalling course.

Wrathful tears choked her. She gulped them down and waited till she could keep her voice steady. "We're doing just fine, Mr. Larrimore. We've got our cows and horses and a good place to live. Pa wanted to bring us out here so we could amount to something, and we're going to. We're not going to turn into outlaws or scum. But if you try what you said" — it was no use; her voice wavered before she blinked and bit down hard on her lip — "if you do what you said, I'll kill you. Leave us alone."

He fell back as if she'd struck him. The pupils of his eyes contracted to tiny points in irises the color of charred ash. His odor of horses, sweat, and tobacco took on a pungent sourness that reminded her of rotting mushrooms.

"God help you, Katie MacLeod! Arizona's never hung a woman, but you may be the first."

"I'd hang before I'd let you have my family."

The rims of his broad nostrils crimped white. "Missy, if it wasn't for those kids hangin' onto your skirts, we might just find out about that. You need a curb bit and a tight rein to keep you from bolting straight to hell. And damned if it might not be fun to break you!"

"Get off my place, Mr. Larrimore, and don't come back, ever!"

"I was in this valley before you, girl. I ride where I want. And don't get any high and mighty notions when my cattle range over this way. If I have to send hands to protect 'em, your cows and horses could sure get mixed up with mine."

"And you call Bill Radnor a cattle thief!"

The rancher laughed, not a whit shamed. "Hard names won't skin me, Katie girl. You think on what I've said. When you get a little sense, my offer may sound right tempting. I won't hold a mite of fractiousness against you. Mares or women, it's them with spirit that turn out best once they quit pitchin' and rarin'." Clamping his hat to his head, he strode to the big claybank, who rolled his eyes and side-stepped as Larrimore dug a toe in the stirrup and settled into the saddle.

Shell Brown and Beau Murphree were already on their way. They touched their hats in farewell, and Beau ventured a quick, admiring smile before they mounted and followed their boss. Watching the sun glint on their weapons, Katie leaned on the stacked wood, knees suddenly weak.

She could scarcely believe it had happened, that Larrimore had ridden up, tried to make her sell him a mare, accused Bill of thievery, asked her to run his household, and served notice that he considered this his range even though he already hogged the whole central upper San Simon Valley! Most monstrous of all, he'd threatened to try to get legal control of the younger MacLeods. He'd the same as said he'd have carried her off forcibly if it weren't for the children! When she told Bill —

She couldn't tell Bill. He'd confront Larrimore. One or both men might die. Even when John Diamond read the horse tracks and asked who'd been here, she must simply say that Larrimore had hoped to buy one of the Steel Dust mares. For the time being, she seemed to have convinced him that it would be disastrous to try to compel her to live at the Pitchfork. But if he finally admitted that she wasn't going to change her mind — Katie shuddered and buried her face in her arms till she reasoned herself out of near panic.

He knew, of course he knew, that if the court gave him custody of the children Bill would intervene. She doubted that Larrimore would risk a pitched battle. As for his appropriating her grass and water, she'd deal with that when and if it happened. A lot of what he'd said today must have been to scare her, to try to coerce her into yielding to his will.

She'd stood up to him, no matter how faint and sick she felt now. She had friends. He couldn't just get away with anything he felt like doing. But, oh, how she wished that Bill weren't an outlaw! She was sure it was a game to him, excitement and danger. The way he scattered money, it meant nothing to him. She drew comfort from the fact that Bill was out right now helping Deputy Sheriff William Breakenridge collect taxes. That surely proved there was no warrant out for him.

Gradually calming herself, she cut out the curtains, having to pause often to rest her arm and fingers for the canvas was heavy. Hemming was difficult, too, requiring a stout darning needle, but by the time the fishing party returned, she had finished one curtain and started on another.

"We've got supper!" shouted Jed, proudly exhibiting five medium-size trout. Water and life had given their kind a beautiful sheen when Katie had glimpsed them in the creek. Now they were dull as flotsam, and Katie felt a pang of regret, though they would make a delicious change of fare.

"Better put them in a bucket of water and wedge it in rocks at the edge of the creek," Diamond advised. "That'll keep them fresh." Jed hurried to do his bidding. "I caught the biggest one!" exulted Melissa with a toss of her yellow braid.

"You did," agreed Diamond. Melissa ran inside. They could hear her greeting Rosie as if they'd been separated for days. Diamond's smile faded as he turned to Katie. "Who was here?"

He frowned as she told him, though she said only that Larrimore had wanted to buy a mare. "He wanted to look over your place," said the gambler. "Even way over here against the mountains as you are, he won't welcome anyone else between the Peloncillos and the north edge of the Chiricahuas." Scanning her closely, Diamond probed. "He didn't hint that you maybe weren't welcome?"

Telltale color heated Katie's face. "He let me know that his cattle would graze here when they need to."

She wasn't used to dissembling. As the frosty eyes searched hers, Katie felt herself blushing more and more deeply. "What else, Miss MacLeod?"

"Nothing!"

"Then it was considerable." Jed dashed up and the gambler said, "We'll talk about it later." Ruffling the boy's fair hair, he chuckled. "All right, lad. Fetch some more manure and I'll get after the corn patch." He whistled and grinned at Ignacio, who had just come in sight as he settled a large squarish rock into the shallow trench he'd dug to mark the line of the wall. "At this rate, Nacho, you'll have the wall up long before the first sprouts are tall enough to lure the critters."

"That is my intention, Don Juan." The old man chuckled. "It is my aim to merit a portion of those fish. If it is agreeable, Katie, I will stuff them with herbs I gathered up the canyon and grill them outside over mesquite."

"That sounds wonderful!" Nacho had already lived up to his reputation for skill with stones. If he could cook, too, Katie might escape some of the monotonous grind of preparing every meal. This prospect took away some of the unpleasant aftertaste of Larrimore's visit. She would deal with him when and if she had to; till then she wasn't going to let him keep her in a temper.

It was still hot, but the slant of the sun was no longer so merciless and the breeze seemed cooler. The horses had stayed near their guest, hobbled Raven, so Katie didn't have to go far to catch Chili and Honeybunch. Melissa helped hitch them to the wagon, and they drove down to the creek to collect rocks for the wall.

By the time the sun pulsed on the dark rim of the mountains before plunging from sight, Nacho had laid the foundation layer of stone, which ran about thirty yards north of the house before it turned south to extend even with the end of the bedroom cabin. Well along with the second tier, he stopped almost reluctantly to attend to the fish. Diamond finished the corn patch and brought the spade to the barn. When he returned, he had dusted off his boots, though they were far from gleaming with their earlier sheen. He had doffed his gloves, rolled down his sleeves, resumed his black string tie and brocade waistcoat, and except for a face ruddy from unaccustomed sun, he gave no sign that he'd done a farmhand's work that day.

Pausing in the door, he glanced from Katie, who was making biscuits, to Melissa, who was feeding the baby, and last to Jed. The boy had helped Melissa take the cows and horses to water, and then, exhausted, had curled up on the rag rug with Ace, who was similarly weary.

Watching the brown cheek nestled to the puppy's domed head and spotted ear, Diamond's eyes softened before he turned to Katie. "I'll be riding now, Miss MacLeod, if that is your wish."

"You have to stay for supper. After all, you brought the line and hooks." Since Nacho was there, Katie added hospitably, "You're welcome to stay the night."

His eyebrows lifted. "Thank you, no. If you'll be advised by me, you won't allow any man under ninety to spend a night here, except in direst necessity."

Katie's cheeks burned. She avoided his condemnatory gaze by carefully arranging biscuits in the Dutch oven. "When someone travels by in the evening, sir, it doesn't seem neighborly not to ask them to stay. In Texas —"

"In Texas, you had your folks. Out here — well, Miss MacLeod, you'll need to be careful. A pretty young woman will draw men like bees. Some are bound to have loose tongues. You can give a man a meal, let him water and rest his horse, but make it clear from the start that no man sleeps here, not even a preacher."

She could see the reason in what he said, though it went against the ingrained custom of making travelers welcome. Diamond smiled as if to take the edge off his remonstration. "I'll be pleasured to eat before I go." He took the heavy Dutch oven and settled it expertly among the coals, raking more around and over it. The beans were already bubbling. "If you'd step out with me for a moment, Miss MacLeod, I'd like to make some suggestions about the garden."

She scrubbed the dough off her hands, dried them, and preceded him as he stepped courteously aside. Katie went to stand at the edge of the tilled earth. Dry though the top soil was, the plow had reached moister levels, and that rich fragrance was enhanced by the

213

manure so deeply spaded in. Her palms had the heat of beginning blisters. She knew if the man beside her hadn't taken over, those blisters would have swelled, burst, and exposed raw skin, leaving her with painful hands for days to come.

"Thank you." She motioned across garden and corn patch. "It's good to have it all ready to plant. We're getting a late start as it is. Now, sir, what did you want to tell me about the garden?"

"To plant it." At her startled look, he said grimly, "Without provoking your sister's curiosity, I wanted to know why you blushed so furiously when denying that Larrimore had more on his mind than trying to buy a mare."

Crimson again, she said, "That's none of your business, Mr. Diamond."

Ignoring that, the silver-haired man mused, "So he did say something that made you uncomfortable." Diamond's voice hardened, cut like a blade. "Did he insult you?"

"No!" Katie flashed. "Well — yes, I suppose he did, but not the way you mean."

Diamond considered. "I studied him while he watched you play your harp, Miss MacLeod. Did he ask you to marry him?"

From the gambler's eyes, Katie knew her face had given her away. "No. He — he wants us to move to his ranch — wants me to help raise his daughter."

"I take it you refused."

"Of course I did!"

"There's no 'of course' about it, my dear. Larrimore's more than old enough to be your father, but he's *muy macho* as the Mexicans say, and most likely the wealthiest man in the county. You wouldn't have to carry rocks and spade in manure if you lived at the Pitchfork. His headquarters is safe from Apache raids, and he'd take the load of raising the children off your shoulders. I guess I'm well nigh as surprised as he was that you turned him down, even if he didn't offer marriage. And he'd probably do that in time."

Gaze sweeping from the creek to the Home Mountain, rose-purple now from light cast from beyond the western ridge, Katie said, "This is ours, Mr. Diamond. I'd rather work and have it than be rich and under Ed Larrimore's thumb." Since this man had already guessed so much, and because the fear was a weight on her heart, she blurted, "I won't turn seventeen till October. Could the court at Tombstone take away the children, give custody of them to Mr. Larrimore?"

Diamond's eyes widened. "The law would have that power. Larrimore threatened to do that?"

"I think I convinced him that he'd better not, but it — it scares me all the same."

"Larrimore won't try anything like that as long as Bill Radnor's in the county." Diamond frowned. After a lengthy pause, he spoke with slow deliberation. "There's one way you wouldn't have to worry about anyone pulling such a trick."

"What?"

"You could marry me." He raised a hand against her shocked outcry. "I wouldn't claim my 'rights' and I wouldn't move in. Nothing would change except that you'd be protected from someone's trying to get control of you and the youngsters."

Katie didn't like this man's profession and was jealous and fearful of his influence with Jed, but not for an instant did she doubt his word. "Why would you offer to do such a thing?"

"Mostly for Jed, though I have a deal of admiration for you, Miss Katie — if you'll permit me to call you that. Let's say you're the daughter that I wish I'd had." He smiled and it seemed to her the frost of his eyes had warmed. "I wish you'd call me John or Jack — or even Don Juan."

She said doubtfully, "Maybe I can if you'll tell me why you're so fond of my brother."

John Diamond fixed his gaze on the slate

and amethyst hulk of Harris Mountain. He didn't speak for so long that she thought she'd angered him. "I had a son who was his age the last time I saw him. His mother took him east to her Philadelphia family while I was fighting Yankees. Her father was a senator and managed to get a divorce for her on grounds of desertion. She married a lawyer, and I daresay everyone has conveniently forgotten that once she was married to a riverboat gambler she met on a trip to New Orleans."

His tone was as emotionless as if he were talking about someone else. Katie still didn't like the growing bond between him and Jed, but neither could she keep from feeling sympathy. "Your son?" she ventured. "After the war, didn't you try to see him?"

"I tried. He was at a military academy where his mother had sent him to eradicate any of my undesirable traits and to get him out of the home she was making with her new husband. Anyway, James didn't want to see me."

Appalled, Katie blurted, "You should have managed somehow, John! Goodness, there's no telling what kind of lies he heard!"

"Doubtless it was for the best," Diamond shrugged. "The last grudging information my wife gave me about James was that he was doing well at West Point. Promotions come slow since the war, but he's likely a first lieutenant by now. He could even be married and a father. It's strange to think that he could be at some Arizona post and I'd never even know it."

"Maybe he'll try to find you someday."

"Maybe." Diamond's mouth quirked in a wry smile. "But it's too late for us to go fishing."

Yes. Too late for the shared experiences, the worship on one side and nurturing on the other, that truly made father and son. Jed hadn't had that with Pa. Impulsively laying her hand on Diamond's arm, she said, "I don't see how it can be bad for you and Jed to be together as long as — as —" Lamely, she finished, "I don't want him to be a gambler, John." Peculiar how easily that name came now, and what a sense of comfort and trust it gave her to use it.

He took both her hands in his. "Katie, sweet, leave it to me and he won't be a gambler. Nothing wrong with his being good at cards, though. In fact, if he's going to play at all, he'd better be good. If it's all right, I'll come out every week or so, take a hand with whatever you're doing, and spend some time with Jed. But I won't stay the night. And mind no one else does, either."

"I'll be glad for you to come, John." She smiled. "It'll be good for the children to have an uncle."

"Better for me." He touched her cheek and a wave of affection flowed between them. She felt almost as if, in the sharing of confidences, he had become her kin. She couldn't even be annoyed that he'd proposed to her for Jed's sake, not her own.

She turned toward the house. John Diamond pressed her hand, smiling in a way that made her smile back in spite of her pique. "Thank you, Katie," he said, and they went in together.

IX

Crisp on the outside, succulent within, flavored with an artful stuffing of what Nacho explained was wild onion, beeweed, horsemint, and *cañaigre*, or wild dock, the trout made a feast along with the biscuits. Beans were used only, as Jed said, "to fill in the chinks." John produced a big, colorful tin of gingersnaps from his saddle bag, and, carried away by the festive mood of having worked hard and accomplished much, Katie recklessly opened another can of peaches.

Nacho had grilled the fish on the grate made for heating laundry water, and Melissa and Jed had begged to have a picnic, so logs were placed around the fire for seats and a blanket spread for Rosie. Jed sat close to Diamond, blissful yet so weary that his eyes kept shutting. An owl *tu-whooed*. Coyotes shrilled somewhere across the creek, and at their yips, Ace growled deep in his small chest, a tiny rumbling. Hackles raised, he dashed to the edge of firelight, barking a warning.

"See, Katie?" Jed beamed with pride as he scooped up the puppy and received his lavish kisses. "He's going to be the best watchdog you ever saw!"

"I'm sure he will," laughed Katie, "but you'd better keep him inside nights until he grows quite a bit."

Finishing his coffee, an extravagance the MacLeods would do without except for special occasions so that they could hoard the container of aromatic beans given by one of the stores, Diamond got to his feet. The glow of the fire harshly graved the angles of his face as he looked out into the deepening night.

"I have to ride soon, but I'll make a deal with you, Katie. If you'll play your harp, I'll wash the dishes."

Dismay flashed across Jed's face before he said gamely, "I'll dry."

"And I'll help as long as Rosie doesn't fret," offered Melissa.

With so many hands, it only took one trip to carry everything into the house, though Nacho went back to set up his tent by the light of the fire before he smothered it and cleaned the grate. With pillows enabling her to sit forward in the rocker so she could reach the harp, which set on a box in front of her, Katie was so tired that she didn't think she could stay awake, but as she played, the sweet notes refreshed her: *"I would go, I would go with you beyond the Irish sea . . ."* Overwhelmed with longing for Bill, she didn't care if he was an outlaw, prayed only that he was safe and would get through his stint as deputy tax collector without serious trouble. A joke that was to him, sort of a game. Probably running cattle out of Mexico was a game, too. She only hoped that before it was too late, he'd learn to take some things in earnest.

Breaking into her reverie, Diamond asked, "Do you know 'The Yellow Rose of Texas,' Katie?"

Of course she did. And "Green Grow the Lilacs" and "The Wagoner's Lad." When Nacho came in, he listened raptly till she finished "Sourwood Mountain" and then asked if she could play a tune if he sang it first.

He had to sing it more than once, but at last she played it through without many blunders, plaintive and haunting with the song of birds.

"It is the mockingbird's tune," Nacho smiled, and struck a jaunty pose. "He's perched in a mass of queen's wreath.

Here in the middle of the flower wilderness
Nobody sings quite so beautifully as me!
Nobody sings as enchantingly as me . . ."

Katie's fingers were by now as tired as the rest of her had been earlier. John threw out the dishwater and spread the rag to dry across the pan's rim. Kneeling by Jed, who dozed

222

on the rug by Ace and Rosie, the man dropped a hand on the boy's shoulder, a hand reddened from lye soap and hot water. Kate took a certain wicked satisfaction in thinking that after hours of using the spade, topped off by this, his hands might not be so supple tomorrow in dealing the cards.

"Good night, Jed," he said. "I'll be back next week or so. Take care of Ace. Train him right and he can be a lion dog and a cow dog and a watchdog — just about any kind of dog you want him to be."

Scrambling up, grasping Ace in one hand and Diamond's arm with the other, Jed pleaded, "Aw, Uncle Jack, you don't have to go, do you? There's lots of room up in my loft!"

"Thanks, son, but I've got business tomorrow." Tousling the fair hair, Diamond gave the boy a hug and got to his feet. Bidding the rest of them good-night, he took his hat from a peg and vanished into the night.

"I'll help him saddle up!" Jed cried, sleepiness forgotten. Ace tumbling after him, he pelted outside. Nacho gazed at the baby, murmured his good-nights, and followed.

Melissa tested Rosie's diaper. "She's dry."

"Then let's just go on to bed and hope she sleeps through the night," said Katie, yielding to weariness.

By the time Jed came in from shouting his last farewells, Katie and Melissa were already in bed with Rosie tucked in her box next to the wall. Jed's loft was above the kitchen, but even so Katie could hear him talking to his puppy.

With the dog, small as he was, and with Nacho under the big oak, Katie felt much less nervous than she had the night before. In spite of anxiety over what Larrimore might try in the future, she was happy that so much had been accomplished; she was glad John Diamond was their friend.

Roused by a strident clamor, Katie jerked upright before she realized the dawn greeter was Chica. The sound woke Rosie, too, who made up for letting her sisters sleep all night by shifting almost immediately from whimper to howl, accompanied by flailing legs and fists. Pacified by dry clothing and the milk Melissa sleepily hastened to prepare, Rosie was cuddled by Melissa while Katie built up the fire and made mush. Jed came down the ladder, Ace hugged to his chest. Nacho was already at work. When called for breakfast, he said, "Thousand thanks, Katie, but I will work while it's cool and rest and eat when the sun is well up."

The family soon was at work except for Rosie. On the serape spread between the garden and the dogtrot, she played with her toes or rolled over and tried to get her knees up beneath her. These locomotions propelled her to the edge of the blanket, and Katie, making furrows with the hoe, had to keep one eye on her sister. Jed and Melissa hitched up the wagon and hauled rocks.

Katie planted onion sets and seeds brought from Texas, chilies, runner beans, and pinto beans, and mounded hills among the corn for melons, pumpkins, and squash. Until it rained, water would have to be carried from the creek or well to irrigate the garden, so she made shallow ditches to carry the water. As she worked, she pondered all that had happened yesterday.

Hard to believe that Larrimore had asked her to preside over his home; harder to credit that he'd threatened to get himself made the younger children's guardian; hardest of all to accept that she'd actually said that if he tried to take them over, she'd kill him. Would she? Part of her protested that of course she couldn't, but another part cried out that, pushed to it, defending herself and her family, she would.

Shivering in spite of the heat, she told herself it wouldn't come to that. Not as long as Bill Radnor was in the county. How long would that be?

A day at a time, she told herself, and responded to Rosie's fretting.

It was cooler under the big oak than in the kitchen, so for dinner they loaded their plates with beans and mush and settled on the logs arranged the night before. Ace, whose nose kept him eagerly investigating, sniffed at a small ridge a little beyond the grate, and then began to burrow and dig in a tangle of dead brush that seemed to have blown against the slope.

"Look!" Jed shouted, setting down his plate and running forward. "Look what Ace found!"

The pup's endeavors had exposed a small wooden door set in frame surrounded by narrow rock walls. After a startled moment, Katie followed as Jed opened the door. "This must be Barney Sykes's surprise," she said, stooping to peer into the dark cavity, drawing in the moist pungency of the earth. "It's a cellar!"

Four split log steps led down to a packed earth floor. The walls of the small room were mortared stone. Upright logs with cross poles supported a ceiling of more poles. A large divided bin in the center gave out the clean scent of pine.

"This is wonderful!" Katie said to Melissa

and Nacho, who had followed her. "Feel how cool it is? We can store our food here, and it'll be a lot safer from animals than it would be in the barn."

"Also," said Nacho, "it might be a very good place to hide."

Sobered by that, Katie returned to the sunlight. Jed, praising Ace, heaped the brush back in place. "I guess Mr. Sykes did that to show how well it can be hidden," Melissa said.

Katie nodded. "If Ace hadn't found it, we'd never have known it was there, though Mr. Sykes would have shown us when he helps Mr. Carson bring the furniture."

They resumed their meal. Today, Nacho consented to rest beneath the tree during the hottest hours. Jed and Melissa went up the creek with their fishing poles, and Katie settled into the rocker, rested her feet on a log, and started hemming another curtain. Even with the dog and Nacho's comforting presence, she'd feel better with the dark closed out at night.

A week sped by. Nothing could make wash day pleasant, but Katie found the outside grate wonderfully convenient. Shaded by the giant oak, breeze carrying away the steam of the boiling sheets and Rosie's things, Katie rubbed out persistent stains on a washboard in a tub resting on a crate. Soapy water would kill plants, but the rinse water went on the rosebush and garden. Jed grumbled, of course, about carrying the many buckets of water it took to do the laundry, but Katie reminded him that they'd had to carry it farther in Texas and that they were lucky to have a well.

"But it rained in Texas!" Jed retorted. "We never had to water the garden or corn!"

"Patience," counseled Nacho. "This is the dry time, but by San Juan's Day, the summer rains should start."

"When's that?" asked Jed suspiciously.

"The twenty-fourth of June. Besides, *niño*, I am taking a load of wood to town tomorrow. I have two large canvas water bags in some things Señor Carson is keeping for me. I used them when I delivered water in Tucson. Now they will be useful for with them we can fetch irrigation water from the creek faster than enough buckets can be hauled up from the well."

Nacho returned with the bags, a bundle of scraps for Ace, and greetings from Bride and most of Galeyville. "Señor Carson thinks he will bring your furniture next week," the old man said. "And Doña Bride, she says you must come for the Fourth of July."

"I don't see how we can." Katie hated to quench the eagerness in Melissa's and Jed's eyes, but it would be worse to let them hope. "The cows will need milking then and —"

Interrupting the children's united groan, Nacho grinned. "I can milk, Katie, and Chica and I, we are old enough to prefer quiet and peace to such fiestas."

Perhaps he was afraid he'd be tempted to drink. "That's kind of you, Nacho," Katie said, and turned a quelling glance on her brother and sister. "Don't plague me, you two! I can't promise just yet."

"We'll work real hard," Jed bargained.

Melissa made a pert face. "We already do!"

"Now listen, you two —" Katie began.

"You two!" mimicked her sister. "That's about all you ever call us any more, Katie! Like we were in the army or something!" Jed nodded vigorous agreement.

Thinking back, Katie was abashed to recognize the truth of this plaint. "I've got so much on my mind —" Horrified at this echo of her father's usual excuse, Katie bit it off. "I guess you're right. But 'you two's' shorter than 'Jed and Melissa.'"

"What's wrong with 'pardners'?" demanded Jed. "You say this place belongs to all of us, but you talk like we're the hired hands."

That stung. She worked hardest of all. She was responsible for them, had to plan and make sure everything necessary got done when it should. But the children had worked faithfully — and they *were* children. Putting aside chagrin, she hugged them.

"Pardners!" she said.

Nacho's water bags balanced on either side of a ridgepole fastened across the pack frame. Each held seven gallons of water. Chica stood with her eyes closed while the water was tipped into the small canals. This turned onerous hourslong drudgery into a much easier task. When the first tiny seedling nudged through the soil, Katie hugged Chica and felt like doing the same to Nacho.

After ten days, it seemed that he had always been with them, and she hated to even think how different it would have been without him. He wasn't quite through with the wall because he had to keep his customers supplied with firewood. Sometimes he returned very late to Home Mountain Ranch, but Katie was relieved and pleased that never did he smell of whiskey.

The cows and horses usually grazed within sight. Katie didn't want a mare or heifer to hide out and have her young where it or she, in a weakened state, might fatally attract wolves or lions or coyotes. The first animal born at the ranch was a fine heifer calf with the same gentle, fawnlike face as her mother, Queenie. As if following her mother's example, Lady Jane produced her calf that evening, and before dark, Jenny was nuzzling a knobby-kneed bay filly who even at birth had the strong jaw of a quarter horse.

"A *señorita*," Nacho said, and that became her name, Rita for short. By the end of the week, besides Betsy's Spots and Queenie's Princess, three other calves of varying shades of light brown with white lured each other into awkward races or played "King of the Hill," trying to hold a slope against all comers. Lady Jane's Buttercup was too indolent for much of this exertion, and Ribbon's Bow usually joined her in following their mothers for all the world like well-bred young ladies disdaining to play with hoydens. Inquisitive Cinders had produced the only bull calf. He had inherited her dusky face, so Jed dubbed him Prince Coal, which swiftly degenerated to Coalie.

The calves were winsome with their big ears and melting eyes, but the colts were even more delightful. Short, fuzzy tails and crimped manes gave them the look of just having unfolded from some kind of damply nourishing seedpod. Golden sorrels like their mothers, with fiery manes and tails, Goldie and Red Rover frolicked with Rita when they weren't suckling Honeybunch and Babe. Chili alone still moved heavily, swollen till it seemed her flanks would burst. This was her first colt. It was sure to be a big one. Katie was troubled, but there was no way to bring the colt till it was ready.

It was three or four days before the cows' milk could be used by humans. Like mare's first milk, it contained special strength-giving nutrients that protected the young from diseases. Even when the milk was all right for human use, Katie didn't try to limit the calves' suckling. There was still plenty of milk for drinking, rich-tasting although the cream was skimmed off for butter and kept in the cellar in a bigger pan of water that also cooled the milk.

Eyeing the thick golden cream, Melissa sighed. "We won't get any butter, will we, Katie? We have to use it to pay back Bride and the stores and saloons and Mr. Carson and —"

Jed watched intently. That neither child begged or fussed moved Katie to recklessness. "We'll pay everybody back, but we're going to enjoy the first churning of butter." Craftily, she saw a way to make watering the garden a less dreary chore. "If we grow enough vegetables to help with our debts, we can use a little more of the butter. Besides, even when we take whole milk in to sell, we'll have lots of buttermilk. And we can make cottage cheese and —"

"And I can make us a delicious soup," offered Nacho. "We have had yucca blossoms fried with wild onions and pigweed, but when there is milk —" He smacked his lips. "Make biscuits or cornbread for supper, Katie, but leave the rest to me! Jed, shall we try to catch a trout by tickling its belly?"

Stuffed trout was a toothsome change from beans, but a big kettle of richly creamy yucca soup disappeared to the last sopping. Chuckling at compliments, Nacho said, "You can't use the datil yucca's blossoms this way, though its fruit is good unlike that of this soap tree yucca or palmillo. You must use only the flower petals. The centers are bitter. Boil them, mash them, add milk, salt, pepper and chopped wild onions, and stir till it's thick."

"I could make it," said Jed though he never helped with the cooking unless dragooned.

"Yes. And the Indians have another good way to use the blossoms. They can be dried, roasted, and stored to be ground later and used in soup."

"I'll gather lots," enthused Melissa. "This is the best soup I ever tasted — and it doesn't even have a bone in it!"

As if the mares welcomed the protection of

the corral for their foals, they often entered it at twilight. Katie walked down to admire the three colts tugging at their mothers' leathery teats. Shiloh stayed outside as if asserting that he was growing up and didn't have to tag after his mother.

"Chili!" Katie glanced quickly around. "Oh, Lord, maybe she's having trouble! This is her first colt. Did you see her this afternoon, Jed?"

His brow puckered. "We saw all the horses up the canyon while we were getting the trout. There's sort of a meadow above a bunch of little waterfalls. She was there, Katie. I saw how big she was and thought how tired she must be of packing all that weight."

"I should have noticed earlier." Gripped by dread and guilt, Katie desperately scanned the enshrouding twilight. "I've got to hunt for her. Jed, run see if Nacho will help look."

"I'll come, too — me 'n Ace! Maybe Ace will smell her! Let us, Katie!"

Ace smelled *everything*. Still, reluctant as she was to put any trust in the bumbling, ever-questioning puppy, Katie had no better inspirations. "All right, you can come, but stay with Nacho unless you catch up with me. We certainly don't need to have to go searching after you."

"You won't," said Jed haughtily. "And I

bet, Miss Smartie, that Ace finds her!"

He rushed off. Katie started toward the darkening canyon. She hadn't been up it since the day Bill had taken her to the magical point overlooking the whole canyon and plain, but she thought she remembered the meadow and the falls. She tried to tell herself that Chili had simply hidden to have her foal, that she would be just fine. But even if the colt came properly, there was danger from predators drawn by the blood scent.

It was getting too dark to discern more than shapes. Katie listened intently, walking as quietly as she could. How many noises there were! Cicadas shrilling; coyotes in their first chorus of the evening; the soughing of wind in the trees mixed with the sibilant murmur of the creek; the low trilling cry of a night-hawk; a poorwill's lamentation; the eerie questioning of owls.

Thank goodness the moon was still close to full. Its luster brightened the sky behind the distant mountains to the east. It would rise before the night got much darker. All the same, Katie was glad when Nacho and Jed caught up with her. Nacho had been carrying the puppy but set him down now.

Ace scurried to investigate every stone and bush. Katie groaned. "He doesn't know what we want him to find," Jed defended. "Maybe

I'd better carry him to the meadow."

A keening howl raised the hair on Katie's nape. "That's a wolf," said Nacho.

Hurrying through shadows and blue-silver patches, they could see the moonlit open meadow ahead. Ace sniffed and gave an uneasy whine. Jed let him down. Nose to the ground, the pup ran into the trees.

His humans followed, struggling through low-spreading boughs and bushes, sometimes bending almost double, often tearing loose from thorny vines or branches. Jed soon passed Katie. Smaller than she, he could squeeze through trunks and thickets that she had to go around.

From what sounded far away, she heard Ace whimpering with excitement. Shielding her face with her arms, she pressed on. Nacho was in front of her now, and that made her passage easier. Finally, above the sobbing of her own breath, she heard laborious, gasping breaths, a faint nicker.

"Chili!"

The mare lay heaving in the shelter of a thick-growing stand of young trees and brush. A spasm racked her. Beneath her tail, a bulging object pushed out a little farther. Dropping to her knees, Katie saw that a thick, bloody mass that looked and smelled like raw liver preceded the colt, covered its emerging head.

Instinctively thrusting through the mucousy stuff, cleaning it away from the small nostrils, Katie remembered that this had happened in Texas. Pa had told Mama about it, though only he had seen it. The afterbirth somehow came first instead of following the colt's delivery and the colt had suffocated.

Sure enough, the foal wasn't breathing. There was no telling how long Chili had struggled like this. She might die, too, if she couldn't expel the dead colt. "Come on, girl," Katie urged, smoothing the young mare's sweaty flank. "Try!"

As if heartened by the humans, Chili tensed with a massive contraction. The foal's leg emerged and one tiny, perfect hoof, swaddled in what was left of the protective membrane.

"The other hoof must be turned wrong," said Nacho. "Your hands are small, Katie. Perhaps with the next pain, you can help."

As gently as she could, all the while soothing the mare, Katie eased her fingers past the colt and felt inside the wet, hot passage till she located the hoof of the leg bent at an angle that wouldn't let it come out. Broken out in cold sweat, agonizingly aware of how much even her most careful handling was hurting Chili, Katie maneuvered the hoof to where it could be slipped out.

With a shuddering convulsion from Chili,

the dead foal pushed out, resting on the grass where she would never run, never graze. Chili lay exhausted and panting for a few minutes. Then, whinnying weakly, she raised enough to bite through the cord and clean her foal, swallowing the membrane. When this was done, she nuzzled the little creature, puzzled at its stillness. A beautiful little filly it was, chestnut like her mother, with a brighter mane and tail.

Katie couldn't hold back tears. The loss of the colt was a blow, especially a filly who would have dropped perhaps a dozen Steel Dust foals, but the cruelest thing was the way poor Chili had been so uncomfortable these last weeks, endured an unusually painful and lengthy foaling, and then had no warm, eager little muzzle searching at her flank.

Rising shakily, Chili tried to nose the colt to its feet. "She won't want to leave it," said Nacho. "It will take her a while to know that it's dead. After she does, I can skin it. The hide will make fine leather."

"No!" Shocked at the violence of her feeling, Katie touched the old man's arm. "I'm sorry I yelled, Nacho. It would be sensible to use the hide and even the meat. But this time — this time, I just can't."

He cupped an ear down the canyon though she heard nothing. "Horses," he murmured.

"Two, at the least."

"Our horses are in the stable."

"Yes."

"Katie!" The wind brought her name. That voice! Were her ears playing tricks? "Katie — it's Bill!"

"Here!" she called, when her lips could move, and hurried forward, acquiring more scratches than before in her eagerness. Now she could hear the creak of saddles, the jingling of spurs. Breaking from the trees, she could scarcely make out Shadow. He blended with the moonlight so that Bill seemed to float in space, his white hat visible before he was.

"Did you find the mare?" he asked, springing down and catching her hand. "A damned shame," he said, when she'd explained. "I'll pack the colt so the mare will come along."

"If I'd missed her sooner —" Katie mourned.

"You couldn't have done anything about that afterbirth bein' in the wrong place. You sure enough saved her."

"Ace found Chili!" Jed burst from the darkness and scooped up the puppy who growled deep in his throat till Jed hushed him. "We wouldn't have found her till the buzzards did, but Ace went right to her."

"Good boy, Ace." Bill scratched the pup behind his ears. "You're going to make a mighty fine dog."

"He already is," said Jed pridefully.

The other rider tugged at the rim of his hat. "Evenin', Miss MacLeod. Bill and me have finished our tax collecting and thought we'd stop to see how you were gettin' along in your new place. Your little sister poked a Winchester through a chink when she heard us comin'. Bill shouted out, of course. She told us where you'd gone."

Katie thrilled with pride in her sister but felt compunction. Melissa must have been badly frightened. "M'liss has never fired the Winchester you left us, or the old shotgun, either."

"Have you used the Winchester?" asked Bill.

"No," she admitted guiltily. "I've been meaning to get Nacho to teach us but — well, we've been busy —"

Bill frowned. "When you need to shoot, Katie, there won't be time to learn. I'll come over soon and we'll have a little target practice."

He led his horse as near to the filly as possible. Then he, Breakenridge, and Nacho got her across the saddle. Bill tied the body so it wouldn't slip, and they set off for home.

At an arroyo several hundred yards from the corral, the men let the foal slide into the gulch. "Tomorrow you may want to cover her with rocks to keep off scavengers," said Bill. "But for tonight, let the mare get used to the idea that the filly can't get up or move, that's she's dead."

Chili whickered, nuzzling at the body. Bill caressed her shoulder. "It's a shame, girl," he said gently. "But you're strong and healthy. Next time I bet you have a dandy colt."

Smeared with blood and mucous as she was, Katie wouldn't go inside till she'd washed off in the creek and put on her other dress, which she'd asked Melissa to hand out to her. By the time she came in, Katie was bemused to see that Melissa, very much in charge, had coffee on, and was frying side meat to go with cold biscuits. When she'd forked the crispy meat on the men's plates, she stirred flour into the sizzling grease, added salt, and poured in milk to stir into creamy rich gravy.

The first Melissa had ever made without plenty of lumps, Katie thought, suppressing a chuckle along with a small pang of jealousy. *She wants to show Bill she knows how to take care of him.*

Worn out as she was, Katie was content to let Melissa remain the hostess. The commotion had roused the baby, who wanted milk and attention. Preparing a bottle, Katie settled into the rocker with the smallest MacLeod and gratefully thanked Melissa for bringing her a bracing cup of coffee with lots of milk, just the way Katie liked it. She felt sad for Chili and the tiny horse that would never breathe the air. Perhaps one of the other colts could be encouraged to suckle Chili so she wouldn't be in pain as her milk dried up.

"Can't wait to see Sheriff Behan's face when I plunk this money on his desk," confided Breakenridge. "Over a thousand dollars! I'd never have believed all those men would pay up, even with you along."

"Oh, I pointed out to them it'd look good for them to be taxpayin' citizens in case they ever got into difficulties with the law," said Bill.

The deputy shook his blond head. "You knew to a cow what size herd each man had. And the way you know who's staked out which canyon! I couldn't have found a tithe of them."

"It was fun," shrugged Bill, smiling at Melissa as she poured more coffee. "Best game I've had since I voted San Simon."

"Voted San Simon?" frowned Breakenridge. "How'd you do that?"

"Well, that was while we were still part of Pima County and Bob Paul was runnin' for sheriff against Charley Shibell, who's a friend of mine. Paul's ridden shotgun on a stagecoach so I wasn't too partial to him and sort of

242

wanted him to know it."

Holding out his cup for more coffee, Bill grinned and settled back. He never talked of his exploits. Katie was sure he was trying to divert her thoughts from the dead foal. "I riled up all my friends to vote and was at the saloon in San Simon when it struck me those Chinese section hands ought to be learnin' their citizens' duties. So I showed 'em the ballot box and recommended Charley. Everybody in town voted, but shucks, even with kids and women, there weren't more 'n thirty ballots. I was feelin' sort of blue when the saloon-keeper's dog took some feathers out of the gander belongin' to the owner of the board-inghouse. Now Shepherd W. Towser sounds pretty important, and Hiram J. Gander would fit a judge. I voted every horse, mule, chicken, burro, goat, and dog in town — and they all had the sense to vote for Charley."

Sighing, he gave a regretful shake of his head. "You'd think the election commissioners in Tucson would have appreciated the trouble I took to think up names, but not them! They threw out the precinct. All the same, it sure was fun."

Scandalized, for though she didn't have the vote, Katie had been raised to believe it a proud American birthright denied to many in other countries, she said, "Is that all that counts with you, Bill Radnor? Having fun?" Startled at the bitterness in her tone, she would have instantly apologized — she owed this man too much to chide him — but he only grinned and locked his arms behind his curly black head.

"Best reason I've found yet for bein' alive, Katie. I know Brothers Daggett and Thomas wouldn't approve, but I guess I'm just a puredee reprobate." His gray-blue eyes traveled approvingly around the room. "Looks like home, smells like home, feels like home. And that's quite a wall Nacho's doin'. Turnin' this into a fortress?"

Nacho spread his hands and smiled. *"Quién sabe,* Señor Radnor?"

Katie darted the old Yaqui a surprised look before she remembered that it was only around John Diamond that he'd spoken more than a few English words. Most likely, Nacho found it wise to conceal his knowledge of the language; certainly, the correct way he spoke would strike a lot of people as stuck-up and somehow a little dangerous. Of course, Spanish wasn't Nacho's mother tongue, either; Katie smothered laughter when she pondered that Nacho, considered an ignorant Indian woodcutter in Galeyville, spoke three languages well. This winter when there was time to sit by the fire, maybe he'd teach her and the children Spanish, even a little Yaqui so that he'd have someone to whom he could speak his native language.

"The wall's to keep deer and other animals out of the garden and corn patch," she explained.

"You've already planted?"

"We were late as it was. I plowed the day after we moved in."

Radnor's mouth tightened. "Damn it, Katie, you're not strong enough to hustle a plow! And it's not fittin' for womenfolk anyway — might mess up your innards. Nacho, why in the world —"

"Nacho didn't come till after the plowing. John Diamond did most of the spading, though." She took a perverse pleasure in saying that and watching Bill's jaw drop.

"Diamond? *He* set them elegant hand-stitched boots of his to a spade?"

Katie nodded.

"His hands!" Bill choked. "He's not done a day's honest work in so long that he must have ruined his fingers."

"He wore gloves."

Breakenridge chortled. "What's the world coming to, Bill? You a deputy sheriff tax collector and Jack Diamond spadin' a garden?" He smothered a yawn. "Been a long day. Took a while to find Ed Larrimore and quite a spell to convince him he owed taxes. Be all right with you, Miss MacLeod, if we throw down our bedrolls on your porch?"

"We'd better mosey along to Galeyville," Bill said. Katie thought that letting deputies stay the night at Home Mountain was different from sheltering anybody, but from Bill's determined look, she saw that he agreed with John Diamond.

Rising, Bill grinned at Melissa. "That was the best gravy I ever tasted, young lady. Some man'll be a lucky cuss when you get old enough to think about double-harness." To Katie, he said, "It's tough about the colt, but at least you saved the mare. If you've got a mind to sell any of the other foals, I'd like to get in a bid early."

By this time next year he could use Shiloh part of a day, though the young stallion still shouldn't carry a man's weight for too many hours at a time. The yearling was halter-broke and sweet-tempered though spirited. That winter there'd be more time to work with him. Katie was no expert with horses, but she had helped her father. It was her resolve to turn over to Bill the finest and most well-mannered horse he'd ever have, a gift that would to some degree recompense all he'd done for her. More, it was a gift of love.

"I don't think any of the colts is just right

for you," Katie parried, silently begging pardon of Goldie, Red Rover, and Señorita. Indeed, they were all responding well to being led by a hackamore and snubbed to a post. "But we'll see, when they're older."

Melissa and Jed at her heels, she followed the men outside to where their horses were still enjoying the wild hay Jed had fetched for them. "Good to see you settled in so well, ma'am," said Breakenridge, and laughed. "We won't put you on the tax roll till year after next but I'll bet my saddle that you'll wind up bein' some of the county's biggest taxpayers."

"I hope we are," smiled Katie.

"Glad Nacho's thrown in with you," said Bill, mounting. "He sure won't let you wrestle a plow again. He's honest, and what's more, he's never been known to take a drink."

"What?" gasped Katie.

Bill's voice was puzzled. "He won't drink. Not even beer. Made him sort of outstandin' around Galeyville."

"Why, John Diamond said he wanted to stay with us because he did drink too much!"

Bill hooted. "It's not healthy to call Jack a liar and I won't. Sounds like he wanted to make you think you were doin' Nacho a kindness to let him stay here — and I reckon you are. Nacho loves kids and they seldom turn up in Galeyville. You'll all be in for the Fourth?"

"Melissa and Jed will."

Bill grunted. "So will you, Katie, if I have to rope and tie you. Everyone's countin' on your bringin' your harp."

"The cows have to be milked."

"Leave it to Nacho for one night."

"It's not fair to make him miss the celebration."

Bill groaned. "For Pete's sake! I'll ride out and milk 'em then! That satisfy you?"

Melissa giggled and Katie laughed. "Then you'd better borrow a dress and bonnet. These cows are used to skirts. When Pa tried to milk them once when Mama and I were sick, they kicked the pail over and kicked him, too. He had to shave and put on Mama's dress and bonnet before they'd stand quiet and let down their milk."

Breakenridge whooped. "We could sell more tickets to see you in skirts, Bill, than we could to your hangin'!"

"Nobody's goin' to get rich sellin' tickets to any one," said Bill. "But your cows'll be milked, Katie, so you just get yourself into town bright and early or I'll come get you."

"Don't disappoint us, Miss MacLeod," put in the deputy in his deep, pleasant voice. "I'm tellin' Sheriff Behan I'm needed in Galeyville to keep the peace, but the real reason I want to come is to hear you."

"Gracious!" surrendered Katie. "I'd better start practicing!"

Everyone laughed, but as the horses splashed across the creek and the sound of hoofs gradually faded, Chili gave a plaintive, questioning whicker.

"Go on to bed," Katie told her brother and sister. "I'll be in soon."

Getting a brush from the shed, Katie found the mare keeping vigil over the filly, whose legs were just starting to turn rigid. Stroking Chili, Katie murmured, "It's too bad, girl. A dirty, rotten shame. But Red Rover's such a big guy that I'll bet he'd like your milk."

Why wait till morning? Why not try him now? Katie was exhausted, but she wouldn't sleep well while imagining how Chili would be trying to get the dead colt on its legs. Finding the horses between the arroyo and the corral, Katie went to the shed for a hackamore.

"I'm just borrowing your baby for a little while," she assured Babe as she slipped the hackamore over Red Rover's ears. He followed readily to the arroyo where Chili still puzzled at her colt. Katie smoothed her flanks for a few minutes, and then rubbed Red Rover, hoping there'd be enough of the mare's own smell to induce her to accept him. Bringing him close to Chili, Katie talked reassuringly to them both while the mare sniffed him all over.

At least she's not kicking him away, Katie thought. She kept up her soothing murmurs as the miniature stallion greedily sought and found a teat. Chili flinched. Then she seemed to know this was what was supposed to happen. While the colt tugged lustily, she sniffed at his jouncing tail and nickered softly.

If only the mares would share him!

Something compelled Katie to kneel beside the filly, caress the fluff of mane and tail, the small, exquisite hoofs. *Run in heaven, little horse,* she thought, letting the tears fall. *Run in the sky and sun and clouds.*

Katie smoothed the mane again and stood in the moonlight till the night wind dried her tears.

X

Ranging back and forth between two proud mothers, Red Rover thrived. Babe, fortunately, seemed glad to share her rambunctious son's greedy attentions. Chili, in fact, groomed him oftener and was more solicitous. Perhaps she had some bewildered recollection of a small, stiff body that couldn't suckle or race at her side.

Nacho hadn't chided Katie for what he surely viewed as a waste of meat and a fine, soft hide, but she knew she couldn't, in the future, be so unreasonable. If it had been a calf, she probably wouldn't have found so horrid the thought of eating it and using its skin, but in their way, the calves were as winning as the colts. When a person really stopped to think about it, it was awful to think of slaughtering any animal — turning cows she knew, like Buttercup, Flossie, and Lady Jane, into beef. When it got cold enough in the fall, Pa had slaughtered a hog and steer. Katie had always had to grit her teeth and try not to breathe in the smell of drenched hair, blood, and yes, terror, while she helped her mother scrape the loosened bristles from the scalded hog.

I'll never do that again, she thought in a heady rush of knowing that she could make such decisions now; there wasn't anybody with the power to tell her not to be silly.

Won't you eat ham and bacon? her conscience demanded.

Well — probably. But we're not going to raise any hogs and get to know them before we cut their throats. And beef? *I'll worry about that later, but we certainly aren't going to kill any of* our cows! How much easier it was not to think!

Hod Carson and Barney Sykes delivered the furniture a few days after the filly was born dead. Beds, chests, chairs, benches, a cupboard, and a washstand replaced boxes, and when every smoothly burnished piece was arranged, Hod sighed gustily through his cinnamon beard, crossed his burly arms and strutted from one room to the other, pausing by Rosie's crib.

"See, you can start the mattress up high and lower the slats when the tyke starts pulling up," he explained. His blunt, stained fingers lingered on the rail, which was sanded off so that there were no sharp edges. "No reason why that little one's great grandbaby can't use this selfsame crib. Black walnut like the rest of the things except for some juniper. Rub in some beeswax now and again, and this stuff'll look as good when you're an old lady as it does right now." His smile widened to show the gap left by a missing tooth. "That's more'n I can say for us human critters."

"Everything's just beautiful!" Katie could scarcely believe a whole houseful of handsome new furniture. "And you've even made a strap to hold Rosie in her high chair!"

"Can't have her crackin' her noodle because of my carpentry," he said, and smoothed his ruddy whiskers. "I was tellin' Barney as we drove out that I reckon I never before got so much satisfaction out of a job, unless it was makin' a coffin for that no-account Cherokee Jack."

"Cherokee Jack?" Jed's eyes rounded. "Was he an outlaw?"

Hod started to spit, remembered where he was, spluttered on the tobacco, and said, "Ten-cent pickpocket was more like it, sonny. Made the mistake of leadin' in a mule Lord Bill knew belonged to a widder woman over in Pinery Canyon. Lord Bill made him take it back, and you'd have reckoned if the galoot was half-smart, he'd have stayed out of Galeyville. But no, he has to come back, all puffed up like a toad after rain, and mosey into Shotwell's store."

Hod paused to savor the memory. Balding, mournful-eyed Barney Sykes shook his head over the wickedness of the departed. "Jack poked his six-shooter in Pat O'Day's ribs, cussed him, and allowed as how he was goin' in for civic improvements like runnin' him out of town."

"Pat's a scrawny little drouthy man," said Hod. "But he was a barroom fighter when Jack was still cuttin' teeth. Pat jumped up, somebody grabbed Jack's six-shooter, and the two went to the floor together close to a bunch of single jacks — that's a miner's hammer, ma'am. Pat got hold of one and when he finished, all Jack needed was buryin'. We planted him below camp. Didn't want such a skunk in our regular cemetery."

"Which, if we don't take skunks, may never have many graves," finished Sykes. His glance flickered out the window toward the root cellar, hidden by loose grass and brush. Katie had thought it just as well to keep it concealed just in case it was ever needed for hiding; it only took a minute to toss the covering over the door. "Find your surprise, ma'am?"

"The puppy did." Katie was appalled at their cheerful account of Cherokee Jack's demise, but he had plainly been no loss to the community. "It's lovely to have such a cool place for the milk and cream, Mr. Sykes, and it'll be grand for keeping our squash and pumpkins."

Sykes beamed, for a moment losing his perpetual air of having just lost his last friend. "Reckoned it'd come in handy, Miss MacLeod. And with 'Paches breakin' off the reservation now and again, it don't hurt to have a place to hole up in. Might be an idea to keep some food and a jug of water in there."

"Nacho's already seen to that," said Katie. "The Yaquis had to hide out so often from the Mexican soldiers that he feels better to have a place all fixed. Now, dinner's about ready, so please pull up one of these beautiful chairs!"

After the meal, declaring that fresh butter sure turned cornbread into cake, the two started for town, butter packed tightly into the lard pails they'd brought filled with scraps for Ace. They also carried the jugs Bride had sent for milk. As well as filling them, Katie sent her friend a pail of butter. The glow of happy pride she felt in making some small return for all Bride had done for them more than made up for knowing that the family needed to go without butter till they'd paid back a respectable amount to the people who'd been so generous. True, no one expected that, but Katie was determined that the MacLeods wouldn't be beholden to anyone except for the kindness and concern that could never be repaid.

After waving Hod and Barney on their way, she went past the budding rosebush Diamond had brought and planted, stepped into the house, and gazed around from sage green curtains — the leaf dye had worked — to mellow, gleaming cupboard, benches, table, and chairs. Caressing Rosie's sturdy high chair with her name carved into a flowering vine, Katie was so happy that she burst into tears.

"Katie!" Melissa caught her arm. "What's the matter?"

Sobbing, Katie couldn't answer. Shaking her head, she hugged Melissa and tried to smile. "I — I —"

"Good gracious sakes!" came a voice from the door. "What's going on here, girls?"

Bill! He handed Katie a surprisingly clean handkerchief, frowning as she wiped her eyes. "Did Hod or Barney upset you? If they did —"

"Oh, no! But look!" Katie gestured at the furniture and again traced the carving on the chair. "It's just so pretty. I wish our mother'd had such nice things."

Katie wished she hadn't said that because Melissa's eyes also misted and her mouth quivered. For the first time since Katie had met him, Bill looked helpless. Then, clearing his throat, he said, "Listen. I'll bet she knows you have them, and that makes her mighty glad."

What a perfect thing to say! Katie blinked and smiled, though there was still an ache in her throat. "The cornbread's still warm enough to melt butter," she said.

"Sounds great." Bill pitched his hat on a bench. "If you're going to feed me, I'd better wash up. Reckon we could get in some practice with the Winchester this afternoon? I brought plenty of cartridges."

"If you have the time, we do," said Katie.

While Bill ate, she and Melissa did the dishes. Jed, spying Shadow, hurried in from a ramble up the canyon with Ace. "I'll bet I can shoot better than either of the girls," he bragged. "M'liss is scared of guns and Katie squinches her eyes shut when she fires the shotgun. If Missou had known that —"

"With a shotgun, your aim doesn't have to be real good," Bill said dryly. "I'm not tryin' to make sharp shooters out of any of you. So's we won't scare the baby, let's meander up the creek and find a stump or dead tree to shoot at."

"We can take turns staying with Rosie," Katie said. Nacho had taken a load of wood to town that day so he couldn't be enlisted.

"Since Jed thinks he's so much better than we are, can't he watch Rosie first?" demanded Melissa. "I don't want him teasing and making me nervous."

"Aw —" began Jed.

Bill grinned at him and dropped a man-to-man hand on his shoulder. "Let me give your sisters a few pointers, Jed, and then you'll be free to burn up the rest of the cartridges I brought. You can even try out my Colt. It uses the same .44-40 cartridge as the Winchester — mighty handy."

"I can use your gun?" Jed whooped. "Oh, boy! Wait'll I tell Uncle Jack! He says he'll give me a Colt on my eighteenth birthday and not a day sooner!"

Startled, Bill glanced at Katie. "I'm sorry. Just didn't think. If you'd rather Jed waited —"

"I'm surprised that John Diamond thinks guns are more dangerous than cards," Katie said, unable to restrain a sniff, though she was pleased at this evidence of Diamond's care for Jed. "But I suppose there's no harm in Jed's learning to use your gun so long as he understands that he doesn't get one till he's eighteen."

Bill looked at Jed. "Understood?" As Jed scowled, Bill said, "I wish, son, that somebody had cared enough about me to see I didn't get a man's gun until I was a man."

With a glance at Katie and a long-suffering sigh, Jed nodded and ascended to his loft. Tying on their sunbonnets, the sisters went with Bill along the cow path leading to the canyon.

"Longest walk I've had in years," he chuck-led, spurs chinking, rifle in one hand, shotgun in the other. "But with such pretty company, it's a pleasure. That lightning-blasted cedar yonder should be a fair target, and look, here's a couple of oaks for shade and even a stump to rest the barrel across. Can't beat that for handiness." He looked back at the house. "We're not out of earshot, but the noise shouldn't be loud enough to scare the baby. After you've fired the cartridges in the rifle, Katie can load, and after that, Melissa. Since neither of you've got ambitions to be real sharpshooters, that ought to be enough for one day."

"You start, Katie," urged Melissa.

Bill leaned the shotgun against a tree and gave Katie the Winchester. "Rest the barrel on the stump, and hold the stock with your left hand," he instructed. "Snug the butt against your right shoulder, and get the middle of the stump between the sights. Now then, pull the trigger."

The shot deafened Katie. She'd tried to keep her eyes open, but they'd closed as she fired. Earth flew up from the foot of the stump. "Not bad," said Bill, cocking his head. "If that'd been some scalawag, he'd have trouble walking and he'd sure enough be scared."

Passing a long arm around her, he yanked

down the lever and clicked it back in place. "See, that ejects the spent shell and moves a cartridge into the chamber. Aim a little higher this time."

Almost embraced, aware of the strong arm enfolding her, Katie's heart pounded. It was the closest she'd ever been to Bill. She had a sudden, driving impulse to turn and look up into his eyes. But if she did, she had a certainty that everything would change, that their friendship would turn into something else — much more, or perhaps be destroyed. She couldn't risk that.

Was he, too, breathing faster? She had no chance to be sure for he moved swiftly away. Forcing herself to concentrate, Katie hit the blackened cedar this time and earned a grin of praise, skinned bark from the sides with her next two shots, fired wild, furrowed up dirt, and then, steadying, hit the trunk twice.

After eight shots, her nerves were frazzled, more from a strong, sweet feeling radiating between them than from the sound. Her shoulder ached from the recoil.

"Your turn, M'liss," she said.

To Katie's chagrin, her younger sister, after missing twice, seemed to get the range and hit the trunk with all five remaining cartridges. Of course, Katie thought, it was a big trunk, probably six feet around with parts

260

jutting higher than Bill's head.

Bill whistled. "Jed's going to have to push to keep ahead of you, honey. All right, here's how you load." He opened the loading port just in front of and above the trigger and stuffed in a shell before handing the weapon to Katie. "Fourteen more," he said, unbuckling one cartridge belt and draping it in easy reach over the stump. "The granddaddy of this rifle, the old Civil War Henry, loaded at the muzzle end of the magazine, which was sort of awkward. Still and all, that was real firing power against a single-shot muzzleloader. And you girls are lucky you came along when powder, bullet, and primer are all done up in one neat cartridge case!"

Katie shot a little better this time, scoring the trunk four times out of eight but never hitting the fist-sized hollow in the middle. Melissa got that once and barked the tree or struck it the other times. She loaded and Katie took her last turn, still not getting the hollow but hitting the tree five times out of seven.

"Respectable," said Bill, moving back as Melissa took her stance. "After all, you're not fixing to hold up stagecoaches for a living." He raised a quizzical dark eyebrow. "Tell me, Katie. Would you really have shot Missou if he wouldn't have let you have water?"

Remembering her desperation, she said,

"Yes. I'd have tried to hit him in the leg or shoulder, of course — not kill him."

He shook his head. "I just can't imagine it, you bein' so tenderhearted and all."

"I'm not tenderhearted when it's a matter of my life or my family's — or my animals', either." With an inward shudder, she thought of Ed Larrimore. If she ever fired at him, she'd better kill him. Sensing that Bill was trying to understand her feelings, she groped to put them into words. "I'm not going to kill anything if I can help it, Bill — not even slaughter for beef. But if I have to, and if I can, yes, I'd kill to defend myself and anyone who depends on me. I don't see what's strange about that."

Bill's mouth quirked. "Trouble is," he said as if to himself, "that when a boy wears a gun, he defends himself maybe a little too fast, and first thing he knows, he's the one good people have to defend themselves against."

"You're good, Bill."

He winced and looked away. When he turned to her, his face was hard angles and his eyes masked. "You don't know me, girl. The Arizona Stock Association has a reward out for me, a thousand dollars, dead or alive. Not that I haven't done business with some of the best members. And it's been a long time since I got sick when I had to kill a man."

262

"But if you had to —"

He raised a muscular hand. "Your have-to and my have-to are mighty different. But one thing you don't have to bother your head about. If what I can tell and teach him carries any weight, Jed won't think that strapping on a six-gun is what makes a man. Go send him down and he can use the rifle while Melissa gets in some practice with the shotgun."

Katie obeyed, troubled. No matter what Bill had done, she believed him the most wonderful man in the world. It sounded as if he'd drifted into his way of life because it was exciting and what he considered fun. Couldn't he change if he wanted to? Or was it, as he seemed to think, too late?

Each day, the flow of the creek narrowed till there were many places where it flowed beneath rocks that looked bleached and dry as bones. Clouds, every hue of gray and blue, built up every afternoon. Towering white thunderheads reared above the mountains, reflecting gold and peach and purple, flared at the top into anvils. There were even forks of lightning and thunder that sounded like a huge underground beast stirring itself; but still it did not rain, not even on Saint John's Day, when Nacho said the rains were supposed to begin.

Several times, Bill had come to oversee Winchester practice and stay for dinner before riding home. It was on Saint John's Day that he pronounced himself satisfied. Katie had hit the hollow once, the tree the rest of the time, and Melissa and Jed had done even better. After supper, they all moved out to the dogtrot and watched lightning flash in the brooding clouds that roiled above the mountains.

"In my pueblo of Vicam," remembered Nacho, who now used his good English in front of Bill, an accolade of trust, "this was the greatest fiesta of the year, for San Juan was the patron of our church. We feasted for three days and nights while the *pascolas* made sure we had a good time — they are a little like dancing clowns. The deer dancer isn't supposed to be funny. He is the spirit of nature, the spirit of the wilderness, and has songs, very old, from before the time when angels and prophets sang the boundaries of the Yaqui lands."

"Angels?" Jed's eyes were wide. "Prophets? I thought they were only in the Bible."

"They walked in Sonora, *niño*. Four Yaqui prophets and a band of angels sang and preached, from near Guaymas to between the mouths of the Mayo and Yaqui rivers. They established our Eight Pueblos. Jesus Himself wandered among us and suffered in the wildlands. Our land is as holy as it is fertile. The Mexicans may hold it for a time, but to us God gave it and to us it will return."

"Do you want to go back?" Jed asked fearfully. To him, Nacho had become like a grandfather besides adding another male to the household.

"No." Nacho's face seemed carved from tough roots. He picked up the baby, who was starting to fret, and for a long time, with her cradled against his shoulder, he gazed toward the south.

Stirring reluctantly, Bill said, "Got to be riding. But first, Katie, could we have a tune?"

They had more than one. In the darkening twilight, Katie felt his eyes on her. Why couldn't it be like this all the time? Why did he ever have to ride away? She was whole, complete and happy, when he was with her. When he left, more and more, she felt as if some vital part of her was gone.

Bill got to his feet, lithe and tall. "Thanks, Katie. Guess I'd rather listen to you than win from Jack Diamond with aces full. Reckon I won't see you till the Fourth of July, but remember that I'll take care of the chores that night."

"But that means you'll miss lots of the celebration," Katie protested.

"Bless your heart," he chuckled. "I won't miss anything."

Was he thinking of Bride? He moved off, whistling for Shadow, and as the family went inside, Katie heard the crunch of hoofs and wondered why she felt so desolate, why it seemed so terribly long till the holiday.

Rays of gold and rose fire fettered the sun to the Peloncillos before it hurtled free, trailing its bonds, burnishing the plain, gilding the mountains. Katie's heart swelled with awe and joy, soared like the pair of circling hawks above Harris Mountain. Had the same hawks watched the killing of the Harris family somewhere very near here less than ten years ago? As she often did, Katie wondered what had happened to the girl carried away into Mexico, who later, when rescued, had begged to return to the Apaches, but no time-muffled tragedy could long shadow her pleasure that morning.

It was the Fourth, and they were going to town! Katie wore her "best" flowered black dress, Melissa her blue, and though these were faded and carefully mended, they were clean and painstakingly pressed with the heavy sad irons as were Jed's and Nacho's shirts. The girls wore the ribbons Bride had given them and had blacked their shoes with tallow and soot from the fireplace, but Jed was barefoot.

The walk from Texas had ruined his heavy winter shoes, which were too small for him now anyway. He'd forgone candy to save the money he'd earned running errands and could have paid for some serviceable work shoes, but he had his heart set on cowboy boots. If he didn't weaken before winter, Katie knew she would trade some butter or vegetables to make up the needed cash.

Nacho drove the wagon hitched to Babe and Honeybunch while Red Rover and Goldie cantered wild circles around their mothers or raced each other across the slopes. Jed, disdaining the wagon, was astride Chili, who whickered after Red Rover even oftener than Babe did. The golden sorrel colts gleamed like new pennies, and their manes and tails fairly blazed. No horseman could see them without longing to own one or both. Belatedly, Katie wished they could have been left in the corral, safe from covetous eyes, but it would be four or five months till the mares weaned them. Till then, the foals would never willingly stray far from their mothers.

Holding Rosie in one arm, Katie held tight to the seat with her other hand and envied Jed his comfortable saddle. She glanced with satisfaction at the precious crocks of butter wedged in tubs of water along with jugs of buttermilk and the sweet milk from yesterday and this morning. Between the tubs rode a big kettle of yucca soup, the MacLeods' contribution to the celebration. The tubs were covered with wet canvas left over from making the curtains, and the wagon sloshed up enough water to keep the fabric damp. Safely away from the moisture, wrapped in a serape, was her harp.

How many gallons of milk had been skimmed for cream to make the six pounds of butter! How many hours of milking, separating, and churning till the butter particles could be gathered and drained and the milk worked out of the mass with a wooden paddle? A pound of butter might not seem like much to anyone who didn't know how it was made, but Katie was proud of the gift her family would give to Bride, the Firbanks, Metzgers, Hod Carson, and Mr. Babcock. Other benefactors would get jugs of milk. Katie was keeping track of what she felt the MacLeods owed. No one expected payment, of course, but they could scarcely spurn gifts. As for the men who'd raised the buildings at Home Mountain, there was no way to repay them except through her music.

As they neared Galeyville, riders of horses, mules, and burros passed them, calling greetings, many riding alongside a little way to admire Rosie — and introduce themselves and find out Katie's name. Most of the animals had red, white, and blue ribbons or rosettes tied to their bridles, and a few of the burros had big tricolored bows tied on their tails. Many riders wore matching hatbands or neckerchiefs. All of them knew Nacho, and some tried to draw out of him more information about the MacLeods.

"Not livin' in Galeyville?" one sunburned, tow-headed cowboy asked.

"*No, señor.*"

"Workin' for this lady?"

"*Sí, señor.*"

"How long you intendin' to do that?"

"*Quién sabe?*" returned Nacho.

"Ain't much for gabbin', are you, old feller?"

"*No, señor.*"

Katie hid a smile behind Rosie as the cowboy rode on, and then her amusement waned. The young man's horse wore a Pitchfork brand. Would Larrimore, too, be in town? More than likely. *Don't be a fool,* she told herself. *You're bound to meet him now and again — and town's the safest place for that.* All the same, her stomach roiled to think of him, remembering those hard, smoke-colored eyes.

Early as it still was, sounds of revelry floated from the long single street. Flags flew from most of the buildings, including Bride's boardinghouse, and red, white, and blue bunting draped a big picture of George Washington on an outside wall of Babcock's saloon. Katie handed the baby to Melissa, and while Nacho held Jed's horse and the team, Katie and her brother, with Ace dashing before, behind, and around them, carried butter and milk to the stores, Babcock's, Firbanks' restaurant, and Hod's workshop.

Mr. Babcock invited them to leave their horses in his corral. Nacho was unhitching when Bride ran out, resplendent in red and white gingham with a blue sash. She swept Katie to her in a warm hug. Katie, in spite of her resolve, couldn't keep from wondering if Bride's exuberance came from spending part of the night with Bill Radnor.

"Is it you, love?" Bride laughed. "And that sweet baby! Here, Melissa, let me take her!" The tall, dark-haired woman embraced Melissa, too, but the girl didn't return the hug.

Puzzled and a little embarrassed, Katie said, "Would you get the butter and milk for Mrs. Malone, M'liss?"

"You got everybody else's!" flashed Melissa. "You might as well get hers, too! Just as if I didn't milk and churn and —"

"Melissa!" Aghast at the explosion and the tears that made her sister's blue eyes even brighter, Katie caught Melissa's hand. "I

270

didn't know — I didn't mean —"

The younger girl twisted away. "I wish I was the oldest! Then you'd find out what it's like to be bossed around and never given any credit!"

This was the thanks she got for trying to look after the family, keep them together, make them a home? Too hurt and angry to speak reasonably, Katie clamped her jaws tight to keep from lashing out. It was Bride who said, "Land alive, Melissa! Don't you think I remember what a help you are? Do me a favor, colleen. Put the butter and milk in a pan of water under the stairs, and then let's get over to Babcock's. Reverend Gus Chenowth is holding a prayer service for rain, and I sure hope the good Lord will pay him some mind!"

Melissa, somewhat appeased though she avoided looking at Katie, took the dairy gifts inside. Nacho carried the big kettle of yucca blossom soup over to where huge pots of beans were cooking over grates and set it where it would heat without boiling. Nuzzling Rosie's soft dark hair as the cooing baby reached for her face, Bride rested a warm hand on Katie's shoulder. "Don't take what the child says too much to heart, Katie. 'Tis a prickly age, neither child nor woman. Try not to let her little huffs upset you."

271

Blinking back tears, Katie forced a laugh. "I wish she could be the oldest for a few days! She'd be mighty glad to trade back."

Bride nodded, paused, and spoke carefully. "Am I imagining things, dear, or are you put out with me? It seemed to me that you acted strange the last few days you were here."

Katie, blushing, was tongue-tied with shame. Bride insisted. "Tell me, child. I hate having something in between us, especially when I can't figure out what it is."

Well, it would be better to know for sure, to have it in the open. Taking a deep breath, Katie plunged. "I — I heard you and Bill talking late one night —"

Bride's eyes flashed. Katie felt so miserable that she'd have welcomed a burst of flaying Irish wrath, but after a moment, Bride relaxed and drew her close. "So that's it. Lord save us, you're jealous."

Katie drew back, shocked at the words, and then she thought, *Why, yes. Yes, I am.*

"Oh, Bride!" she said and began to cry.

Pressing Katie's head to her bosom, Bride smoothed her hair and said gently, "To be sure, it's no wonder. What woman wouldn't love Bill, at least just a little, him with that proud black head and way he has of smiling?" As Katie stiffened, Bride went on, "I can put your mind to rest on one score, Katie. Bill's my dear friend. He's looked out for me ever since I came to town, made sure I was respected — and he's respected me. Not that there wouldn't have been more if he'd been willing to marry. But he never asked for that — or anything. I guess I think more of him than of any man in the world, but we're friends and only friends."

"I — I'm so ashamed! You've been so good to me, Bride. Anyway, it's none of my business."

"Of course it is, if you care about the footloose rascal — and you could pick a lot worse, dear. But Bill loves his freedom. Did he tell you he turned down that big estate in England and being a real lord on account of he'd have had to go there to live?"

"He did?" Katie gasped.

"That prissy-prim English solic — solicit — anyhow, some kind of fancy lawyer who came back over here, he couldn't believe it, either. Sat out under the oak at Babcock's with Bill and argued better than an hour. Those that were listening say Bill was real patient till the lawyer fellow called him 'my good man.'" Bride's rich laughter pealed. "Guess that's when the lawyer found out Bill's got a lord's pride even if he won't have the title. The stage was just pullin' out for San Simon and I saw myself how Bill picked up that

273

fine-dressed gent along with his gear and tossed him aboard. The lawyer didn't try to get off, either. He screeched back that Bill was a heathen savage and Arizona was the right place for him."

She broke off as a dozen cowboys, all wearing voluminous yellow slickers, swarmed into Babcock's amid laughter and the jingle of spurs. "Why on earth are they wearing rain gear inside?" Katie wondered out loud.

"They're joshing Reverend Chenowth, dear. They'd just better not tease too hard. Chenowth's a tough old freighter, and they say that he's killed men and then preached their funerals. He's taking up land southwest of San Simon so it looks like we'll have our own parson in the neighborhood even if Brothers Daggett and Thomas decided to settle elsewhere. Ah, here you are, Melissa! Let's hurry and get a seat."

"What happened to the newspaper?" Katie asked, for the little shanty was gone.

Bride shook her head sadly. "Och, only three issues of it did we get! A burro tied out in front dragged down the whole shebang, and the poor editor, he was that disheartened that he left for Tombstone."

Jed with Ace in his arms was standing between Nacho and John Diamond outside the barber's. The gambler raised his hat to Katie and she smiled back, glad that they were friends. Knowing that Jed would be looked after, Katie didn't try to hustle him into the service. She stepped inside the shadowy room, still morning cool in spite of being occupied by all the town's women and a good sampling of the men. Disappointment flooded Katie as she saw that Bill Radnor wasn't in the crowd. Could he have forgotten that he'd promised to milk the cows that evening so she wouldn't have to leave the festivities early?

Gray-haired Sarah Metzger smiled and made room for the newcomers by nudging Myra Firbank to move toward the end of the front bench. Mrs. Metzger said she'd sold the butter and milk almost the instant they were on the counter. "The butter brought five dollars," said the kind-eyed woman.

"I sold mine for ten," boasted Myra Firbank. "Set it on the table, and Hi Phillips bought the whole pound for him and his friends to slather on their pancakes!"

"I was offered more," Mrs. Metzger returned mildly. "But I thought five dollars was fair. Especially since it was a gift."

"It wasn't exactly a gift," demurred Katie. "You both gave us so much that we're just grateful we can give something back."

"That's to be commended," nodded Sarah Metzger. "But from now on, I want to pay you for whatever you bring in."

"So do I," said Myra Firbank less convincingly.

"And so do I!" Bride echoed.

"I'm keeping track," Katie assured them. "When we're even — and gracious, if butter brings at least five dollars a pound, that won't take long — we'll be glad to sell you all we can."

The room hushed except for the rustle of the cowboys' slickers as a tall gray-haired man with piercing eyes stepped behind the sheet-draped bar. The fascinating lady framed above him was also covered, and so were the gaming tables and array of bottles.

"Brothers and sisters," Chenowth said in a voice that filled the room, though it was neither loud nor harsh, "it's gratifying to see that some of you have so much faith in the might of prayer that you're all decked out for a gully-washer. Now the Lord loves a cheerful giver so I reckon He loveth a cheerful asker, 'long as there's no mockin' intended." He paused. Under his gaze, the cowboys sat up straight and stopped grinning. "This is the day we celebrate our country's independence, and I won't hold you long. Maybe you've heard about the preacher who told a cattleman that the Lord would send rain when it was needed bad enough. The cattleman looked around at his bony cows and dried-up range and he said, 'Brother, if the Lord don't know we need rain right now, He's a dang poor cowman.' "

Chuckling with his audience, the ordinarily dressed minister went on. "The Lord's a good cowman and a good shepherd, too, even if some of us can't figger out why He bothered about those stinkin'-hoofed, snot-nosed, range-foulin' critters. So we're gathered, dear brethren and sisters, to ask Our Heavenly Father to bless us with bountiful, soaking rain — not a sluicin', floggin' deluge that'll carry off what little soil manages to stick to these rocks — not a rizzly, drizzly pitty-pattin' shower or a Methodist sprinkle — but rain steady as a mother's love, the kind that sinks down to every root, gets the creeks to runnin', and makes this old desert bloom like the rose of Sharon and the lily of the valley. Before we get to that, though, I want you to ask yourself if you're worthy to entreat favors of the Lord." His eyes fixed on young Billy Clanton. "Billy, last time we talked you was about of a notion to repent."

The freckled face reddened. "I'm sorry, preacher, but I reckon I'm too late."

"While you're breathing, son, it's never too late to ask God's forgiveness." The boy looked miserable. Chenowth frowned. "You don't doubt God will forgive you?"

"Preacher," blurted the youngest Clanton, "God may forgive me, but the grand jury won't!"

That brought such laughter that Chenowth stiffened and scanned Billy, who squirmed unhappily. Apparently convinced that the boy meant no disrespect, Chenowth quelled the merriment with a cold gray stare. "No earthly jury can do more than hang you, son. You'd better be makin' your peace with the Judge who can send you to the eternal lake of fire." Billy swallowed and glumly studied his boots. The minister sighed and lifted his arms to bring the congregation to their feet.

"Divine Father," he prayed, "Ruler of the universe Who holdeth the thunder and lightning in Your hands, we implore You to open the heavens and send us rain. Bless us and the beasts of the field and the birds of the air, the crops and trees and thirsty grass. However, Lord, Thou knowest best. We don't presume to dictate, only to advise, for Thine is the kingdom, the power, and the glory. Amen."

"Amen," the crowd echoed.

Most went up to thank the preacher and shake his hand, but one grizzled rancher whispered to his wife, "Sal, there's just no use prayin' for rain when the wind is in the west."

As Katie followed Bride out into the brilliant light, she looked up and down the street, studying each cluster of people, each knot of horsemen. She didn't see Bill Radnor, but Ed Larrimore came out of Shotwell's store and crossed the street, tipping his hat perfunctorily at some point in between Bride and Katie.

"Good to see you in town, Miss MacLeod. Shows the 'Paches haven't wiped you out yet. Too bad you can't race one of them Steel Dust mares today, but of course you can't when she'd have a colt trailin' behind."

Jed dashed up, grasping Katie's sleeve. "Katie! There's going to be a race down on the flat. There's a hundred-dollar prize! Can't I ride Honeybunch? You know she won every time Pa matched her. If I win, I'll give you all the money except for enough to buy some boots."

"I'm sorry, Jed, but you know perfectly well that Goldie would follow and either get hurt or kill herself trying to keep up." She smoothed his fair hair back from his flushed forehead. "Maybe next year you can race Shiloh."

"Next year!" Just as tears had earlier glinted in Melissa's eyes, so now they did in Jed's. Katie began to wish they hadn't come to the celebration. If it was going to be one struggle after another with her brother and sister, this outing, which should have been such a treat,

279

was going to be an ordeal. Jed's lips quivered. "You're mean, Katie! You — you care more about the horses than you do about M'liss and me!"

It was a good thing she was holding Rosie or Katie couldn't have kept from slapping him. Neither he nor Melissa had the slightest notion of how hard it was for her, to have to make the decisions, to be the one to say no.

"I'm not going to let you kill one of the colts," she snapped. "And if you can't behave yourself, Jedediah MacLeod, we'll start home right now."

Larrimore dropped a blunt-fingered hand on the boy's shoulder. "You a pretty good rider, lad?"

Jed squinted up in puzzlement for the sun was in his eyes. "I don't fall off much, sir."

The rancher glanced at Katie. She didn't see where this was going, but in justice to her brother, she had to nod her head. "He's been riding ever since he was three. One of our horses would put down his head and let Jed grab his ears and climb on his neck before the horse raised his head and let Jed slide down to his back. He can stick like a burr, Pa always said."

"I've got a two-year-old gelding I'd like to race," said Larrimore. "But my men are all too heavy. I'd pay you to ride him, win or lose, but if you win, you get half the prize." He slanted a challenging smile at Katie. "That is, if it's all right with your big sis."

The less they had to do with Larrimore, the better Katie would like it. She seethed at being put in such a spot, but she knew Jed was a good rider. Deciding that she didn't have the right to deny him the chance to win or earn enough money for his much-desired boots, she gave Larrimore a chill look but said, "I suppose you can race, Jed, but do be careful."

"Oh, I will, Katie!" He gave her an enthusiastic hug. "Where's your horse, sir?"

"Papa!" shrilled an indignant voice behind them. "You can't let that little boy ride Glencoe! Glencoe's mine!"

XI

Turning, Larrimore smiled indulgently at a girl of perhaps seven. Her blazing green eyes were the color of her much beruffled taffeta dress and her mass of curly red-gold hair was caught back by a matching ribbon while a straw bonnet, gay with red, white, and blue bows, dangled at her back. Involuntarily, and with a pang, Katie looked at Melissa's dress, so faded that the blue was almost white, and at Jed's patched shirt and bare feet.

Still, no matter how well Larrimore would provide for her family, there was no way Katie would dream of living at his house. She devoutly hoped that he'd abandoned any thought of ever trying to get custody of the younger children.

Hurrying from the Cosmopolitan Hotel like a mother hen after a single chick was a plump, dark woman who stopped a little way from the child and beamed fondly on her. She would be the one who sewed the elaborate dress, brushed out those coppery curls, but the girl didn't give her so much as a glance. "Sure, Glencoe's yours, sweetheart." Larrimore's voice, often so harsh, had no rough edge for his daughter. "But you must want to see him run and win."

"Why can't *I* ride him?"

"Because you're going to grow up to be a lady, and ladies don't race horses."

A pointed little chin jutted out. "Then I don't want to be a — a gol-durned lady!"

"Hallie!" The tolerance was gone. "If you're goin' to act up, I'll have Chapita keep you in the hotel till we're ready to go home."

"Papa!" For the third time that morning, Katie saw tears glisten in childish eyes. It made her feel a little better to know that even a real parent could have trouble with offspring, though you could tell with half an eye that Hallie was spoiled rotten as a carcass left out three days in the sun. Unlike Jed and Melissa, Hallie let the tears slide down her cheeks. "If — if my mama was still alive, she wouldn't let you be so horrid!"

"Your mama would have you behavin' yourself," he growled. "And if you can't, you lope back to the hotel."

Green eyes looked up through star-pointed lashes as Hallie caught her father's hand and hugged it to her cheek. "Don't be cross, Papa! I — I'd just die if I couldn't watch the race with you!" She looked Jed up and down. "What's your name, boy?"

"Jedediah Franklin MacLeod." At first, Jed had seemed dazed by the little girl's almost fairy elegance, but her imperious tone straightened his spine. He stared at her with a truculent glint in his eyes. "What's yours?"

She gasped. Probably she'd never been asked that question before. After a startled upward peek at her father, who wore a bemused grin, she smoothed her hair ribbon and scowled at Jed, who was the taller by three or four inches. "I'm Harriet Elizabeth Larrimore. I live at the Pitchfork. It's the biggest ranch in Cochise County, maybe in the whole world. Where do you live?"

"I live at Home Mountain, and we have Steel Dust horses and Guernsey cows."

"What's a Steel Dust horse?"

"You don't know?" Jaw nearly unhinged, Jed gaped at her. "Why, everybody's heard of Steel Dust!"

"I haven't."

When he decided this was true, Jed gave her a look of pitying scorn. "Why, he was just the best quarter horse ever foaled in Kentucky, Harriet Elizabeth Larrimore! Won every race he ever ran till he was matched against the Shiloh our bay yearlin's named after. Steel Dust reared up in the chute and got a bad splinter in his shoulder — couldn't run the race. Fact is, he went blind and never raced again, but he sired colts right up till he died down in South Texas about ten years ago when he was thirty-two."

"Texas!" sniffed Hallie. "No wonder I never heard of him."

So jolted that it took him a full minute to recover, Jed curled his lip. "Stupid old girls don't know much about that kind of thing, I reckon, but that stallion was so famous that folks lots of times call any quarter horse a Steel Dust." His eyes narrowed. "Why, you prob'ly never even heard of Sam Bass's Denton mare!"

"No, and if she was some dumb old Texas horse, I don't care!" Hallie appealed to her father. "Papa, are you really going to let this — this young little boy ride Glencoe?"

"I am if we get down to the course in time," said Larrimore. He called down the street to Beau Murphree, who was wearing a red shirt with a white and blue silk bandana. "Beau! Toss the lightest saddle we've got on Glencoe and bring him along. We've got us a rider!"

Jed's chest thrust out. He stalked down the hill as if he could already feel the aristocratic lift of high-heeled cowboy boots. Nacho followed, carrying Ace to protect him from hoofs, wheels, and feet.

"Let me take the baby." John Diamond had watched the whole encounter from in front of Shotwell's. Falling easily into step beside Katie, he hoisted Rosie against his shoulder and slanted Katie a wryly amused glance.

"Your kid brother may not wind up a gambler, Katie, but will you like it much better if he races and other folks lay their money on him?"

"I'm beginning to think I won't have much to say about what Jed does," said Katie with a bitter stare at Larrimore. "Any man who comes along can do more with him than I can."

"Seems like that ought to tell you something, Miss MacLeod," said the rancher. "The kid needs a daddy."

"He needs a mother, too," Katie retorted. "I'm certainly not much of one — though I could do a lot better if I didn't get so much — help!"

John Diamond made a coughing sound, hastily covering his mouth. Larrimore gave Katie a bland smile. "Glencoe ought to win easy as long as Bill Radnor don't race that gray horse of his, and I've not seen hide nor hair of Bill today. He may be celebratin' down in Mexico."

"He was celebrating in Evilsizer's a couple of hours ago," said Diamond. "Way his cards were running, he needs to win a horse race." The gambler shielded his eyes beyond the brim of his hat. "Reckon he thinks so, too. There he is, down by the starting post."

Katie saw him then, taller than anyone, crossed belts of his .44s slung negligently from a waist that looked more slender because of

286

the breadth of his shoulders. Laughing with his friends as he lounged beside his horse, he glanced around, saw Katie's party, and swept off his light gray hat.

The sun struck black fire from his hair as it might have from a crow's wing. Katie felt herself drowning in those smiling eyes that just now seemed more blue than gray. That smile, she knew, was equally for Bride, even for Melissa, but her lungs filled with a rush of bright, intoxicating air that tingled and sang through her. For the first time since Melissa's flare-up, she was glad they had come to town.

Billy Clanton caught up from behind her, riding abreast of Radnor. "How come you missed the preachin', Bill? You need rain over at your Roofless 'Dobe Animas ranch as much as we do here."

"Well, I should have been there, but I was tuckered out," grinned Bill. "Stayed up all night tryin' to find better cards than some very young clubs." He looked ruefully at Diamond. "You didn't have that trouble, Jack."

"Luck," shrugged the other.

"Figgerin' to make up your losses on the horse race, Radnor?" demanded Larrimore.

"Might just."

"Who's runnin'?"

"Hi Phillips thinks his bay might beat Shadow, Billy Clanton wants to see what his new claybank can do, and Wesley Reed from over on Cave Creek will ride his black gelding. You have a horse?"

"Yeah. Glencoe, a two-year-old dun. That cream color the Mexicans call *huevo de pato,* duck egg."

"He's my horse," proclaimed Hallie.

"I'm going to ride him," asserted Jed.

Bill looked from one to the other. "Well," he said, smiling at the girl, "it's a good thing you got a jockey, Hallie. You're fixed up plumb too pretty to ride yourself." To Katie, he said, "Bride's loaned me the rig I need to keep your cows happy, so don't you cut your time short in town, Katie."

Nodding, he rode ahead to make room for the flow of people on foot or horseback who streamed down the hill and followed the creek around to the comparatively level stretch of ground where worn earth showed other races had been run. This was a holiday at the mine, of course, and Katie greeted her friends from the boardinghouse, who were as usual engaged in an amicable exchange of insults. "Did 'ee hear about the shifter in Bisbee who could no wise get un Irishers to understand their job?" crowed Hal Trego. "Finally boiled it down to 'Keep that hole full!' to un and 'Empty that chute!' t'other."

Pat and Liam Shaughnessy snorted in unison. "Why, ye spindle-shanked Cornish runt!" jeered Pat, including Tim Penrose and Jerry Polfax in his withering glance. "Ye do be prayin' your Methodist prayers so long and loud before ye go in the mine that the good God must weary of ye!"

"We needs must pray," shot back Trego, "when we have to work with 'ee thick-skulled carousin' Irish!"

Bride turned at that. "Mind your tongue, Hal Trego, or you'll be hunting another place to board!"

"Twas of Irish men I spoke, Bride," the Cornishman said with a twinkle of green eyes. "Irish women, 'ee be very different. Beautiful, kind, and quick to forgive."

"Now listen to the man!" marveled Liam, Pat's brother. "Cornish or no, he's been at kissin' the Blarney Stone!" The miners eddied into the crowd forming on either side of the course. Most of the cowboys who'd built the MacLeod house and outbuildings came up to ask Katie how the family was getting along, and from the way they lingered, Katie had to realize, with a gratifying thrill of feminine triumph, that dark, husky Joe Hill, ferociously black-moustached Charlie Snow, flaming-haired Slim Jones, and the others were more interested in her than in how the garden was doing.

Jed slipped a piece of rope into Katie's hand, and she looked down to see that Ace was attached to the other end. "Watch him for me, will you, Katie?" Jed asked. "I'd better get acquainted with Glencoe." He went over to caress the pale yellow gelding and talk to him softly while Beau held the reins.

Hallie marched up to them and defiantly patted the horse, too. In a carrying voice, she said, "I just hope, Jedediah MacLeod, that you can ride Glencoe as well as I can! And mind you don't saw on his mouth or use your spurs or —" Was that a deliberate slip? Looking down at his bare feet, the rancher's daughter exclaimed in mock sympathy, "Oh, you can't use spurs. You don't have any boots."

Apparently feeling she had the best of the encounter, the girl let Chapita chide her back to her father, as sapling-thin, smooth-cheeked Hi Phillips reined in his bay. "Sure good to see you, Miss Katie," he said. "You're lookin' pretty as a heart flush."

Overcome at his boldness, he crimsoned and rode on toward the starting post, where Billy Clanton was checking the cinch on his rangy claybank. A dark-haired young man soothed a nervous black gelding. Off to her right, Katie heard a weathered, graying man reply impatiently to his wife's murmur, "Sufferin' catfish, Isabelle! Wesley's not goin' to get hurt runnin' a race after journeyin' from California to the Gila in the thick of the Indian troubles, and then down to Cave Creek! Lot more likely to get hurt handlin' a whipsaw or broad axe. He's earned a little fun."

So that was Stephen Reed, settled in the first deep canyon of the eastern Chiricahuas. Near him were two brown-haired middle-aged men who spoke with marked accents. One had clearly been drinking and the other was admonishing him in what Katie thought was German.

"The Duffner brothers, Otto and Max," said Bride in Katie's ear. "They built a 'dobe house over on Silver Creek with portholes for shooting through if they're raided. They're the Reed's closest neighbors. Came out here to get Otto over his drinking, but they haven't had much luck. As well as prospecting, they haul freight. According to Nick Babcock, every barrel Otto's delivered has a tight seal but is a quart or two low. Nick finally went over a barrel real good and learned how Otto stayed in free booze. He'd drive one of the barrel hoops up an inch or so, hammer a spike through the wood, drain out a bottle full, and then stopper the hole with a wooden peg before he hammered the hoop back in place." Bride laughed. "Nick thought if Otto wanted a drink that bad, he was welcome to it. Just adds a little onto Otto's tab when he slips Max's tether and visits the saloon."

Bride also pointed out Brannick Riggs and his family. "Brannick's from Alabama — fought for the South. They settled in the Sulphur Springs Valley about ten miles south of Fort Bowie a few years ago. Sell dairy products and vegetables to the fort. Beef, too, since William, one of the boys, went to work for Colonel Hooker — he's got a big ranch north of Willcox. William learned the cattle business and the Riggs got the start of their beef herd from the colonel, though they could've bought rustled Mexican stock a sight cheaper from their neighbors, the MacLowerys. Apaches never bother the Riggs. Brannick's given them food when they were hungry and they remember that. Stephen Reed's part Cherokee; that may be why Indians haven't raided him. That tall white-whiskered man behind Isabella Reed is Phil Morse, who has the sawmill on the west side of the Chiricahuas. Good gracious! What's Johnny Ringo doing with that red paint?"

"Daubing it on a cord strung above the finish line," said John Diamond, flipping open his silver watch case to entertain Rosie. "He's a judge. Reckon he aims to be sure there's a red mark on the winner's chest so there can't be any arguments."

Barney Sykes, Nick Babcock, and withered, frizzy-haired Jake Trimble were the other judges. Ringo and Trimble stood on either side of the finish line. At the other end of the quarter-mile track, Sykes and Babcock were lining the horses up with the starting post when Bill Radnor swung down from Shadow.

Lifting a front hoof, he examined it and shook his head as he straightened, throwing up his hands to the other racers. "Loose shoe." His voice carried to at least some of the onlookers. "I'm out, boys."

"We've got the race good as won!" said Larrimore. "Radnor's gray was the only one had me worried."

Ike Clanton yelled, "What's the jockey weight for this race, anyhow? That Mac-Leod kid can't weigh seventy pounds drippin' wet!"

The judges exchanged startled glances. "Guess nobody thought about that," Babcock admitted sheepishly. He turned to the riders. "If you want Larrimore should get another jockey —"

"Shucks," said Billy Clanton, reckless blue eyes laughing, "if the kid can win, let him!"

Hi Phillips said, "Suits me."

Thin, dark young Wesley Reed hesitated. "All right," he said finally.

"How about you folks who've laid bets?" asked Babcock. When no one spoke, he grinned. "Looks like you're all standin' pat. Let's run this race!" Striding to the other side of the starting post, he drew his six-shooter while Barney Sykes made sure the horses were in line.

"When I fire, go!" called Babcock.

He fired into the air. Ace yipped and pressed against Katie's legs. As if propelled by the blast, the horses burst forward. Men tossed their hats in the air. Women waved theirs. Whoops of encouragement shrilled into a roar. Rosie began to cry. Diamond backed out of the throng with her and watched from a little distance. He must have been a good father, Katie thought with the part of her mind that wasn't fixed on the race. How awful that he'd probably never see his son again!

Billy Clanton's claybank and Hi Phillips's bay plunged into the lead, flying blurs of yellow and dark red. Jed crouched so low to Glencoe's neck that the amber mane whipped back to cover his bright hair. The dun's stride lengthened. Seeming to soar rather than run, he flashed past Wesley Reed's black gelding, for a split second drew level with Katie and her companions, and surged ahead, gaining on the leaders.

The crowd doubled its frenzy. "Look at his

294

belly smoke the ground!" yelled Larrimore above the tumult of cheering and cursing. In the excitement men had forgotten not to swear in front of ladies — and for that matter, some ladies other than prostitutes were using words one wouldn't have expected them to know.

"Come on, Jed!" Bride shouted. "Leave those *spalpeens* eatin' your dust, darlin'!"

The thunder of hoofs drowned by boisterous clamor, Glencoe streaked by Hi's bay, gained on the claybank. For heartbeats, the two were neck and neck. Then Glencoe rocketed ahead, a smudge of pale yellow, snapped the cord at the finish line, and finished three lengths ahead of Billy Clanton.

No argument about who won this race! It was clear that even without the advantage of Jed's weight, Glencoe would have won. Even the losers cheered themselves hoarse. The riders let their mounts slow before they looped them back to the starting pole.

"The winner is Glencoe, owned by Ed Larrimore, ridden by Jed MacLeod," announced Nick Babcock. "But all you boys ran a good race." He handed Jed a leather pouch that clinked and obviously weighed the boy's arm down.

The other riders congratulated Jed. Then he was surrounded by everyone that had bet on Glencoe and some that hadn't. Cheeks flushed, eyes brilliant, Jed cried, "It was Glencoe! All I did was hang on!"

"That's right," Katie heard Hallie mutter. "I could've done that!" But the little girl looked at Jed with grudging admiration and, with a queenly air, said to him, "You rode pretty well — for a Texan."

Jed shot her a withering glance and then loftily ignored her. Slipping down, he caressed the sweating neck and praised the dun till Beau took the reins. "Here's the prize, Mr. Larrimore." Jed proffered the heavy bag.

The rancher took it, carelessly shook about half the big silver pesos and dollars into his hat and gave it to Hallie. "That's yours, sweetheart, you're the owner." He handed the pouch back to Jed. "Here's your share, son. Thanks for winnin'."

"I'd have done it for nothing," Jed laughed.

Hallie held the money-laden hat to him. "Take this, too. Get you some boots."

Jed crimsoned. "You better get you some manners — though I reckon they can't be bought. I can pay for my own boots." Scooping up Ace, who licked at him in joyous relief, Jed ran to John Diamond. "Uncle Jack! Let's go buy those boots you wanted to get me but I knew Katie wouldn't let me keep!" Over his shoulder, he called, "You can have the rest of the money, Katie! Slitherin' snakes, we're rich! Come on, Nacho!"

"Nacho or I'll keep the baby till she starts to cry — or needs a woman," Diamond grinned. He and the old Yaqui walked off with Jed between them and Rosie's small bonnet bobbing over the gambler's shoulder.

Katie noticed that Hallie stared after Jed, surprise and a sort of wistfulness on her face. Probably, in offering the rest of the prize money, she'd intended to make peace, not insult Jed further, but it wouldn't hurt her to learn to consider other people's feelings.

"Heavens to Betsy!" exclaimed Bride. "I've got to get back and see about that turkey I have roasting! I forgot to stoke the fire before I left."

"I'll run ahead and do that," Melissa offered. Gathering up her skirts, she did indeed run.

"I have to see someone," said Katie to Ed Larrimore. She paused, forcing the words that she knew came out sounding ungracious. "Thanks for being so generous with my brother."

"He earned it. Natural-born rider." Larrimore regarded her with a tight little smile edging his mouth. "When he's a couple years older, he can sure hire on with me." Hallie caught in her breath at that and her eyes glowed.

"I'll need him at Home Mountain," Katie said.

"We'll see."

Their eyes locked. She felt his will push at her like a physical force. She was glad when he moved off, trying to match his stride to his daughter's. Even so, she had to trot to keep up, and even more did the hapless Chapita.

Blast the man! thought Katie. Between him and Diamond, she was going to have a hard time keeping Jed at home. It wasn't just that she needed his help — and there was so much that a strong boy of fourteen or fifteen could do that she couldn't — but she didn't want Jed thrown too soon into the company of rough men, growing up on the outside while still a child within. Billy Clanton seemed like that to her, as did Hi Phillips and Slim Jones.

Even, amazingly, even a bit, Bill Radnor. That might be why he had such a thirst for danger and fun. He'd become a man so early that the boy had never grown up. He was standing now with the Clantons and the judges. "What'll you take for that claybank, Billy?" Nick Babcock asked as Katie approached. "I need a saddle horse. Even if he didn't win, he's fast enough for me."

"Thirty bucks and he's yours." Billy tipped his hat to Katie, brashly admiring. "Howdy,

298

Miss MacLeod. Nice race your kid brother ran."

"It was big of you not to fuss about his weight."

Billy shrugged. "Wouldn't have made much difference, man or boy. When that dun hit his stride, the wind couldn't catch him." He raised an eyebrow at the balding saloon owner who'd been examining the horse. "Look at his teeth if you want. I'd guess him about four years."

Babcock opened the horse's mouth and scanned strong, yellow teeth, then gave a nod of approval. "I'll take him. Write me out a bill of sale." He produced a crumpled envelope and a pencil. As Billy scribbled laboriously against his saddle, Babcock gave a delicate cough. "Uh — Billy, you're sure that bill of sale's good?"

Handing it to the buyer, Billy chuckled. "That bill of sale's just fine around here or traveling' west. Might not be quite so good, though, was you to ride east of Lordsburg."

Babcock handed back the paper. "No hard feelin's, Billy, but I want to ride wherever I have a mind to."

"Fine by me," shrugged the yellow-haired young man. "There's plenty will want him if you don't."

He swung into the saddle and rode off with

his brothers and Hi. The judges strolled off, discussing the race. Bill Radnor lifted an eyebrow at Katie. "Who rubbed your fur the wrong way, Katie? You look all huffed up about somethin'."

"I want to see that loose shoe."

"Now, Katie —"

"Easy, Shadow," she said to the horse, stroking his neck before she picked up his right forefoot and tested the shoe. It didn't have the slightest hint of being loose. Releasing the hoof, she said flatly, "You cheated, Bill Radnor. You dropped out because you thought you'd win. You the same as handed Jed fifty dollars."

"I could afford to," said Bill sunnily. "I won four hundred dollars by betting on Glencoe."

Katie groaned. He went on earnestly, though his mouth quirked at the edges. "That worked out lots better on account of I couldn't get any bets against Shadow."

Speechless, she could only shake her head. "Come on, Katie," he said commiseratingly but with irrepressibly dancing eyes. "If we don't hurry, we won't get there in time to hear the preacher read the Declaration of Independence."

"He might better pray for the lot of you!" Katie sputtered, but as Bill walked beside her, leading Shadow, the pure bliss of being with him washed away her anger. She couldn't believe that anyone, anywhere, was happier than she was this Fourth of July.

While flags all along the camp's one street furled and unfurled in the sunlit breeze, the Reverend Gus Chenowth read the Declaration of Independence in a sonorous voice. Tears glistened on the cheeks of many of the foreign-born miners and Katie's own eyes misted. As much as reality, this country was a dream, a promise, what it was to become still taking shape, still as malleable and infinitely varied as its people. It would probably be years before whites and Apaches could live as neighbors; she could see that people born citizens of Mexico would still feel that's what they were in spite of the United States having acquired the lands they'd always lived on. It would be a long time before lynchings of black men in the South stopped. But at least there was no more slavery. At least there was hope. Didn't the long litany of long-forgotten and now unimaginable British oppressions in the colonies bear witness to that?

Throughout the reading of the lengthy document, the throng stood patiently. *"And for the support of this Declaration, with a firm reliance on the protection of divine Providence, we mutually pledge to each other our Lives, our*

Fortunes, and our sacred Honour." When Chenowth intoned the name of the last signer, hats sailed into the air amid wild cheering.

"Begorra, man!" Katie heard Liam Shaughnessy say to Tam O'Neal as he gave him a rib-crushing hug. "It be one of the grandest things about this country, that here we can celebrate whippin' the bloody English!"

The minister raised his arms for silence as a man stepped up beside him. "Well, the devil's a preacher if that's not Breck!" Bill shouted a greeting and the stocky, blue-eyed deputy waved back.

"Boys!" Chenowth's booming voice checked the merriment of those who hadn't seen his gestures. "It's fittin' that whilst we're all gratefully minded of our luck and privileges in being citizens of this republic, we should have the opportunity to do our duty. The deputy's here to tell you about it."

Breakenridge stepped forward. "It's good to be among so many tax-payin' citizens," he said, grinning, and paused till the whistling and clapping died down. "We need some folks for jury duty, and I reckoned some of you fellows wouldn't mind visitin' Tombstone for a spell. If you're game, let me know." He added with a flash of strong teeth, "I'm hopin' for volunteers, but if I don't get 'em, I'll sure summons you."

"Might be kind of fun to get on the other side of the jury box," mused Slim Jones, he of the red hair and biscuit-baking prowess.

"They say there's an almighty pretty new singer at the Birdcage Theater," said Hi. Both of them put up their hands, Barney Sykes volunteered, and so did Joe Hill, the husky, dark-haired rancher from close to San Simon.

"Thanks, boys," nodded the deputy. "I'll let you know when court's going into session." He led the clapping for the sacrificial lambs on the altar of trial by jury. As the applause subsided, Hal Trego jumped on the porch.

"Since this be 'un minin' camp," he bellowed, "right after we eat, there'll be 'un single-jack drillin' contest at the big boulder just up the road toward the smelter. The prize be five hundred dollars, given by 'ee honorable owner of 'ee Texas Mine, Mr. Wessel."

The crowd cheered lustily and, drawn by tantalizing odors, advanced on the plank tables set up under the big live oak trees shading the street near Babcock's saloon. In addition to a few wild turkeys Bride and other women had roasted, there were dishpans full of a whole beef roasted slowly in a pit, the gift, someone said, of Bill Radnor. Several huge cast-iron kettles of spicy beans simmered on grates and Katie's kettle of buttery rich yucca soup rested half on a grate, half on some bricks. A couple of giant chuckwagon coffee-pots set on glowing coals while men with gloves stood ready to pour. There was a barrel of lemonade for those who wanted something cool. The table was heaped with biscuits, cornbread, pies, cinnamon rolls, cookies, and cakes. Mrs. Reed and Mrs. Riggs set out a big variety of preserves, pickles, and relishes. There was even wild honey oozing from the delicate waxy comb. Bride, the saloons, and the restaurants had loaned the stacks of tin and enamel plates, cups, and eating utensils.

As soon as Reverend Chenowth asked a blessing, lines formed with a scattering of small children and their mothers urged to go first. Katie sought out John Diamond and relieved him of Rosie, who needed both changing and milk though she still hadn't whimpered, so enthralled was she with the sights and sounds. Ace at his heels, Jed raced up.

"Look, Katie!" He tugged up his patched pants leg to exhibit handstitched black boots. "They're just like Uncle Jack's! Aren't they dandy? Wait'll I show that ole Hallie!"

"Beautiful," said Katie, slanting Diamond a look that told him she was sure he'd commissioned the boots and had planned sooner or later to give them to Jed. "They won't be too good for farmwork, though, with those high heels."

"I can go barefoot at home," said her brother, "but when I'm riding, these heels will sure hold the stirrups!" It was clear that milking cows and plowing didn't play a big part in his dreams of the future — but what ten-year-old boy would get enthusiastic about that?

He hastened off, doubtless to strut in front of Hallie Larrimore. Katie couldn't repress a grin. In spite of their thorny beginnings, the two youngsters were obviously intrigued with each other.

Bearing Rosie to the boardinghouse, Katie changed her. The baby fell asleep before she emptied her bottle. Tired out, and no wonder. Katie put her in her box tucked into a corner surrounded by padded chairs turned on their sides so there'd be no way Rosie could pull out of her bed. Most likely, though, she'd sleep for hours. Babies took a lot of care, but were so sweet and warm and trusting to hold that they were more than worth it. Tenderly giving a pat to her small sister's elevated rear, Katie hurried out to take her place in line with those already coming back for seconds.

Pat Shaughnessy won the single-jacking contest, kneeling on the dressed top of the granite boulder, swinging the four-pound hammer at more than a blow per second, flicking away a dulled drilling steel every minute and inserting a longer one that would make another two or three inches while Barney Sykes sluiced away cuttings with water poured from a can. The hammer had a wrist thong that let the driller's fingers relax on the backstroke till the end of the swing when they gripped the handle again for the powerful downstroke.

"The divil can hammer with either hand," grumbled Tam O'Neal, who'd had the bad luck to break off a steel in the hole. Pat, gasping and pouring sweat, threw an arm around Tam's shoulder.

"Niver mind, lad!" he grinned. "Ye'll all drink at my expense till the money's gone!"

A baseball game between miners and cowboys ended in a tie. As shadows lengthened and the breeze blew a trifle cooler, Bill Radnor carried the harp out of the saloon for Katie and placed it on a crate near her chair. There must have been four hundred people sitting on porches of the businesses across the street, on stumps and wagons, and those who couldn't sit, stood.

With spirits running high, Katie feared that her music wouldn't hold the crowd, but by the time she had played the last note of "Comin' Through the Rye," even Billy Clanton seemed spellbound. Filled with that exhilarating power of gripping an audience, honoring requests when she could, she played till her fingers were sore. While she rested, Hal Trego got his fiddle and Bill Radnor produced his French harp.

The street quickly filled with dancers. Billy Clanton swung Melissa; even younger girls were partnered. Most of the men had to make do with miners or cowboys who wore bandanas tied around their sleeves.

Ed Larrimore was advancing on Katie. Springing up, she caught Bill's arm. "Please — will you dance with me?"

"You bet I will!" Pocketing the French harp, he took her hand and whisked her off beneath the rancher's nose. "Oh, so that's the reason your feet started to itch all of a sudden," Bill chuckled. "And I thought it was my charmin' disposition." He squinted at the lowering sun. "One sashay around the street and I'll make tracks to milk your cows."

"In Bride's dress and bonnet," she reminded him, dimpling. "I'll play a few more songs, if people want them, and then we'll start home in the wagon." Bill could reach Home Mountain in less than half the time it would take them in the wagon. If he hadn't taken on the chore, the MacLeods would have needed to leave well over an hour ago in punishing heat. "Thank you, Bill, for giving us such a wonderful holiday."

"My pleasure." How could his look reach down to fondle and warm her heart when she knew anyone he wasn't mad at, man, woman, child, or dog, would get the same flashing, free-hearted smile? But she was in his arms, she let him spin and whirl her wherever he would, and she was sure that if she lived to be a hundred, she'd have few memories more gladsome than dancing with Bill Radnor on this first day she knew that she loved him.

XII

Katie's shoulders ached from scrubbing things on the washboard and wringing them out, but the washing, thank goodness, was done for another week. Sheets flapped from the line stretched between the big oak and a lesser one, and garments and smaller things dried on nearby bushes. As soon as the two tubs of rinse water were carried to the garden, she, Melissa, and Jed could go inside, have a meal of cold cornbread and buttermilk, and stay in the house till the heat began to wane.

July was hot in Texas but lacked this parching thirstiness, air sucking moisture from mouth, eyes, and nostrils, searing the lungs during the merciless hours from late morning till around three or four when clouds bulked gray and purple or towered in luminous thunderheads that still had not brought rain.

Mercifully, this high desert cooled when the sun set — sleeping was comfortable, and early mornings deliciously brisk. Moreover, the house was much cooler than those of milled lumber, and Katie daily blessed Bill for getting his friends to build with logs. When enough buckets had been carried from the last tub to make it light enough to lift, Katie and

309

Melissa emptied it, among the rows of growing corn and set it at the edge of the porch, where it would catch the runoff should it rain.

As she straightened, Katie caught a distant glint, shielded her eyes, and made out a group of horsemen coming from the east about even now with Blue Mountain. Even though it was unlikely that Nana's raiding would bring him here, an icy chill shot down Katie's spine. Heart pounding, she gripped Melissa's arm. "We'd better get Rosie and the guns and hide in the cellar!" Nacho had taken a load of wood to town and wouldn't be back till night.

"They're not Apaches," Jed scoffed. "That one in the lead's dressed in blue like a soldier. Maybe they're from Fort Bowie." Reassured but wary, Katie loaded the shotgun while Jed levered a cartridge into the chamber of the Winchester.

"You two —" Katie broke off and laughed. "Pardners, I mean! Take Rosie to the bed-room, Melissa, and if there's trouble, hide with her under the bed. Jed, why don't you get up in the loft with the rifle? I'll keep the shotgun by the door. Probably all they want is a drink and something to eat, but we'll be careful till we're sure they're all right."

"Bet I can shoot two or three of them before they even know where I am." Jed's bravado was marred by the way his voice cracked.

"Just keep away from 'em, Katie, so I won't have to worry about hitting you."

She gave him a swift hug. "Don't shoot unless they get really mean." He went up the ladder, the rifle almost as tall as he was, then rushed back for Ace, who was beginning to growl deep in his throat.

"Hush up, boy," Jed told him, scrambling up the ladder. "You've got to learn to be quiet when we're hiding."

Smoothing her hair, buttoning the top of her dress, and rolling down her sleeves, Katie groaned at the prospect of building a fire to heat the beans. At least they were cooked and only needed warming. Cold cornbread and buttermilk with leftover stewed apples would scarcely do for company, and she'd need to grind and brew some of their treasured coffee. Provided the travelers were peaceable, however, she certainly wasn't going to complain.

Now she could hear the clop of hoofs, the creak of leather, and the chinking of metal. She opened the door and waited, right hand poised to seize the shotgun even after lemon yellow stripes on sky blue trousers confirmed that one of the men in the lead was a cavalryman. Her father had fought the Yankees, and though the MacLeods hadn't suffered directly from nine years of Reconstruction, she still couldn't feel that men in blue uniforms were friends.

He wore a white helmet and was close enough for her to make out the single bars on vertical yellow cloth shoulder patches. His black boots reached to the knee, higher in front than in back. He was clean-shaven, but though she was sure she'd never seen him before, something about his bearing and the harsh angles of his face were familiar. His eyes — she caught in her breath and stared.

The eyes scanning her from beneath straight black brows were John Diamond's — a hint grayer but dark-lashed and deep-set. He rode a chestnut gelding, but the older man beside him was mounted on a sturdy mule. A big nose split his weathered face in half, and gray was winning over light brown in a wild and frizzly beard. He wore a rumpled old duck suit and white canvas helmet. On his right, mounted on a splendid bay, was a middle-aged man with shrewd blue eyes and a neatly trimmed, rather sparse beard and moustache.

Behind this front rank rode a tall, deep-chested young man with sandy hair and a smile that widened when he saw Katie. Beside him, in a deep blue uniform coat with big chevrons on the sleeves, jogged the most villainous-looking person Katie had ever seen. Small and wiry, his flowing, waving black hair had a coppery sheen where the sun struck it. His right eye, a piercing black, fixed on Katie as

312

if peering down the sights of a rifle, but it was the other one that disconcerted her. Grayish-white, it stared to the left as if watching for something no one else could see. A large blond man with a florid moustache brought up the rear along with a broad-shouldered Mexican.

Reining in by the porch, the man on the mule doffed his helmet and gave Katie a slow smile that softened his blue-gray eyes and lines graved deep from cheekbones to jaw. "Good day to you, miss. If you could give us something to eat and let us rest our horses, we'd be glad to pay you."

Katie stiffened. "You're welcome to what we have, sir, but I would never charge *anyone* for food."

"Including the army?" he chuckled, dismounting. "Maybe I can persuade your parents to a different view."

"Our parents are dead, sir." At his startled look, she added, "They didn't die here, but back in Texas."

"You're with an older brother?"

"My brother's younger, sir, and so are my sisters."

"Good heavens! Children living out here alone?" Frowning, his gaze swept from the garden wall to the solid outbuildings and corral. "Children never cut those logs and hefted them into place."

"Our friends did."

"Friends from Galeyville?" asked the trim-bearded older man on the fine bay. The good-humored wrinkles at the corners of his mouth and eyes tightened to grim ones. "If those cattle thieves are corrupting a bunch of orphans, they're even worse than I figured."

"They haven't corrupted us!" Katie's voice was husky with indignation. "Everyone in town, miners, business people, and — and cowboys, helped us get started. If you're going to say bad things about my friends, I don't want to feed you!"

"Please, Henry!" said the man in the rumpled duck suit. "Miss, with your permission, we'll water our horses and my mule and hobble them in the shade. I'm General George Crook, back in Arizona after some years up north. This gentleman is Colonel Hooker. I imagine you've heard of his Sierra Bonita Ranch north of Willcox."

Katie had also heard of Crook, the tough but fair commander who'd had remarkable success at, in his own words, reconciling Apaches to "raising corn instead of scalps" before he was sent to fight Cheyenne and Sioux the year before yellow-haired Custer's defeat at the Little Bighorn. With the northern tribes settled on reservations, it had evidently been decided that Crook was needed in Arizona. Called "Gray Fox" by Apaches, he was renowned for enlisting Indians as scouts. Their tracking skills and knowledge of the terrain had greatly aided him in both Arizona and the Department of the Platte.

Awed at meeting a legend, even if he *was* a Yankee, Katie realized that she was rudely staring and turned her gaze to the men who had dismounted and stood holding their headgear and reins. Nodding toward the one with Diamond's eyes, Crook said, "If you will give me the favor of your name, miss, I'll present Lieutenant James Corrigan."

Corrigan? But Diamond was probably a made-up name like so many of those heard in Galeyville. Trying not to gape at Corrigan, who looked to be in his late twenties, Katie said, "I'm Katie MacLeod. This is Home Mountain Ranch." She raised her voice. "Jed, come on down! M'liss! It's all right!"

Crook's mouth twitched. "I'm glad you've decided we don't eat children, Miss MacLeod. With Nana loose over in New Mexico, I'm stationing detachments along routes he or other raiders may use should he veer into Arizona. It's my hope that you and other civilians will sleep sounder in knowing there are at least a few soldiers closer than Fort Bowie."

Corrigan inclined his head. His hair, thick and black, grew back from his temples exactly as Diamond's did. Katie smothered a question about Corrigan's father. She'd tell Diamond about the amazing resemblance and leave it to him whether to try to meet this rather stern and formidable young man.

"Tom Horn," said the general. Like Crook, the smiling young man was over six feet tall. His unlined face and rosy cheeks made him seem little more than a boy, and as Katie said, "Pleased to meet you," he blushed and fumbled the broad rim of his hat.

"Al Sieber's my chief of scouts." Crook looked with affection at the big fair-haired man with the luxuriant moustache who stood as if favoring his left leg. "He half-raised young Tom with a little help from Mickey Free, here, who can track a shadow in the rain."

Free was the slight man with the strange cocked eye. Katie chilled to see that the scabbarded knife at his belt had a blade twelve inches long. She couldn't guess whether he was Indian, Mexican, or both. "Merijildo Grijalva is another of my best scouts." Crook glanced at the dark man, who had smiling black eyes and white, even teeth. "He was carried off captive by the Chiricahuas and raised as one. Mickey was captured as a boy and brought up by Pinal Apaches. Tom lived with Chief Pedro up on the reservation, so

316

they all know Apache ways." Corrigan's mouth thinned disapprovingly. Crook gave him an amused look. "Most of my superiors and many of my juniors consider it folly to rely on Indian scouts, but only through them and men like these can marauding bands be pursued and made to know their raiding days are over."

"I'll take Apaches over white cow thieves anytime," grunted Hooker. "When I came into the country nine years ago, I rode into Cochise's camp. Told him when his people were hungry, they were welcome to kill one of my steers. They would have anyway, but my making the gift turned them friendly. I've never been raided or bothered. It's that bunch at Galeyville that needs to be cleaned out." Seeing Katie's face, he shrugged heavy shoulders. "I'll say no more about them, Miss MacLeod, except this. You might tell Bill Radnor that since the sheriff won't do anything about him, I'm offering a reward for proof that he's dead."

Fear squeezed Katie's heart. This man was powerful and meant what he said. "Then you can't come under my roof," she answered. "It wouldn't be there except for Mr. Radnor. I'll bring your food out under the oak."

Instead of riling, the rancher was studying the cows, who were resting in the shade not

317

far from the corral. "Look like some nice Guernseys there. I've been bringing in Durhams and Herefords to improve my stock. Herefords do better than Durhams and cross well with range cattle, but I also keep dairy cows. When that bull calf's weaned, I'd like to buy him. No disrespect, young lady, but you've got no menfolk I can ask."

Katie's cheeks had warmed at the word "bull," but at least Tom Horn had taken the general's mule to water and Merijildo had taken Hooker's bay, so only the two older men were in earshot. "You're right, Colonel Hooker, I do have to talk about things a lady's not supposed to mention. Maybe I could swap Prince Coal to you if you'd send one of your best bulls down to range with my cows a while early next summer."

Hooker stroked his neat beard. "Trouble with that, speaking frankly, Miss, is that a cow brute will mount those heifer calves before they're big and strong enough to be mommas. But I guess there's no way you can keep range bulls from gettin' at 'em, either. When there's any choice about it, you want a heifer's first calf sired by a bull that's smaller than she is so she won't have trouble calvin'. I've got a dandy small Jersey. One of the boys can bring him over next June. I'll pay you some boot for your Prince Coal, though, if

318

he grows into what he looks like he will."

"There's one thing you have to promise." Katie's face burned now in earnest because she knew how peculiar her request would sound. "If you decide not to keep Prince Coal for breeding, I want to buy him back. I have to be sure that you won't sell him for beef."

Hooker's jaw dropped. "When I buy a critter, I reckon it's up to me what I do with it."

"Then you can't have him."

Keen gray eyes searched her face. His expression gentled though his brow was still furrowed in puzzlement. "You aim to make this kind of deal for any stock you sell?"

"Yes."

He gave a long, slow whistle. "Well, it'll be mighty interesting to see what happens. Anyone who makes pets out of their livestock is headin' for grief, if not ruin and disaster. What'll you do with a cow when she's too old to calve?"

"She can just graze and enjoy life."

"Holy cow!" he breathed and shook his head, then broke into surprised laughter that shook his ample chest and belly. "You named this place wrong, Miss MacLeod! You'd ought to call it the Holy Cow Ranch. Everybody will, when this news gets around."

"If you'll excuse me," said Katie with all

the dignity she could summon, "I'd better build a fire to heat the beans and mix up some cornbread. Would you like some cold butter-milk?"

"I can't think of anything in the Territory I'd like better," said the general.

Hooker chortled. "That's because you're not a drinking man, George. But for sure there's nothing better on a hot day. Seems crazy to me that most ranchers don't have a drop of real milk on their tables."

Crook grinned. "You know what they say about Arizona — that it's got more cows and less milk, more rivers and less water, and you can see farther and see less, than anywhere in the world."

"That's not so!" Katie swept her arm from Blue Mountain toward the canyon and across the plain to far-off blue mountains. "This is beautiful! And — and it's home."

"It is," said Hooker soberly, though there was a twinkle in his eyes. "That's the main thing." He frowned suddenly. "Probably you haven't heard about the president."

"The president?" echoed Katie, turning back.

"President Garfield was shot July second in a Washington, D.C., railway station. He's still alive but not expected to recover."

Shrinking, for even though she had no love

for Yankees, it was a terrible thing that a president be shot, a terrible repeating of the murder of Abraham Lincoln. Katie whispered, "How — who —?"

"A man named Charles Guiteau. Apparently he blamed the president because he hadn't received some office he'd been seeking." Hooker shook his head. "It will be a national disgrace if our presidents must serve with the knowledge that they're likely to be assassinated."

"Guiteau should've been killed in the same minute he fired at the president," growled Al Sieber. "No use wastin' taxpayers' money on a trial for a skunk like that."

"Summary execution would do little for our national honor, either, Al," said the general. "All we can do is pray for the president and his family and carry out our duties."

Katie hurried to the house before shocked tears spilled over. She knew nothing about James A. Garfield except that he was a Republican and only inaugurated that spring. Still, he was the president, and a human being, and that such a thing could happen made the earth seem to shift beneath her feet.

Doubtless any man there would have instantly given his life for the president, but their appetites were not affected by his plight. They drank all the buttermilk, slathered hot cornbread with the butter Katie had planned to apply to what she considered her debts, consumed the beans that would have fed the family for three meals, and devoured stewed apples made delicious with thick golden cream.

"As rich as my Jerseys' cream," praised Hooker. "The drawback is they don't give much of it. An old farmer who bragged on his Jerseys said he could put a silver dollar in the bottom of a bucket of Holstein milk and it'd be so watery a person could see the coin. The Holstein milker snorted and said the milk from a Jersey wouldn't even cover the dollar."

Jed, unimpressed by a general who'd wear a plain old suit and ride a mule, had found a new hero in Corrigan. He admired the light cavalry saber, what the officer explained was a .45-70 Springfield carbine with the barrel protruding from the open end of its leather boot, and the Colt .45 caliber single-action revolver. Jed laughed delightedly when the lieutenant placed the white cork helmet on his head and it slipped down over his ears.

"We were just issued these miserable things," said Corrigan. "They're cooler, but they shine almost bad as a mirror. At least we keep the chin strap looped up most of the time and don't have to wear the fancy spike on top except with dress uniform."

"If the helmet accidentally tumbled into some mud and it was several hours before you found it," said Crook offhandedly, "it might wash off to a nice, safe tan." The general settled more comfortably on his log and raised a bushy eyebrow at Hooker. "Would you, Colonel, set my mind at rest? Is it true a flock of turkeys gave you a stake to begin the Sierra Bonita?"

"Pure gospel, sir." Hooker leaned back against the oak. "Like most who went to California, I got poorer instead of richer, so I hit on the notion of buying turkeys with all the money I could finagle and driving them over the mountains to Carson City, Nevada, which was prospering from the mines. I could buy them for a dollar fifty a bird and hope they'd fetch four or five dollars each. Well, I had one helper and some mighty good dogs. We brought those turkeys along just fine till we were coming down from the sierra not far from Carson. Wound up on a precipice we couldn't get down nor very well go around. The dogs scared the turkeys till they finally just flapped their wings and took off. I stood there and saw my last dime, and it borrowed, sailing away with all my hopes. Didn't know how in the world I could face my wife and three kids. Talk about discouraged!"

"Did you catch the turkeys, sir?" asked Jed, diverted momentarily from admiring the lieutenant's spurs.

Hooker nodded. "We went down in the valley. Those dogs were a marvel. We gathered up that whole shebang, shooed 'em into Carson City, and sold 'em at five dollars apiece. That was in eighteen sixty-six, and army posts and Indian agencies in Arizona were buying beef from California. Those turkeys raised me enough cash to move here and go into business as a contractor."

"I respect you, Henry," said Crook. "I know you for an honest man. But contractors who don't want the Apaches to be self-sufficient bear a heavy share of blame for ongoing depredations. Why, in eighteen seventy-three, with only a few hoes condemned by the quartermaster and sticks hardened in fire, the Apaches on the White Mountain reservation raised five hundred thousand pounds of corn and thirty thousand of beans as well as melons, barley, and wheat. They sold wood and hay to the army. The Tontos on the Verde were doing so well that speculators got them forced down to San Carlos, which is much drier and less fertile. I did all I could to stop that, and the insane policy of placing bands that were traditional enemies on the same reservation."

"For a man who paid for Deltche's head, sir, you seem strangely inclined to sympathize with the savages," said Corrigan.

"I paid twice for Deltche's head, and for six others," returned the general amiably. "Deltche murdered several families and some other people so I promised to spare his warriors if they brought in his head. One head turned up at San Carlos and another at Verde. Since the bringers seemed sincere, I paid them both."

"Head's too heavy on long journey," said Mickey Free. Taking out his long knife, he cut around an imaginary skull. "Cut around throat, then down back of head, pop skull out —"

"Mickey," cut in the general, "that's no tale for children. Nor was my talk of heads. Your pardon, Miss MacLeod."

Jed, mesmerized, tugged at Mickey's sleeve. "You — you mean you brought in a *face?*" he whispered. "Kind of a mask?"

Mickey nodded. To Katie's horror, he let Jed hold his knife and examine it before sticking it back in its sheath.

"If you'd been left in charge, General," Hooker said, "I doubt I'd be selling any beef to San Carlos. The Indians knew you were like Al Sieber here — that when you said you'd kill them, you would, and when you said you were their friend, it was true. Your scouts earned money and went on being warriors. But you were sent north, and since Cochise's death, things have gone from bad to worse." He made a disgusted grimace. "I've sold a lot of beef to the army and agencies, but I never tallied an eight-hundred-pound steer as weighing thirteen hundred."

Crook nodded. "Of course there are outbreaks. Of course innocent settlers are killed. But those who cheat the Indians and drive them to despair are as guilty of these murders as the Indians who commit them."

"Strong words, sir," frowned Corrigan.

"Lieutenant, my experience with Indians began before you could toddle. Ninety-nine-hundredths of Indian woes are caused by traders and agents. The worst Indian is a model of honor compared to those Christian gentlemen who fatten on their misery."

Tom Horn's smile had faded. "How will you handle the Apaches, General?"

"As much as the government allows, I'll see that they can raise their own food and stock and sell the surplus. And I'll urge they be given the vote."

"The vote!" choked Corrigan, leaning forward. "Sir, you can't mean it! What do ignorant heathens know about our government?"

"That it lies to them." The general's beard jutted forward. "They should be armed with the vote to protect themselves and live under the same laws as everyone else. Believe me, Lieutenant, they understand justice very well."

Corrigan's back was stiff as a ramrod. "You will forgive me, sir, but I saw my best friend scalped at the Rosebud. You can't expect me to applaud the bestowal of citizenship on vicious barbarians."

"Barbarians?" Crook's musing voice had a rueful tinge. "Among the things I never learned at West Point was that one day I'd offer bounties for the heads of enemies — a barbaric custom if ever there was one. You've heard what Chivington's Colorado volunteers did to Cheyenne bodies at Sand Creek. No, Lieutenant, we can't deny Indians the vote on grounds of our moral superiority." He added less gruffly, "Your problem, Lieutenant, is that you haven't been fighting Indians long enough to appreciate them. And bear in mind that Apaches differ from Sioux and Cheyenne as much as Germans differ from English. Apaches very seldom take a scalp. They care more about results than winning glory."

"I defer to your greater experience, sir." Corrigan sounded not at all convinced.

327

"You won't go wrong there, Lieutenant," said Al Sieber. As Katie and Melissa gathered up the emptied plates, he, Mickey Free, and Tom Horn moved to the shade of another tree and began to play cards. Crook, Hooker, and Corrigan began to talk about the effect the president's critical condition was having on the country, while Jed lingered near the young officer.

Katie supposed it was better for Jed to emulate a soldier than a gambler, but she wasn't thrilled at the prospect of his pursuing either career. Washing the dishes in water heated by the sun, she inwardly groaned when Melissa said, "Did you notice how much the lieutenant looks like Mr. Diamond?"

"Mmf."

Melissa rinsed a plate and dried it. "If you ask me, it was pretty silly to make them eat outside! If you fed them, why did it matter where? It put us to a lot more work, carrying food out and toting everything back. If you ask me —"

"I didn't!" Katie's voice wavered. "No one who wants Bill Radnor dead is coming in this house as long as I have any say about it! And if you don't feel the same way, Melissa Jane MacCleod, I'm mightily ashamed of you."

Melissa's eyes opened wide, meeting Katie's. "Why, you — you're in love with him!" she said in a gasp. "That's not fair, Katie! I love him, too!"

"Fudge!" Katie's cheeks burned. "You're only thirteen years old!"

"You're only sixteen. He's a grown-up man."

"I know that better than you do, it seems." In spite of her humiliated resentment, Katie felt an unwilling rush of sympathy when tears sparkled in her little sister's deep blue eyes. "Honey, for you, it's sort of like Jed worshiping Mr. Diamond. Right now, he's all wrapped up in the lieutenant. Of course, you love Bill — Mr. Radnor — for all he's done for us but —"

"I could say the same about you!" retorted the younger girl, mouth twisting as she hastily rubbed her sleeve across her eyes. "Oh, why did you get to be the oldest?"

"You're welcome to it," snapped Katie, wiping her dripping forehead against her own rolled-up sleeve. Melissa's tears spilled over. Katie made a supreme effort to step out of her sixteen-year-old self and speak like a woman. "Listen, dear. Mr. Radnor's twenty-nine. We're both too young for him, even if he wanted to settle down." Silently, bitterly, she added, *At least that's what he thinks.* "I don't suppose either one of us will ever forget him, but there are lots of young men and someday —"

"You don't love him as much as I do or you couldn't say that!" Melissa's flush almost hid her freckles. "If I can't marry him, I won't marry anyone!"

Perhaps because that vow was frequently in her heart, Katie gave an unwise and derisive laugh. "Don't be a silly goose, M'liss."

"You can't be my sister!" Melissa cried. "If — if you were, you couldn't be so horrid!" She gulped, flung the dish towel over a chair, and fled to the other room, screaming over her shoulder, "You don't look like us! You don't favor Mama or Pa. I bet they took you to raise when your real folks died or ran off and left you."

Shaken like a tree in a storm that had loosened its roots, Katie leaned on the edge of the table to keep from falling. Her insides contracted and knotted as if she'd been kicked hard in the stomach. *M'liss didn't mean it,* she tried to tell herself. *She's mad and hurt and wants to hurt me.* And had certainly succeeded. *You can't let her upset you like this,* Katie scolded. *And you can't wrangle. You have to make her respect you or you'll have pure hell while she's growing up. But I'm not grown up myself,* a part of Katie wailed. *I can take care of Rosie, but M'liss and Jed, especially M'liss —*

She would just have to do the best she could. Drying her eyes, Katie swallowed, fought back tears, and started scrubbing the bean pot. She was pouring the rinse water over the rose-bush when Melissa marched in and resumed her task of drying and putting up dishes. Her eyes were red and swollen, but her pointed little chin thrust upward. Every motion jerked with offended pride.

Had they still been sisters only, Katie could have harbored her angry hurt till time or chance smoothed things over, but if she expected to control her brother and sister, she had to first control herself, prove to herself and them that she was worthy to advise and lead. She couldn't, though, put her arms around Melissa. Those scathing words, ripping open a festering wound, still seared her heart: *"You can't be my sister!"* At worst, Katie had never doubted she was Mama's child. Now even that certainty was undermined. Whatever the truth, it couldn't change the present and Katie's respon-sibilities, but it mattered, mattered terribly.

So all she said to her sister was what she could say in honesty. "Melissa, I'm sorry I called you a goose. I shouldn't have and —"

Melissa tossed down the towel again, but this time to throw her arms around Katie in a hug that squeezed out her breath. "A *silly* goose is what you said, and you were right! I don't know how I could say such nasty, wicked, awful things! Of course, you're our

331

sister, Katie — no one else could put up with me." She drew back, stricken. "Katie, don't cry! Please don't! I — I'll try to do better!"

They held each other, kissed and laughed and cried, but the nagging question had buried itself to batten on Katie's deepest anxieties. Even as she settled down with some mending while Melissa fed the baby, she somberly admitted that, though she'd forgiven her sister's words, she never could forget them.

But as if heaven had forgiven some sin of the earth deserving drought, that night wind swirled though the house with a rush of coolness, lightning splintered the sky, thunder resounded like an iron monster trapped in the mountains, the smell of parched grass and dust changed from acridity to fragrance, and the rains came.

XIII

Hailed by the warble of finches, a cardinal's merry whistle, and the lilting song of a towhee, the sun rose next morning on a land revived, leaves brightened, even the dull green of yuccas and mescal fresher. Dried grass, pale yellow to rich gold, looked full of energy rather than withered and lifeless. The sky smiled. Most bracing of all was breathing in scents that made the air almost tangible, the grateful pungency of leaves and hopeful, expectant earth.

Rain came that afternoon and the next. Toads *thunk-thunked* at night over the sibilant rasp of cicadas and rejoicing coyotes. Calves and colts frolicked with new exuberance. Tiny sprouts of green softened the earth and pushed up through sere growth. Squash and melons, discouragingly small before in spite of water fetched daily from the creek, now swelled plumper by the day and corn seemed to spear upward as one watched.

Diamond paid a visit in time to enjoy with them their first squash flavored with green onions and chilies. "I think he's your son, John," Katie said after telling him about Corrigan in a few private moments while Jed was tending to the gambler's horse.

"He and his mother must want to forget it." Diamond's mouth jerked down. "Corrigan is her family name. Whatever she's told him about me, it won't be good."

"That's all the more reason to talk to him, try to set things straight."

"I wrote to him — sent money — on Christmas and his birthday till he went off to West Point. He never answered."

"Maybe his mother didn't let him see the letters."

"Maybe."

"John —"

"He's a man. Old enough to decide if he wants to know me."

"But could he find you if he tried?" Katie hesitated, then broke a cardinal rule of frontier etiquette. "Is Diamond your real name?"

After a heartbeat, Diamond said, "It's the name I wrote him under."

Tears brimmed in Katie's eyes. "If you reach out, the worst he can do is tell you he wants to forget you. At least you'd know you'd tried. Please, John, give your son a chance to meet you."

"I'll ponder it," he said, as Jed ran in with Ace at his heels. Smiling at the boy, the man said, "This rain should have the trout swimming around instead of hiding under the rocks. Shall we go up the canyon and see if they're biting?"

Nacho usually took butter and milk to town when he was delivering firewood, but Jed was campaigning to use up the rest of his prize money. "I want a saddle and a red shirt," he said grandly one night at supper. "And I'm going to buy you and M'liss some pretty dress material, Katie, and something for Rosie."

"This next lot of butter and milk and vegetables will put us even with Bride and Mr. Carson and the stores," Katie mused. This was about the third time Jed had pressed the matter. Besides, she hadn't seen Bill in so long that her dreaming, hoping, secret self felt starved. "Our everyday dresses are patched till there's no place to sew a new piece. That's your money, Jed, and we'll pay you back, but it would be *lovely* to have new dresses."

Jed gave a shake of his yellow head. "We're pardners, remember? Shucks, I'm a hog anyhow, getting boots and a saddle and red shirt."

"A nice hog!" Throwing her arms around him, Melissa gave him a resounding kiss before he could wrench away.

"I'll win a lot more races," Jed said airily. "Shiloh'll be old enough to run next Fourth of July."

Katie started to say the young stallion would belong to Bill Radnor then, but caught herself. Jed's sharing his money made her realize that he and Melissa should have a voice in what happened to animals that were theirs as much as hers. Clearing her throat, she said, "We probably owe Bill Radnor our lives. For sure, we owe him this house and all." Melissa gave her a look that was pure female, and Katie blushed but doggedly went on. "What would you think of giving Shiloh to him when he's old enough to ride?"

"Give away Shiloh?" Jed cried. "Pa reckoned he'd be another Steel Dust!"

"I think we should," cut in Melissa. "Bill's been wonderful to us, and you know that, Jedediah MacLeod."

"But —" Jed chewed his lip and at last gave a sigh. "All right. I guess we should. But let's agree right now that Red Rover stays at Home Mountain."

Katie nodded. So did Melissa. "Hey!" Jed blinked, chuckling. "Do you know us pardners just made up our minds about our first big problem?"

"We did," laughed Katie, relieved and happy. "To celebrate, let's make molasses candy!"

Nacho offered to take care of Rosie, and if need be, the evening milking, so on the first of August, the other MacLeods drove Jenny and Babe to town. Red Rover, Shiloh, and Señorita larked ahead, cantering back now and then, manes and tails streaming like banners of red and black, to make sure their mothers were indeed coming. Ace rode in Jed's lap but had grown enough that his legs hung over the boy's knees. Jed had shined his boots with soot and grease and buffed them till they glittered except for where the toes were scuffed too deeply for the most earnest burnishing to avail. Katie had trimmed his hair and washed ears that he'd skipped during his bath.

Melissa wore her bee pin, and arranged her single fair plait over her shoulder so that she could admire the azure blue ribbon Bride had given her. "I hope we can find material that matches my ribbon and get enough for a bonnet, too." Her eyes, the same blue, glowed like summer twilight, and she gave an impatient bounce. "Will you get cloth to match your ribbon, Katie?"

"If I can find it." Katie didn't dare count on locating that special hue of golden green, though she hoped a becoming dress that fit and showed — well, that *fit* — would make Bill Radnor realize she wasn't just a child. The last time he'd been to the ranch was the Fourth, when he'd donned Bride's skirts and bonnet and done the milking.

Would he be in town today? Katie's heart plunged at the chance he might not be. When she went so long without seeing him, she ached as if some part of her were missing, something from deep inside. She worried, too, especially since Colonel Hooker had said he was offering a reward for Bill. Still and all, fretting wouldn't help. For the first time ever, she was getting to pick out material for a dress and she was going to enjoy it! "Getting a new dress is going to be so wonderful that I'll love it whatever color it is." Holding the reins in one hand for a moment, she reached around Melissa to pat Jed's cheek. "You must be the best brother in the whole world, Jed — or at least in the Territory!"

His chest inflated. "Shucks, when I grow up and win really big races with my own horse, I'll buy you girls lots of clothes!"

"Your wife won't let you," said Melissa practically. "But that's all right. We'll have husbands by then who'll buy our dresses."

Katie opened her mouth to remind her sister that in spite of the hoarded savings she had helped to accumulate, their mother hadn't been permitted more than two dresses at a time, a good one that became everyday when the everyday one was worn past mending.

Instead, Katie said, "Whether I marry or not, I'm going to have some way to have my own money, whether it's from butter or eggs or my share of whatever's earned on our ranch or farm." Involuntarily, her fingers bit into

338

the reins. "When you get married, Jed, don't you dare keep all the money and make your wife beg for every penny she needs!"

"Sufferin' sidewinders!" Jed hunched over Ace and whispered loudly in a floppy, spotted ear. "If women are all like my sisters, or worse yet that stuck-up Hallie Larrimore, you and me'll stay bachelors!"

Katie had managed not to think about Ed Larrimore for a couple of days, but the name evoked her fears. Determinedly, she fought them with laughter. "We'll have you so well-trained that the nicest, sweetest girls will fight over who gets you," Katie teased.

As if mention of the rancher had conjured up signs of him, she saw several cattle with the Pitchfork brand heading along a draw. Every now and then, some came in sight of Home Mountain and had to be chased back east. So far, they seemed to have ranged there naturally, but Katie was afraid that Larrimore might order his hands to deliberately push his cattle onto Home Mountain graze. It wouldn't take a herd long to clean out grass that would sustain the Steel Dusts and Guernseys all year.

Warding off fruitless worry over what Larrimore might be planning, Katie glanced proudly over her shoulder. Milk, buttermilk, cream, and butter filled crocks, jars, buckets, and jugs wedged securely in tubs of water covered by soaked canvas left over from the curtains — very useful that wagon top had proved! "The box of chilies and squash is a present for Bride," she said. "A real present, because a pound of butter and a jug of milk finish paying what we'd have owed for board if she'd charged us — not that there's any way we can ever pay her for taking us in the way she did. But isn't it marvelous, pardners? Now we can save up for another saddle so we'll each have one, and shoes — you need some plain ones, Jed, so you can save your boots — and winter coats, and flannel for Rosie's winter clothes and —"

"The first thing we save for better be another rifle." Jed scanned ahead, behind, and on both sides. "I heard Mickey Free tell Tom Horn that old Nana's sure to raid up into New Mexico this summer. We're mighty near the line — not that Apaches pay any mind to things like that. Did you know Mickey was the stolen boy who brought on all the big trouble with Cochise in Apache Pass back in 1861 when Lieutenant Bascom and some other officers hung some Chiricahua Apaches? It was Pinal Apaches who took Mickey. When he was only thirteen, he got a job freighting between El Paso and Tucson. His boss taught him English and gave him the Green River knife. He's killed a lot of men with it and —"

"Jed!" Katie shuddered. "I don't want to know any more about Mr. Free."

"Me, either!" Melissa's bonnet jerked with the emphatic dip of her head. "The way he looked at my hair made me think he wanted to scalp me."

"He'd rather take heads or face skins."

"Jed!" To save her, Katie didn't know whether her brother was trying to comfort or terrify them. "I guess we can stand your all the time telling us what Mr. Diamond said, or even that Lieutenant Corrigan, but I draw the line at Mickey Free." Changing the subject, she spoke in a guileless tone. "Since there's no school close enough, we'll need to find an arithmetic book and a couple of readers, maybe a speller and a geography and a history."

"Katie!" Now it was Jed's turn to screech before he cast her an accusing glance and brightened. "You can't teach us all that stuff. You can do sums and read and write a little like Mama taught you, but that's all — and that's plenty."

"It's not. We can all read a little — we can teach ourselves more. If you can read, you can learn most anything." She thought of an ally in Jed's education. "Ask Mr. Diamond about it. He'll say you need to learn everything you can."

"He already did," Jed admitted glumly. "I

might as well tell you since I bet you're fixing to say something to him. He said he'd be glad to come several times a week this winter and teach us. I tried to beg him out of it, but I'll bet he's already ordered a passel of books."

"That's kind of him," Katie said.

Wasn't it sad that a man who enjoyed children so much, especially a boy, hadn't been able to help raise his son? Had John sought out the lieutenant? She hadn't heard from Diamond since the day she'd tried to persuade him to get in touch with Corrigan. If that had gone well, she was certain John would have shared his good news; since he hadn't, she feared the news was bad. Would Bill be in town?

Delighted with the squash and chilies, Bride insisted they have coffee and cinnamon rolls before they began their shopping. "John Diamond will be mighty sorry to miss you," she said. "He's gone to Tombstone for a few days." She didn't have any real news of the president. "His doctors won't say whether the poor man's able to make decisions." Bride's high brow furrowed. "It's worrisome for the country to rock along without someone in charge. And sure, 'tis a disgrace to the country when the elected president can be shot at, even if he be a Republican."

A knock sounded at the door. "Is Clan Mac-Leod in town?" called Bill. Katie's heart stopped and then raced joyfully. He smiled on them all and pulled up a chair. His eyes were clear and bright, matching the blue silk scarf at his throat, and his black hair looked freshly combed.

"You smell like you've just been to the barber," Bride teased, pouring his coffee. "A good thing Diamond leaves now and then so you can catch up on your sleep."

"Will you help me pick a saddle, Bill?" urged Jed. "I was going to ask Uncle Jack but —"

"I'll be glad to," Bill said, and slanted a merry look at the sisters. "Why don't we all congregate for dinner at Firbanks Restaurant? My treat. You don't get to town that often."

Jed handed Katie eighteen dollars of his remaining prize. "Go ahead and spend it," he said. "Maybe you can buy your shoes and Rosie's flannel."

It was the most money Katie had ever held in her life, the silver coins big and solid. It was such a heady, powerful feeling that she divided the money evenly with Melissa. That was half the pleasure, possessing the money and knowing it was yours to use. Katie intended to buy coffee from her share, and the baby's flannel, but imagine having nine whole dollars!

Promising to stop by before they left town and to bring Rosie when the weather cooled, Katie and Melissa floated off to the joys of examining bolt after bolt of cloth and trimming and trying on any shoes that looked as if they might fit. For Katie, the pleasure was multiplied by knowing she'd see Bill at noon.

There weren't many shoes since Galeyville had so few women, but because choice was limited, it didn't take Melissa long to choose scalloped side button boots with an elegant, incurving Louis XV heel over a laced pair with a low, flat heel. Though she winced to see half her sister's money go for boots alone, Katie held her tongue. It was the first time Melissa had enjoyed such extravagance, might be the last, and the boots were well-constructed and should wear a long time.

Her own larger, narrower foot presented her with the temptation of bronze kid fedora slippers with a beaded top and dashing coxcomb bow, but though ravishing, they were so frivolous that she smothered a sigh and returned to Metzger's store to debate between walking boots scalloped along the buttoned side or Common Sense boots with a lower heel. Virtuous at conquering her mad urge to own the bronze fedoras, she allowed herself the scallops and had seven dollars left.

"I have a nice bargain on colored cotton

hose," suggested gray-haired Sarah Metzger. "Ten cents a pair or a dozen for a dollar, and they come in cardinal, garnet, wine, and navy as well as brown, tan, and black."

They split a dozen, Katie daring one garnet pair while Melissa bought all the cardinal ones in her size. It was a shock to learn that Rosie's hose cost more than theirs, eighteen cents a pair for cotton, twenty-five cents for wool, but she'd need them that fall, so from her money Katie bought a pair of cotton and four of wool and smiled ruefully at Mrs. Metzger.

"Isn't it funny that we don't seem to need much out on the ranch, but when I start looking around a store —" She shook her head. "It's a good thing I don't live where I'd be in stores every week."

"You can save on flannel," said the older woman. "Unbleached Canton is eight cents a yard."

"But the scarlet's so pretty!" Melissa stroked it. "Think how it'd look with Rosie's dark hair. I'll help pay for it, Katie. Do — do you suppose we could buy enough to make us petticoats?"

"Let's decide on our dresses," Katie said. "Then we'll see how much we have left. I still need to buy a pound of coffee."

"Maybe Jed —"

"He didn't have to give us any of his money,

M'liss. Anyhow, just remember! Next time we can trade or sell our butter and milk so we'll have money again."

"Just as a matter of business," proposed Sarah Metzger, "if you're giving me such a nice order, I can discount a little."

Scotch gingham was twice as expensive as American, but Melissa kept returning to a bolt of blue squares in several shades striped with white and navy. Eight yards cost a dollar and twenty cents. Three spools of thread at five cents each, fifteen yards of medallion braid for trimming, and carved jet buttons came to another dollar. Counting out her money, Melissa gave a sigh of happy relief and said to Katie, "I have a dollar and eighty cents left. Please, let's get Rosie the flannel and some of this beautiful embroidered scarlet flannel edging!"

"M'liss! It — it's a dollar twenty-five a yard!" Katie gulped.

"But she'd look so sweet!"

"I'm taking nine yards of this flowered sateen." Katie selected the domestic at twelve and a half cents, half the cost of the French imported. "See, these leaves really do match my ribbon and I love this soft green background with the bronzy-yellow blossoms. I'll need four spools of thread, rick-rack to match the leaves, and these little dark green buttons.

Oh yes, we'd better have several yards of elastic for garters and petticoat waists."

"We can get flannel petticoats?" Melissa squealed.

"You can for sure, honey. We have three-eighty left. Let's see now — twelve yards will make our petticoats and all the winter gowns Rosie'll need. At twenty cents a yard" — she couldn't keep from giving her sister a hug — "we can do it and pay for a yard of edging."

"With fifteen cents left over," figured Mrs. Metzger. "And then there's your discount. Tell you what, I'll throw in the coffee."

"Oh, that's too costly!" protested Katie.

Sarah Metzger leaned on the counter. Her gray eyes were unusually bright. "Didn't you bring in a pound of butter and a jug of milk, paying up for what we were glad to give you youngsters for a start? You'll take the coffee, Katie MacLeod, or I won't sell you the rest of this truck!"

"I'll bring you some more butter —"

"You'll not! What you'll do is bring that baby in to see me in her pretty red gown. Mmm. That roll of red edging is so close to gone that I might as well throw in the rest of it. Only a foot or so, but it might let you edge two gowns."

Stowing their booty in the wagon, which was in front of Babcock's corral while the horses were inside it, Katie and Melissa turned to find Bill and Jed approaching, their brother resplendent in a red shirt, staggering under the weight of a carved leather saddle trimmed with silver conchos.

"Look what I got for twenty dollars!" he whooped. "Mr. Shotwell loaned a cowboy fifteen dollars on it, but the cowboy got killed. Business is kind of slow right now so Mr. Shotwell was glad to make five bucks. There was a red plaid shirt I thought Nacho would like, so Mr. Shotwell knocked off a dime and since mine was his best pleated flannel, he took fifteen cents off it. So," he said triumphantly, gasping as he heaved the saddle over the side of the wagon, "I did what Bill said — bought six pair of socks so I won't ruin my boots." He grubbed in his pocket and produced a dollar and several coins. "You can have this, Katie."

"You're a dear, but we've got everything we need." Before she could enumerate their successes, Melissa reached in her bundle and brought out the fancy-heeled boots. "Aren't they pretty? And we got red flannel for Rosie and the most beautiful embroidered edging and —"

Setting one hand under her elbow and another under Katie's, Bill steered them across the street. "Let's order our dinners! While we're waiting, you ladies can describe your shopping foray. I never eat breakfast and I'm starving."

Myra Firbank, regarding Bill with the same fascinated revulsion she might have paid an outsized diamondback rattler, said there was turkey and dressing, poppyseed rolls — with butter, thanks to the pound the MacLeods had brought that morning — and fresh-baked peach pie.

When they had ordered, Bill said, "This is a special celebration, Mrs. Firbank. If you have champagne punch, I think my guests could have a small glass apiece."

Mrs. Firbank stiffened. Her sharp black eyes went wide. "Mr. Radnor! You can't be depraved enough to turn these motherless innocents into wine-bibbers! Even if we had alcohol, which we don't, being good Baptists, I wouldn't serve it to young 'uns, especially females. In all my born days, I never heard of such a scandal!"

Bill bowed his head as if chastised, but Katie saw the wicked gleam in his eye. "Ma'am, I guess I have to beg your pardon. Reckon I hadn't thought about the possible results of my careless notion." He shook his dark head in sympathy. "It must be a martyrdom for anyone with as tender a conscience as yours, ma'am, to live in this rough community."

"Mining towns are where the money is," shrugged Myra. "And there's too much competition in Tombstone and Globe." She added forgivingly, "There's sarsaparilla to drink, or lemonade, and of course there's coffee."

The MacLeods decided on lemonade, which was made from a bottled essence. Bill requested coffee, strong and black. "Shame on you!" Katie said as soon as their hostess vanished into the kitchen. "You knew perfectly well, didn't you, Bill, that she didn't have champagne punch?"

"I suspected as much." His eyes glinted. "But I couldn't resist enlivening her day. Besides, you never know till you try." He turned to Melissa. "So you found red flannel for Rosie. What did you find for you?"

As soon as they'd finished their last crumb of flaky sugared pie crust, Jed and Melissa went off to gloat over their acquisitions and buy some candy. Katie hadn't rushed, hoping for a private moment. Bill's smile changed as he looked at her.

"So the kids are happy, Katie. Did you get everything you needed?"

I need you. Katie looked down so he couldn't see the yearning in her eyes. "Does anyone ever get everything they need?" she asked, trying to make it a joke. "Do you?"

He didn't answer for so long that she stole

a glance. His face had turned somber. "There's wants, Katie, and there's needs. I reckon I have more of my wants than I do my needs, but that's my own fault. What is it you need?"

She couldn't tell him how much she longed for him, so she answered with another hunger that would explain why her eyes had filled with tears. "I — I'd give anything in the world if my mother were alive, if I could have a chance to get her to love me —"

Startled, Bill stared across the table. As a tear splashed into her plate, he laid a big hand over hers. "She had to love you, Katie," he said roughly. "Anyone would. You're imagining things if you think she didn't."

"If she did at all, there was more shame than love." The thought of Melissa's several outbursts seared Katie anew. "I — I don't look like my brother and sisters or much like my parents. If I was really mother's child, I think I was the reason that she married my father."

"Katie, that's nonsense!"

She shook her head, drawing her hand away. "She always acted as — as if she owed him something. It was so important to her that she'd earned money to help buy the Guernseys and Steel Dust horses. I can't remember her ever asking Pa for anything." Bitterness, grief

351

for a woman who'd worked so hard and had so little, welled up in Katie.

What a waste, those stocks and that money hoarded in the cabin! "She never asked — and he didn't give her much. That hurts most of all. That I can't make it up to her sometime — that I won't be able, ever in this world, ever in my whole life, to give her nice things."

"Katie, you're raising her children." Bill's voice was husky and he reached across to touch her face. "That's the finest gift she could have."

His tenderness helped. If he ever loved a woman, he could show a lot of it. Katie managed a weak smile. "Lord knows I'm trying. But it'd be easier if I were a few years older." *And maybe then you wouldn't think I was a child.*

The shadow of a powerfully built squarish man filled the door before it was pushed open. Hallie Larrimore came in, her father looming behind her. He looked so big there, a dark, faceless, formidable shape, that sheer physical fear washed through Katie, draining her strength.

The rancher's eyebrows climbed at seeing Katie with Bill. Stopping at their table, Larrimore took off his hat.

"Miss Kate," he said, with a bare nod to Bill. "You fortin' up in town till they catch Nana or the old devil heads back to Mexico?"

"Nana?" Bill rasped. "Has he worked over this way?"

The rancher shrugged. "Who knows? He probably only had about a dozen warriors when he left the Sierra Madre, but he picked up more on the Mescalero reservation. Maybe around forty all told, for sure no more than seventy. The army's got ten times that many troops and scouts chasing him, but that old fox has faded into those mountains he's lived and hunted in since he was a cub, and he's seventy-five now. Take the Black Range, the San Mateos, and the Mogollons, and you've got twenty thousand square miles of the roughest country anywhere."

Bill scowled. "Yes, and all Nana has to do is dodge the soldiers. He's not trying to wipe them out. In fact he won't fight a pitched battle unless he's cornered. Suits him to raid a ranch or little town or kill travelers. He knows all the springs, caves, trails, and good ambush sites, and you can bet he has caches of food and supplies all over."

"Colonel Hatch — he's the commander of the Military District of New Mexico — is taking advantage of the new railroads and telegraph lines," Larrimore said. "Three sides of Nana's mountains are cordoned by them so troops, dispatched by a wired order, can be sent by train to wherever Nana was last seen or is expected."

"Fine, but the west is open — the San Carlos reservation."

"That's dandy with Colonel Hatch, though he'll station a few detachments along the border," Larrimore growled. "Once the hostiles are out of New Mexico, they're somebody else's headache."

"Like ours."

"It's plumb ridiculous!" Larrimore's eyes smoldered like charcoal fanned by wind. "Forty raggedy-ass — excuse me, Miss Kate — forty heathen makin' mock of hundreds of U.S. troopers!" He turned to Katie. "You'd be a sight safer at the Pitchfork than at your place."

"I wouldn't feel safer."

Dull red crept to the roots of his wiry gray hair. "You won't be so pert, missy, if the 'Paches get hold of you."

"From all I hear," retorted Katie, somewhat, but not very, ashamed of her underhanded jab, "Apaches heading south from San Carlos are a lot more likely to take the easy way past your land and the San Simon Valley than to swing into the little pocket by Home Mountain and have to journey through the mountains or travel across the plain till the valley stretches south."

"They move with two scouts ahead and two

behind," said Larrimore. "You can bet if they knew about you kids and those horses, at least a small party would swerve your way. Their numbers are way down, and they always have raised lots of captive children. Your brother would make a warrior. You and — what's her name? — Melissa are strong and young, able to give the band children. The baby would be too much trouble. They'd just brain her."

Katie stifled a gasp of outrage. Bill said, "That's enough, Larrimore. People can't stop living just because there are Apaches on the loose. In fact, here you are with your daughter."

"Yes, and if you'll look across at Babcock's, you'll see half a dozen Pitchfork horses besides mine and Hallie's Glencoe."

"Parties with a lot more than seven fighting men have been wiped out," said Bill.

Larrimore's thick dark eyebrows meshed over his flat nose. "When I crave your advice, Radnor, I'll ask for it. Just because I'm tryin' to talk some sense into a headstrong filly —"

Katie intervened. "I thank you for your concern, Mr. Larrimore, even if what you said was horrid."

"Well," he grunted, tossing his hat on a table in the corner, "if you change your mind, you're welcome at the Pitchfork."

"Tell your brother I'll let him ride Glencoe

sometimes," put in Hallie. She wore a gold taffeta riding habit and plumed cavalier hat, totally unsuitable for her age, the occasion, and the thorny wilderness. In spite of her patronizing manner, her eyes glowed with eagerness. It was clear she'd welcome company her own age at the ranch, and Katie felt a rush of sympathy for her.

"Thank you," returned Katie with a smile. "You're very kind, Hallie, but our Steel Dust horses are good enough for us."

The Larrimores were scarcely seated when Deputy Sheriff William Breakenridge strolled in with Johnny Ringo. They paused to exchange pleasantries with Katie and Bill, then settled at the adjoining table.

"So you've really got a warrant for me, Breck." The reddish-blond outlaw sounded a little hurt. "Shucks, I was just funnin' with the boys like they did with me when they cleaned me out and told me to go grow more wool."

"All well and good, Johnny." The deputy pushed back his yellow hair and sighed. "However, Webb says he'd laid down four aces when you drew on him and said you reckoned two guns beat four aces any time."

"It did," grinned Ringo. "Dave Estes and me walked out of Evilsizer's with five hundred dollars that bunch had cheated us out of. I'm plumb disappointed that they've got no sense of humor." Lawman and outlaw ordered coffee and dinner from a disapproving Myra before Ringo said plaintively, "Tombstone's no fun these days. Last time I was there I tried to get any one of those Earps to shoot it out at ten paces, one of them holding to one edge of my handkerchief while I had the other. Doc Holliday was game, but the mayor broke it up. I don't mind your arresting me, Breck. That's your job. But I hate having to go in to Tombstone."

"Still, Johnny, that's where you're needed." Breakenridge pulled out his watch and glanced at it. "Soon as we eat, I need to start back."

"I've got things to attend to," said Ringo. "You go ahead and I'll catch up with you if I have to ride all night."

Shocked into unabashed staring, Katie saw the deputy's blue eyes search the other man's. "All right," he said after a minute. "I'll see you on the trail."

They talked of other things, then, and with their conversation muffling her lowered voice, Katie said to Bill, "I guess I should ask Jed and Melissa if they'd rather stay in town. I'm sure Bride would be glad to have them, and Rosie, too." She swallowed. "I'll tell Nacho that Nana's still raiding. He may decide to move in for a while."

"He won't leave you, Katie. Why don't all of you come to town till Nana's back in Mexico?"

"And when will that be? One month? Two? Three? The cows have to be milked, and with the calves and colts and horses, we have too many animals to keep long in Babcock's corral. And there's the garden!"

She was giving reasons, and they were true, but with instinct deeper than thought, the primeval drive that made most creatures protect their homes where their young were reared, she knew that if she left the ranch now, abandoned plants and growing corn, the fragrant rosebush twining beside the door — if she abandoned her place, it would never be hers. She would lose it. This she felt in her bones, even as she admitted that the Chiricahua Apaches must feel the same way, even more so, about this vast region, plains, mountains, canyons, that they had roamed freely, lands sacred and beloved. In a strange way, she could understand why they would kill her and any whites, though that didn't make her less afraid or more willing to die.

"Katie." Bill's eyes probed deep in hers. "Didn't your father die — and take your mother with him — because he tried to rescue his savings?"

Katie flushed. "That was different. The fire

358

was there for sure, but chances are that tucked against the mountains the way we are near the mouth of Whitetail Canyon, raiders won't come our direction. People can't just stop living because of Nana."

"Quite a few have," reminded Bill.

Suddenly remembering that his ranch was in New Mexico, Katie caught in her breath. "Is your place near where Nana is?"

"Nana's reported a good hundred miles north. I'm close to the border. My stock will be all right unless Nana makes his dash for Mexico through the Animas Valley." When Katie still frowned, Bill said, "Look, I'm not taking crazy chances. Don't fret about me, Katie. You just be careful. If Nana comes your way, let him have the stock and he likely won't bother you if you're forted up in the house with weapons."

He paid for their meal, leaving extra coins that caused Myra to smile on him and call, "Hurry back!" as they went outside.

"I have to talk to Jed and Melissa," Katie decided, glancing around. "They must be visiting Bride."

"Katie." Bill's voice was strained. "Under the circumstances, and with Nacho there, I reckon it would be all right for me to stay at your place as long as Nana's on this side of the border."

Mightily tempted, she finally shook her head. "Thanks, Bill, but no. I'm choosing to stay at Home Mountain. If that's a bad choice, I don't want you to suffer for it." She hesitated. "Jed might stay with John Diamond. He thinks the world of him. Would you look after Jed till John gets back from Tombstone?"

"My," Bill grinned. "Diamond will be glad to hear he's come up in the world! Two months ago you were afraid to let the boy go fishing with him! Maybe Mrs. Firbank's right. We may be corrupting you."

"Or maybe *you're* changing," Katie retorted. She only wished that were true.

XIV

This was going to be the prettiest, nicest smelling homemade soap ever! Katie vowed. She poured a basket of wild mint and hoarded yellow rose petals into the boiling, slippery mass, the result of lye water leached from ashes and simmered for several hours with all sorts of accumulated fats she'd gotten from Bride — bacon rinds and grease, drippings, tallow, and some cracked bones that were too big for Ace to tackle, for marrow yielded good fat. The soft soap could be used at its present stage, but in order to make bars, Katie would have to boil it hours longer and add some of their sparingly used salt. The mint and petals would be strained out with the impurities, but their odor would remain. She'd sprinkled the cheesecloth-lined molds with more leaves that would look nice in the finished bars.

Giving the thick liquid a vigorous stirring, Katie wondered anxiously if the lye were strong enough. Mother had always tested it by seeing if it would float an egg. Lacking eggs, Katie had hunted for a small hunk of wood that she estimated to weigh an equal amount. It had floated jauntily on the strong brown fluid, but this was the first batch of soap Katie had made without her mother's supervision.

It was less than a year ago that they'd carried out this rite under an oak tree above the Nueces, seven hundred miles away and a lifetime ago. Katie's eyes stung from more than the lye. Mary MacLeod, that autumn of 1880, the autumn that was to be her last pleasuring in scarlet, gold, and tawny foliage, was just beginning to show the rounding of the baby whose life would begin as Mary's ebbed.

Could it be only five months since her children had buried her beside her husband and started westward? So much had happened that it seemed as if years had passed. Yet Rosie, on the serape spread under the far side of the giant tree, was only beginning to push up on her knees, get them beneath her, and rock precariously till she collapsed. She, like the colts and calves frisking on the slopes, would grow up without a memory of the old home. Nor would she remember her mother as Katie did now with a rush of mingled love, grief, and puzzled, questioning resentment.

No use in that; no use at all to wonder why Mary had treated her so coldly. Better to remember how, when Katie had asked her brother and sister if they would stay in town while Nana was depredating, Jed had said, "Hey! We're pardners! You bet we're stayin' at the ranch!" and Melissa had quickly hugged her. "Of course we're staying with you, Katie. You're our sister!"

Well, Nana, pursued by troops stationed in both New Mexico and Arizona, hadn't veered across the territorial border, but the Mexican border had been a regular battlefield that August. First, down in a canyon that connected the San Simon Valley with the Animas Valley, a pack train of Mexican smugglers had been ambushed. John Diamond, who'd brought the news, scoffed when he said that it was rumored that the Clantons, Mac-Lowerys, and others in on the raid had looted seventy-five thousand dollars in big silver 'dobe dollars.

"Four thousand is more like it," he said. "A couple of days in Galeyville and they were flat busted."

With a sick, dazed feeling, wondering how laughing, good-natured young Billy Clanton could kill men from hiding, Katie whispered, "Bill Radnor?"

Diamond shook his head. "He didn't have any part in it, Katie. He's lifted a lot of Mexican cattle, but that's sort of a game both sides play along the border. I've never heard of Bill killing anyone who didn't have a fair chance. Besides, when that happened, he was playing cards with me."

363

She heard that with relief and a flash of pain. Why didn't Bill ride out to see them? Willowy, bashful Hi Phillips had stopped off, and so had sandy-headed Charlie Hughes. Slim Jones of the flaming hair and moustache had even made biscuits because he happened by on a wash day. She hadn't seen Bill, though, since the day he'd bought their dinners and scandalized Myra Firbank. Though Katie was glad he hadn't been at his ranch in the Animas Valley where he might be in Nana's path, it hurt to know he'd been in Galeyville and hadn't made the effort to visit.

Putting that aside, Katie searched the gambler's face. "Did — did you locate Lieutenant Corrigan?"

"I wrote to him at Fort Bowie. The letter came back."

"Maybe —"

Diamond flicked his perfectly manicured fingers. "It was marked REFUSED in very large letters. It was initialed." A muscle in his jaw knotted, but when he spoke, it was with an attempt at lightness. "Don't look so tragic, Katie. The lieutenant obviously gets along very well without his disreputable father."

"If he only knew you!"

"It seems he has no concept of his monumental deprivation." When she started to protest, Diamond's flippant tone took on a raw edge. "Leave it, my dear. He doesn't want to know me. Probably it's best."

"It can't be!"

"Oh, Katie-Kate," he said caressingly. "You want your happy endings, don't you?"

She'd watched him through a blur. "It — it's just so awful! When someone's dead, there's no way to make up or change things. Why can't we be kinder to each other, now, while we're alive?"

"Pure human cussedness, sweet Kate, and fear people will judge us weak and try to take advantage." His hand brushed hers consolingly. "Never mind. I'm glad you persuaded me to try to reach James. At least I know I offered my hand and it was his choice to keep strangers."

Diamond went on to say that Old Man Clanton hadn't long savored his triumph over the smugglers. About the middle of August, driving a herd of three hundred stolen cattle through Guadalupe Canyon, which lay part in Mexico, part in the United States, he and four friends were gunned down as they started to cook breakfast in a rainy gray dawning. John thought regular Mexican troops had thus punished Clanton's thieving on their side of the border and the ambuscade in what was becoming known as Skeleton Canyon. Whoever had done the killing, the cattle had been run back to Mexico, there were five new graves on a little hill in the Animas Valley, and a number of Mexicans had been found riddled with bullets in the San Pedro Valley. Nana wasn't the only one to avenge blood with blood. With a chill of sadness, Katie thought again of Billy Clanton. He was only a few years older than she; she was sure there was good in him; but what end could he have now except a violent one?

Wisps of hair clung damply to Katie's forehead. Brushing them back, she scooped up Rosie, who gurgled and patted her face. "Wet again!" Katie sighed, then nuzzled the soft neck. "But you were a sweet girl not to fuss. Let's get you changed and have some dinner."

Melissa, who cramped painfully a day or two when her flow started, was, at Katie's insistence, having an easy day, sipping hot ginger tea as she hemmed the five yards of her dress skirt, which now lacked only trim. Katie had only gotten as far as gathering the waist on her own gown. She'd helped Melissa with buttonholes and setting in the sleeves and collar, but once Melissa's dress was done, Katie could concentrate on her own. They had to start Rosie's flannels, too. With the coming of September, nights were growing cool.

Jed, after carrying plenty of wood and kindling down to the grate, had gone to help

Nacho cut wood to pack into town next day. Nacho had made a pair of connected canvas cases to fit on either side of a horse behind a saddle. These held milk and butter, and there was room on top to secure a bag of squashes and chilies or roasting ears. Jed and Melissa took turns accompanying Nacho and got proprietary pleasure in selling Home Mountain's products — enough, Katie hoped, to give Jed sufficient pride of ownership to combat the allure of hiring on with Larrimore in a few years.

What did the rancher intend to do about them? Katie wondered as she changed the baby and prepared her bottle. He probably thought she'd get tired of the endless work and responsibility and give up. No man in his senses would lightly run afoul of Bill Radnor. Surely, though, the longer the Mac-Leods survived and the older she got, the weaker his pretext for guardianship would be.

A seventeen-year-old more frequently than not was a mother and mistress of a household. Katie would turn seventeen the sixth of October, just a month from now. If Larrimore was going to carry out his threat, it seemed to her that he'd have to do it soon.

Should she tell Bill about Larrimore's threat? Katie chewed her lip as she handed Rosie to Melissa to feed and dished up their own quick dinner, left over from last night, fresh corn stewed with squash, peppers, and ground acorns. During August, they had gathered five bushels of several kinds of acorns Nacho had told them were good for eating. These made a tasty addition to their food and cost nothing but labor. Katie's satisfaction in this feat dimmed as she wrestled with whether or not to tell Bill about Larrimore's intentions.

Her head throbbed as if a searing mass expanded and contracted in the back of her skull. It blotted out the sound of hoofs till Melissa half-rose to peer out the window. "It's Bill!" she cried. Forgotten were her cramps, though she did place Rosie on her blanket and prop her bottle before dashing outside.

Katie followed, torn by contradictory feelings, joyful to see him yet tormented over whether she should confide in him. The key lay in how long the rancher would leave her undisturbed. There was no way of telling.

At the sight of Bill, the writhing muddle left her mind. All she could think was how lightly he swung down from Shadow, how lithe and graceful he was, unlike many horsemen who lumbered when unmounted. Though she knew they were given to a child, Katie envied the hug and kiss he gave Melissa before he caught her own hands and gazed down at her, black head tilted, eyes the shade of the autumn-hazed mountains.

"By the Lord, Katie! If you're not as pretty as green grass after a drouth!" He nodded at the bundle tied behind his saddle, leafless limbs sticking out of burlap wrappings. "Up in the high country of the Mogollon Rim, trees are already bare. I got these off a Mormon settler. Two apples, two pears. It may be a good thing I had 'em behind me as I came down through the reservation because the Apaches thought I was crazy. They don't hurt crazy folks even when they're all riled up like they are now over the Dreamer getting killed."

"The Dreamer?" Katie echoed. "The one who raised up the spirits of the great chiefs?"

"The same. He told his people better times were coming and that their dead would return to life if they joined with him in a kind of Wheel Dance. So many Apaches from different bands were joining him that the agent and army commander at Fort Apache sent for him to come in and talk. When he didn't, the army went after him. He agreed to go peacefully, but his followers were angry and kept harassing the troops. When they began to make camp, some Apache scouts mutinied and started firing on the troopers. The Dreamer was killed in the skirmish. That was late in

August. So there's been hell to pay. Three soldiers and four civilians killed within a few miles of the fort, ranches attacked, more people killed, and even Fort Apache was under fire for a couple of hours, which sure isn't the Apache way of fighting. Just about never attack forts."

"Did — did you see any Apaches?"

"No, but I felt them. And you can bet they saw me. I didn't hear about the trouble till I met an army patrol, and by then it was just as risky to go back as ride ahead."

"I — I wish they hadn't killed the Dreamer." Katie thought of Jesus. "I don't think any good can come from bothering with people's religion."

"Well, after Nana's raid, the Apaches are stirred up and the army's nervous. At least three of the scouts who fired on the soldiers are going to be tried, and they'll certainly hang." He shook his head. "The Dreamer was one of the first scouts General Crook enlisted when he was in command in this territory last time. Up till now, the White Mountain Apaches have usually gotten along pretty well with the whites. After all, they didn't get hustled out of their home country like the Chiricahuas and Nana's Mimbres. They're mad now, though. I sure wouldn't care to be living up close to the reservation." Apparently noticing Melissa's frightened face, he turned to study the trees. "Reckoned they'd grow just fine between the garden and the corral. Won't give Rosie much shade next year, and no fruit, but in a couple more years, they ought to do both."

Relief that he'd come safely through banished Katie's headache. Whyever he hadn't been to see them, it wasn't because he'd forgotten them, didn't care. Overwhelmed with thankfulness that he was alive, Katie threw her arms around his neck as far as she could reach — and planted a kiss on his throat, which was all she could attain, even on tiptoe.

He froze, took a quick step back. Katie felt his arms tense, knew he was about to inflict the ultimate humiliation of disengaging himself. Blushing, she hastily drew back, only too aware of Melissa's glare.

"That's — that's so good of you, Bill!" She tried to sound normal, but her words rushed, tumbled out breathless. "But you shouldn't have gone to so much trouble and traveled through the reservation. You'll have to let us pay you."

Melissa nodded, demanding his attention. "We've been selling butter and milk and vegetables, Bill, so we have money."

"Glad to hear it in case I need a loan," he chuckled. "But the trees are an investment.

I'm sure countin' on eatin' pies made out of the fruit. Speakin' of food, don't I smell something tasty?"

"It'll be better with biscuits." With the night cool lingering inside through the shortening days, it was no longer uncomfortable to build up the fire at noon, though to enhance Bill's dinner, Katie would gladly have done so on the hottest day. "I'll get them baking while you take care of Shadow." When Melissa seemed inclined to stay and chat with Bill, Katie said more sharply than she intended, "If you'll get the fire going, M'liss, I can start right in mixing biscuits."

Melissa thrust out her lower lip. Before she could argue, Bill said heartily, "While you ladies are working so hard, I can dig at least one tree hole. Do you trust me to locate your orchard?"

They both nodded. "It'll be special for you to plant the trees," Melissa said. "Anyway, you'll have to dig where the rocks come up easiest. We didn't fetch all the rocks in the wall from the creek, you know."

"The way you're talkin' I sure hope there's butter to go with the biscuits," grinned Bill.

"There will be," promised Katie.

"And cream for your coffee," added Melissa.

An hour later, Bill finished his sixth biscuit,

third bowl of stew, and sighed contentedly as he thanked Melissa for another cup of coffee. Melissa seemed to have forgotten all about her cramps, Katie thought sourly, though she knew her sister was no malingerer.

After raking coals to one side for the Dutch oven and building up the fire at the back to create more embers, Melissa had run out to "help" Bill get one pear tree planted. When she'd finished her stew and biscuits, she'd flourished her new dress at Bill, showing where the trim would go, and put on a pair of scarlet hose that showed when she modeled her scalloped new boots.

"Real fancy heels," Bill praised. "Sounds like you young 'uns stretched Jed's money till it squealed."

Thus encouraged, Melissa brought forth the red flannel and lavish edging. "See, we'll make Rosie some warm winter gowns, and there should be enough of this scrumptious embroidery to use around the hems of two of them." Holding the vivid soft material to her cheek, Melissa said rapturously, "Katie and I'll get petticoats! With flounces!"

"Melissa Jane MacLeod!" Katie was sure she had turned as red as the flannel and blurted before she could stop herself, "Are you going to show him your garters?"

"Katie! You — you mean old copper-headed rattlesnake!" Eyes brimming, Melissa tossed the flannel on a chair and started to bolt, but Bill rose and pulled her to him, patting her shoulder.

"It's all right, honey. Your big sis just wants you to act like a lady, but shucks, I'm family." Above the bright, bowed head, his gaze reproved Katie; she wanted to sob and run away, too, especially when he teased Melissa gently, "I'll sure watch when you wear your new dress to see if I can't spy just a bit of that flounce. Now if you could pour me some more of that good coffee —"

Sniffing but vindicated, Melissa did so. Shamed, feeling unjustly put in the wrong, Katie, stiff-backed, marched out to give the soap a good stirring and heap more wood beneath the grate.

Why, why, did she say childish things like that when she wanted Bill to think she was grown-up? *Because you aren't grown-up!* jeered part of her mind. *You're jealous of M'liss, jealous that Bill pets her when he jerked back from you like you had cholera! You couldn't get your arms around him and you couldn't kiss anything but his neck — if he'd wanted you to kiss him, he'd have bent down so you could. For goodness sake, quit fussing at your sister! Try to act like someone who'll be seventeen next month.*

Katie blotted more than steam from her face

before she went inside, cleared the table, and began to wash the dishes. In a lull of Melissa's chatter, Katie asked, "Is there any news about Nana?"

"You haven't heard?" Bill asked, amazed.

"No one's gone to town in a week, and we haven't had any visitors since then."

"You are behind the times," said Bill. "By now, Nana must be holed up snug and safe in the Sierra Madre. Faded across the border like smoke about a week before the Dreamer was killed. Lots of times that wily old fellow was as close as eight miles to the different bunches of troopers that were after him. Victorio's avenged."

Katie thought of James Corrigan and the scouts. "The Apaches killed a lot of soldiers?"

"About five from the best count. During the two months the army chased him, they fought seven real battles. Nana must have covered three thousand miles, struck at least a dozen ranches and settlements, and left at least thirty civilians dead, more than likely others, travelers, who'll never be found."

The menacing, ever-present weight that Katie had tried to ignore lifted from her now, but she was stunned at the havoc wreaked by such a small party and the futility of the army's efforts. "Did Nana lose many warriors?"

"He never left dead or wounded so there's

no telling, but chances are he didn't lose a tithe of those he killed."

Melissa's eyes went wide. "You mean he'll just hide in Mexico till he wants to raid here again?"

"Nana's old. He's avenged his son-in-law and can rest content. But there are younger war chiefs in his band. And you can bet the reservations are buzzing over his success and worked up over the Dreamer's killing." He glanced unhappily from Katie to Melissa and down at Rosie, who had fallen asleep. "If anything happened to you kids, I'd never forgive myself."

"We'd have built without your help," Katie said. Did he remember how up on the mountain he'd showed her the world? "But whatever we patched up wouldn't have been much shelter in an attack. Thanks to you, we have good, thick walls and all of us can shoot."

"Likely it won't come to that." Bill rose and stretched. "There are lots easier ways to Mexico than by here." He brightened. "Given a little time, General Crook can probably straighten out conditions at the reservation and convince the leaders that their people will be better off there than chased by soldiers on both sides of the border."

There was a hint of sadness in his voice. Katie turned toward him, impelled to ask, "If

376

you were an Apache, would you stay on the reservation?"

"No. And I'd kill every white-eye who got in my way."

"Bill!" Melissa shivered, pausing with a bowl and dishtowel in her hands.

"Forget it, honey." He ruffled tendrils escaped from her single braid. "Most Apaches aren't as mean as I am. Say, I hope you gals haven't stoked me so full that I can't dig those other tree holes."

Pulling on his hat, he ambled out, leaving his gunbelts on the table. Silence deepened between the sisters. Melissa's chin jutted at an unforgiving angle. Why do I have to be the one to make up first? Katie thought with a wave of resentment. M'liss didn't have any business to prance around like that, bragging about our petticoats, kicking up her foot so Bill could see her heel and those red hose, too!

But mentioning garters was certainly worse. Swallowing hard, Katie opened her mouth and said so. Melissa didn't melt. "You — you don't like for Bill to pay me any attention!" she accused. "You're a nasty, jealous cat!"

Startled, for this was the first time Melissa had ever refused to make peace, Katie stared at her sister, who avoided her eyes. Drying the last cutlery, Melissa hung up the towel and ran outside.

"I'll move the rocks out of your way," she called to Bill. Soon they were talking and laughing. Blindly, Katie dumped the dishwater and went down to test the thickness of the soap. It was clever of Melissa not to let Bill know she harbored a grudge. That way, his sympathies would be on her side. It wasn't fair, not fair at all!

The ropy, sullenly bubbling concoction had thickened to the consistency of gluey mud. The fire was ashes and shards of charcoaled limbs that glowed red as the wind fanned them. The kettle was far too big and hot to pour from. Katie longed to go watch Bill plant the trees. She was starved for the sight of him, the deep vibration of his voice that permeated her like rain laving thirsty soil, refreshing each nerve and fiber till she felt she was only truly, completely alive when she was with him.

Tantalized by knowing she could fill her senses with him just by passing into Rosie's yard — and Melissa had been so hateful that she didn't deserve consideration — Katie battled the yearning. It was no use telling herself that she had as much right as Melissa to pleasure in his company. She wouldn't be able to enjoy it with her younger sister so resentful. Best get on with the soap making. Katie could certainly have used help, but she resolved not to call Melissa.

Rosie might wake up and wriggle into some disaster, so Katie went to the house and moved her into the box Nacho had made from beautifully grained hand-polished mesquite when she outgrew her first one. This box had carrying handles cut into each end, slanting sides about two feet high, and rounded rims and edges. Rosie made a few sleepy sounds when Katie settled her, but her afternoon nap was still a long one. Besides, Melissa would hear her if she cried, so Katie could give her full attention to her task.

The big cast-iron ladle already leaned against one of the benches that held the molds. Katie got the milk buckets and the outside washstand. Setting the stand close to the grate, Katie placed the buckets on it and covered them with cheesecloth secured by rocks. The iron handle of the ladle would heat immediately. Katie wrapped it with an old cloth and began to scoop up the steaming liquid and pour it into a bucket, compelled to stop and scrape off the cheesecloth when it became clogged with rind, petals, mint, and bone. When one bucket was about two-thirds full, Katie used rags to protect her hands as she poured it into the other bucket for a second straining. The bane of homemade soap was bits of dark, scratchy matter that rubbed into the laundry you were trying to do, or rasped your skin.

This twice-strained liquid, now cooling, poured sluggishly into the molds. Nacho had used the two from home as models to fashion three more, and Katie had also lined all the cream pans.

It was slow, tedious work. In spite of a playful breeze, sweat beaded Katie's eyebrows and trickled between her breasts and her aching shoulders, plastering sleeves and bodice to her flesh. Still, she could smell roses and mint and there were no ugly little flecks in the soap, only petals and sprigs of mint. Best of all, the first poured lot was congealing, turning opaque at the edges.

Katie was exhausted when she finished, but there was enough soap left on the sides and bottom of the kettle and buckets and hardening in the cheesecloth strainers to do tomorrow's washing if it was kept fluid. Sighing as she picked up the buckets, Katie wondered if Bill had planted the last tree. Drawing water from the well, she dumped it into the kettle along with the cloths that she used to wash the inside of the big iron pot. Several more buckets rinsed off the last of the soap; a tub turned upside down protected the sudsy water from leaves, twigs, and whatever might fall into it.

There! Katie stepped back and moved weary shoulders to unkink the knots. She had a start on wash day, and praise be, the soap *was* hardening. Even after Bride had her share, there'd be plenty for the family and about a dozen bars to sell.

She didn't hear Bill till he whistled softly. "Holy smoke, Katie! You opening up a soap factory? How in blazes did you fill those molds without scaldin' yourself down to the pin-feathers?"

No doubting the concern in his voice and eyes. He didn't think she was terrible — or at least not too terrible. Blinking, Katie sternly controlled the impulse to throw herself into his arms and have a good, thorough, all-out cry instead of the smothered snufflings and leaking tears that occasionally escaped her when she was alone. Such a relief it would be to cling to him as Melissa had, face pressed against his heart! But that would be acting like the child she was trying to convince him that she wasn't.

"I ladled the soap into a bucket and poured it out of that," she said. "It took a long time, but it wasn't particularly hard. Did you get all the trees planted?"

"It took a long time." His tone was solemn, though laughter sparkled in his eyes. "But it wasn't particularly hard." His grin flashed and he dropped his mimicry, showing her his hands. Blisters had broken and she noticed that his boots were badly scuffed. "My hands don't fit a spade anymore. I can't believe you plowed that ground, Katie! A jumble of rocks with dratted little soil holdin' them together!" He rubbed his back and grimaced. "Sure reminded me of why I don't want to be a farmer. But the roots are in good and deep, I brought up loam from the creek, and there's durn near enough rocks to build another wall. Melissa tossed the little ones over the wall, and I dumped the big ones."

"Maybe I can get Nacho to start a house with them," Katie said in sudden inspiration. "He swears that tent is fine, but I'd feel better if he had something solid with a proper roof."

"If he piled it up by the garden, he'd already have one wall raised." Bill hesitated and looked at her searchingly. "Are you all right, Katie? Sisters are bound to have these little tussles, I guess."

"*Sisters* do." Unable to conceal her woe, Katie turned her head and stared at the glimmering creek without really seeing it. "The trouble is, I need to be some kind of mother to M'liss. I — I'm just not wise or kind or old enough!"

In spite of all her efforts, she ended in despairing sobs that, because she was trying to suppress them, wrenched her whole body. Catching up her skirts, she started to run. Bill stepped in front of her. Her cheek did fit above the strong, solid beat of his heart. One arm was around her shoulders; the other cradled her head.

"Poor, brave little darlin'." Bill's soft words were muffled in her hair. "Listen! Even grown-up real mothers flare up and bite their kids' heads off a sight worse than you do. After all, they're human."

"They can do it because they are mothers," Katie lamented.

"And you have to do better?" The deep, strong rhythm of Bill's heart and the rumbling of his voice were blessedly comforting. What a wonderful father he'd be — not cold and harsh like her father, if he had been that. Bill shook her gently. "It's a miracle the way you've managed. Raised a garden in spite of drouth, paid off the start folks gave you before you'd take money for your butter and stuff, held your little family together — why, you've done fine, honey!"

Honey! That was what he called Melissa. This embrace was under false pretenses, and though the child in Katie craved to linger, savor the bliss of his closeness, the woman in her rejected caresses given to console an orphan girl.

Moving away was like tearing flesh from frozen metal. "You've been wonderful to us."

Katie was astonished that her words didn't crack, even managed a small laugh. "So have Bride and John — so has everyone. With so much help, we *had* to prove we were worth helping."

Why did he look at her that way, lines deepening between his straight dark eyebrows? "Katie," he said. "Oh, my pretty Katie!"

A current pulsed between them, a force that drew like a magnet, questing, primeval, heedless of reason. Lightheaded, though her legs were suddenly heavy and molten, Katie couldn't breathe.

Helpless, she closed her eyes and waited. His hand brushed her waist before it jerked away. A stifled sound burst from him, but when he spoke, it was lightly. "Come inspect your orchard, ma'am. If it suits you, I'd better be riding."

Dashed from heights of believing with her body and senses that he must surely see her as more than a waif, Katie couldn't face him. A hot tide rose to the edges of her hair. Had she been mistaken?

No! That magical flow between them was still there. If she could have been sure that it was only her age that disturbed Bill, Katie would have ventured rashly; but what if he'd withdrawn because he cared for some other woman?

Forcing a smile, Katie said, "You'll stay to supper, won't you? Nacho and Jed will be home any minute. They'd like to see you. And we'll have roasting ears — with butter."

"You're mighty tempting." As soon as it was out, his eyes changed, but he gave a chuckle. "I'm supposed to meet Sheriff Breakenridge in Galeyville, though. Never a good idea to keep a deputy waiting. Gives them time to think of all kinds of things better let lie."

The trees were planted where they'd have room to grow without crowding. Touching a bare branch, Katie said, "I can hardly wait till spring. How lovely they'll look when they're in bloom! And to get fruit, too. It's almost too much."

"I can think of other things useful and pretty." Bill's grin was his familiar devil-may-care one. "Just you remember, I get some pie!"

"You'll get the first ones," Melissa promised, coming out the door with Rosie in her arms. She walked with Katie to watch Bill toss his saddle on Shadow, and both of them waved him off.

When he paused, flourishing his hat, on the last knoll from which he could be seen, Melissa said, "My cramps are a lot better, Katie. Thanks for letting me rest this morning.

And for — for letting me help Bill plant the orchard. Just to get even a little, I've cleaned the roasting ears. They're ready to boil as soon as Nacho and Jed get home. You come in and rest from that horrid, sticky work, and if you'll watch Rosie, I'll milk and get supper.

Because Bill had brought the trees, because he had planted them, four spindly bare-branched trees had been transformed into a dream of bounty, succulent red and golden fruits nestling in luxuriant green leaves. But trees grew — and so did girls.

Hugging both her sisters at once, Katie said, laughing, "I haven't broken anything, M'liss! I'll help with the milking. But you know, it'll be plain heaven not to worry about cooking after stirring that soap so long!"

"That's what I thought," Melissa nodded. With Rosie murmuring happily, they went inside together.

Weary though she was, Katie played the harp late that night, making the music express her longing for Bill and her love. Nacho said to her softly, "Your harp, tonight she is a woman, Katie. First she is joyful and then she is weeping."

XV

As pale yellow kernels lost their savory milkiness and matured to firm gold, hardening the shucks, the feasts of roasting ears and stewed green corn were over. Stripped of leaves carried, after they dried, into the shed for fodder, the naked stalks were topped by curing ears that would later be shucked in front of the fire on winter nights and ground into meal in the small steel handmill.

Nacho built a deep, wide trough down one side of the cellar. Here, melons and squash were placed in sand to keep as long as possible and would be joined by some of the pumpkins after these finished ripening. Others would be cut in chunks and hung up to dry from the kitchen rafters, joining strings of red and green chilies and bundles of wild mint, Mormon tea, and *cota,* all of which made excellent tea.

They had already eaten all the chokecherries they'd gathered in July, but the rains had plumped the ripening wild grapes up the canyon and the hackberries along the washes. Dried, they would give a taste of tart sweetness and could be stewed into corn meal and molasses for a sort of pudding. Black walnuts and piñon nuts would soon be ready, and little by little, the hay in the shed mounted up as cut grass cured and was hauled in. If Katie could help it, none of their animals would go hungry that winter when snow was on the ground.

It still wasn't quite necessary to have a fire at night for comfort, but they all sat closer to the hearth now while Rosie, in one of her new red flannel gowns, played or napped in her mesquite box till she announced with increasing loudness that she needed a change, milk, or just some loving.

Katie and Melissa mended or sewed, a kerosene lamp between them. Jed cracked acorns or hulled beans till Ace beguiled him into a rough-and-tumble, and Nacho mended gear or stitched at the tiny moccasins he was making for Rosie. Old face cragged with shadows, he told of magic hills in the Yaqui country, where one could enter and receive the gift of singing, prospering, being lucky in love or war, anything you chose. "But you do not go to hell or heaven when you die then," he explained. "Your soul belongs to the enchanted world." He conjured serpents with rainbows on their foreheads, wild sheep possessing powers flowing from *yo aniyo,* the "ancient and honorable realm" that existed even before prophets and angels sang the boundaries of the Yaqui land. He also beguiled them with stories of the nuns for whom he had worked in Tucson.

"Ambrosia, Emerentia, Monica, Euphrasia, Maxine, Hyacinth, and Martha." He named them with smiling, half-rueful tenderness. "Tucson welcomed them with fireworks, the ringing of bells, and an eagerness that helped the sisters open a school less than two weeks after they arrived."

"They must have been good teachers," Katie praised. "Your English is better than ours."

"I wanted to learn. They taught me." Nacho grinned. "Their regular students had twenty-nine subjects. I'm grateful that I didn't have to study natural and intellectual philosophy and how to make artificial flowers and fruit. Katie, do you suppose you could play a song on your harp if I hum it for you first?"

Most evenings, she did play for half an hour or so before bedtime, while Melissa rocked the baby and gave her what they hoped was her last bottle till morning. Katie didn't want to forget any of her mother's songs or any of those of that Mary MacLeod, far back in time, who'd made her songs standing in her door, "neither within the house nor without," thwarting the law. Melissa still had no wish to play, but perhaps Rosie one day would, perhaps a child of her own —

Ever since she met Bill, Katie evoked him

as she lay down to sleep. To begin with, she'd relive that first time she saw him on his tall gray horse, head thrown back, eyes shining like storm clouds with sun behind them. After he took her on top of the mountain — would they ever go there again? — she'd summoned up that moment when awareness flowed between them, when she'd believed for a heart-stopped moment that he'd take her in his arms. Then came dancing with him on the Fourth of July. Now she remembered the sound of his heart beneath her cheek, the melting strength of his arms. *"My pretty Katie,"* she heard him say, his words sweeter than any notes of her harp. *"Oh, my pretty Katie!"*

The sensible part of her mind warned her that it was foolish, useless, and dangerous to love Bill Radnor. He could be killed any minute or drift with the wind, answer the lure of some new frontier. Worst of all, he saw life as a game, played for thrills and fun.

He didn't seem to take his Roofless Adobe Ranch any more seriously than the name sounded. No way at all could she imagine him behind a plow or milking cows, except as a one-time joke in Bride's dress and sunbonnet. As for his being a miner, Katie winced at the thought of him disappearing into a dark hole, out of the sun and wind that seemed his element. He would scuff his handstitched boots and wear blisters on his hands to plant a few trees for the family he'd so carelessly yet effectively succored, but it was impossible to picture him ever planting a whole orchard.

It all came down to dreaming. Dreams sweeter to Katie than the reality of any other man could ever be. Strange. Though she blushed when she fleetingly allowed herself to imagine beyond the ravishing enchantment of a kiss, she knew she'd love anything Bill wanted to do. Shy and awkward she would surely be, but he could teach her and she longed to be taught, to become his woman, shaped and made one with him by his loving alone.

When Larrimore intruded in her thoughts, though, she was terrified at what she feared he might try to do. Even if he didn't force her, even if he allowed her to escape, she froze at what would go before. She would feel dirty if he touched her, degraded and *owned,* as if he'd seared her flesh with his cruel brand. Never, never, no matter what happened would she live in his house!

Though the menace of him worried her more than had Nana, Katie tried not to think about him, assuring herself that he wouldn't risk trouble with Bill. All she could do was hope that the rancher valued his connection with Bill too much to lose it.

One morning, Shiloh was nowhere to be seen, but Nacho found fresh tracks that he didn't think were made by the other Steel Dusts who were grazing up the canyon.

"Shod, so the horses belonged to white men," Nacho said. "I will follow on Chica, Katie, and see what has happened." He frowned. "I cannot think that anyone in Galeyville would steal from you."

"It could be Larrimore." Katie chewed her lip. "I think I'll ride toward his ranch and find out. My friend, it's best you stay here. No cowboy will shoot me, but they'd kill you."

Reluctantly, the old man nodded. "Some don't count Mexicans or Indians in their killings. But Katie, don't go to the ranch itself. Should Señor Larrimore take it in his head to make you prisoner, it could lead to many deaths."

"Let me come," Jed implored. "If we run into trouble, I'll streak for Galeyville and bring help."

"That is where you should go in the first place," said Nacho grimly.

"I don't want to cause a fight," Katie said. "I hope we can get Shiloh back without either John or Bill hearing about it."

Nacho got a hackamore on Red Rover and

led him into the corral, going to fetch the rifle and shotgun while Katie and Jed caught and saddled Jenny and Chili. Jenny, Shiloh's mother, might scent her independent young son, or he her, and they might try to get to each other. When Melissa ran out, holding Rosie, to learn what was happening, they hastily explained, thrust their weapons in the scabbards, and were on their way, not attempting to follow tracks on the rocky ground because, inexpert as they were, that would slow them up inordinately.

"What if we don't catch up before we get to the Pitchfork?" Jed asked.

"We'll worry about that if it happens that way," Katie returned briefly.

It occurred to her, chillingly, that Larrimore might have planned on her following. Perhaps he thought if he had her in his house, he could persuade her to move in — or he might intend more than persuasion, believing that if he forced her, she'd be too ashamed and broken to do anything but accept his "protection."

Scanning the rolling flat for a glimpse of riders, Katie feared they were too late. From the tracks, Nacho thought Shiloh had been stolen before dawn, at least an hour ago, by three or four men who had found him grazing at a distance from the other horses.

Though Katie and Jed rode as fast as they

could without recklessly endangering their mounts, the gilded blue of the Peloncillos didn't seem much nearer, but they were gaining on Cienega Peak, its stony side washed white by sun. Larrimore claimed all the land from there to Mexico, the whole San Simon Valley that stretched between the Chiricahuas and that humped chain of mountains across the New Mexico line. His headquarters was over there someplace on the river — the river that he'd dammed so that it had been dry when the MacLeods journeyed that way.

Suddenly, Jenny threw back her head, drinking the wind, and gave a long, carrying whicker. Katie's eye caught motion as horsemen rode out of a wash. Jenny whickered again. There was an answer, faint with the wind against it.

Katie and Jed loosened the reins to give Jenny and Chili their heads as they galloped toward the knot of riders surrounding Shiloh, held by a halter improvised from a rope. Pulling up, Katie centered the Winchester on Shell Brown, the green-eyed Pitchfork foreman. "We'll have our horse, Mr. Brown."

The thick-bodied blond man grinned. "Jeff! Milt!" he called to two of the three riders behind him. "Settle your loops over this pair. We'll tie 'em in their saddles and send 'em home."

Jed pulled out the shotgun, pointed it at the cowboy who'd reached for the rope coiled at his saddle horn. The man froze. "Go ahead, Milt!" snarled the foreman. "The kids won't shoot."

Katie's lucky shot knocked off his hat. Levering in a new cartridge, she said, "I'll shoot you first, Mr. Brown."

The green eyes blazed. His hand was on his revolver before he jerked it away and swore. "You know we can't kill a boy and a half-grown woman!"

"I'm glad to hear it since you don't mind stealing from them. Did Ed Larrimore really think we wouldn't try to get Shiloh back?"

"He thought you'd run to —" Shell bit off the sneering answer. "The boss thought you'd come calling," he shrugged. "And that once you saw the Pitchfork, you'd decide livin' there soft and easy beat slavin' away on that little back-pocket spread of yours."

What he meant was that he'd tried to provoke a confrontation. She feared one or the other would be killed, and even if Bill shot the rancher, more than likely Larrimore's men would get him the next instant — unless Bill rode to the Pitchfork with a small army of his own. Katie had a horror of men dying because of her. All because Larrimore couldn't stand to have the MacLeods' small ranch over in this far corner of what he considered his domain! For a moment, she thought it would serve him right to get killed, but then she remembered Hallie, who'd be left with no parent at all, and young, likable Beau Murphree.

"Well, you can just tell Mr. Larrimore that he can't scare us," said Katie and laughed with fierce, challenging joy. "You're right — you can't gun us down, but we can certainly shoot you if you try to keep us from taking Shiloh. Jed, ride in and get him."

Shotgun across the saddle, Jed rode to Shiloh, reached for the rope. The cowboy holding it glanced at Shell. "Boss?"

Shell spat. "The brats have us in a tight. No use anyone gettin' hurt right now."

Jed took the rope and led Shiloh toward his mother, who nuzzled him anxiously. His nostrils flared red and he was sweaty, but he hadn't been hurt.

Veins pulsed in the foreman's temples. "Radnor's primed you kids to murder — and you won't always be kids." Menace filled his voice, but after a last hard stare, he swung his horse, snatched up his riddled hat, and started east.

Katie and Jed watched till the men faded into the distance, their presence betrayed only by an occasional glimmer of metal reflecting sun. Jed leaned over and stroked Shiloh.

"Ready to go home, boy?"

For once, Shiloh was glad to stay near his mother. As they jogged toward the ranch, Katie frequently glanced over her shoulder. When she caught Jed doing the same thing, their eyes held before they burst into laughter that on Katie's part, at least, was almost hysterical.

"This is one time that being kids came in handy!" she gasped.

Grudgingly, Jed nodded. "When I tell Uncle Jack —"

"You mustn't! Don't tell anyone!" As Jed stared, Katie leaned over to grip his arm. "I think Larrimore wants to provoke Bill Radnor into riding up to Pitchfork headquarters all set for a fight — and I doubt that fight would be a fair one."

Jed blinked. "But what if Mr. Larrimore tries something else? If he'd steal our horse —"

"He was trying to make something happen, Jed. Maybe he'll quit when he knows we won't be bait for him and that he can't bluff us."

"What if he doesn't quit?"

"We'll worry about it then. For now, Jed, keep still about this. We don't want our friends getting hurt on our account."

"We sure don't," Jed agreed, and they rode along in silence.

Katie knew how furious Larrimore must be at the failure of his plan. Fortunately, she worked too hard and slept too soundly to torment herself endlessly over a hazard she could do nothing about. It was a little like the risk of an Apache raid. One might come and completely shatter this home and security, but it would be useless to let that hovering peril haunt autumn days as crisp and delicious as the apples John Diamond brought on his way back from a gambling sortie to the booming town of Globe.

He brought sobering news, too. President Garfield had died September nineteenth without ever leaving his bed after he was shot in early July. Chester A. Arthur was now president, and it was said he was so outraged by the lawlessness in Cochise County that he was thinking of asking Congress to authorize the use of troops to restore order.

"Not that the troopers don't have enough on their plates, what with the White Mountain Apaches still furious over the way their prophet was killed." Diamond scowled, and Katie knew he must be thinking of his son. "Most of them surrendered after more troops were brought in, but some of the fiercest — unreconstructed, I guess you might call them — are hiding in those mountains. Trying to comb them out would be like reaching into a den of rattlers."

He had other surprises in his saddlebags, several McGuffey's readers, a big geography with fascinating engravings and maps, an arithmetic, a Webster's dictionary and speller, and unbelievable luxury, books to read for pleasure! *"Ben Hur*'s by Lew Wallace, the governor of New Mexico, who probably spent a lot more time writing the book than he did in trying to stem the Lincoln County War. His wife hates the territory so much that she's suggested that Mexico should be forced to take it back. It's amusing that the governor chose to write about ancient Rome rather than Billy the Kid or that range war, but you'll enjoy the chariot races."

Giving the fat volume to Melissa, he handed Jed another one. "This is Mark Twain's *Tom Sawyer*. Don't let it give you any pesky ideas, my lad." The last book, *Scottish Chiefs* by Jane Porter, was placed in Katie's hands.

"A fitting book for Clan MacLeod," Diamond laughed. "I was lucky to chance into a schoolteacher who'd decided to give it up and start prospecting. The books had to go to help build up his grubstake."

Overwhelmed, Katie opened the book, and saw so many words she didn't know that she gave a rueful shake of her head. "It's wonderful to have all the books, John, but I'm afraid it'll be a long time before we can read the stories."

"I'll wager you'll surprise yourselves," he said. "When winter comes and you won't have much outside work, you can study the school books a few hours every day. Feed me dinner and I'll come once or twice a week to help you along. At night, you can take turns reading to each other. There's the dictionary for words you don't know. By time for spring planting, I'd bet you — if I didn't know how disapproving you are of bets, Katie — that you'll have finished all these books and be ready for more."

"I would like to study, too," said Nacho. "The sisters taught me to speak, but I can only write my name and cannot read."

Admonished by the fact that an old man born to a different language was willing to work at learning more of hers than was necessary, Katie said, "We'll do our best."

One morning as Katie started down to the shed to milk, she saw something white moving on a distant slope to the south. "Is that a wagon, M'liss?" she called, shading her eyes.

Melissa peered outside. "Don't know what else it could be." They watched for a few minutes, but it seemed to have stopped. Melissa pointed. "Look! A bunch of horses way over there! And there's some riders!"

Their father had never run more cattle than he could easily brand himself, but on their way west that spring, the MacLeods had passed a good dozen branding outfits, most of them with a canvas-covered chuckwagon far enough from the commotion to keep dust out of the cook's supplies and pans.

In a breath, the sisters gasped, "It has to be a roundup!"

Who could it be but Larrimore? Katie's neck prickled as she strained to see. There sat the wagon and those horses had to be the *remuda*, the extra horses, for during the intense, heavy work of roundup, riders often changed horses three or four times a day.

Of course, Pitchfork cattle wandered up the canyons and into the mountains for water and shade. Perhaps a camp was really needed at that location, but telling herself that didn't ease the all-gone sensation in Katie's stomach. Setting up a camp this close to Home Mountain Ranch was clear notice that Larrimore regarded this whole range as his.

Surely, though, after the way she and Jed had rescued Shiloh, the rancher wouldn't try to take the MacLeods' horses and cattle. As if they liked the protection of the north ridge of mountains stretching out into the flats, the livestock kept pretty much between them and the creek, grazing both sides of the stream up into Whitetail Canyon.

Since his abduction, Shiloh had kept closer to the other horses. Only Prince Coal, inheriting an urge for solitary exploration from his mother, Cinders, ever wandered in the direction of the intruders. Even if the Guernseys hadn't worn the Running M that James MacLeod had dreamed of seeing on vast herds, there was no way the fine-faced, delicate-boned purebreds could be confused with regular range stock. The calves and colts weren't yet branded.

Swiftly making sure that all the Home Mountain animals were in sight, Katie called to Nacho, who was just emerging from his tent. "We're going to have to keep our animals on this side of the creek, Nacho. See over yonder? It must be a Pitchfork camp."

Nothing ever seemed to surprise or perturb the old Yaqui. He nodded. "Have no alarm, Katie. We will keep the herds away from Señor Larrimore's branding irons."

Stepping out for kindling, Jed heard and let out a whoop. "I'll saddle up Chili and stand guard! I better have the Winchester. I wonder if Hallie's over there."

"Of course she isn't! Her father would never let her come to a roundup. It'd be a good idea for you to be on horseback so you can chase our horses or cows back if they start wandering," Katie granted. "But you leave the rifle inside."

"Aw, Katie!"

"I mean it, Jed!" Grown men wouldn't knowingly hurt a boy, but if there was some kind of fracas, who knew what could happen? Katie, in truth, was a lot more worried that being around a camp would entrance Jed even more with being a cowboy, even if some of the Pitchfork hands had tried to steal Shiloh. If Larrimore were there, he might even manage to flatter Jed and make him think it'd be grand to live at the Pitchfork.

Sternly regarding her young brother, Katie said, "If anything happens, Jed, you let me know right away and we'll decide what to do. Don't you even think about going off by yourself."

"You never let me have any fun!"

Katie ignored that and got on with the milking. Half-expecting Larrimore, she went about her tasks with frequent glances out the window. She was churning, feeling the particles of butter starting to come together, when she heard hoofbeats. Springing up from the churn, she ran to the door.

"It's Flossie!" Jed panted, reining up Chili. "A scrubby, ugly old bull came bellowin' across the creek." Jed knew womenfolk weren't supposed to hear about such things. He colored, stammering. "I — I tried to run him off, but he charged us. Then he — he got Flossie. And now he's hanging around, just like he owns our cows!"

Flossie was the only cow that hadn't calved that summer. Aghast at such a mate for one of the fine Guernseys brought out here with such difficulty, Katie yanked off her apron. "Don't get close to that bull, Jed, but stay in sight of our cattle. I'm going to the camp and tell them to come get that brute! Finish churning, M'liss, and don't let Rosie get off her blanket."

"Shall I go with you?" asked Nacho, who had been chopping wood.

"They won't hurt me, but if I make them mad, they might take it out on you. Just help Jed if that bull tries to drive Flossie away."

The other horses had followed Chili. It took only minutes to bridle Jenny, lead her to the stable, and toss on Pa's old saddle. Katie couldn't ride up to a bunch of men with her skirts rucked up, astride, and it wasn't terribly far. Right foot in the stirrup, she hooked her left knee around the horn and, without getting her sunbonnet, rode toward the dust and smoke by the distant wagon.

As she approached, several men were driving maybe a dozen cattle out of a small canyon.

A considerable way south, riders pursued elusive animals along the flank of a mountain. A little distance from the branding fire, several riders held a bunched herd of perhaps fifty or sixty cows and calves. Beau Murphree, in purple scarf and red shirt, sent his buckskin cutting horse into the mass. As soon as the horse knew which beast Beau wanted, he followed it through the herd, matching every dodge, skillfully edging it clear of the other animals. Once in the open, Beau swirled the loop of his rope over his head, cast it, and as the circle closed around the calf's hind legs, Beau jerked upward, tightening the rope. Sliding on his belly as the buckskin hauled him toward the fire, the calf was seized by two men who heaved him on his right side. While one cowboy planted a knee on the calf's head and twisted back its foreleg, the other sweating, dirt-streaked cowboy threw off the rope, grabbed the lower hind foot, and sat down behind the calf, bracing his boot against the upper part of the other hind leg. Beau tipped his hat to Katie and rode in for another catch.

The second the calf could no longer struggle, a brander smoothly pressed a cherry red iron on the flank. Katie's nostrils stung with the odor of scorching hair. The calf gave a piteous blat, more scared than hurt, probably, since a practiced brander seared the hide just enough to make it peel and leave a permanent mark. At the same time, another cowboy deftly nicked a bit out of the top of one ear and the bottom of the other, then used the sharp knife for the two swift cuts that made the calf a steer.

Larrimore made a mark in a small notepad as the victim lunged to his feet and was met by his anxious mother, who sniffed him, licked him, and as she led him back into the herd, cast a reproachful look at the men who'd hurt her baby.

That was when Katie noticed that the cow wasn't branded with a Pitchfork like the one her son now wore, but with a mark Katie would have called a horseshoe. She also had one ear slashed at the bottom, the other on top.

"Well, if it's not Miss Kate," drawled Larrimore, as Beau caught a full-grown cow and yanked her off her feet so the flankers could pounce on her. As the cow bawled, the iron sizzled, and the knife flashed, Larrimore made a mark and shoved back his hat from thick gray hair. "Right neighborly of you to come by. Light down — if you can — and have a cup of coffee."

Katie could scarcely believe her ears. Acting as if he hadn't sent his men to run off a Steel Dust! Ignoring that his trick hadn't worked. Angry as it made her, a cool part of her brain warned her to let it go and stick to the matter at hand. "A Pitchfork bull's over with my cows. I want you to come get him."

A heavy eyebrow rose. "I'd call it a favor, loaning you one of my bulls."

Katie's fingers dug into the reins. "You know good and well I don't want scrub range stock mixing with our purebred dairy animals! I'm getting the loan of a good Hereford from Colonel Hooker!"

He shrugged square shoulders and tallied another calf. Then, mouth quirking, he watched her with eyes the gray of sodden ash. "Missy, there's no way under God's sun to keep an old range bull away from a cow when she's ripe and ready if he's close enough to smell her. Let me tell you, girl, those critters can pick up that scent just like they do water. To them, it's damn near as important."

"One never came this way before you set up this camp! What are you doing way over here?"

"Brandin' my cattle."

"And other people's, too," Katie shot back. "I see a lot of earmarks out there that aren't like what your man cut on that calf — whose mother didn't wear your brand, either!"

"I've bought out a couple of little shirttail brands," the rancher said easily. "I'm late brandin' the calves on account of I kept the

407

men close to the ranch whilst Nana was rampagin' around. But now I'm makin' a clean sweep through here. Figger any cows this side of the mountains are mine on account of if I don't own 'em, they've probably been stolen."

Stolen! The nerve of him! But again she judged it better not to confront him over the theft of Shiloh. "Our cattle aren't stolen, and they certainly aren't yours."

"Hell, I'm not talkin' about a few dairy cows." Larrimore tallied a yearling bull calf that had dealt Beau and the flankers plenty of grief before he was thrown and subdued. "But I need every head I can chouse out of the canyons. Got a contract to deliver a thousand head to the San Carlos agency. Good time to clean out this wild stuff with other brands."

Katie knew that such "little shirttail brands" as he hadn't been able to buy out cheap, he'd run off with guns. He would certainly have done the same to the MacLeods except for Bill Radnor's protection.

Not much more subtly than one of his bulls, Larrimore radiated male dominance. Concentrated in his hard stare, it battered Katie, threatened to overwhelm her. Forcing herself to meet that almost contemptuous gaze, Katie said, "Come get your bull, Mr. Larrimore."

"I can't spare a man. Guess Cookie's helper can do it if a couple of you help head the critter this way. He gets wind of some needy cow over here and he'll plumb forget about yours." The rancher called to a red-headed boy of about fourteen, all arms and legs, who was doing the bidding of the lame, bald-headed cook and consequently subjected to a continuous flow of language hot as the branding iron. "Tom! Catch up a horse. There's a Pitchfork bull favorin' one of this young lady's pet cows. I want you should fetch him here."

Coiling the rope a flanker had just tossed off a heifer, Beau glanced wistfully at Katie before he sent the buckskin back into the herd. Tom was apparently glad to escape his camp chores and the cook's cussing for he speedily caught a spotted pony from the rope-enclosed *remuda* and hefted on a saddle.

"Girl." Larrimore's rocklike jaw set, nearly making his face a square, the flattened nose adding to that appearance. "I've let things slide, figgerin' you'd see how crazy it is for a bunch of kids to try to hold down a place out here. Looks like you're plumb hard-headed, but you better get this through your pretty noggin. One way or another, you'll be out of here by spring." Without glancing at his notepad, he made another tally.

Spine chilling from neck to tailbone, Katie whispered, "Try to take the children and I swear I'll kill you."

Those charcoal eyes flared like coals fanned by a sudden breeze. Flat nostrils swelled as he laughed. "That won't be easy, Kate. But you don't have to lose the kids. I'll buy you out anytime. You can take the youngsters and go wherever you want."

"We're already where we want to be."

He shook his massive head. "It won't do, missy." Though he hadn't seemed to be paying any attention to the branding apart from keeping the tally, he abruptly shouted, "Don't use that iron, Slim! Too hot — you'll blotch the brand." Turning back to her, he said, "You're a high-headed filly, Kate. It's kind of amusin' to watch you prance, but my patience is about used up."

Dread gripped Katie, turned her hollow inside. Reading her fear for Bill, the rancher said, "I've heard Radnor's talkin' about headin' up to Alaska, tryin' for some of that gold. What with President Arthur wantin' to send troops after rustlers and Colonel Hooker offerin' a bounty for him, Galeyville's gettin' a mite hot for roostin'." Larrimore spat into the fire, which hissed back at him. "If Radnor winters outside of hell, I'll bet it won't be here."

"We won't move. We won't sell."

He glanced toward the herd. Katie had seen three brands that weren't his, each representing someone's dream, somebody's pride and hopes. "Now where," he mused, "have I heard that before?"

Tom was waiting. Katie reined away and started for Home Mountain, too upset for conversation. "Sure is a pretty mare," ventured the young wrangler. He looked appreciatively at Señorita, who waited for her mother a safe distance from the turmoil of the roundup. "Nice filly, too. Say, ma'am, could these be Steel Dust horses?"

A nice, intelligent boy even if he did work for Larrimore. Soothed by his admiration for the horses and the fact that he'd called her "Ma'am" though she couldn't have been more than a year or two his elder, Katie smiled. "They're descended from Steel Dust and Shiloh both."

"Shiloh, too!" The boy's hazel eyes glistened. "Boy howdy, ma'am, that's the best blood there is for quarter horses. My daddy had a Steel Dust gelding once. Won a lot of races around Waco."

"You're from Texas?"

"Yes, ma'am." He still had the blunted nose of childhood, dusted with freckles, a softness to features unhoned by time and weather. His clothes were tattered, the runover boots looked too big for him, and his hat was stained till there was no guessing its original color. He looked hastily away but not before Katie saw a droplet start down his cheek. He smudged it away, gulping. "Ma died last year — fever and chills — and Pa, well, seemed like he just didn't have the heart to work the farm anymore. He'd always hankered to do a little prospecting so he headed west on our Steel Dust horse. Left me with his sister in Waco so's I could get an education."

His voice broke off. After a moment, Katie said, "Looks like you decided to follow him."

"I tried." Tears coursed unheeded now. "Struck out on my own pony about a week after he left so's when I caught up with him, he couldn't send me back. He'd said he was going to Silver City. When I came through El Paso, Nana had just killed them surveyors and jumped that stage. I was scared, let me tell you, and hid good at night, but I kept going. Found what was left of Pa along the road, him and the gelding picked to their bones. Way I knew Pa, he had a prayer book that was his mother's and it was all torn up in the bushes."

Katie's own eyes blurred. "Tom, I'm sorry —"

He didn't seem to hear. "Ground was too hard to dig. I dragged Pa into a wash and covered his bones, what the varmints hadn't dragged away."

"You didn't want to go back to your aunt?"

He shook his curly red head feelingly. "No, ma'am. Aunt Lillian, she meant well, I guess, but that week I was there she thrashed me with a willow switch seemed like every time I moved or opened my mouth. Brought blood. We never whipped a mean mule like she whipped me. I just kept riding west till I hit a Pitchfork branding camp a couple of weeks ago. They fed me good and Beau Murphree spoke for me to Mr. Larrimore." He added dolefully, "Sherm Walcott — he's the cook — is mighty hard to please, though. When I draw my pay, I'm leavin'."

Filled with sympathy for this orphan who didn't even have brothers or sisters, Katie almost said he could stay at Home Mountain, but checked herself. That wouldn't work if Melissa or Jed didn't want him, though he could certainly earn his keep. "If you're not too tired after you finish your chores tonight, why don't you come over for a little while?" she invited. "We came out here from the Nueces, so you could call us homefolks."

Tom swung toward her, tear-streaked face beaming. "I'll come, ma'am, long as Sherm don't padlock me to the bean kettle! Say, is that your place up ahead?"

With a rush of pride and thankfulness, Katie saw it as he must, the long double cabin, the substantial shed and big corral, and along the slopes above the creek, Steel Dust horses, Guernseys — and one scrubby Pitchfork bull.

"That's Home Mountain Ranch," she said. "And there's Ed Larrimore's bull. That's my brother, Jed, on the chestnut. We'll help you get that brute moving."

The bull was so reluctant to leave his new-found female that finally Katie, Jed, and Tom drove Flossie into the corral and barred the gate. Only then, snorting and occasionally charging a rider who got too close, did the bull, who was a nondescript dun color, allow himself to be headed back toward the camp.

Halfway there, as Larrimore had predicted, he paused to snuff at some intriguing scent, snuffed again, and with a swing of his tail, broke into an eager trot.

"Much obliged for the help," called Tom, waving his hat. "Don't give up on me tonight, ma'am. I'll come soon as I do the dishes!"

Jed shot his sister a puzzled glance. "You asked a Pitchfork hand to Home Mountain?" he asked as they turned homeward.

"Gracious, Jed, Tom's just a boy. And wait till I tell you about him!"

By the time she had, Jed said slowly, "Guess it's not much fun bein' a cook's helper even if you are workin' on a real ranch. Must have been awful, findin' his pa that way."

Katie nodded. After a few minutes, Jed sighed and pushed back his fall of yellow hair. "Reckon we're lucky we're together. Katie, why don't we ask him to come live with us?" Swallowing, Jed made the great concession. "He can bunk in the loft with me." Having been magnanimous, he now saw a bright side. "Say, if there were two of us menfolk, you and M'liss couldn't boss me around so much!"

Glad Jed was learning that working for the Pitchfork wasn't necessarily bliss and thinking it likely he'd be more contented at home with an older boy around, Katie said, "We'll talk about it after we get better acquainted and M'liss and Nacho get to meet him. For now, let's turn Flossie out so she can graze. I guess we'll have to watch our stock till Larrimore moves his camp."

"Was old cat-eyed Harriet with him?" Jed made an atrocious face, but there was an eagerness in his voice that made Katie hide a smile.

"Of course not, Jed. Her father's trying to raise her into a lady."

"Huh!" scoffed Jed. "She takes on airs like the queen of England, but she's just a silly, stuck-up brat. I'd like to show her my boots, though. And my saddle."

"You'll get to sometime," Katie said, swinging down to open the gate. "I hope," she murmured to Flossie as the dainty heifer with the dark shadowings on her deerlike face strolled languidly past, "that you won't have a calf by that nasty old bull."

Unsaddling, she rubbed Jenny down and turned her loose to canter back to the other horses. As always, Katie watched the horses with proud delight, but as she turned, she saw the distant haze of smoke and dust arising from the branding.

The smile died on her lips. Larrimore would push and threaten. He'd done that before. But this time she had a feeling that he wouldn't put off much longer whatever he meant to do. *"One way or another, by next spring, you'll be out of here."*

We won't, she vowed. Yet she was full of foreboding as she started for the house, and a flood of desolation swept through her as she wondered if Bill was really going to Alaska. Much better that he did, though, than be ambushed by Larrimore or someone else. Should she warn him about the rancher?

Once again, she fought it over in her mind. If she did, if Bill knew how Larrimore was crowding her, Bill would certainly have it out with the Pitchfork's owner. Spring was a long way off. She decided to wait.

XVI

It was dark, chores were done, and the family was gathering by the fireplace that evening when Ace leaped out of Jed's arms and set up a clamorous barking. From outside, a voice hailed, "It's me, ma'am! Tom Buford!"

Jed ran out to show the visitor where to hobble his pony. "I bet I won't like this Tom," sniffed Melissa. "It's too bad about his daddy getting killed and all, but most boys that age are just horrid!"

"Is that why you put on your new dress?" teased Katie. Most becoming it was, the blue bringing out the color of Melissa's eyes and a special dash added by the carefully stitched braid at the collar, sleeves, and bottom of the full, full skirt.

"Katie!" Melissa's cheeks pinked as she bent to her sewing. "I had to put it on so I could let out the bodice and hem of my old one! What do I care what a *fourteen-year-old* thinks? Boys that age are still children!"

Katie refrained from observing that thirteen-year-old girls were also children and that the nearest example had heretofore shown no interest in refurbishing the old dress. "I can't imagine that *I'll* want this Tom Buford living with us," went on Melissa. "And you just remember, Katie! He's not to be invited unless I want him, too."

"Fair enough. But give him a chance, M'liss. He's an orphan, like us."

"There you go, trying to make me feel ashamed if I don't like him," retorted Melissa, stitching so vigorously that she pricked her finger, winced, and stuck it in her mouth. "He's closest to my age, so I'm the one he'll pester and aggravate and — and —"

She pressed her lips tight together as the door opened. Tom had somehow managed to wash his face and hands and wore a somewhat cleaner shirt than that of the morning. It was clear that his Aunt Lillian had expended more effort in whipping him than in mending his clothes. The overlarge leather vest was his only garment that wasn't full of rips and holes.

Stooping to pet Ace, he gazed around the room, lit by lamp and fire, scented with crackling juniper and the good, lingering odors of stew and biscuits. He blinked when he saw Melissa, who was busily not looking at him after her first swift glance. When his eyes came to Rosie, playing in her box with a cardinal's feather Nacho had found, he tiptoed over, quietly as he could in the clumsy, over-size boots, and stared down in wonder.

"Is — *it* a yearlin'?"

418

"*She* is almost seven months old," Melissa informed him. "Can't you tell she's a girl by her face?"

"No, ma'am," he said humbly. Was he being diplomatic or did the new dress and soft light truly make Melissa look old enough to him to merit the grown-up title? Katie stifled a chuckle at the way Melissa visibly began to melt. "I don't know much about babies," he said. "But this one looks soft and pretty as a young calf's ears."

"Calf's ears!"

He reddened, searched for less offending words. "She — she's prettier'n a baby skunk. Hair's just as black and fluffy and —" Under Melissa's glare, he floundered to a halt.

Coming to his rescue, Katie said, "Tom, the baby's called Rosie and that's Melissa. And this is Señor Flores."

"I'm Nacho." The old man stretched out a welcoming hand. "Tom, you are welcome." That he spoke his good English testified that Nacho felt an immediate trust and liking for the boy.

"Pull up a chair," Katie urged. "Would you like a glass of milk?"

"Real milk?"

"Of course," interpolated Melissa. "We have a dairy."

He sipped the milk, at first responding

419

timidly to Melissa's interrogation and Katie's gentler questions. To put him more at ease, Katie played the harp a while, lively tunes she thought he'd know from Texas, "Green Grow the Rushes, Oh!," "That Is the Way with a Texian," "Here, Rattler, Here!," "Red Rosie Bush," and others. Tom listened, entranced, so obviously grateful to be in the midst of a family that Katie's heart went out to him even more.

"Let's pop some corn," she suggested, returning the harp to its corner and covering it with the ancient plaid. "Jed, please fetch the older butter from the cellar. And let's make molasses candy, too."

"Oh, it's a party!" Melissa cried, dropping her sewing and scrambling to start mixing the candy.

Tom slowly looked from one of them to the next, last of all at Rosie, now drowsing on Nacho's shoulder as the battle-and-age-scarred Yaqui patted her back. "Looks like to me," he said, "that you have a party all the time."

They crunched buttered popcorn and pulled molasses taffy amid shrieks of laughter when the candy ropes broke or stuck to someone's fingers. It was far past bedtime and Katie did at last tuck Rosie into her crib, but the jollification was such fun that no one worried about rising before dawn.

However, when Nacho, after a scary tale of a witch, rose to make his good-nights, Tom sighed and got up, too. "Best be ridin'. Sherm's already sore because I left. He'll expect me up extra early in the morning." Picking up his old hat, he seemed to fix each one of them in his mind, especially Melissa. "This was the best time I ever had in my life. I'm sure obliged to all of you for havin' me."

"Would you like to come live with us?" Melissa blurted. Flushing, she clapped her hand to her lips. "Oh, I forgot!" She looked appealingly at Nacho.

He smiled. "I hope you will join our *familia,*" he told the boy. "It is a good one."

Thunderstruck, Tom scanned their faces. "Ma'am?" he said to Katie, begging her to confirm what he thought his ears had heard.

It seemed a bit headlong to invite a stranger into their midst without a little more consideration, but after all, if they were agreed — Besides, there was no way Katie could bear to quench that blaze of hope in the hazel eyes.

"We can't pay wages," she said. "You'd be — well, like family."

The young jaw firmed. "I don't want charity. I'd sure work hard."

"There's lots you can do," Katie assured him. "We can pay for your clothes and things like that. When you need much cash money, you could hire out to somebody for a while."

"Or help me cut and sell wood," said Nacho.

"I've got my saddle and horse," Tom said. "There's ten dollars comin' to me when I finish out the month with Mr. Larrimore." He grinned a bit ruefully. "When the fall cattle work's done, Beau Murphree asked if I'd like to stay on and help break a hundred head of broncs. I was goin' to do it rather than have no job, but I rode third saddle some for Beau before roundup started and I sure wasn't lookin' forward to a winter of it."

"Third saddle?" frowned Melissa.

Tom nodded. "Beau rode first saddle — you know, after the horse was roped and fastened up by his hackamore to the snubbing post, Beau'd tie up his left foot so he couldn't kick or paw. Talked nice and kind to him, moved real slow and easy. He'd toss on a saddle blanket, let the horse smell it, and took it off and on till the horse knew it wasn't goin' to hurt him. Then came the saddle. After the horse got used to the cinch, Beau, talkin' gentle all the time, got up in the saddle and down from it till the horse figgered that wasn't too bad. Next, Beau let his foot down and untied him from the snubbing post. When the horse bucked himself plumb to a standstill, Beau climbed up and rode him a little. Then we found a log the horse could drag some and tied him to it for the night so that he'd learn a rope around his neck meant he wasn't goin' anywhere. Next day, Chuck Willard rode second saddle. Beau wanted to make it easy for me, so I rode third saddle the third day — and those horses bucked and pitched like crazy!"

Shaking her head, Melissa said wisely, "Tom, don't you ever let anyone do that to you again! Beau told me what a lot of fun it is to see a kid try to figure out why he gets bucked. When Beau rides first saddle, the horse is tired out and he's still pretty tired the second day. But the third day — well, he's rested and aggravated and here comes a brand new rider. What you do is ride a horse from start to finish."

Tom went red to the tips of his ears, but after a second he grinned. "Beau's been good to me. Reckon I can't grudge him his little prank. But I sure am glad I won't be breakin' horses with him all winter. I'll finish my month and draw my pay. That'll buy some clothes. And then —" Again, his shining eyes went from face to face and rested last on Melissa's. "Then, if I'm still welcome, I'll come — home."

Melissa regarded him with an indulgent protectiveness she'd never shown Jed. "You'll be welcome. And you be careful, riding back to camp in the dark."

Far from resenting her bossiness, Tom looked first surprised, then gratified. "I will," he said. "Good night. And — and thanks. I'll sure do my best to make sure you're never sorry."

Jed went out with him. Katie couldn't resist a mild tease. "Looks like you've taken Tom to raise, M'liss."

"He needs it! Look at the way Beau took advantage —" Seeing Katie's grin, the younger girl said haughtily, "Anyone can see Tom's a nice boy. And he'll earn his keep."

Katie said demurely, "I'm sure he will."

The chuckwagon, smoke, and dust remained on the horizon for two more days. Mid-morning on the next day, the smoke vanished in a dusty pall that gradually moved eastward. This was soon followed by the wagon. Katie heaved a long sigh of relief. Larrimore haunted her thoughts. She still couldn't decide whether to say anything to Bill. But surely the rancher wouldn't do anything till roundup was over and he'd completed the drive to San Carlos. She breathed easier just knowing that he wasn't camped a few miles away.

The family was eating dinner the following day when Ace started barking. Ever since

Nana's raid, these alarms always made Katie's heart go into her throat. She jumped up and ran to peer out the window, Jed and Melissa getting there ahead of her.

Three horsemen splashed across the creek. "Why, it's Hi Phillips!" cried Jed. "And Slim Jones and Charlie Hughes!"

Hurrying outside, tagged by her brother and sister, Katie smiled a greeting and was about to ask these men to have dinner in the house they'd helped to build when she saw that the horses were lathered and heaving and Slim hung to his saddlehorn, his face so pallid that his red moustache looked even fierier than usual. One thigh was soaked. Blood dripped from the boot.

"Miss Katie," said thin, smooth-cheeked Hi. "We sure do hate to bother you but Slim's goin' to cash in if he keeps gettin' jolted and Ed Larrimore's after us. Is there someplace you could hide Slim? Sure hate to ask but —"

"The cellar." Katie's mind worked as if it belonged to some onlooker, someone who wasn't scared, both for Slim and of the rancher.

Hi swung down and so did sandy-haired Charlie Hughes, his freckled face and snub nose making him look even younger than he was. "Show us where to put Slim and we'll be on our way."

425

"Your horses look done in," said Katie. "Listen, you all hide — take your saddles with you. We'll run the horses up the canyon so Larrimore will go after them, and get them to travel in the creek long enough that with any luck, he'll lose their tracks."

Slim roused enough to mumble, "Too — too dang'rous for you, Miss Katie —"

Charlie rubbed his forehead. "We ran off some cows we reckoned were as much ours as Larrimore's. Sure can't mix you up in it."

"Get in that cellar!" she fairly screamed. Nacho was already uncinching a saddle. Jed and Melissa did the same. Charlie and Hi eased Slim out of the saddle and supported him between them while Katie raced ahead to open the cellar. "Help yourself to the milk," she said. "And don't open the door, whatever happens! When it's covered up with branches and leaves, they'll never see it!"

"But we'll be afoot!" protested Charlie.

"No, you won't!" Katie hissed. "When it's safe, you'll ride out on Steel Dust horses. There's water in the trough the milk sets in, and some cheesecloth. Fix Slim up the best you can and I'll come when I can."

While Jed and Melissa grabbed bridles and hurried to catch Steel Dusts, Katie pulled off Slim's saddle and put it inside the cellar beside the other two and the bridles Nacho tossed in. Bareback on Jenny and Babe, Jed and Melissa urged the weary horses toward the canyon — they'd have to stay after them to make sure they didn't stop with the Steel Dust herd. Katie and Nacho disguised the door, piling up dead branches and brush as if they had simply been blown by wind into that angle of the slope.

Fortunately all the space between house and cellar was used so much that the way to the cellar was no barer than the earth around the grate where the washing was done. Nacho kicked dirt over curled bits of bloody dust, examined the location carefully, and said, "Why don't you go to bed, Katie? I will tell Señor Larrimore you are ill."

In truth, she was, of fright and worry over the men. They had all helped create this home. If Larrimore caught them, they'd live no longer than it took to toss ropes over a limb, and they were all so young! She didn't think any of them was five years older than she was. Remembering the cow with the Horseshoe brand, she was convinced that Larrimore had often done exactly what he would hang these men for doing.

"Thank you, Nacho," she said. "I'd rather be on my feet when I talk to Mr. Larrimore, and I'm sure he'll insist on seeing me. Oh, I hope Jed and Melissa can get those horses run off to where he can't find them!"

Nacho peered out at a cloud of approaching dust. "The young ones know the canyon well. If they lose the horse's tracks in the creek and drive them up one of the side canyons, the chance is good that the *señor* won't find them. He will, you see, expect our friends to follow the main canyon over the pass to the Sulphur Springs Valley. He will not expect to find them in places with no way out, where they would be trapped."

"I hope you're right." Katie scraped the plates into Ace's pan. "Please, Nacho, find something to do near the house. I'll feel a lot better if you're close."

"I will split kindling." He didn't have to tell Katie that an ax was a formidable weapon. "We should try to keep Señor Larrimore here as long as possible."

Katie shivered. "I know." The more time Jed and Melissa had to conceal the horses, the better. "They'll see the tracks heading toward the canyon, but if they know Slim is wounded, they might search the buildings. I'll try to make them suspicious so they'll do that."

"Good." Nacho touched her hand. "I will be right here, Katie."

He went out. She poured hot water into the dishpan over a bar of soap. The cellar would be pitch black with the door closed. She prayed that Slim's life wouldn't soak into the floor along with his blood. At least, now that he wasn't jolting in the saddle, Hi and Charlie should be able to stop the bleeding.

The sound of hoofs increased from a muffled beat that seemed no louder to Katie than the thud of her heart, gradually swelling into a drumming that reverberated through her whole body. How long since Jed and Melissa had chased the horses away? Twenty minutes? Half an hour? It couldn't be much more than that, though every minute had crept by interminably. Wiping a plate, Katie went out to stand by the rosebush as the riders reined up their horses.

Larrimore rode his white horse within a few yards of Katie before he stopped. Shell Brown was just behind him. The foreman's pale green eyes roved over Katie in a way that made her feel handled. Neither man took off his hat, though Beau Murphree did.

Eleven men sat horses whose necks and haunches were dark with sweat. To Katie, they seemed strangers, though she recognized several she'd seen at the branding. Their eyes glittered in hard faces. They were hunters now, not cowboys — hunters of men. Even Beau's usually merry brown eyes had that intent primeval lust for the chase.

"Have you seen three cattle thieves?" demanded Larrimore.

"I saw three men." Katie gestured. "You can see the tracks making for the canyon."

Larrimore's flat gray eyes scoured the corral and outbuildings. "I hit one. Sure you haven't hid him away some place?"

Katie shrugged. "Look all you want." Even to Larrimore, she couldn't bring herself to tell a straight-out lie. "But if you have to hunt in the bedroom, don't wake the baby. She's cutting teeth and is cranky."

Larrimore scowled. "You must be getting sense, girl. You're a sight more obligin' than I reckoned you'd be."

"I'd rather not shoot you unless I have to. You're not going to find anyone, so what do I care if you look, just so you don't rouse the baby or do any damage?"

Still puzzling, the rancher stared at her fixedly as if trying to penetrate her brain. "You're sayin' them birds swung by here and went on up the canyon?"

"You don't have to believe me. Look for yourself. And then kindly get off our property."

He showed strong square teeth, swinging from his horse, dropping the reins in front to ground-tie him. "I'll check the house, boys. Shell, make sure the shed's looked over good

— prod the hay with a pitchfork. And don't forget the privy. No matter what Miss Innocent here says, I think it's likely the one we shot is tucked away someplace in spittin' distance."

"Well, don't spit on my floor," Katie said sharply. "And I'll thank you to hurry up so I can get on with my work."

Marching inside, she finished drying dishes while Larrimore went up the ladder, which creaked with his weight, scanned the loft, and strode into the bedroom. Katie could hear Shell dividing the men to search the outbuildings. Good. The time they wasted here would give the children more precious minutes.

So that Larrimore wouldn't catch her alone inside on his return, Katie took the dishpan outside and dumped the water far enough from the house not to draw flies. Watching the cellar from the corner of her eye, she gave thanks that it had gone unnoticed. If Slim just didn't bleed to death —

Wiping out the dishpan, she got the water bucket and was starting to the well when Larrimore stalked from the kitchen, spurs clunking dully. "I sure figgered you for a softer heart," he growled. "Can't imagine you lettin' that fellow ride on with a bullet in him."

"They didn't want to cause us trouble." That was true enough. "Why don't you leave hunting men up to the sheriff?"

"Missy, you been here long enough to know Behan's not strainin' himself to chase cow thieves. And that deputy of his, Breakenridge, he's great pals with Bill Radnor. This is the first time anyone's had the gall to steal Pitchfork stock. I aim to see it's the last."

"Were they Pitchfork cows?" asked Katie rashly. "Or did they wear other brands like most of those you rounded up just south of here?"

He bent a grim stare at her. Something flared in his eyes. Involuntarily, Katie stepped back. He was so close she could smell his salty, acridly male odor, so close she could see the pores in his ruddy face, the pulsing veins in his temples. He gave a small, harsh laugh. "Today, girl, maybe tomorrow, I aim to hang those thieves and leave 'em dangle. Then, when my herd's gathered for San Carlos, I'm trailin' them up. After that —" His voice turned husky, sending a twisting stab of fear into her vitals. "Well, Kate MacLeod, I'll have all winter to deal with you. And you can make it just as hard or easy on yourself as you want."

He had started out set on asserting claim to Home Mountain. But once again, Katie sensed that he desired her, too. "No fair court would give you custody of the children!"

"Any court will rule this is no place for a bunch of kids who're being made pets of — or worse — by rustlers and outlaws." He put up a hand to stop her retort. "Never mind flyin' off the handle. There's no use arguin' and I don't have time. Got any biscuits or cornbread we can eat while we ride? And if you've got some good cool buttermilk, I'll pay you twice what you get in town."

If only he wouldn't think to inquire where the milk was kept! "I've got cornbread." Katie hoped she didn't sound as breathless as she felt. "Jed took our dairy things to town yesterday so there isn't any buttermilk." Anticipating his next question, she added hastily, forgetting her qualms about lying and just hoping fervently that he didn't know much about milk. "We were hungry for cottage cheese so I let the rest of the milk sour and used it up that way." Backing to the house as the Pitchfork men strode, disgruntled, from the outbuildings, she almost babbled. "I — I'll get the cornbread."

Bringing out the Dutch oven and a knife, she divided what was left from dinner. She'd planned to have it for supper, but baking again was a small price to pay if it got these men away without their finding those hiding in the cellar. Even through the debris-covered door, they could probably hear.

She handed out the crusty golden bread. The cowboys, a little calmer now, tipped their hats and thanked her. Most went down to the creek, dropped on their bellies, and drank before remounting. Wolfing the bread, they started off after Shell Brown, who had located the tracks.

"Pretty good, missy." Larrimore crunched a bite, savored it, and swallowed. He would, she thought, enjoy a woman in the same way, consume her without a thought to her as a person. "Glad you had enough sense not to harbor them thieves." He glanced at the sun. "We'd ought to catch 'em before dark. They've used them horses for at least a couple of days. Ours were fresh this mornin'." He reached in his vest. "What do I owe you for the bread?"

"Nothing." *I just hope you choke on it.*

Setting his foot in the stirrup, he heaved himself into the saddle, massive-chested, the muscles of his thighs showing like iron cords. "Unless we catch that gang in the canyon, we won't be back this way," he said. "My guess is we'll chouse 'em down out in the valley. May have to haul 'em back to a tree big enough to hang them." He smiled on her bleakly. "But it won't be too long, girl, till I come back. You'd better have the right answer."

He spurred away. If only those horses were

well up some small canyon! Leaving the wood-
pile where he'd worked while the Pitchfork
men were there, Nacho said, "I will see how
the young man is, Katie. Meanwhile, singe
the spines off a cactus pad and watch that the
cowboys do not double back. The pulp side
of a split pad makes a good poultice for
wounds."

Katie knew he was trying to keep her from
the possible shock of finding Slim dead. She
didn't argue but followed his instructions,
building up the fire to burn off the countless
hair-fine spines, and putting on coffee and
beans. Before the men rode on, they'd need
food, something to give them fresh energy.
Getting out a sheet so worn in the middle that
it would accept no more patches, she tore off
several strips for bandaging and washing the
wound, got the concoction brewed from
crushed creosote leaves that Nacho kept on
hand for treating cuts on cows, horses, and
humans, and paused outside to scan the mouth
of the canyon.

All she saw was a diminishing haze of dust.
Jed and Melissa, she was sure, would have
no trouble hiding when they heard the riders
coming. All the same, she'd feel a lot better
when they were safely home. Steadying herself
for what she might find, she turned toward
the cellar.

★ ★ ★

Once pressure could be applied to the artery pumping blood through the jagged hole in the thigh from which a bullet had ripped its way, the wound had clotted. Someone had cut away the garment from the hurt. In the light from the door, Slim's freckles stood out on his ashen countenance, but he tried to raise himself when Katie knelt by him.

"Miss Katie —" His voice was faint and labored, and his chest rose and fell rapidly. "You shouldn't have risked it — but I — I sure do thank you —" He managed a grin. "That buttermilk, it tasted better'n any whiskey."

"There'll be coffee before long, and beans and mush," she promised. "Just you rest easy, Slim, while we get this wound dressed." Nacho was already dousing the torn flesh with the creosote solution. Slim flinched and bit his lip while the old Yaqui bound the split cactus over the wound, applied a large pad made from the sheet over that, and, while Katie held these in place, securely wrapped the cloth strips around the leg from which the Levi's had been cut away.

"Think you can ride, Slim?" asked Hi.

"Sure." The whisper was almost inaudible.

"The bleeding could start again!" Katie looked up from the limp form to Hi and Char-

436

lie. "You can stay here till he's better."

Hi shook his head. "No, ma'am. We've put you in enough danger already. When they don't find us in the canyon, the Pitchfork may have a closer look around. Our best chance is headin' through that little gap north of your place and makin' for an abandoned adobe over by Apache Pass. We can hole up there till Slim can stick a saddle to Tombstone or Tucson."

"Why not leave him here, at least?" Katie urged.

"Ma'am, thank you kindly," gasped Slim. "But I better go with the boys. I — I'd rather hang than bring grief on you — but I'm not real keen on hangin' at all if I can dodge it."

Katie looked appealingly at Nacho. He considered and drew her outside, past earshot so no one would hear his fluent English. "Packed and bandaged as it is, Katie, I think it will not bleed much. Let us bring them food. They can eat while we catch some horses." He hesitated. "Katie, you may not see those horses again."

All too well she knew that. Were it possible, she knew the men would return the mares, but all kinds of things could happen to prevent that. "We just have to take that chance," she said, though the thought of losing three of the Steel Dusts turned her sick. "Their horses may have spooked too far to locate, and anyway, they're worn out." She called into the cellar that food and coffee were on the way, and when these were set on a bench so the men could help themselves, she and Nacho took bridles and went for the horses. She hated to lend them, but it was the only chance the young men had. Even if the mares were never returned, that would be better than knowing these friends dangled at the end of ropes in some lonely canyon until buzzards and predators cleaned their bones.

Half an hour later, the three rode slowly toward the gap beyond Home Mountain, Slim hunched in the saddle between his companions. The colts had been penned in the corral to keep them from following their mothers. Fortunately, almost weaned, they could do without milk.

"Here come Jed and Melissa," Nacho said gently.

"Thank goodness!" Katie swallowed the knot in her throat. The main thing, the matter of life and death, was that the young men get away. And that the family was safe.

As if he knew what she felt, Nacho said, "Go meet your brother and sister, Katie. I will make sure the cellar has no betraying signs and cover up the door." He added, "I have seen men hang. Whatever happens, Katie, this is a good thing you have done."

He seldom touched any of them except Rosie, but now he took her hand and pressed it to his weathered face before he turned away.

XVII

To Katie's relief, Larrimore didn't return or he would surely have wondered where the other Steel Dusts had gone and why the colts were alone in the corral.

"We kept the horses in the creek as much as we could once we got in the canyon." Melissa's eyes glowed in her flushed face. "I reckon once Mr. Larrimore lost their hoofprints he just decided they couldn't have gone anywhere else but across the valley."

"Yeah," grinned Jed. "We took Slim's and Charlie's and Hi's horses up a little side canyon and a lion or something spooked 'em. They got away from us. The boys may have a tough time findin' them."

Neither blamed Katie for letting their friends take the Steel Dusts. "What else could you do?" asked Jed roughly, smudging at an eye. Melissa nodded.

That made Katie feel at the same time both better and worse. Of course, what troubled her most of all was wondering if their friends had gotten safely away, if Slim had survived the bleeding and exertion.

On the fourth day after the men had disappeared through the gap, Bill Radnor rode through it on his big gray horse. Before she could see his face, Katie, with a quickening heart, knew him by the way he rode and the tilt of his dove gray hat.

The Steel Dust mares streamed in front of him, chestnut and golden sorrels, tails and manes tossed by wind and speed. Jed hurried to let out the colts and there was a joyous reunion. Melissa ran as fast to welcome Bill, meeting him several hundred yards beyond the corral. He reached down and swept her up in front of him so that they were laughing and talking when they stopped in front of Katie.

Her heart had raced toward him, though her body had not for she was holding Rosie, who was fretful with cutting teeth. Easing Melissa down, Bill followed lightly, ruffled Jed's hair as the boy rushed to take charge of Shadow.

"Son, if your big sis asks me to stay to dinner, you can pull off his saddle and rub him down."

"Of course you're invited!" Katie was so glad to see him and there were so many questions she wanted to ask that they tumbled over each other. "Where'd you find the horses? Is Slim all right? Did you see Larrimore? Where —"

He raised a long brown hand, chuckling.

"Whoa! Let me hold that girl baby while you get me some buttermilk, and I'll tell you the whole story." The laughter faded from his eyes, and he bent a severe gaze on her. "That was a fool thing to do, Katie. If Larrimore had found those boys, he'd likely have hung them on your big oak to teach you a lesson, maybe burned you out."

"Slim had to get that bleeding stopped. And their horses were done in."

"I know, but they chose to play that game."

"It's not a game!" she flamed at him. "It's stealing and it can get men killed!"

The sun left his eyes. "Guess I won't stay for dinner," he said, turning.

Katie caught his arm. "Of course you will! You don't need to get mad because I tell you the truth. Here, take Rosie, and come inside."

Their eyes battled. *I love you!* she wanted to cry. *How could I stand it if you got yourself killed in what you call a game?* After a moment, he shrugged, took Rosie, and let her stand on his arm while he supported her back.

"I guess I can't expect you to look at it my way, Katie." Bill followed her into the kitchen and sighed as she pointed an imperative finger at the rocker. He settled into it, stretching out his long legs. As always, when entering the house, he'd yanked off his spurs outside the door. "But the way cattle change owners from here to the border *is* a game, a pretty rough one sometimes. Most of the cows in that bunch Slim and the others made off with wore the brands of little outfits Larrimore drove out or bought out for next to nothin'. It's like his land. He never bought it or filed a claim. He's just there and able to run everyone else off."

"And hang men who take cattle he claims!"

"Yep." He thanked Melissa for the buttermilk she'd fetched from the cellar and grinned at Jed, who was sitting close on the rug with Ace in his arms. "To answer some of those questions you fired at me, Slim caught the stage for Tucson yesterday. He's limpin', but the wound's healin' clean. He'll laze around till he can straddle a horse and take out for places that'll be healthier for him than Cochise County. Hi and Charlie sloped for Mexico."

"Where did you see them?"

"I was at MacLowerys' when Larrimore came foggin' along. He thought Slim might be there. The MacLowerys let him look, and he rode on in one mighty sour temper. When he allowed that he searched your place, too, I reckoned you'd had something to do with the boys gettin' away that slick on winded horses. I kind of jogged around checkin' places where I've holed up on occasion and found them at that old adobe near Apache Pass. Slim thought he could make the ride to Tombstone, and we all figgered the sooner they changed climates the better. Little way from Tombstone, we left your Steel Dusts with a friend who sold us a couple of horses for Hi and Charlie. I borrowed one for Slim. We had a big feed at Nellie Cashman's, Hi and Charlie hit the trail for Mexico, and I hung around yesterday till Slim was tucked in snug and safe on the stage."

Bill's smile faded, and he shoved back the waving black hair falling over his forehead. "Can't think of any way Larrimore can find out you loaned the boys those horses — that's why we switched outside of Tombstone and my friend sure won't talk. But I'm passin' the word that men who get themselves in a jam better leave you out of it."

"Slim and the others didn't want to stay," Katie defended, mixing cornbread to go with the hearty stew of corn, squash, and chilies thickened with ground acorns. "I made them hide. There wasn't anything else we could do."

Bill looked from one of them to the other, including Nacho, who had come to lean in the door. "No, I reckon there wasn't. But you won't get put on that spot again if I can help it. It's not fair to take advantage of kids —"

"Kids!" Katie set her hands on her hips.

"I'll have you to know, Bill Radnor, that I'll be seventeen next week! That — that's grown-up, almost!"

"Almost," he agreed, eyes twinkling, though for a flash he had looked — well, stunned and something else. Jubilant? "For sure, it's a very special birthday for a young lady. We need to celebrate." His brow furrowed for a moment before he snapped his fingers. "Say, you've never been to Tombstone, have you? Let's go, the whole family!"

Tombstone! Rich, wicked, exciting, the county seat and biggest city in Arizona — the biggest place between San Antonio and San Diego, for that matter! Katie couldn't have been more astounded had he proposed a trip to fabled New York or San Francisco. She clasped her hands, scarcely able to breathe, and then she remembered.

"We can't. There's the milking, and the trip would be hard on Rosie and —"

"I have been to Tombstone," said Nacho. "I have no wish to return. I will do the milking, Katie — yes, in your old dress and bonnet! — and take care of Rosamunda."

"See?" laughed Bill. "It's all settled."

"No, it isn't," said Katie, though heaven seemed less wonderful than a visit to the town with Bill as an escort. "We could take our food, but we'd have to stay at a hotel. It would cost a scandalous amount."

"My treat." Bill waved her objections aside. "And it'd be purely a sin to take a food basket when there's all those fancy eateries with thick tablecloths and thin soup. There's always a play or music or something going on at Schieffelin Hall or the Miners Exchange, or a benefit at one of the churches."

Letting this soak in, he nuzzled Rosie's neck while she squealed and yanked his hair. "Must be some things you need to buy," he went on persuasively. "You can go in all the stores. We'll eat in the Maison Doree and Can Can and at the Grand Hotel. But we'll get our best grub at Nellie Cashman's Russ House. If she had room, she'd have you stay with her, but she's got her widowed sister and five kids there so I reckon you'll do best in the Grand."

It sounded wonderful beyond anything Katie had ever dreamed of enjoying. It also sounded horrendously expensive. Ignoring pleading looks from Jed and Melissa, she said as firmly as she could, "We can't possibly let you pay for all that!"

"Great jumping rattlers!" he began, then broke off as a smile spread across his face. "Katie, I know a way that you can pay for the whole shebang! In fact, I'll let you treat me. And I bet you can have money left over for your shopping."

"We won't sell any horses!"

"Don't have to. Just bring your harp." As she stared, he chuckled. "Oh, I sure won't book you into the Birdcage. They have some good performers but it's a saloon. No reason in the world, though, why you can't play at Schieffelin Hall or the Miners Exchange or in one of the churches. Famous entertainers visit Tombstone all the time, Katie. There's lots of money being made and folks don't mind spendin' it. Why, they'll beg you to stay and play for a week!"

"I — I can't do anything like that!"

"Sure you can. You played in Galeyville, didn't you? To a lot rougher crowd than you'll find in Tombstone!"

"It's different! Tombstone's a city! And you say they have all these real singers and actresses, maybe even from New York!"

"From Paris and London, too," he said. His dark eyebrows arched. "I reckoned you were proud of that harp of yours — proud of the songs your kin made long ago in those misty Western Isles."

"I am proud of the harp! It's just that — that I'm scared."

"And you so grown-up, too," he teased, then shrugged. "All right. Let me take you."

Jed and Melissa had hold of her on either side. "Oh Katie, please!"

Bill shook his head and said piously, "Hard as these kids work, Katie, how do you have the heart to keep them from having a frolic?"

Defeated, she glared at him. "I'll play! That is, if you can find anyone who'll listen! But don't you go working some of your tricks, Bill Radnor, and fix it so the money I earn is really yours!"

"Would I do that?"

"You bet you would!"

He gave a sorrowful shake of his head. "Doggone, you're more suspicious than a rancher around a sleepered calf."

"What in the world is that?" At his embarrassed look, Katie said hastily, "Never mind!"

"It's a calf that's earmarked, but not branded," said Jed loftily. "Tom told me about it. They found quite a few during the roundup. The cowboy who does it figgers on slipping the calf out of the herd later on and burnin' his own brand on it, while he doctors the earmark to fit his."

Katie groaned. Bill said hastily, "I swear, Katie, every nickel you get will be earned fair and square from admissions. I'll start back after dinner to get everything fixed. All you have to do is figger out a program, make out your shopping list, and get ready to roll Tombstone on its ear!"

"Her birthday's the sixth," Melissa supplied.

"Fine. We'll start real early the fifth, leave Fanchers' ranch real early again next morning, and get to Tombstone around noon. If we start home the ninth, that'll give you two and a half days in town. Long enough?"

Katie put her hand to her dazed head to clear it, but she still couldn't believe this was happening. To be escorted by Bill to all the finest places in the territory's largest, richest city? Not only visit the stores but actually have money to spend beyond that hoarded from selling milk, butter, soap, and vegetables? She'd been planning, for Christmas, to buy some of that beautiful but frightfully expensive edging for Melissa's red flannel petticoat; Jed needed work shoes; they ought to have another shotgun or rifle in case of an attack; they needed another saddle; and Katie stopped the mental list right there since it already would cost more than the total of their small savings and a wildly optimistic guess at what she could earn for playing a few times.

If she could earn anything at all! In spite of her reception in Galeyville, she found it hard to believe she could attract an audience in Tombstone, where there was so much entertainment on top of saloons and gambling halls that were open twenty-four hours a day.

Bill thought she could do it, so she would try. Not only in hope of making enough to pay for this marvelous excursion but to honor her forebears and sing their songs in this country so far from their islands. If she kept her mother's songs alive, Rosie would have at least that much of Mary.

Counting days, she looked at Bill in consternation. "We'd be gone six days!"

"Five and a half," he soothed. "We'd be back by afternoon on the tenth."

"It's too long to leave Rosie."

"Now what can you do for her that Nacho can't?" Bill asked. "I think she likes men! Look at the way she's hanging onto me!"

It was true that Nacho could calm the baby when no one else could, walking her tirelessly and crooning. At such times, Katie wondered, with smarting eyes, if he thought of his slaughtered children. He nodded reassuringly.

"Have no fear, Katie. I will not leave her — she will even go to the shed with me for the milking. Chica and I will both be glad of a holiday."

There was nothing for it but to nod, so excited and happy she couldn't speak. Jed let out a whoop. Melissa swooped to kiss Bill's cheek, and they sat down to dinner amidst a gladsome babble of plans and questions.

"How will we get my harp there?" Katie asked in sudden alarm. "And we only have two saddles! Oh dear —"

"I'll bring a pack mule," Bill said.

"I will fashion a box for the harp so it will be protected," offered Nacho.

"And I'll bring an extra saddle," finished Bill and suddenly thought of something. "Say, my handsome young friend, Russian Bill, got himself hanged over in Shakespeare for stealin' a horse. First critter he ever stole, far as I know, and he durn sure never killed anyone. His heart was set on bein' a real outlaw." Bill sighed. "Wasn't too long ago the mayor got a letter from the U.S. Consul in St. Petersburg tryin' to get news of a lieutenant of the Imperial White Hussars last heard of in Arizona. The kid's mother was a lady-in-waiting at the court of the czar. Anyhow, to make the poor lady feel better, a letter went back saying her son had been prosperous and respected in these parts but had met with a sad and fatal accident. Guess that's one of way looking at it. Nobody in his right mind ever stuck his head in a noose on purpose. But the long and short of it is that Bill left his saddle and gear to me and I picked it up a few weeks ago, folks in Shakespeare bein' smart enough to reckon they'd better not appropriate somethin' of mine. All this bein' a longwinded way of sayin' that you might as well take Russian Bill's saddle and save your money."

"Can I have it?" Jed demanded.

"If it suits your sister."

Katie wasn't charmed at inheriting the saddle of a young man who'd wasted his life so tragically, but good saddles were costly. She gave a reluctant nod.

"If Tom Buford comes to stay with us by then," said Melissa, "may he go to Tombstone with us?"

Extra expense, but it would be a dream for Tom, too. Besides, thought Katie basely, if he were along, Melissa might fuss over him instead of Bill.

She nodded again and the clamor broke out afresh.

It was a good thing Bill had brought a big, strong mule, Smiler, for Katie would hate to see diminutive Chica burdened with the crated harp. Smiler seemed amazed at getting off with such a light load, but Bill said to him, "Don't get too spoiled, my lad. On the way back, you'll have a lot of plunder to carry."

Katie's heart lurched when she kissed Rosie good-bye and placed her in Nacho's arms. Rosie did pucker up, dark eyebrows knitting, but Nacho hoisted her to his shoulders and soon had her giggling as he trotted around like a horse. Ace whined when Jed told him to stay. Nacho picked him up, too, and promised to keep him in the house or under close supervision so he couldn't follow and perhaps get lost or eaten by predators.

They rode for the first canyon south of Whitetail Canyon, where Bill said a trail led over the mountain into Pinery Canyon and southwesterly across the Sulphur Springs Valley. They'd take South Pass through the Dragoon Mountains, stay with the Fanchers, and reach Tombstone next day.

They followed a streambed where sycamore trunks gleamed white, leaves dusky flames of orange and brown against cedar and evergreen oak. Near a waterfall, the trail began to climb more steeply. The horses needed to rest several times before they reached the long backbone of the ridge. As they paused, Katie gazed across at another crest of the mountains and beyond to the shimmering plain and distant purple ranges.

This reminded Katie of that other vantage point where Bill had taken her to survey the country on the other side. That was only five months ago, but it seemed she had never lived anywhere else. She had no wish to remember the hardscrabble Nueces ranch where Pa hoarded his money and Mama her love.

Watching Bill as he rode ahead, picking the

way, Katie felt as if her love for him made her shine like a lighted lamp. It was a delicious sparkling day, crisp enough in early morning to make the sun welcome. For the journey, Katie and Melissa wore their old "best" dresses, but their new ones were carefully rolled with their nightgowns, hose, and new petticoats in canvas bags tied behind their saddles.

Before approaching a habitation or other travelers, they would hook their right legs around their saddlehorns, but it would be ridiculous and not very safe to hold that position any oftener than they had to. They rode with their skirts covering their legs as modestly as possible, but their carefully polished new shoes were in plain view as well as glimpses of scarlet and garnet hose.

Melissa, it seemed to Katie, lost no chance to edge momentarily ahead of Bill, flaunting her curved heels and scalloped side-buttoning, but Katie was far too blissful to take much notice of that. Melissa had been clearly disappointed when Tom Buford hadn't arrived in time to accompany them. He'd surely come soon, and then Melissa would be so busy mothering and bossing him around that with any luck at all she'd decide Bill was an old man, to be loved only as an uncle or brother.

Cheered by this prospect, Katie left her

sister to chatter flirtatiously with Bill while she herself gazed from the crest of the ridge toward that point from which Bill had shown her all the world she could ever want.

They spent the night at a small ranch on the edge of the Dragoons. Tawny-haired Sally Fancher was expecting her first baby. When Bill remarked that next day was Katie's seventeenth birthday, Sally dimpled at her gangling dark young husband. "I'll be sixteen on Christmas Day," she said. "And then we'll have been married a year. My folks made us wait till I turned fifteen, but they gave in then and we had a lovely wedding. Everyone came from miles around." Were her violet eyes a little wistful as she smiled at Bill? "You came, Mr. Radnor. Do you remember that you danced with me?"

"Every time I could grab you before Matt here did," said Bill gallantly.

Katie hoped this would show Bill that she was no child by any reasonable standard, but as they rode along next day, having promised to stop on their return, he suddenly burst out, "It's a damn shame!"

"What is?" Katie blinked.

"Little Sally! Think she'll be light on her feet this Christmas? Or for too doggone many of the next thirty years, if she lives that long?"

"But she's so happy!"

"Wait'll she's nursing one baby, got one at her knee, and is carrying another!"

"Bill! Melissa shouldn't —"

"Hear? She better, if it makes her stop to think, and so should you! Hell, we know it's not good for heifers and fillies to breed till they got their growth. Same for a woman. That poor kid's bones and teeth'll be drained by a string of babies. Sure, young Matt worships her. Sure, they'll have their good times. But why couldn't she have a few more years just to be a girl? Just to be pretty and dance?"

Melissa asked the question burning on Katie's lips. "How old do you think a girl ought to be to get married?"

"Twenty-one," he said promptly.

"Bill!" the sisters wailed.

"Well, then, not a day under eighteen, and then only because if she stays home, she'll get worked ragged helping take care of her mother's younger kids. If *I* were a gal, I'd never get married at all."

Again Katie let Melissa blurt the question. "Why?"

"So I could do what I wanted and have some fun." There it was again, Katie thought balefully. With Bill, it all came down to fun. He spread a hand, expanding on the matter. "Look at Nellie Cashman. She was born in

Ireland and came to San Francisco with her sister. Sis marries, starts havin' babies. Nellie joins the 'seventy-seven gold rush to the Fraser River up in British Columbia and cures lots of miners of scurvy by rushin' in potatoes. She sojourned in Virginia City and ran Delmonico's in Tucson before she came here, all the time helpin' folks and not a breath of scandal around her name. Meanwhile, sis's husband lives long enough to give her five kids and then cashes in. Sis, naturally, comes to live with Nellie. So I ask you: which one's had the best life?"

"Sounds to me like Miss Cashman works more than she frolics," said Katie.

"When you enjoy it — and she sure does — that can be fun, too," said Bill. "She's Catholic, and when some men were goin' to be hanged a while back, she was their confessor since there was no priest. And then there's China Mary. There's four to five hundred Chinese in and around Tombstone. She's the boss and go-between. Anyone wants to hire a Chinese, they come to her and she guarantees there'll be no stealin' or she'll make it good herself. Mary makes a lot of money, but she's loaned or just given stakes to down-and-out miners, and there's a good many would be dead if she hadn't taken 'em in and nursed them. Take French Marie, now" — Bill broke off, reddening. "Well, better not take her, but if I was a gal critter, I'd never marry."

"Since you're not," Katie incredulously heard herself asking, "do you intend to?"

Those blue-gray eyes swung to her. Between them coursed that wild, sweet fire that melted her bones. He *had* to feel it, too; at least something — "Why," he said, "that depends."

"On what?"

He turned away, breaking that powerful flow between them. "A whole lot of things. Better save your voice, Katie. I've got you booked to play tonight at the Miners Exchange."

"Oh, my goodness!" Katie had been practicing every night, but panic flooded her. "I don't think —"

"Katie," he said, "when you look back at all those faces, you just remember each one paid a buck to get in and half of that's yours!"

In spite of three volunteer fire departments, there'd been a serious fire that summer and cindery ruins stretched along Fourth Street north of the wide main thoroughfare, Allen Street. Bill kept a firm grip on Smiler, maneuvering amidst buggies, horsemen, buckboards, and creaking lumber and supply wagons.

A Wells-Fargo stagecoach rumbled by, a man with shotgun perched beside the driver.

"Stages get robbed a lot," said Bill. "It's got so bad bullion's being cast in two-hundred-pound bars so that they're harder to tote away on horseback."

Smiler had reason to live up to his name when he saw sixteen of his brethren toil by, hitched two abreast to an ore wagon on its way, Bill said, to the mills in Charleston and Contention. This team met one of twenty-four mules coming the other way, hauling one huge cargo wagon and three smaller ones, the last one of which carried trail necessities — bedding, grain, and camp provender. Mounted on the left-hand wheeler next to the lead wagon rode the driver with a blacksnake whip in his right hand and the jerk line in his left.

"How can he manage that whole team?" gasped Jed, discovering yet another fascinating occupation.

"He's got a swamper to run alongside the mules and urge 'em along when the going gets rough," said Bill. "But mostly Angus there does it by some pretty complete cussin', that whip, and the jerk line. See how it runs through a ring in the collar of each mule on the nigh side clear up to the nigh leader? The leader's the smartest critter in the whole she-bang, Angus included. When Angus wants to swing left, he pulls steady on the line, but when he keeps jerking, the leader turns right.

The lead mule on the off-side gets steered by that jockey stick stretched from his bridle bit to the hames of the left leader's collar. Most drivers make big pets out of their wheelers and pointers — they're the pair just in front of the wheelers — because they're the ones that have to make the sharp turns while the leaders and others do a wider swing. Look out! Angus is fixin' to spit!"

To the disgusted wrath of several ladies on the boardwalk, a stream of brown juice splattered in front of them. "You — you *hog!*" one of them shrieked. Angus calmly shifted his cud and spat again. The ladies retreated into a store.

Wide-eyed, marveling, Jed asked, "Won't they dig out all the silver before long, Bill?"

"Oh, it seems like there's plenty of ore yet, but in March they started gettin' water in the mines. So far they think it's good — helps wash out the tailings, but if it gets too deep, they'll have to put in pumps like they use in Cornwall, and if that doesn't work —" He shrugged. "Well, Tombstone will go the way of a lot of other boomtowns. Meanwhile it's struttin' its stuff. That two-story frame on the corner with those fancy eaves hangin' out over the boardwalk is all gussied up now with crystal stemware and big mirrors. They call it the Crystal Palace, but it started out as the Golden

Eagle Brewery. It's in the Wherfritz Building. Doc Goodfellow used to have his office there next door to the coroner — real convenient, but he's moved across from the back entrance of the OK Corral." He cleared his throat, looking embarrassed. "Be sure you keep on the south side of Allen Street. You're perfectly safe there except from Angus' tobacco juice. But the north side" — he jerked his head to the string of saloons, gambling dens, and dance halls — "that's no place for any of you, and I do mean you, Jed, same as your sisters. Don't you go up Sixth Street, either."

"Is that where the bad ladies live?" Jed demanded eagerly.

Bill gave a brief nod as if hoping the girls wouldn't notice and gestured at a row of one-story adobes straggling along Fourth Street south of Allen. "That's Rotten Row. Most of the lawyers have offices there, convenient to where the courthouse is bein' built and the saloons. They kinda wear a track back and forth."

Reining up in front of an imposing two-story frame building, he hitched Smiler and Shadow to the post and began untying the clothing bags. "I'll put these inside and get our rooms. Then we'll leave the horses back down the street at the OK Corral. I'll take the harp over to the Exchange while you tidy

461

up, and then we'll start off with a good dinner at Nellie's."

Two tall men strode by, one exceedingly thin with a narrow, pallid face, dingy blond moustache, and cold gray eyes. The other was pale, too, but didn't look sick. An outsized yellow-brown moustache drooped beneath his jaws on either side of a thrusting chin. When he tipped his hat to Katie, she saw that his hair was yellow, but what she really noticed was the silver star pinned to his vest.

"Good morning, ladies," he said, including Melissa with a faint smile that didn't reach eyes the color of slate and just as hard. Though he scanned them for no more than a second, Katie felt shamed — dirtied somehow, as if he'd looked through her clothes to her body. His attention rested speculatively on Bill. "Howdy, Radnor."

"Howdy, marshal." There was no warmth in either Bill's voice or his eyes. He stepped up on the boardwalk with his burden. "Howdy, Doc," he said to the emaciated man, who nodded and gave him a bleak smile as Bill entered the hotel.

"That must be Wyatt Earp!" Jed breathed as soon as the men high-heeled out of earshot. "Breck says he was marshal of Dodge City when it was roughest, and now he's a U.S. deputy marshal here. He'd a sight rather be

462

sheriff — that's where the money is, collecting fines and taxes, 'cause the sheriff gets to keep a part. Earp's got four brothers. They're all in Tombstone. Virgil's the town marshal and —"

"Who's the skinny man?" Melissa asked, shivering. "He's got the coldest eyes I ever saw!"

"Has to be Doc Holliday. He's got consumption and would liefer die from a bullet than coughin' up his lungs." It was clear that Jed had asked William Breakenridge plenty of questions. The boy peered along the street to another two-story frame rising above the brick and adobe buildings beside it. "There's the Bird Cage! It was just around the corner where Bill shot Marshal White —"

Katie put her hands over her ears as best she could while holding Jenny's reins and Señorita's halter. "Good heavenly days, Jedediah MacLeod! I don't want to hear such things and you shouldn't know them!"

"Aw, sis, it was an accident! The marshal asked for Bill's gun. Bill was handin' it over when Wyatt Earp ran up from behind and grabbed him. The six-shooter went off — into Marshal White. Bill stood trial in Tucson — it was the county seat then. Marshal White left a sworn statement that Bill hadn't shot him on purpose. Even Earp testified to that.

The judge called it a — a misadventure and let Bill go."

If she made herself face it, Katie knew Bill had killed, and not just by accident. It shook her that he could ride into a town where such an awful thing had happened, chatting amiably and set on having a festive holiday.

Stricken and subdued, she was thankful that she didn't have to talk when Bill emerged and said he and Jed could take all the horses over to the stable and corral.

Katie slipped down before he could help her. With a puzzled glance, he lifted Melissa from the saddle and swung her to the boardwalk.

"The clerk'll take you to your room," he said. "Jed and I bunk right down the hall. What's the matter, Katie? You're lookin' kind of green around the gills."

"I — I — it must be all the racket."

"There's plenty of that, but you won't mind it so much after you tuck away some of Nellie's good cookin'. Get yourselves all prettied up and let's start celebratin' your birthday!"

Leaving Shadow and Smiler hitched, he took the reins of two mares and set off down the street, Jed close behind.

"Katie!" Melissa gave her a shake. "It was an accident!"

"Yes, but — He's killed other men."

"If he hadn't they'd have killed him." When Katie gasped at her young sister's cold-blooded view, Melissa shook her head. "Katie, for goodness sake! Don't mope around and spoil everything!" She tugged at Katie's arm. "Come on in! I want to see our room. Isn't it grand to stay in a big hotel? I never dreamed we would, ever!"

Katie allowed herself to be urged inside. Truly, it was out of the question to ruin this treat for her brother and sister. But she would have given anything not to know that just down the street and around the corner, Bill Radnor had killed a man. It didn't help much to remember that she had several times aimed a weapon and would have fired if she'd been forced into defending herself, her family, or their animals. Bill, she was sure, recklessly put himself in positions where someone was bound to be shot, and this weighed heavy on her heart.

XVIII

Melissa bent down to feel the flowered blue carpet, opened the tall wardrobe with its mirrored door, peeked in every drawer of the marble-topped chest, studied herself in the great oval mirror of the dresser, peered through the lace curtains at the street below, and then, with a blissful sigh, stretched out on the big bed with its tall carved headboard and blue brocade bedspread.

"Isn't it elegant, Katie? It seems a shame to have such a lovely room and not just stay in it."

In spite of her heavy-heartedness, that made Katie smile. "All right. You just stay here and gloat over the room while we have a nice dinner and go shopping."

Melissa bounced up at once. "Katie! You know perfectly well I couldn't bear to miss a thing! I hope my dress isn't wrinkled too much!"

Thanks to being folded around petticoats and nightgowns, the dresses shook out quite acceptably. They washed in the gold-rimmed porcelain basin with water poured from a matching pitcher, dressed, and combed their hair.

"I don't want an old braid." Melissa tried her bee pin several places before fastening it at the throat of her stand-up collar. "Will you tie my hair back with my ribbon?"

Katie obliged, allowing the crimped yellow locks to fall softly over Melissa's ears, framing her face, before catching them back and securing them with a romantic bow in the ribbon Bride had given her. Holding out her full, full skirts, Melissa twirled in front of the dresser mirror that reflected her from radiant smile to scalloped boots.

"Oh, Katie, I'm so glad you're having a birthday — that is, I'm glad Bill wanted to celebrate!" She clapped her hand to her mouth. "Gracious, I forgot!" Rushing to her sack, she rummaged at the bottom and handed the result to Katie. "Happy birthday!"

"What nice handkerchiefs!" Katie exclaimed. "Goodness, M'liss, I didn't know you could take such tiny stitches! And you didn't embroider just my initials, but my whole name!"

"See how I twined roses around the K?" Melissa asked proudly.

"Lovely!" A good thing Melissa had identified the lopsided knots; Katie had been about to call them sunflowers. "Mama used to say nothing made her feel more like a lady than having a pretty handkerchief. There, I'll put one in my pocket."

The sisters hugged. Melissa danced back, scrutinizing Katie. "That goldy-green exactly, perzactly matches your eyes, and I'll bet your waist is smaller than mine." She let out a wistful breath, glancing from Katie's breasts to her own gently budding ones. "Do you think I'm ever going to grow a bosom?"

"Of course. You'll probably have to let out your bodice before Christmas, certainly before *your* birthday in April."

Katie could especially sympathize with her little sister because today marked an important milestone in her life. Mama thought seventeen was when a girl — *woman* — could start doing her hair up. Mama, married herself at fifteen, had made it clear that she didn't want her daughters to even think about marrying till they were eighteen, and she said there was no use in their trying to look grown-up till they were. As a matter of convenience, Katie usually wore her hair pinned back in some sort of careless knot from which ringlets willfully escaped, and she'd privately experimented, but she'd never, in public, worn her hair *up*. She had brushed it till it clung to her hands, and now, holding the ends as she bent over, she swirled the thick auburn mass into a coil and pinned it in place high at the back of her head, using her mother's tortoise-shell pins.

The image that gazed back from the mirror seemed almost a stranger's. Had her eyebrows always winged up like that at the outer edges? Her cleft chin and high, slanting cheekbones had no trace of baby fat; even her nose looked shapelier, and her mouth and eyes no longer seemed too large for her face. "Ooooh, Katie!" Melissa's awe was flattering. "You're beautiful! But you need a locket or brooch. Here, you wear my pin."

Katie stopped Melissa's fingers as they worked on the catch. "Thanks, darling, but only girls named Melissa get to wear bees."

"Maybe you could tie your ribbon around your neck."

"Like a cat?" smiled Katie. "Tonight I'll make it into a huge bow to wear at the back of my head. That'll be almost as good as jewelry."

"No," said Melissa, "it won't." She looked downcast before her eyes glinted with hope. "If Bill knows you don't have any jewelry, he'll —"

"Don't you dare breathe a word!"

A knock came on the door. "Aren't you ready *yet?*" called Jed. "Jumpin' Jehosephat! We left the horses and uncrated your harp and washed up and —" He dodged as Katie opened the door. "Holy smoke, sis! If you were a filly, you'd sure enough be a golden sorrel!" He gaped at Melissa. "What's happened to you? All of a sudden, your teeth aren't too big and your hair looks pretty!"

Melissa inspected him with a sniff. "At least I guess you washed your face," she conceded.

"Hey! I shined my boots!" He thrust a toe forward.

"Lead the way, Jed." Bill took a sister on either arm, sweeping them toward the curving stairway. In his white shirt and blue silk scarf, he looked incredibly tanned and handsome, and as always those storm-colored eyes reached into Katie and twisted not only her heart but the nerves and veins of her very core. "There's not a man in town wouldn't bust his buttons to be escortin' such pretty ladies," he said. He quirked a judicious eyebrow at Katie. "Pilin' your hair up like that sure makes you look like a grown-up woman, but I'm glad some of those curls broke loose!"

Pleasure in his admiration couldn't dispel Katie's wretchedness over Marshal White's slaying. *How can you act as if everything's fine when you killed a man just a few blocks from here?* she wanted to cry. Unable to think of a response to his banter, she was relieved when Melissa said, "It's the first time Katie's had her hair up, Bill. She does look like a lady, doesn't she?" Quickly, she gripped his arm with her free hand. "But, Bill, it's only three years and six months till I can wear my hair up, too!"

"Huh!" snorted Jed. "And by then I'll be old enough to hire out for a cowboy!"

"Whoa!" chuckled Bill. "One shock at a time!"

He ushered them past swinging doors that revealed glittering crystal chandeliers reflected dazzlingly in countless mirrors and an ornate and crowded bar that seemed miles long with a painting behind it of a gauzily draped lady. Merriment spilled into the richly carpeted foyer off which opened a dining room with three sparkling chandeliers hung from an intricate centerpiece. Silver, fine china, and crystal graced tables spread with starched white tablecloths.

"We'll eat here this evening," Bill said. "Usually they've got fresh oysters and fish rushed from California by train as far as Benson and then staged in. If you're hungry as I am, though, you don't want to wait on the waiters and chef to fuss around, so let's get on to Nellie's."

The adobe Russ House was across from the Contention Consolidated Mine and handily catty-corner from the firehouse, facing across Tough Nut Street to miners' shacks conjured of boards, metal, brush, adobe, and canvas. Several urchins were brawling in the street, yelling with more vigor than they punched. A trim-waisted, dark-haired young woman dashed out, pulled the boys apart, and said, "Here now, boyeens, what be the matter?"

"He hit me first, Miss Cashman!" accused the carrot-headed one. "He called me a name!" retorted the scrawny dark one.

"Wheesht! What a clamor and you the best friends in the world! Shake hands, the pair of you, and I might just cut you each a nice piece of fresh-baked pie."

"Well —" Grubby hands met, and the boys skipped through the door.

"Miss Nellie!" called Bill. "If I can pick a fight, will you give me a hunk of pie?"

Turning, Nellie Cashman's dark eyes lit up and a smile softened her rather long face and determined chin. "Lord Bill! I'll give you a whole pie if you'll chip in to send Peggy MacNeal and her children back to her family in Ohio. Her husband was killed last week in a cave-in — drank up most of his wages so Peggy's got nothing to fall back on."

Bill pulled out a wallet and extracted a pad, scribbled for a moment, and handed the paper to Nellie. "Fill the check in for whatever the lady needs, Miss Nellie. I want you to meet the MacLeods, Katie, Melissa, and Jed. They have a dairy and horse ranch northeast of Galeyville. Katie's seventeen today."

"Happy birthday, dear," smiled Nellie, shaking hands with all of them. "Come right on in and have a seat while I give those little rapscallions their pie. Thank you, Bill, for helping Peggy. You never let me down."

"Who could?" said Bill, grinning. "When you decide something needs doing, we all know we better shell out."

The Russ House was clean, cheerful, and packed with miners, some of whom were vacating a table as Bill ushered his guests within. "It's a joke around town that kids put on fights in front of Nellie's so she'll break up the ruckus with a hunk of pie," Bill said, picking up a menu. "Nellie's cookin' is good as her heart. Order whatever suits you. I'm having chicken and dumplings. They're the best you'll ever taste."

He was right. In Texas, chicken had appeared on the MacLeods' table only when a circuit-riding preacher stopped by or a hen was so old she quit laying and was consequently tough and stringy. Delicious steamed greens and corn fritters completed the main meal. As their plates were cleared away, Bill stepped to the door and signaled.

A dark, distinguished-looking man in a peaked sombrero trimmed with silver lace and a hatband of 'dobe dollars came in, holding a guitar. He swept off the huge and resplendent hat, bowing to Katie, and in the same moment, Nellie appeared, bearing a cake with blazing candles.

"May this be a wonderful year for you," Nellie said, setting the imposing creation before Katie. "Bill, you said not to make one of those cakes that are all whipped air and egg whites, so this is my special sour cream chocolate cake with caramel-nut filling and fudge frosting."

"Mmmm!" Jed smacked his lips.

"Blow out the candles, Katie." Bill took his seat, smiling on her in a way that made her heart feel as if he held it in his strong brown hand. "Get them all at once and your wish comes true."

I wish — that you had never killed anyone? That you weren't a rustler? No use in wishing for what couldn't be undone. *I wish — no matter what you are, no matter what you've done, I wish you will love me — that there will be a way, somehow, someday, for us to be together.*

She closed her eyes and blew. Everyone, including the miners, clapped and cheered. She dared to look then. Only threads of smoke spiraled from the candles. Bill's eyes met hers, and in that moment, the man he had summoned struck his guitar and his deep, mellow voice filled the room.

"Awaken, my love, awaken." Bill's soft voice was to Katie as melodious as the singer's. He translated whenever the man paused.

On the morning you were born,
were born the flowers.
On the day you were born,
nightingales sang . . .

With the last notes, Bill murmured, " 'Of the stars from the sky, I would take down just two — One with which to greet you, the other to say good-bye.' " Such sad, beautiful words that Katie, already overburdened, couldn't fight back all her tears. One rolled down her cheek before she scrubbed it away and took such a draught of strong coffee that she almost choked.

The musician played on, haunting tunes so full of longing that she was sure they were love songs. Unable to look at Bill, she took a bite of cake. It was delicious, but she had no appetite. Jed and Melissa devoured two pieces each while Katie had half of hers left. She didn't want to leave it and hurt Nellie's feelings, but it stuck in her throat and was increasingly hard to swallow.

Bill motioned to the buxom blonde waitress

475

who was helping Nellie serve tables. "Wonder if you could box up the cake, ma'am?"

"To be sure," she nodded. "Nellie has a box ready — said you'd paid for the cake when you ordered it special and that you're to take it with you."

"The custard's mighty good," Bill said to the children. "Why don't you have some while I have a talk with your sister?"

"And more coffee, please," Melissa said to the waitress as if she dined in good restaurants every day.

There was no escape. Bill drew back Katie's chair. As she rose, wondering what he wanted to talk about and afraid of breaking down completely, ruining what he had planned to make a happy day, he tried to press silver into the singer's hand.

"*Gracias,* Lord Bill, but no." The man bowed again, let his dark eyes rest meltingly on Katie. "To play for such a young lady's birthday celebration is my pleasure, my gift to her. *Señorita!* May you have love, money, and time to enjoy them."

"Thank you. The songs — I'll never forget them. They are a lovely gift."

"Not so lovely as you," he smiled. He went out, ducking to avoid knocking off the sombrero. Bill set his hand beneath Katie's elbow and steered her into the street. Walking past the firehouse and miners' dwellings, he said, "What's the matter, Katie?"

Mutely, she shook her head. He stopped, turned her toward him, hands on her shoulders. "What is it? What took the shine out of your eyes and your day?"

The warmth of his hands made her knees dissolve. She yearned to go into his arms, press her face against his chest and weep, wanted to be held and consoled. "I — oh, Bill, you killed a man here! How can you ride in all joking and lighthearted?"

"So that's it." He released her, gazing at the hill beyond the town where mine shafts were next to office buildings, workshops, and smoking chimneys. "I wanted these days to be nothin' for you but happy." His tone was so quiet she could scarcely hear above the dumping ore carts on the slag heap adjoining the firehouse. "Instead, because of what I am —"

"You can change!"

His eyes were like a winter sky hazed with coming storm. With coldness around her heart, she saw him, not as her friend but as Bill Radnor, gunman and outlaw, feared on both sides of the border. "I can't change what I've done."

Beseeching him, she said, "You can start over."

He sighed. "It's not that easy, honey. I've

got a name. If I hung up my guns, I'd be dead in a week." He set his fingers beneath her chin and made her look at him. "There's one thing I want you to know. I never killed anyone who didn't have a gun in his hand."

She nodded miserably. "I'm sure you didn't. Sure you wouldn't."

He sighed. "Katie. Will you do something for me?"

"Anything I can."

He touched her face. "Put what can't be mended out of your mind and make the most of what's happenin'. Have a happy birthday, darlin'. That's the best thing you can do for me."

Somehow, she did feel better, just having talked with him. She was sure that, though his urge for excitement might lead him into a gunfight, he didn't think that killing was fun. "All right, Bill. I *will* have a wonderful birthday. It already is."

"Fine. Now why don't Jed and me go buy that hoe and rake and other rifle you need while you girls do your shopping?" He brought out his wallet and pressed a number of greenbacks into her hand. "Don't argue. You can pay it back after your concert tonight. The seats are sold out, and there'll be folks jammed in the aisles anyplace they can stand. So, young lady, you'd better get back to the hotel in time to rest before dinner and your performance."

Katie's stomach churned at the thought of playing for a crowd used to famous musicians, but the money in her hand gave her courage. The miners and cowboys in Galeyville thought she was worth listening to. These people had paid a dollar apiece to hear her. She would sing her mother's songs, pluck notes like jewels from the old, old harp; if that did not content them, at least she'd do her best.

Proceeding down the boardwalk, which was shaded by wood awnings supported by posts, the sisters wandered through every store on Allen Street, not only feasting their eyes, but buying to such purpose that in one mercantile, the owner dispatched his assistant to the hotel, bundled with Levi's for Jed and Nacho; a Turkey red oilcloth tablecloth; sewing needs; muslin for chemises, drawers, and summer dresses for Rosie; a handsome gray Stetson for Nacho's Christmas; and a snugly soft blanket for Sally Fancher's baby.

Coming out of one store, they almost bumped into Billy Clanton, unsteady on his feet, whiskey strong on his breath. He stared at them blankly, then tugged off his hat. "Well, if it's not the MacLeod ladies! Welcome to Tombstone!"

"Thank you, Mr. Clanton." Katie hesitated. "I'm sorry about your father."

"We brought him out of the Peloncillos and buried him at our place," Billy said. His blue eyes glistened, and he ducked his head. " 'Scuse me, ladies. I see a friend of mine yonder." He cut across the street toward the Oriental Saloon, paying no heed to a cursing Wells-Fargo driver who veered just in time to miss him.

Affected by the encounter, sorry for Billy, though his wild old father had certainly brought his death on himself, Katie wondered what would become of the boy. Did he have a chance to choose a different life, grow up before he was killed? Such thoughts reminded her too much of her worry over Bill. With conscious effort, she concentrated on how to spend what was left of the afternoon.

Groceries could wait till next day, for the hours were flying. Katie gave Melissa five dollars, and they roamed separately in the largest emporium, where after much comparing and deliberation, Katie, for Christmas, bought Melissa a lacy blue Shetland wool fascinator and enameled locket as well as the embroidered scarlet edging to sew on her petticoat. For Bride there was a fringed, embroidered cashmere shawl the color of the Irish sea. Jed was hankering for a good pocketknife, and Katie finally chose a bone-handled one with four blades of Rodgers steel. Thinking of long winter evenings, she also bought him a set of dominoes.

Bill — Anything she got him must be able to fit in a saddle bag. She'd already bought linen to make handkerchiefs for him and John Diamond, but the heady feeling of having money to spend, though she had yet to earn it, made her recklessly determined to buy him something elegant, something he'd have to like even though he could buy anything he wanted. A pair of solid gold link sleeve buttons hand-engraved with horseheads caught her eye.

Merciful heaven! They cost $4.50, a dollar more than the imported Swiss gold watch beside them, more than the Persian shawl she'd wistfully admired, or that delectable bronze lace bonnet faced with velvet and trimmed along the edge with gold satin roses!

But surely he would like them. It gave her a thrill of pleasure to buy such a gift for her love. She chose a silver-plated magic pencil for Diamond, and it was time to get back to the hotel. Wonder of wonders, there was still ten dollars in her pocket.

As Bill had predicted, the Miners Exchange hall was jammed. Mr. Truitt, the manager, had found a padded stool of just the proper height for Katie to play the harp that rested on a small bench. As the curtains were drawn, she was seated with her left side toward the audience, skirts modestly arranged, the mass of her hair held back by the high enameled comb that was Jed's birthday gift.

Greeted with applause that shook the rafters as the sleek, tail-coated manager introduced her as "The Scottish Flower of the Chiricahuas," Katie, in a surge of panic, almost rose to flee. Then she saw Bill in the front row, Melissa and Jed on either side and — yes, that was John Diamond!

And there was Deputy Sheriff William Breakenridge next to Johnny Ringo, and Billy Clanton at the back with the MacLowery brothers. Most of the men were miners, though, like those at Bride's house who had become her friends. She knew the songs they liked — her hands knew. These people wanted to listen, and suddenly her fear was gone. She *wanted* to play, to give them the old harp's music.

Beginning with "Greensleeves," she ended with "Jack-a-Diamonds," able to smile past her harp to the gambler. Her fingers were sore and tingling. Rising, she bowed her head to the uproarious clapping that continued as the curtains shut. The clamor redoubled. When the cheering diminished not in the slightest after her fourth bow, the manager spread his hands.

"Could you give them one more, Miss MacLeod? They've never carried on like this even for Eddie Foy!"

Katie didn't know who he was, but if the audience liked her that much, she'd manage one more song. Nodding, she resumed her seat. She gave the standing crowd "Auld Lang Syne," and the curtains billowed shut a final time. The audience thronged the stage. Her hand was pumped, kissed, and patted till Bill and John Diamond came to her rescue and escorted her backstage, where she was more sedately praised by young Mayor John Clum; bearded Ed Schieffelin, who'd discovered Tombstone's rich lode; William Breakenridge; Sheriff Behan; young, husky Reverend Endicott Peabody, shepherd of the Episcopalians, who would don boxing gloves with any man who thought his collar made him a sissy; several grandiloquent lawyers; and Dr. George Goodfellow, a lean, rangy young man with a moplike brown moustache and merry eyes.

"How's the sawbones business, Doc?" asked Bill.

With a rueful smile at Katie, the doctor shrugged. "Thanks to practicing in Tombstone, I'm going to be the world's foremost authority on gunshot wounds. Did a little assessment work on a miner this morning. His body was rich in lead but too badly punctured to hold whiskey." At Katie's shocked face, he said quickly, "Forgive me, Miss MacLeod. I fear I'm not exposed to ladies often enough to remember that some subjects aren't fit for their ears." He eyed Bill with a curious professional eye. "You've fully recovered from that bullet through the hips? It would have killed anybody else."

"Oh, that loosened my hinges and bolts a tad, and I creak a little when it rains," shrugged Bill. "But I wasn't born to die by a bullet, or rope, either, in spite of some folks's fond hopes."

"How can you say that?" demanded Goodfellow.

"I just know it. I'll die quiet in my bed."

"Want to bet on that?" asked Diamond.

Bill grinned. "Not much point in it, Jack, since either way I won't be around to pay up or collect. And speak of collectin', here comes the manager."

Rotund, pink-cheeked Mr. Truitt handed Katie a canvas bag, which rustled and chinked at the same time. "Your share, Miss Mac-Leod. One hundred and forty-five dollars! If there'd been room, I could have sold twice as many seats." His voice took on a wheedling note. "You couldn't play another engagement?"

Dazed at these riches, Katie still didn't hesitate to shake her head. "I'm sorry, sir, but I'm already fretting over our baby sister, wondering how she is. We can't possibly stay longer than we've planned."

"When word gets around, I could charge two dollars a head," he urged.

"Thank you but no."

"Well," said Truitt reluctantly, "when you come to town again, remember, please, that I gave you your first chance, sight unseen, harp unheard. You *will* see me before making other engagements?"

"Of course I will." Katie gave him a radiant smile and her hand.

"Let me carry that bag for you, Katie," Bill said. "All those 'dobe dollars make quite a load. Truitt, I'll come for the harp tomorrow." As they went out into the crisp night, Katie gasped.

"The lights! Look at them, all along the streets!"

"Gas lamps," said Bill. "Tombstone's doin' its best to keep up with the big cities — not that it has much competition in the Territory."

A muted roar came from saloons and dance houses, and the street swarmed with begrimed miners coming off a shift while cleaner ones trooped toward work. Like saloons, the mines operated without a pause, running three shifts a day.

It was a town that never slept, was never silent. The afternoon's shopping had been dreamlike near-ecstasy, the evening's magnetic flow with the audience a complete intoxication. Suddenly, Katie was so exhausted she could hardly move one foot ahead of the other, and she was grateful for Bill's hand beneath her arm.

"Uncle Jack," Jed importuned. "There's over half of Katie's cake left. Come in and have a piece, won't you?"

"Thanks, son, but your sister's as ready to fold as I am when I've got a busted straight. How's about I join you for breakfast?"

"That would be nice," Katie said, and Bill nodded. "Make it nine, Jack. Katie needs a good night's sleep."

"I'll bid you good-night then." They were nearing the Crystal Palace. "I — uh — have an engagement." He rummaged inside his perfectly tailored black coat, extracted a small velvet box. "Since Melissa has a bee, Katie, it seems only fair that you should have a harp."

Lights blazing from the French windows and doors of the Palace struck fire from a golden harp encrusted with sparkling stones. "You can wear it as a pin, or there's a loop and a chain to make it into a pendant," Diamond explained. He kissed her cheek. "Bride sends her love. She'd have given her eyeteeth to come watch your triumph, but she couldn't leave her boys."

Katie stared transfixed at the glittering harp. She'd never seen anything manmade that was so beautiful. "John, it's too much! I can't —"

"You'll never be seventeen again," he laughed. "Wear it in health, Katie-Kate. Just pretend I'm your uncle."

In spite of her awed pleasure, up in the room, Katie was so sleepy that she could scarcely wash her face and undress before falling into the luxurious bed.

"It seems strange without Rosie," she sighed. "I wonder what she and Nacho are doing."

"They've been asleep for hours," said Melissa practically. "She'll have such fun with Nacho that she won't miss us at all." As she brushed out her yellow, yellow hair, the soft glow of the lamp made her look, in that graceful pose, almost a woman. "It was the grandest day! I just wish Tom could have come with us. He hasn't had many good times."

"He'll have plenty with us," Katie promised, snuggling into the vast pillow.

It had been a wonderful day, once Bill had made her tell him what was wrong. There was still a knot of sadness in her about that. But still, the most perfect day of her life had been when Bill took her up Whitetail Canyon and along the mountain — when they had been there high above the world.

Melissa blew out the lamp, sprang into bed, and gave Katie a squeeze. "Happy birthday, Katie!" They kissed good night, and Katie sank quickly into exhausted, blissful slumber.

XIX

When they entered the sumptuous restaurant next morning, Diamond was already seated, a steaming silver coffee urn before him. He rose, wincing, to pull out Melissa's chair while Bill did the same for Katie. Though Diamond was impeccably groomed, his shirt spotless and starched as the tablecloth, Katie thought the lines in his face had deepened since he last came to help them with their studies, and his eyes were red-rimmed.

"Ringo and I were up so late I never went to bed. Glad to see the rest of you look fresh as daisies." He slanted an amused look at Bill. "Even you, Radnor."

"I turned in early," Bill said virtuously. "Didn't crave a headache. But I reckon you and Ringo couldn't pass up a chance to show house dealers five of the same complexion when they were holdin' straights."

They breakfasted on omelettes with mushrooms, broiled oysters, and cream biscuits with marmalade. Sitting between Diamond and Bill, Katie seized a moment when the others were planning the day, to softly ask, "John, have you met your son?"

"No. I don't expect to. Lieutenant Corrigan

489

is in command of a detachment camped in Horseshoe Canyon in the San Simon Valley. If he wants to see me, it's only twenty miles if he rides over the mountains and comes down Cave Creek Canyon."

"It's only twenty miles the other way, too, John."

"I won't force myself on him."

"He just doesn't understand —"

"And isn't about to try."

"He's your only son."

"I know that better than anyone."

She laid her hand on his arm. "John, please!"

"Leave it, Katie." His tone was brusque. "He's a grown man. He knows what he wants." The gambler drained his coffee and got to his feet. "Enjoy your stay in Tombstone, Clan MacLeod. I'm heading for Galeyville. If it suits you, I'll come over Wednesday and we'll work on division and multiplication."

Jed pulled a face. "I'd rather read *Tom Sawyer.*"

Diamond tousled Jed's hair affectionately. "You've got to have enough arithmetic to conduct business, son, and help keep the Home Mountain dairy and Steel Dust accounts. See you Wednesday." His burnished metal eyes met Katie's. "Seventeen's special, my dear. Have a happy year."

490

Katie's heart ached for him, though she was exasperated at his stubbornness. Men! Left to themselves, they wouldn't do much but ignore each other or fight. No time to brood over it, though. It was ten o'clock! Never before had she sat down to breakfast at nine. It felt positively sinful, but oh, the huge bed and pillows had been so comfortable! For the first time since Melissa yielded her crib to Jed and started sleeping with Katie, there'd been room enough that Melissa's restlessly flung-out arms and legs hadn't roused Katie several times a night. Also, since Rosie was born, this was the first time she hadn't demanded attention. *But I miss her so — if seems a week since I cuddled her, felt her pat my face . . .*

"Better wind up your shoppin'," Bill said. "Have the groceries stowed in bags or boxes branded good with your name so I can pack Smiler in the morning."

Katie had figured up what Jed told her Bill had spent on the Winchester, cartridges, and hoe. He'd also advanced Jed three dollars. Katie opened the money bag Mr. Truitt had given her the night before, took out a bundle of greenbacks, and handed Bill the bag. "That should make us even."

"There's no rush."

"I'll feel better to have it paid back. Jed,

why don't you come with M'liss and me?"

"Aw —"

"Leave him to me," said Bill, grinning. "It'll keep me out of trouble. We'll meet you at the Can Can around noon. They have lobster, shrimp, and fish rushed in by stage from the Mexican coast. The corvina are especially good."

Katie tucked the bills deep into her long pocket and, with Melissa, set forth to stock up on groceries.

Two-storied Schieffelin Hall was an imposing sight, just around the corner from the *Epitaph* office and the two-story adobe in which Doctor Goodfellow had his surgery in sight of the Episcopal Church a block away. Catty-corner from the Hall were Fly's Photo Gallery, the back entrance of the OK Corral, and the lot where the City Hall was being raised.

Again, there was standing room only. Again, Katie's nervousness changed to the wish to give music to a crowd so eager to hear her. A harp string broke, causing great dismay, but someone appropriated a string from a player piano and she was able to play on. Her share of the proceeds was two hundred dollars, a sum so staggering that she couldn't imagine such riches for a few hours that had been pleasure for her, something she would gladly have done for nothing.

"Want to open a bank account?" asked Bill, chinking another heavy bag as they walked toward the hotel after the throng of admirers finally dispersed.

"No. I'll keep whatever silver there is after paying the hotel bill and hide it in the cellar. Didn't you say we'd have breakfast at Miss Nellie's in the morning?"

"If that suits you."

"I want to leave a hundred dollars for her to help people."

"Katie!" Melissa yelped. "You wouldn't buy a new dress for your concert even when we saw that lovely green velvet that was just your size!"

"I can't wear a velvet dress on a ranch. We've bought everything we need for months and months, and we've had a wonderful, wonderful time. It doesn't seem right to keep all the money when the town gave it to us."

"Honey," said Bill, scratching his head, "Some Tombstone folks have been known to lose more on the turn of a single card than you made at both concerts."

"All the same, I want to give the money to Miss Nellie."

"When that word gets around," said Bill, "I bet it'll be a long time before she has to ask high rollers to contribute to her shorn sheep and lame ducks. Get some rest, Katie. It's Maison Doree for supper and then Miss Boyd and her play."

They had supper with Julius Caesar, the three-chinned, florid-faced owner, hovering at their table, suggesting delicacies. Seated in a box next to Bill, Katie hung on every gesture and word of Miss Nellie Boyd and her Dramatic Company of New York and Chicago fame. The evening passed like the enchanted dream this whole holiday had been. Katie had expected the hotel bill to be outrageous, and indeed it was, but there was still close to ninety dollars left after she gave Nellie Cashman a hundred and got a warm hug and kiss in return.

"I wish we lived here," said Jed, glancing back wistfully as they faced eastward with the Dragoons sprawling down the middle of the Sulphur Springs Valley and the Chiricahuas so far away that they hazed into the sky almost without a line to mark them. "Billy Clanton bought me a sarsaparilla, and Deputy Breakenridge showed me around the sheriff's office, and Mr. Schieffelin took me down in his Lucky Cuss Mine. Jeeminy! The first ore out of it assayed fifteen thousand dollars to the ton! I'll bet if we lived around

494

here, I could find a lode!"

"Jed," scoffed Melissa, "You're such a baby! First you want to be a gambler, then it's a cowboy, and now a prospector. Keep changing your mind like that and you'll never be anything."

"I've got time to do a lot of things," Jed retorted. "I'm sure glad I'm not just an old girl who can't do anything but get married!"

"Katie and I don't have to get married," Melissa informed him loftily. "We've got a dairy and Steel Dust horses and — and anytime we need *lots* of money, Katie can play her harp!"

To Katie, silver clinking in the bag with her clothing, it still seemed a dream, but magical as it had been, she was glad to be going home. Her arms ached for Rosie. She wanted to caress Shiloh and Jenny and the other horses, croon to Flossie and Cinders and the cattle. All she truly wanted was at Home Mountain — except for Bill.

Sally Fancher pressed the baby blanket to her cheek, gentian eyes glowing as she impulsively gave Katie a thank-you kiss.

"Matt," drawled Bill, producing a bundle. "If it's all right with you, I'd like to give your wife a little somethin' for puttin' up with us all goin' and comin'."

"Why, sure," said Matt, looking, beside Bill, very skinny, young, and awkward. His jaw dropped a bit when Sally eagerly unwrapped the same exquisite Persian shawl that Katie had fancied. Seeing his wife's pleasure, however, Matt swallowed.

"Mighty thoughtful of you, Bill," he said manfully amidst Sally's exclamations of delight.

Bill said gruffly, "Everybody always gives the baby a present, but I reckon the mama should get one, too."

Katie loved him so much in that moment that she thought her heart would burst.

They reached Home Mountain in mid-afternoon. Bill had promised to have Smiler back in Galeyville that evening, so as soon as he'd helped unload, he departed. Desolate, Katie couldn't bear to watch him out of sight. After being in his company for almost six days, she felt dull and dreary without him but gave herself a determined mental shake.

How dared she mope when she had enjoyed such a transcendent birthday trip? With shame and a stab of grief, she thought that her mother had never pleasured in such a time; in fact, she suspected that Mary MacLeod's only solaces had been her harp and her children. *The other three*, Katie thought, but instead of her usual bitterness, Katie felt compassion for a desperate girl not as old as she was, who had, Katie was positive, married without love to give her baby a father. Which led to an appalling thought.

If James MacLeod had perished alone, if Mary hadn't provoked early labor by trying to save him, without his dour presence, might she not have been different to Katie — have been free at last to love her?

That would never be answered, never, but Katie was glad that her old bitterness had faded, that her main regret now was for Mary's constricted life, and not for herself. Cuddling Rosie, Katie stood on the walkway and watched the joyful reunion of the horses. The cows were ambling along the ridge, slowly grazing their way toward the corral, while Prince Coal bolted amongst the other calves, trying to lure them into a frolic.

Delight in the animals, pleasure in Home Mountain Ranch, the sweetness of the little body in her arms filled Katie. This *was* home. It was good to be here. But as she went inside to tuck Christmas presents away before they were discovered, holding the golden cufflink buttons, she sent a flow of love to Bill and allowed herself the dream that someday this would be his home, too.

Nacho, much to Melissa's disappointment,

said that Tom Buford had ridden over to say that he didn't want to be a burden to the Mac-Leods and had consequently decided to work through October for the Pitchfork. That way he could not only buy the clothes he needed but come with a little money in his pocket.

"Shucks!" scowled Jed. "Katie, why don't I ride over to tell him you made so much money with your harp that he doesn't have to worry about stuff like that?"

Before she could answer, Nacho said gently, "He will feel better, Jed, if he comes with money he has earned. Later, when the ranch prospers with his help, that will be different."

Time now to break ears of corn from withered stalks and store them in the cellar; time to snap the pumpkins from the vines and leave them in the sun till the shells hardened, when they, too, would be stored in the cellar.

When Diamond came, except for necessary chores, they gave the day to lessons. In between, Katie made sure they studied for an hour or two each day, even if it was spelling or reciting times tables and posing addition or subtraction problems to each other while at night, by a cheery fire, they sat around a tub and stripped cobs of corn. When Katie didn't play the harp before bedtime, or Nacho didn't tell stories, Katie or Melissa would read from *Tom Sawyer* or *Scottish Chiefs,* pages they had previously read to themselves, sounding out words they didn't know.

According to Diamond, a few days after his return from what was now referred to as "Katie's Birthday," Bill had left town and not returned. He was frequently gone for weeks, Katie knew, but still it fretted her when she knew he was away.

She was hanging out clothes one morning late in October, smiling at the chatter of the jays, and perky little juncos, gray and rust, who would stay the winter. The *chulos,* or coatimundis, watched her curiously from the lower limbs of the big oak. Charming creatures they were, with long, pointed clever noses, neat little rounded ears, and sinuous tails as long as their furry grayish-tan bodies. They had talonlike digging claws and resembled a raccoon-monkey cross.

"They must have wandered up from Mexico," Nacho had mused, when Ace barked them up the tree on their first appearance several weeks ago. "I've never heard of them this far north before. Probably yearlings. Females and their young born this summer will stay in a band, the females standing guard and looking after any young one that needs help. They play and visit, *chulos* do, and groom each other while they gossip. But the males are only with the group from breeding time till the females get cranky with them after the young are born. The male yearlings have to leave, too, then. These traveled far."

"Why don't the males stay together?" Jed asked.

Nacho shrugged. "Who knows? They forage alone, and *chulos* eat just about anything. The only males who stay in pairs are brothers."

"Poor little guys," said Jed. "Can't we put out something for them to eat, Katie?" So scraps were put out for the *chulos* daily, and Ace learned to tolerate them. In fact, he seemed to have decided they were companions of a sort.

When Ace started barking, Katie thought he'd decided to pester the *chulos*. A reprimand died in her throat as he ran barking toward the creek, frightening the *chulos* higher up the tree. As always when the dog sounded an alarm, Katie's heart skipped a beat. She was poised to dash for the house when a lone rider topped the eastern slope. It was a black horse, and with relief, she recognized Diamond's lazily erect posture long before she could see his face. Draping Jed's Levi's on a bush, she hurried inside to make biscuits, a little puzzled to see John today since he'd held lessons only the day before yesterday. She heard Jed greeting his idol and was cutting out biscuits when Diamond came in.

She knew by his grim expression that something was wrong. A floury hand went to her throat. "Bill?"

He shook his head. "No. Far as I know, Bill's fine, though he's not been in Galeyville of late. Katie, I know you had a fondness for young Billy Clanton. He's dead. So are Frank and Tom MacLowery."

Katie's head whirled. Billy Clanton with his yellow hair and blue, blue eyes, always laughing till that last time she'd seen him — reckless but somehow very likable. Now he wouldn't have a chance to grow up.

"How —?"

Diamond took her hands. "Doc Holliday and Ike Clanton got in a fuss around midnight on the twenty-fifth. Next day, Wyatt Earp pistol-whipped Tom MacLowery. Then, early in the afternoon, the Clantons and Mac-Lowerys were fixing to leave town when the Earps and Doc Holliday braced them. Tom and Ike weren't armed. According to Ike, who got away, they all put up their hands when Virgil Earp told them to and Tom opened his coat to show he was unarmed, but Wyatt and Morgan opened fire. According to the Earps, Billy Clanton and Frank MacLowery pulled six-shooters. Holliday killed Tom with a double charge of buckshot from his sawed-off shotgun. Morgan Earp's first shot hit Billy, but he fought from his knees and wounded Virgil Earp in the leg. He also shot Morgan through the shoulder. Wyatt's first bullet took Frank MacLowery in the belly, but it was a bullet in the brain that finished him, either from Holliday or Morgan. Billy kept firing, bad hurt as he was. Virgil Earp shot him in the chest, and that knocked him on his back. Some men carried the kid to Doc Goodfellow's office. Doc gave him a shot of morphine to ease his pain. Sheriff Behan tried to stop the fight while the Earps were coming down the street, but they were set on a showdown."

"I — I know the Clantons and MacLowerys were suspected of stealing cattle," Katie said, feeling sick.

Billy Clanton, eighteen years old, badly hurt, deserted by his brother, his friends dead, battling to the last four of the most deadly men in the West. A terrible image filled her mind: Billy, face twisted with rage and agony, defying his enemies like a cornered wild creature, dying possessed by hatred. Somehow, his passing into eternity in such a state was more horrible than his dying. God have mercy on him. Whom would he meet in the world he passed to, his terrible old father, or the mother who'd surely have grieved if she knew in the afterlife what trails her sons were riding?

Katie fought back scalding tears. "Can — can the Earps just shoot them down like that and get away with it?"

"They'll stand trial. But they're saying they thought the men were all armed and that they were conspiring to murder them." Diamond shrugged. "With the Earps all law officers of one kind or another and Holliday deputized, it's not likely they'll be punished. One whisper is that the Earps and Holliday were involved in trying to hold up the Benson stage back in March when it was carrying eighty thousand dollars. Whoever did it killed Bud Philpot, the driver who'd changed seats with the shotgun messenger, Bob Paul. It's rumored that the Earp outfit was afraid that the Clantons and MacLowerys might be able to give evidence that would link them to the murder and attempted robbery. But rumors are just that. Rumors."

He hesitated. "I wanted to give you the straight story, Katie, before you heard all kind of puffed-up stories that might have had Bill Radnor dead, too."

"Thank you, John."

Numbly, she fitted biscuits into the Dutch oven, placed it in the coals, and heaped more around and over the iron cover. Bill wasn't killed this time; but three young men she had known had died in seconds in view of Schieffelin Hall, where only three weeks ago she'd played her harp. It was in just such a way, in such an ordinary moment, that any day, any hour, Bill could meet his death.

Two days later, they were moving pumpkins to the cellar late one afternoon when Nacho stiffened, shading his eyes as he scanned the southern horizon. "A rider." He squinted. "That looks like Tom Buford's pinto pony."

"Maybe he decided to quit the Pitchfork early," said Melissa. "Katie, isn't it lucky we have that apple pie made?"

"He won't get all of it," warned Jed. "Hush up, Ace. That's our new pardner."

"Let's hurry and get these pumpkins in," appealed Katie, for her brother and sister looked ready to abandon their work and run to meet Tom. "Once they're stored, we can take the rest of the day easy."

Thus occupied, they didn't really watch Tom's approach. They stowed the last plump orange globes as he splashed across the creek, and only then did they go to meet him.

"Apaches!" He slid from the saddle, held to the horn as if his legs were trying to fold. The freckles blotched across his nose seemed to stand out on his sunburned skin, and the hazel eyes were dilated. "They hit head-quarters yesterday noon. Came out of no-where! Didn't waste much time at the ranch house — just ran off some good horses that were in the corral. But Hallie had gone off alone after Mr. Larrimore, who'd left for Tombstone that morning. The Apaches got Hallie and they're headed for Mexico!"

"Mr. Larrimore's in Tombstone?" Katie faltered, unable to take in what Tom was say-ing.

"I guess he was tickled to hear what they're sayin'— that Lord Bill's dead. Word is that the Earps killed him over in the Whet-stones. Tried to collect the reward on him from Colonel Hooker, but seems like Hooker didn't believe it and wouldn't pay."

Melissa gave a wild cry, threw herself on Katie. "He can't be dead! He can't be! Not Bill —"

Tom's face dissolved in swirling, writhing vapors of red and black that exploded in Katie's brain. *Hooker didn't believe it. There'd been no body.* She clung to that. When she could form words and push them through her tight throat, she whispered, "Did — did any-one see it?"

"Only the Earps and Holliday. They jumped him in his camp by a spring, him and some friends. The Earps claimed he was wanted for robbery — that a stage driver recognized him. But some think they were afraid he'd try to get even for Billy Clanton and the MacLowerys. They were his friends. What's sure is that no one's seen Lord Bill."

Whether he was dead or had simply left the country, Larrimore could move to get custody of the children now. That must be why he'd gone to Tombstone.

"What about Hallie?" cut in Jed.

"She slipped away from Chapita, rode after her daddy on her Glencoe horse. You know how feisty she is. She was mad at Mr. Larrimore for not takin' her along." The boy swallowed. "Seth Riley and I were makin' a last hunt for unbranded calves yesterday and camped out. Didn't know what was goin' on till Shell Brown dragged into our camp this noon shot full of arrows. He'd ridden out to warn some homesteaders not to settle on Pitchfork range. On the way, he saw Hallie, and while he was tryin' to catch up with her, the Apaches, about thirty of them, rode down the valley with the horses they'd stolen."

"Is he sure they — they didn't kill Hallie?" Again it was Jed asking.

"She was alive last he saw of her, tied in the saddle. Don't see how Shell can pull through. We did what we could for him and left him in our camp while Seth took out for

506

Tombstone to tell the boss and I rode here. If one bunch broke off the reservation, maybe more will. They haven't ever really quieted down since their Dreamer was killed."

Nacho stiffened. "Some are here now," he said very quietly. "I just saw a rock move across the creek where a few of the horses are. And that bush —" Katie was rooted to the ground. Nacho pushed her and Melissa. "Get inside! Tom, bring your horse in."

"But they're going to steal Shiloh and Red Rover and Chili and Babe!" Jed cried.

"Better that than getting ourselves killed." Nacho was shooing all of them along. "If we don't try to stop them, they'll probably run off the easy pickings and leave us alone. There aren't enough Apache warriors to risk any needlessly."

So frightened that she could scarcely breathe, Katie looked vainly for the other horses or the cows. Thank heaven, they were grazing up the canyon or behind a slope. The raiders couldn't guess there were more animals, and probably they wouldn't search, since they were surely hurrying to reach Mexico before pursuing troops caught up with them.

"We must get the weapons ready and pull out the chinks from the firing holes," Nacho said.

Tom patted the rifle in his saddle scabbard.

507

"Glad I spent some of my pay on a Winchester!"

As if watching herself in a bad dream — and surely it was a bad dream — surely, surely, Bill couldn't be dead — surely Apaches weren't really out there in the field — Katie got a Winchester, levered in a cartridge, and took a firing hole where she could watch bushes and rocks moving, shadows gliding from one high clump of bear grass to another. Melissa stood beside her with the shotgun. Nacho took the other front firing hole.

"If some do attack — which is unlikely — let them know at once that we are well-armed. Tom, you will break out a window pane and shoot through that, keeping to the side. Jed, keep watch at the rear. The garden wall provides good cover if they decide to use it."

Katie remembered all the terrifying stories she'd heard about Apache raids. Older children, especially boys, were often adopted into a band, but a baby would be in the way. And someone her age, if not killed, would be a drudge to her captor's wives unless she became one of them.

No! She mustn't think of such things! Thank goodness, they'd bought plenty of cartridges and shotgun shells in Tombstone. There was food in the house, two buckets of water, milk for Rosie. Even if the Apaches laid siege, with any luck, they could be held off till they decided the risks weren't worth the poor kind of plunder in most frontier homes.

In spite of this reasoning, Katie's hands shook as she grasped the rifle. She gasped as one coppery figure quickly looped a rope halter around Babe's head and vaulted to her back. Instinctively, Katie braced the rifle against her shoulder and peered down the sights.

"At this distance, you will probably not hit anything," warned Nacho. "But you are more likely to shoot a horse than a man."

Trembling, Katie watched another warrior capture Chili, watched others slip nooses around the necks of Shiloh and Red Rover. "Let's try to stop them!" Jed yelled. "If there's only five or six of them —"

Nacho caught the boy's arm. "Look."

A band of riders waited on a knoll, perhaps a score of them. Surrounding the house, at different vantage points, breech-clouted brown bodies detached themselves from rocks and brush. Rifles glinted as they rejoined the party.

Unnerved, Katie whispered, "How could they come up on us like that? If you hadn't seen those down by the horses, Nacho —"

The Yaqui shrugged. "They scatter out when approaching possible danger or prey,

with scouts moving in from different directions. One seldom sees them till they're ready
to be seen." Katie hadn't realized how tense
the old man was till he let out a sighing breath.
"They have four fine horses — but we have
our lives."

"I should have stopped those 'Paches!"
mourned Jed. "I'm the only man in the family.
It was up to me."

"Fudge!" Katie held him tight, tried to
speak strongly. "We've still got the other
horses and all the cows. We're mighty lucky
when you think what could have happened."
Still, her heart ached for the loss of the horses,
especially Shiloh, spirited, handsome Shiloh,
who was to have been her gift to Bill.

Oh, Bill! *It's not true, Colonel Hooker
wouldn't pay. The Earps lied about it or were
mistaken.* People didn't die of grief — at least
not if they were young and strong, she knew
that. But to believe him dead would kill the
woman part of her, strangle the part that
dreamed and laughed and loved.

Wrenching herself from this agony, deter-
mining to believe him alive till she was forced
to admit otherwise, Katie was aware for the
first time that Rosie was howling, indeed,
had been crying since they rushed into the
house. At the moment, though, Jed needed
comfort worse than his baby sister, whose

world could be made right so simply with being held and soothed, given some milk, having a diaper changed.

"At least the horses are so good that the Apaches won't eat them down in Mexico the way they usually do once a journey's over," Katie said, releasing Jed with a hug.

Tom started outside with his horse, but paused to say, hazel eyes clouded, "I sure am sorry you lost those horses."

"We were still lucky." Katie shuddered. "Poor little Hallie!"

That made Katie remember why Larrimore had probably gone to Tombstone and that chilled her almost as much as the Apaches had. It proved that Larrimore, at least, must credit the account of either Bill's death or his permanent quitting of the country. It was possible that Larrimore had better information than did Colonel Hooker. *No! She wouldn't, couldn't believe it.*

"It was payday when the Apaches hit," said Tom, returning. He had only ground-hitched his horse by trailing the reins in front of him. "Most of the hands had gone to Galeyville or San Simon to blow off steam. Beau Murphree's sent riders to both towns to collect the men, and another to Tombstone to tell Mr. Larrimore. Soon as Beau gets a party together, they'll go after Hallie. I told him

I'd come back and help once I'd warned you."

"You can't follow that raiding party so close," Katie admonished and remembered with sudden hope. "Lieutenant Corrigan's detachment should be along the way the Apaches ride." Whatever Larrimore planned for her family, she suffered at the thought of a child younger than Jed being stolen away by a band of painted, half-naked warriors. "Maybe he can —"

Nacho shook his head. "The lieutenant has — what? Ten men? Twelve? There were perhaps thirty in the band that stole Hallie, the twenty-odd warriors that attacked us will be following, and who knows that there may not be another small group or two driving off all the livestock they can to feed their people through the winter in the Sierra Madre? Until he has reinforcements — and most of all, scouts who know the country and Apaches — all the lieutenant can do is get his command slaughtered."

So many horrors. *Bill — oh, Bill!* Pulling herself together with a supreme effort of will, Katie said, "You'll get yourself killed or captured if you leave now, Tom, and it'll soon be dark. If you have to go, wait till morning."

"Please, Tom," begged Melissa. "If those Apaches got you —"

"The other rescue groups can't start today,"

said Nacho. "Get a good supper, a good night's rest, and leave at dawning. More than likely you will meet up with Pitchfork cowboys or another posse."

Tom gave in reluctantly and went to help Jed bring up the cows for milking. There was no laughter around the table that night. Jed refused his apple pie.

"I'm not sick," he muttered in response to Katie's anxious question. "I — I just wonder if Hallie's got something to eat."

"They plan to keep her," said Nacho. "So she won't starve."

Jed got up hastily from the table, caught Ace in his arms, and went up the ladder to his loft. Melissa stared at Katie. "I thought he didn't like Hallie."

"Like her or not, this is awful." *And Bill — oh, Bill!* Scarcely able to see through blurring tears, Katie got up and began to clear the table.

XX

Next morning, Jed didn't come down to do his chores; neither was Tom stirring. Katie thought the boys had overslept, tired out by the strain of the attack, and decided to let them sleep. While Melissa tended Rosie, Katie brought up the cows and set to milking.

In spite of her resolve to consider Bill alive, worry for him was a crushing weight. It desolated her further to see how Honeybunch and Chica, the burro, restlessly haunted the oaks where their companions had last grazed. Jenny was out of sight, but she surely hadn't tried to follow Shiloh because Señorita was down among the oaks, questing forlornly with Goldie for their master of races and games, Red Rover.

At least they and the cows were safe. Katie got some comfort from pressing her forehead first against Queenie's sleek warm flank and then against Cinders's and Lady Jane's, milking on one side while Spots and Prince Coal tugged greedily at the other. When she went inside, Katie made herself speak cheerfully to Melissa. "We have two mares left, and the fillies can have colts in three years. Colonel Hooker has some fine stallions —"

"Damn Colonel Hooker and damn you, Katie!" Melissa gave the cornmeal mush a furious stir and began to fill the bowls. "How can you think of having anything to do with the colonel when he — he was ready to pay for Bill's being killed? Don't you ever think about anything but building up herds and this ranch?"

Stricken, cut to the heart, Katie could find no words. She looked at her sister for a moment and then carried the steaming hot water kettle outside to scald the milking things. When she returned, the aroma of coffee filled the room. One of the luxuries Katie had bought in Tombstone was enough coffee to permit them to drink it every day.

"I hear thrashing around in the loft," said Nacho. "Jed could be having nightmares. It may be time to wake him."

Melissa, avoiding Katie's eyes, was giving Rosie her bottle. Katie held up her skirts, climbed the ladder, and called softly from the top rung, "Jed! Time for breakfast, honey!"

Lit only by one tiny window, the loft was dark. What she thought was Jed's huddled form went into a convulsive struggle. A muffled whine came from the bundle. Tom, in the other corner, jerked upright.

"Where —" he began, and then rolled from his blankets, fully clothed except for his boots, which he hastily pulled on. "Good gravy, the sun's up! I've got to hurry!"

Katie gripped the ends of the ladder. "Do you know where Jed is, Tom?"

For the first time, Tom realized something was wrong. "He's not downstairs?"

Katie shook her head. Hauling herself to the loft floor, she hurried to the pallet. Her brother was gone — his boots, hat, and Winchester, and a couple of his blankets. With trembling fingers, she loosed a squirming Ace from the shirt that had been tied snugly around him, the strip of sheet that had formed a muzzle fastened around his nose and secured behind his ears. A scrap of paper lay on the pillow.

Too dark to read. Taking it and the puppy, followed by Tom, Katie descended, nearly oblivious to Ace's frantic slathering of her face and neck. "We'd better keep him in," she said dully as she let him down. "He might follow Jed."

Even before she read the labored printing, she guessed where he had gone. *"I want to get the horses back, and Hallie, too,"* the wavery letters ran. *"I knew you wouldn't let me go with Tom, Katie, but I've got a dandy idea. Uncle Jack says Apaches will gambell on anything. I will try them. Don't fret. I'll be karefull. Take kare of Ace. I hobelled Senyorita so she couldn't follow Jenny and me.*"

Reading it aloud, Katie stared at it as if the words might change. No wonder she hadn't seen Jenny that morning! Tom started for the door. "I'll go after them. With luck, I can catch up with Jed before he gets close to the Apaches."

"Wait!" What she must do came to Katie's mind without conscious thought. She exchanged glances with the old Yaqui. "You'll go with me, Nacho?"

He nodded. "Tom," said Katie, "I have to go after Jed. He's my brother. Nacho understands Apaches, so he's coming. But we can't leave Rosie and Melissa here alone, not with Apaches on the loose. Please, you stay here."

"Katie!" Melissa cried.

"We can't just let Jed get himself killed," argued Katie.

"No, but" — Melissa seized her — "Katie, what if the Apaches kill you? Or make you a slave?"

"The Apaches won't kill Jed unless they have to," Nacho said. "A boy that fearless would make them a valuable warrior."

"Jed's not fearless." Katie tried futilely to swallow the lump in her throat. She tried not to think of things she'd heard Apaches had done to women. They didn't rape, but there were mutilations, tortures — Still, it was impossible

517

to stay here while her brother rode into danger. She sucked in a long breath. "Jed had to go — and so do I."

"Mr. Larrimore will get the army after Hallie," cried Melissa. "They can bring Jed back, too."

"The army's not supposed to enter Mexico," Katie pointed out. "Even if they do, they may never find the Indians." The anger that had flashed between the sisters that morning washed away in their tears as they embraced.

"May we use your pinto, Tom?" asked Nacho.

"Katie," the boy urged, "let me go. That's no trail for a gir — I mean, lady."

"I can't wait here and wonder about Jed."

Melissa poured coffee and splashed milk on the mush. "Eat before you go. And at least stop by Galeyville and get Mr. Diamond and some of the other men to ride with you!" She burst into sobs. "Katie, I — I just couldn't stand it if you d-didn't come back."

"You'd stand it. You'd look after Rosie and Tom would help, and so would Bride, and all our friends. We can't ride through Galeyville, honey. That would lose us an hour — enough to let Jed find the Apaches before we can catch up with him."

Nacho spooned up his mush and swallowed down the coffee, turning to the door. "While

Tom and I get the horses, fill our canteens, roll some blankets, and put food and cartridges in our saddlebags. You'd better change, Katie, into the old clothes of mine that you were going to mend."

Rosie, in the bedroom, was crooning to herself. Katie ran back to get her. Pressing her face to the baby's silken hair, she prayed they would soon all be together again — and if Bill lived, she would never ask for anything more, even the return of Shiloh and the other Steel Dusts. Leaving the baby on the rug, Katie hurried back to strip off her skirts and pull on Nacho's ragged trousers and shirt. When she returned, Melissa was stuffing the saddlebags with Tombstone delicacies, sardines, cheese, and dried fruit. Katie bundled up cold biscuits from last night. She and Melissa carried out the bags, rolled blankets, and canteens, and helped Nacho and Tom fasten them to the saddles.

"Oh, Katie!" wailed Melissa.

Katie held her tight. "We'll be back. Take care of Rosie. Tom, you take care of both of them."

The hazel eyes were moist. "You bet I will!"

Katie put on the hat Tom had loaned her, set her foot in the stirrup, swung into the pinto's saddle, and was off beside Nacho on Honeybunch at a fast trot, waving back from the top of the first slope.

Let us find Jed, she prayed, and the wind soughed the refrain in her ears. *Let us find him. And little Hallie — let her be safe, let her be rescued.*

If only Bill were here! He knew the canyons of Sonora as well he did those of southern New Mexico and Arizona. *If only Bill's alive . . .*

As they neared the turning to Galeyville, the trail being fairly well defined now by travel back and forth to Home Mountain, Nacho said, "Look! It is Don Juan!"

Diamond hailed them with an upflung arm. Raven stretched himself into a smooth lope. When he came within earshot, Diamond called, "The children — are they all right?"

When he heard what Jed had done, he groaned, but said after a moment with fatherly pride. "It might just work. Apaches love to gamble. And they honor courage above everything. If a white boy rode up to them of his own will and proposed a wager —"

"What if he lost?"

Diamond grinned. "I don't think you have to worry about that."

"John! You weren't just fishing all those afternoons!"

"A boy needs educating so he won't be cheated," said the gambler blandly, then said in quick alarm, "That changes things. Beau Murphree left town at dawn with all the Pitchfork cowboys he could sober up and a dozen other men, heading after the Apaches. I didn't hear about it till Bride roused me, scared to death about you, so of course I started out right away for your place. Jed might pull off his stunt alone — but not if a big bunch of cowboys and citizens go storming down."

At Katie's frightened look, he explained, "If there's a good ambush site, the Apaches will wipe them out for a windfall of horses and gear. If it's not to the Apaches' advantage to attack, they'll simply fade away — but if they're pressed, they'd likely kill both children." Diamond scanned her face. "What if you can't catch up with Jed before he gets surrounded by Indians? It won't do any good for you to be made captive or killed."

"I — I hoped we'd find him first. From his tracks, Nacho thinks he doesn't have more than a four-hour start on us."

Slowly, Diamond said, "But his scheme may be the best — maybe the only — chance for Hallie."

Katie's mouth went dry. "I'll bet Ed Larrimore's in Tombstone right now trying to get custody of the children," she cried, overwhelmed by fear and bitterness. "He waited till he heard Bill was dead!" Staring at her friend, she demanded pleadingly, "Do you believe that, John? Do you think Bill's been killed?"

"Katie, I don't know."

She rode for a time in tormented silence. Hallie's imperious small face rose before her. Spoiled and indulged, used to every comfort, what was happening must terrify her more than it would a girl more harshly raised. Jed had borne the brunt of her pique over his riding Glencoe, yet he'd gone alone to try to save her. A deep breath escaped from Katie.

"Surely the army — if they have scouts —"

"They can find the tracks. And Hallie's body."

"John!"

"The only thing — apart from Jed's plan — that might work would be to offer ransom. Apaches know that soldiers won't kill them like varmints the way Beau Murphree's bunch would if they got a chance. Apaches have got used to parleying with men in uniform. Negotiations have repeatedly been set up that way. A small group of soldiers and scouts make contact with the hostiles and set up a meeting with higher-ups or agree on terms that have induced the Apaches to return to the reservation. If Larrimore sent a ransom offer through a detachment, chances are good the

Apaches would listen. I'll bet they'd rather have a hundred head of cattle or some mules and horses than one little white girl."

"That's what we can do!"

"What?"

"There aren't enough of us to scare the Apaches into killing prisoners and running. Nacho can make them understand that we're offering livestock for Hallie — and Jed, too, in case his idea doesn't work. Larrimore's bound to be willing to trade cattle for his daughter."

Nacho said, "Many Apaches speak some Spanish. I can make them understand." He nodded, smiling for the first time since they'd found Jed gone. "It could succeed. But we must try to overtake Murphree and his cowboys, persuade them to wait."

"More than likely, Lieutenant Corrigan and his men also are on the trail south," said Diamond. "I hope he has a good scout or two. They'll advise him not to crowd." The gambler sighed. "If he'll listen. The lieutenant, I fear, still goes too much by West Point battle tactics, which have nothing to do with this kind of trouble."

Since Diamond and Nacho both seemed to believe there was a chance they could rescue Hallie, they had no choice but to try. It eased the strain about overtaking Jed, but now it was vital to keep the Pitchfork men from endangering the children.

"Maybe I should ride ahead and try to get Beau to hold off," said Diamond. "It'll wear Raven down, but most likely one of the cowboys would change horses so I wouldn't have to keep pushing him."

Katie bit back a protest. Diamond's company and his cool appraisal of the problems had mightily heartened her; she didn't want him to leave them. But he was right, of course. She was starting to wish him well and urge him to be careful when Nacho said, "There are two men over there by that big wash. They seem to be piling up rocks."

"Must be burying somebody," surmised Diamond. "Shell Brown must have cashed in. This sounds like where young Tom was camped, just where the Chiricahuas end, and the valley opens out all the way to Mexico."

As they neared, Katie recognized Sherm Walcott, the bald, lame cook she'd seen at the branding. The other hand, a chubby blue-eyed boy, looked scarcely older than Tom Buford. Shell had still been alive when Beau's party found him that morning, so Beau had ordered the cook and the lad to stay with the foreman till he died and bury him decently.

They knew Diamond, and when he explained his fear that Beau's expedition could get Hallie killed, Sherm nodded. "That what I argied, but they were all het up and tore off hell-for-leather. Bud, why don't you hurry on fast as you can 'thout breakin' your hoss's leg in a burrow? Tell Beau Miss Katie MacLeod, old Nacho, and Jack Diamond want him to wait — that they've got a plan to get back our little gal."

Bud swung into his saddle and was off at a canter. Tears glistened in the gruff, stove-up old man's faded eyes. "Bless you, ma'am," he said to Katie. "But you'd ought not to go near them savages. Let the men take care of it."

"Jed's my brother. And Hallie — well, after what she'll have been through, she might feel better if a woman's there."

"A woman," Sherm repeated. "You are that, Miss MacLeod, and so I'll tell Ed to his face! Here you are goin' after his girl while he's in Tombstone claimin' that you're too young to have charge of your life and your family's. Drat him, he got that gossipy tee-totalin' Myra Firbank to write a letter sayin' that Lord Bill would have had the MacLeod fillies guzzlin' champagne punch if Myra'd had any! And of course everybody in the county must have heard by now how he took you all to Tombstone." The cook spewed a stream of tobacco at a yucca as if it were to blame for Larrimore's doings. "By grannies, this ought to make even Ed plumb ashamed of himself!"

Though Katie had suspected why the rancher had gone to the county seat, to hear it confirmed shook her. After a fearful glance at Diamond, Katie shrugged. "What's important is to get the children back. Wish us luck, Mr. Walcott."

"You bet I do!" They were already trotting south, past Shell Brown's mound of rocks.

The long, rugged, eastern rampart of the Chiricahuas faced the western ridges of the less lofty Peloncillos. The broad plain stretched for miles in between, spires of soaptree yucca rearing withered stalks above whispering, swaying grass that was grazed down in the upper valley but luxuriant and stirrup-high as they proceeded southward. The Apaches, fleeing at speed, hadn't tried to cover their tracks. Horses, ridden and driven, had trampled a wide swath as near the Chiricahuas as possible without encountering rough terrain.

"This way," explained Nacho, "they could make for cover if pursued and also stay closer to the streams that run in several of the canyons." He shielded his eyes. "Up ahead — perhaps that is Señor Murphree. But the small group — do they not have blue coats and wear yellow stripes down their legs?"

"We're near Horseshoe Canyon," said Diamond. "That's where Lieutenant Corrigan's based. Perhaps that's his detachment."

Peering beneath her hand, Katie said in relief, "Bud's caught up with them — that's his red shirt and black hat. He's on that white-stockinged sorrel. And here comes Beau."

"Who else would wear a purple shirt?" murmured Diamond.

They met the Pitchfork's top hand some distance from the other horsemen. Galloping up, Beau scowled at Katie even as he doffed his hat to her before turning his perplexed wrath on Diamond.

"What's all this about some plan you've got? While we argue about what to do, them 'Paches are scootin' into Mexico. Once they hole up in the Sierra, the whole U.S. cavalry can't find 'em!"

Diamond explained, and as he did, Beau's exasperation turned first to jaw-dropped amazement and then to grudging admiration. "It could work," he admitted. He slanted a marveling glance at Katie. "And your kid brother hit on that notion all by himself!" He rubbed his lean jaw. "If Shell's dead, I guess I'm actin' foreman. If it comes to dickerin' for Hallie, I know Ed would give his whole damn ranch and all that's on it rather than lose his girl. Offer whatever you have to. But say, can't I come along?"

Diamond said diplomatically, "The fewer there are of us, the better our chances to negotiate will probably be. Might be a good idea for you to try to find Ed Larrimore and keep him from tearing off half-cocked."

"Guess you're right. I'll send the boys to see how much stock we've lost, and I'll head for Tombstone. Ed's goin' to take it hard, Shell gettin' killed. They grew up together, went through the war." The light brown eyes rested on Katie. "Miss MacLeod, you — well, be careful. We'll be prayin' you come back safe and sound with our little girl."

Galloping back, he spoke briefly to the officer and the Pitchfork cowboys. Then he was off at a lope, evidently planning to head through Tex Canyon Pass into Rucker Canyon and make for Tombstone. The cowboys scattered northward in twos and threes. They would scour the draws and canyons on either side of the valley to determine how much Pitchfork stock had been killed or driven off.

The approaching officer was indeed Lieutenant Corrigan. Katie stole a swift glance at Diamond. How would they meet, this father and son who hadn't seen each other since the officer was a child? They had to recognize what each saw in the mirror — hawk features, frost gray eyes, graceful tapered fingers. Corrigan, like his men, excepting Mickey Free, wore a black armband, mourning for President Garfield, Katie supposed. The detested white cork helmets had been replaced for winter with broad-brimmed black felt hats bearing the insignia of crossed sabers.

Addressing Katie rather than his father, the stiffly erect young officer said, "Murphree's cowboys seemed to understand him, but I am far from clear as to what you intend. Kindly explain yourselves so that I may ascertain my course of action."

"You are not allowed to cross the Mexican border, sir." Diamond's tone was cold as his son's.

"If I choose to risk my commission, sir, that is my affair," returned Corrigan so starchily and in such a similar voice that Katie almost smiled in spite of the gravity of the situation.

Quickly, she told the young man what they hoped to do and tried not to plead as she added that the Apaches might be more disposed to deal with him since they were accustomed to bargaining with officers and viewed them with more trust than they did civilians.

She held her breath as the lieutenant considered. It didn't take long. "A child's been abducted," he said. "Another child's gone to rescue her — and with all respect, young lady, it seems that yet a third child proposes to deliver them. I'll come with you, but I won't order my men across the boundary. However, if there are volunteers —"

They could have followed the trampled grass without Mickey Free. That slight but formidable scout with one clouded eye and the coppery glint to his flowing black hair had volunteered along with every one of the soldiers. However, since Free supported the advice of Nacho and Diamond, the lieutenant selected the two with considerable experience of Apaches, and ordered the other six to patrol the valley and warn off any citizen posses that might come storming toward Mexico.

Even though they were still a tiny band, the soldiers bolstered Katie's confidence. Ruddy-faced Sergeant Griffin with his keen blue eyes and floppy sandy moustache told her he had a daughter about Hallie's age and that he had served with Crook during the general's last command in Arizona. Lanky Private Harris, smooth-faced as a girl and angelically blond, was the son of a noncommissioned officer stationed at Camp Bowie before it achieved the dignity of being called a fort. Harris had run errands for Tom Jeffords, the agent, and come to know Jeffords's friend Cochise, who had taken a liking to the boy.

To Katie, the soldiers seemed to represent the might of her country. Here, approaching a foreign land and deadly peril, she was prepared to forget The War Between the States, fought before she was born. Corrigan allowed his men to talk with the civilians, but he stayed well in front with Mickey Free. With cold civility, Corrigan addressed his father as "sir." The one time he called him "Mr. Diamond," the officer hesitated over the name and then rapped it out curtly with a note of scorn.

Corrigan hadn't encountered the Apaches because he'd been on a scout south of the Chiricahuas when a scared freighter told him about the raid on the Pitchfork. Some of the seventy-five warriors who'd fled the reservation had gone ahead with the women and children to refuge in the Sierra, but several raiding parties had lingered to run off stock for winter food and to damage the encroaching whites as much as possible.

"Cochise's son Naiche is a leader," Corrigan said. "There's Juh of the Nednhi, or Southern Chiricahuas, whose home range is the Sierra, and his brother-in-law, a warrior of no great distinction, who is called Geronimo. Looks like they're making for the old trail through the canyon where that pack train was ambushed in July — people are starting to call it Skeleton Canyon because of that. It leads to the Animas Valley and down into Mexico."

Naiche, Juh, Geronimo . . . The strange names sing-songed in Katie's head. She wasn't used to riding so steadily for such a long time. Though being astride made it easier to control the pinto and had been comfortable for hours, her thighs ached now from the unaccustomed position.

Jed wouldn't burden Jenny much. Most likely he'd increased his lead. As the sun grazed the ragged spine of the Chiricahuas' southern rim, Katie gave up hope of overtaking him that evening. "It'll be the first night in his life that Jed's been alone," she said to Nacho and Diamond. As for Hallie — well, this would be her third night with the Apaches. Perhaps she'd be so exhausted she'd sleep sound.

"Jed's a brave little fellow," Diamond said. "He's just the sort the Apaches would want to bring up as one of them. They'll go to considerable trouble to keep from killing him."

Over his shoulder, Corrigan said, "Your concern for this lad is rather surprising, sir. Those of your calling rarely have time for children or domestic life."

"I supported my family as long as I was

allowed to," said Diamond. "And that we were separated was no wish of mine."

"Time permits rearranging the past into what one wishes it had been," observed the lieutenant.

"Some people do that with their present," returned the gambler. "Or they let what was told them about the past decide what happens now."

Up ahead, an eagle and several ravens lofted slowly from the ground, the ravens croaking harshly. These birds were among those that would clean bones now that the buzzards had mostly gone south for the winter. Cold with fear, Katie strained to see what had drawn them.

Corrigan rode ahead with Mickey Free. In a few minutes, they reined up to wait on the others. Mickey called, "They stop here! Eat horse. In hurry — leave hide."

Predators had dragged off parts of the skeleton and gnawed the head and hide. Katie gripped the saddle horn as everything whirled darkly. Soon, though, she could see again. There was no mistaking that bright red-gold, the blood-clotted red mane trailing raggedly from the savaged head.

Red Rover, pride of his two mothers, the most frolicsome and spirited of all the colts. A moan escaped from Katie. At four months, though a strong little creature, he hadn't been able to keep up. She saw him, early gusto turning to weariness, whickering plaintively to Chili and Babe, who weren't allowed to stop for him — saw him driven along till either he fell and couldn't get up, or it was time for his captors to rest — and eat.

Poor Babe and Chili! How they must have grieved, how savagely they must have been whipped to make them leave what was left of their son.

This death of the colt caused what the attack of yesterday and fear for Hallie and Jed had not. For the first time, Katie hated the Apaches. As her group rode deeper into the fateful canyon, she couldn't see for her tears.

XXI

All the rest of the day, they followed the creek that twined through the canyon. Connecting the San Simon Valley with the Animas Valley of New Mexico by cutting through the Peloncillos, the canyon was open to the sky, surrounded by grassy hills studded with juniper, scrub oak, and clumps of sotol, agave, and yucca. Though mostly shaded on the south side by walnuts, junipers, and a few sycamores, this part of the canyon boasted few trees of the height and density of those common in Whitetail.

On the left, floods had bared the bleached white, yellow, and orange rock bones of the hillsides, here and there grooving shallow grottos or carving weird effigies, while higher up, wind and storm-sculpted chimneys and pinnacles reared against the sky.

Near the broad, flat mouth of the canyon, Diamond pointed out a grassy recess surrounded by cliffs and shaded by several big oaks. "The Devil's Kitchen. Joe Glanton, one of the most notorious scalp-hunters, is supposed to have camped there. His sweetheart was murdered by Lipan Apaches over in Texas. After that, he was so merciless to

Indians that Sam Houston outlawed him. He's supposed to have had several dozen men in his gang, cutthroats of all races. They sold Apache scalps to the Sonora governor for fifty dollars each. Scalp hunting was a lucrative business along the border for many years, and Glanton, like most of his kind, was a little careless about mixing Mexican scalps in with those of Apaches. When he joined the Gold Rush to California, he abused the Yuma Indians on the Colorado River so brutally that they clubbed him to death with several of his men. No one mourned him."

Katie knew her friend was talking to distract her briefly from her sorrow for Red Rover and her fear for the children, but it only deepened her foreboding to know this canyon had seen ruthless murders long before the July slaughter of the pack train.

Katie shuddered and for a long time quailed at every round white rock, afraid it was a skull. The trail of many horses crossed and recrossed the creek. At least there was no chance that Jed had gotten lost. This artery of lifegiving water sustained tribes of javelina, bands of deer, and flocks of wild turkeys, and as twilight fell, coyotes began to gossip in the distance and a wolf howled to be answered by another.

When darkness thickened, they stopped at

the first spot that offered grazing for the horses. After rubbing the horses down, the soldiers staked out their mounts with ropes attached to steel picket pins, and the others used hobbles. Before they ate, the cavalrymen put grain in their horses' nosebags. Katie and Nacho had brought cracked corn for their mounts and shared it with Diamond. Grass alone wouldn't sustain horses when they were being pushed like this.

A shoe was loose on Griffin's sorrel. Every cavalryman carried two horseshoes and fifteen nails — Griffin said the field gear a horse carried for a five-day journey weighed over one hundred pounds — so a new nail was hammered in with the head of his steel picket pin. Not wishing to attract either Apaches or bandits of whatever nationality, the small party ate cold food, the soldiers producing packets of hard bread and cans of corned beef and bacon from their ration bags, while Katie, Nacho, and Diamond shared sardines and cold biscuits. Bone-weary, as soon as they'd eaten, everyone rolled up in their blankets, except Free, who was standing first guard. He'd be relieved by Griffin, Harris, and Nacho, whose experience made them the best sentries.

Diamond and Nacho put Katie between them, close enough to reach out and touch either one. Comforting as this was, it harrowed

Katie to think of Jed, all by himself except for Jenny. He must be huddled along the track six hours or more ahead. There was no way he could have missed seeing Red Rover's pitiful remains. At least for tonight, she didn't have to worry about his catching up to the Apaches. Unless they had dallied, they were well across the border. But poor little Hallie!

Sergeant Griffin said that when these Chiricahuas were evading pursuing troopers after breaking off the reservation, they'd kill anything that might give them away, dogs that might bark, horses of a color light enough to be seen at night. If Hallie impeded them before they reached their mountain refuge, they would surely kill her. Hideous as it had been to find Red Rover's ruined body, it would be worse to see a dead child.

Katie feared crossing the border, but it would also be a relief. Once in Mexico, the Apaches would feel safer, for even though they might still encounter Mexican soldiers, they wouldn't expect pursuit from the U.S. Army.

Tomorrow, we may find them, Katie thought. If they want us to. If they don't — She refused to even think about that, admit that once the Apaches wished to, they could vanish, perhaps carrying Jed with them.

A wailing shriek from up the canyon made

her sit up with a muffled cry. The horses neighed in fright. Nacho's hand closed warm on her shoulder. "Katie," he whispered so softly that the soldiers couldn't hear — around them, he was back to his usual speech with strangers: *Sí, señor, No, señor, and Quién sabe?* "It is only a mountain lion."

"It — it sounded like a woman."

"They do. I'll go stay with the horses till the lion goes elsewhere for supper."

After that, Katie didn't think she could sleep at all, but when she next opened her eyes, it was to the first graying light before the dawn.

It was a beautiful canyon to have seen so much bloodshed, in places broad enough for thick stands of big trees and high-grassed meadows where towering oaks, cottonwoods, and sycamores offered inviting shade. A side canyon turned off to the right between high sandstone cliffs, one with a large cave near the summit. The country grew wilder, the creek in places narrowly walled by rocks and boulders.

It was in one such defile that the white rocks became skulls, of both men and animals, some with hair and shriveling skin still attached. For a considerable distance, bones and verte-brae, also scabbed with dried skin and blood, protruded from sand and fallen leaves or were wedged among the rocks.

"The story is that a Mexican youngster escaped this massacre," Diamond said. "He's supposed to have gathered the men who killed Old Man Clanton in Guadalupe Canyon. But most likely regular Mexican troops got the Clanton bunch."

"And then the Clantons were suspected of killing any Mexican who passed their ranch," Katie said wearily. "And then Billy and the MacLowerys were killed in Tombstone. Isn't there ever going to be an end to it?"

Corrigan said, "If President Arthur gets his wish, Cochise County will be placed under military rule. That, I assure you, would bring a change." He flicked a look at his father. "Riffraff and outlaws would mend their ways or seek another refuge."

"This is not a defeated country to have soldiers ordering us around," retorted Diamond. "Besides, if the army has as little success in dealing with outlaws as it does with Indians, it will inspire more laughter than respect."

The two men scowled at each other, furrow of brow and set of mouth so alike that it would have been laughable except for the enmity on the son's part. Katie had hoped that this forced companionship might lead to liking, or at least understanding on

Corrigan's side, but he seldom was close enough for conversation and the remarks he had made were insulting. Diamond was no man to beg forgiveness, and his son's starchy correctness was bound to rub him the wrong way. If anything, this expedition would probably leave them hopelessly estranged. It seemed so sad and useless that Katie would have liked to shake them and order them to stop acting like children.

The canyon widened to an open plain that had to be the Animas Valley. They struck south on the trail worn by smugglers, rustlers, Apaches, and even some law-abiding travelers. "One can go to Janos on this trail," Nacho said to Katie. "That small Sonoran town prospers from the enterprise of smugglers like those whose bones we passed. There is handsome profit in carrying Mexican silver to Tombstone or Tucson, exchanging it for merchandise, and bringing this duty-free into Mexico."

"I suppose Mexicans still feel there shouldn't *be* a border, said Katie, remembering Diamond's lessons. This region had belonged to Mexico till the Gadsden Purchase of 1854, which added the southern parts of Arizona and New Mexico to the vast western empire ceded by Mexico after the war with Mexico ended in 1848.

"What's sure is that Mexico hasn't been able to defend its northern frontiers any better than Spain did before Mexico won its independence," shrugged Diamond. "In the treaty ending the Mexican war, the United States undertook to keep Comanches and Apaches from raiding into Mexico as they've done for centuries. The last Comanches finally came into the reservation in Indian Territory six years ago, but the Apaches —" He shrugged again. "There aren't many left in the Sierra, but they could hide out for years."

Overhearing, Sergeant Griffin dropped back. "According to the scouts, the 'Paches almost starve sometimes in the mountains. They get tired of being on the run from Mexican troops. Give General Crook a chance to clean out the crooked agents and suppliers who're cheatin' the Indians out of their rations and goods, and a reservation will look a lot better to most of the Indians."

At noon, the party rested the horses and themselves, washing down their cold food with water from a spring where they filled their canteens. Katie, stiff and sore from riding so long, winced as Diamond helped her back into the saddle, but she was glad to be traveling again. She wouldn't draw an easy breath till she saw Jed and Hallie, knew they were alive.

She felt as if they'd been riding forever, as if she were trapped in a nightmare that would never end. Mountains marched on either side of them, the higher peaks forested darkly with pine, the ridges buttressed with stone and serried by weather to rock pinnacles and bastions. Sergeant Griffin squirted tobacco and called, "Hey, Mickey! We in Mexico yet?"

The scout laughed, spread a hand. "No matter."

"Of course it matters," rapped Corrigan. "Major Emory, who represented the United States on the Joint Boundary Commission that completed the survey of the border to the satisfaction of both countries in eighteen fifty-five, established markers all the way from the Pacific to the Gulf of Mexico."

"Yes sir," returned the ruddy-faced sergeant, a twinkle in his brown eyes. "But I doubt if anyone rides around looking for the markers."

Corrigan flushed. "The lawlessness of the citizenry on both sides of the border doesn't alter the fact that the markers are — are *official!*"

"Yes, sir." Poorly concealed amusement left the soldier's face. "Figgered this trail was too good to last. Free's heading across the valley for those dratted mountains!"

Nacho murmured to Katie, "I have been here only once, when I came up from the Rio Yaqui, but I think we are in Mexico and that is the Sierra de San Luis. Southeast of it across a broad plain is another small range, and south of that lies the main Sierra Madre."

It sounded so vast, so frightening. Despairingly, Katie looked at Diamond. He reached out to rest his hand warmly, strongly, on hers. "Free was raised by Apaches. He can think and track just like them. Don't worry, my dear. We'll find Jed and Hallie."

Alive? Unable to speak, Katie nodded mutely. Where the tracks started up the rugged mountain, ravens flapped shrieking away from tearing at the bones of another butchered horse. The hide was black. Katie felt guilty at a surge of relief that Babe and Chili and Shiloh must still be alive. The unlucky black had wanted to live as much as her horses did. After what had happened to Red Rover, though, she didn't think she could bear finding another Steel Dust slaughtered.

The Apaches and their stolen herd had gone over San Luis Pass through scattered oak and juniper. From the summit, as the horses rested, Katie gazed across the plain southeast to the rounded mountains Free called the Sierra en Media, Mountains in Between.

"Good spring in middle," he said. "Maybe

Apaches rest few days before go Sierra." He pointed toward a distant mass so far away that it seemed a hazy gigantic shadow melting into the brilliant sky.

Dizzied at the immensity of these wildlands, desert plains studded with isolated peaks or small spurs of mountains, Katie thought it looked as if the earth had erupted to spill these clusters of rock at random across this desolate expanse. Heart sinking, she glanced longingly back at the Peloncillos and beyond them at the purple rim of the Chiricahuas.

If only Jed were safe, could be brought back, and Hallie, too, she'd never ask for anything again beyond the prayerful hope that had become a part of her being — that Bill was living, that he was well, even if she could never see him again.

"Move out, Free," said the lieutenant.

It was late afternoon when they rode out of a canyon on the east side and faced the wide plain between them and the next range. They had traveled forty miles that day, some of them grueling. "We'll rest our mounts two hours," said Corrigan. "Free says it's five miles to those springs, so we should still reach them before it's dark."

Katie almost fell off the pinto. "Poor boy," she said, stroking his sweaty neck. "Once we

545

catch up, you won't have to hurry. We'll take it easy coming back." *If we come back.* "And when we get home" — *if we get home* — "you'll get all the hay and corn you want and can graze and play."

She took off the saddle and bridle so he could have several luxuriant rolls in the sandy wash, led him to water in a pool fed by a trickle still running down the canyon from the fall rains, and hobbled him before she fed him a few handfuls of corn.

Without spreading her bedroll, she turned the saddle sideways and was in a stuporous drowse when several shots rang out, echoing and reechoing up the canyon. For a confused moment, she thought she was at Home Mountain with Apaches attacking, but as she started up, Corrigan shouted, "Get behind the rocks! They're trying to run off the horses. Men, fire at will!"

The lieutenant got off a shot with his carbine as bullets hissed above Katie's head. Jerking Tom's treasured new Winchester from the saddle scabbard, Katie scrambled on hands and knees for the rock ridge that the men had turned into a formidable defensive position, shooting as fast as they could eject shells and push up the levers.

The Apaches had cover, too, a jumble of boulders, but as Katie, kneeling, raised up enough to sight and fire, before she could pull the trigger, an Indian convulsed upward, throwing out his arms, the side of his head blown away. In that instant, Private Harris pitched forward, clawed at the rocks as brains spilled from the back of his skull, drummed his toes, and was still.

"He's dead," Diamond shouted at Katie when she dropped the rifle and started for the soldier. Knowing her friend was right, Katie lofted the rifle, but as she squinted down the barrel, she caught movement in the brush.

"Hold your fire," Corrigan ordered. "They seem to have had enough. It won't help our bargaining to kill more of them than we have to. Just keep ready till we see them leaving."

Blood pounding in her ears, Katie tried not to look at the young soldier whose blond hair was soaked with blood and grayish ooze. He hadn't looked eighteen. She thought of Billy Clanton. A time and place this was where boys killed and were killed. Oh, Jed . . .

Well out of range, two Apaches straightened. They carried a body between them, hoisted it on the back of an animal they led out of a ravine. Mounting, they set off for the Sierra en Media.

"Stragglers," Griffin said heavily. "Hoped to jump us and get more horses and plunder."

"I'm not sure I killed the one they carried off," said Corrigan. "It won't, I fear, make our mission any simpler."

He looked pale and shaken, almost a boy himself in spite of the stubble darkening his jaw. Kneeling by Harris, he turned the soldier over and closed the long-lashed blue eyes that stared without blinking at the sun rimming the crest.

"Poor lad." Griffin's voice was husky. "Thank God, he's an orphan, but he's got a sister married to a packer at Fort Apache."

"Save his effects for her, Sergeant. I'll take them to her — tell her he volunteered to rescue some children." The lieutenant moved his head as if to clear it, glanced to where Diamond, with a rock, was scraping in the silt above the wash, while Nacho undid Harris's folded blanket from beneath the cantle roll and spread it on the ground. "That's right." Corrigan straightened. "We can't leave him for the scavengers."

"We can dig with our knives and picket pins." Griffin opened a long case attached to Harris's saber carrier and tossed a steel picket pin over a foot long to Diamond, then unsheathed his own knife with a heavy eight-inch blade. Nacho got Harris's and the lieutenant used his. Though the young trooper was past feeling, Katie handled him as gently as she could while she alternately dragged and lifted him into the blanket.

Mickey Free, returning on his saddled horse — fortunately, their mounts had been out of range behind a slope — stared at them as if they'd gone crazy. "No waste time," he growled and gestured. "Better try kill Apache fellas. Hide bodies."

"He is right," Nacho said, though he kept on digging. He dropped his pretended lack of English and the soldiers looked at him in astonishment. "If we kill and hide those two before the main camp can hear shooting, the Apaches holding the children won't know what happened. But if these ride in with a dead man —"

"They fired on us first," said Corrigan.

"Sir," blurted Griffin, " 'Paches don't fight civilized."

Enough silt and rocks had been dug out for Harris's swaddled body to be placed in the shallow trench. Katie spread earth over the blanket while the men brought stones heavy enough to discourage birds and beasts of prey.

"I may be a fool," said Corrigan. "Still, I cannot bring myself to fire on a fleeing enemy, especially when they have burdened themselves with their comrade's body. Civilized they are not, yet they have honor. To that we must appeal."

Mickey Free's one black eye glittered. "You are fool!"

The officer glanced from him to Griffin, then to Katie and Nacho. "I will ride on alone to parley. That will at the least make them curious. I have picked up enough Spanish, I think, to make those who speak that language understand your offer to ransom the girl." He looked at Katie. "I will, of course, include your brother should he be in their camp." Strength flowed back into his voice. "Griffin! Free! Make your way up the canyon tonight with this lady and man, covering your tracks. Make a well-hidden camp. If I'm not back by morning, push over the summit and escort Miss MacLeod and Mr. Diamond back to —"

"I came for my brother and Hallie Larrimore," said Katie.

Diamond nodded. Griffin said hardily, "Sir, I volunteered."

With a grunt, Free shrugged. "I come. Speak Apache."

Katie touched the stones heaped over a brave young soldier, prayed silently he was in a place of light and love. In minutes, they were riding.

As they crossed the barren plain, twilight deepened and so did the glow of fires at the middle of the western base of the mountains.

Remembering accounts of Apache fire tortures, Katie shivered, yet somehow, even in her overwrought and fearful state, those fires seemed to speak of cooked food and warmth, people resting and relaxing.

Was Jed there? Hallie? As they had passed no more carcasses, Katie dared hope the two mares and Shiloh were all right, even though the smell of roasting meat floated on the wind. With Free and Corrigan in the lead, the small party was close enough now to see dark figures pass in front of the several fires. The Apaches who had attacked them must have reached camp half an hour ago. In spite of the white flag Free carried, a shirt tied to the tip of a yucca stalk, Katie was rigid in the saddle, braced for a hail of bullets.

Two rocky hills squatted several hundred yards from the fires. As the group rode past them, the hillocks came alive with men, mostly clad in high moccasins and long white breechclouts, all pointing rifles or bows and arrows.

Mickey Free shouted to them in Apache. He was answered by a man in an army jacket that looked strange with his breechclout. Gesturing with his rifle, this warrior indicated that the intruders should proceed.

Surrounded by a score of warriors, they rode on, horses shying nervously at the unfamiliar scent. "Mr. Free," Katie pleaded, "ask them if my brother is safe, if Hallie Larrimore is here."

Free spoke with the jacketed warrior, who made a brief reply. "Boy play cards with Geronimo for girl. Girl scratch, bite, cry too much. Kill if boy no win."

Another Apache yelled something, brandishing a lance. "He one we fight little bit ago. Say friend die. Say we die, too."

Those words pierced Katie, but as she shrank, glad that no one could see how she was trembling, she drew in a long, grateful breath.

There in the firelight sat Jed, bright hair shining, surrounded by Indians as intent as he was on the cards in his hand. Across from him was an Apache, who, as the prisoners approached and dismounted, threw down his cards with a sound of disgust. Rising, he folded his arms.

Frowning brows almost fused above the narrow beginning of his long nose. Prominent cheekbones pressed down the thin line of his mouth. His black hair was hacked off raggedly on a level with an outthrust chin. It was easy to imagine that as he aged, the middle of his face would recede, leaving chin and nose to hook into each other like a hawk's beak. White men's trousers showed under his breechclout. They were tucked into moccasins reaching just below the knee, and he wore a white cotton shirt and a red scarf knotted around his throat.

Fascinated — and intimidated — as she was at seeing Apaches up close, Katie looked past the scowling warrior to her brother, scanning him anxiously. His face was grimy and there were dark hollows under his eyes but he seemed to be unhurt. He didn't get up and obviously struggled to keep his poker face, but at the sight of his sister and friends, his eyes lit up and it seemed to Katie that his tautly erect posture eased.

A small figure pelted from the shadows and cast itself against Katie, knocking off her hat, clinging desperately. "M-m-miss MacLeod! It *is* you, isn't it, in spite of those awful clothes? Where's Papa? Isn't he coming after me?"

Katie sank down and held the child close. "I hope we can take you back before your papa comes, Hallie. Beau told Lieutenant Corrigan to offer to ransom you, so we came on ahead."

"You came for Jed," said Hallie, snuffling. "But *he* came for *me*."

"Yes, he did. Now keep quiet, honey, so we can hear what they're saying."

Still snuffling, Hallie kept a death grip on Katie, who stayed on one knee the better to comfort the bedraggled little girl. She didn't appear to have been much hurt, though she had a split, swollen lip and a bruise on her cheek. Her expensive green serge riding habit was ripped and dirty, her face was cruelly sunburned, and her auburn curls were matted in thick tangles.

The grim-looking Indian rapped out a few sentences and a question. Free turned to Corrigan. "Geronimo say you kill kinsman two hour ago. How dare ride to camp?"

"Tell him his kinsman fired on us," instructed Corrigan. "We come in peace."

"Why?" demanded the Apache through the interpreter. "Why you bring woman dressed like man?"

"We come for the children. Miss MacLeod is the boy's sister. If the children are not given to us, the Gray Fox, General Crook, whom Apaches know well is a chief of his word, will send messages to the Mexican government. He will ask to cross the border, help Mexican soldiers find you."

Geronimo's eyes glittered as the scout translated. Barking a contemptuous reply, he made a slashing motion, pointing his big chin at Hallie, who screamed and burrowed deeper into Katie's embrace.

"Geronimo say maybe you all die here. Apache go deep in Sierra. Gray Fox not find."

"Hunger will," said Corrigan.

Geronimo sneered. He answered at some length in a mocking tone and resumed his seat on a stone across from Jed. "Say we stop game. Important game. Boy ride in, very brave. Make good warrior. Say he play cards with chiefs for girl, his horses. Already win horses from Juh. Now play Geronimo for girl. He win three hands out of five, take her. He lose, he stay, be Apache."

"Oh, Jed!" Katie burst out.

Geronimo glared at her, growled orders. "He say keep quiet," explained Free. "When game over, he decide how treat us. Boy win two hand, Geronimo one. No want noise."

There were no women in this camp, though it seemed to Katie that most of both parties must be here, the one that captured Hallie and the one that raided Home Mountain. Some chewing on meat sliced from joints roasting on skewers, the warriors flocked around the gamblers so thickly that Katie had to bend and twist to keep Jed in sight.

Geronimo frowned at the cards Jed was shuffling with a deftness that shocked Katie. She winged a reproachful glance at Diamond, who quickly changed his proud smile to a bland one. As Jed started to deal the cards, Geronimo raised his hand in a halting motion and called something over his shoulder to Free.

555

"Got more card?" the scout relayed. "Geronimo no like boy's deck."

Griffin raised a sheepish eyebrow at Corrigan, who shrugged and said, "If you've got a deck, hand it over. Otherwise the Apache may not play."

Their horses had not yet been unsaddled or led away. It only took the sergeant a moment to extract a deck from his right-side ration bag. "Helps balance, you know, sir," he winked at Corrigan. "Helps the off-side balance the near side and the carbine."

The lieutenant gave him a quelling look and passed on the deck to Free, who gave it to Geronimo. He tried to shuffle, dropped the cards. After a second try, with a sound of annoyance, he handed the deck to Jed. Jed grinned and gave a careless heave of his shoulders, but Katie had seen the flash of dismay that, just for a second, widened his eyes.

Under his breath, Diamond murmured to Katie, "A damn shame I never got past showing the lad how to use a marked deck."

From the intent faces of the onlookers, Katie supposed there were many bets on the outcome. Free indicated several leaders with his chin. "Juh," he whispered, thrusting his jaw toward a very big, rather corpulent warrior. "Naiche, son of Cochise."

Slender and handsome, this young chief had

chiseled, delicate features that led Katie to recall being told that the great Mimbres Apache chieftain, Mangas Coloradas, had married a beautiful Mexican captive. Three lovely daughters by this best-beloved woman had married chiefs of other Apache bands, among them Cochise, renowned leader of the Chiri-cahuas. Naiche had inherited this come-liness. His face was smooth as a woman's; in fact, not a one of the Apaches had any facial hair. Katie remembered that Nacho had told her they considered moustaches and beards both ugly and dirty — and come to think of it, they probably were, especially with men who took snuff or chewed tobacco.

Chato had a broad face and stubby nose. Middle-aged, heavy-bodied Loco had a badly scarred cheek and drooping eye from an encounter with a bear. The light skin and gray eyes of good-looking Chihuahua contrasted with the coppery or swarthy complexions and dark hair and eyes of his companions. Free said he'd been carried off as a child from Mex-ico and was one of the bravest, most respected chieftains. The scout named no more Apaches then, for Jed was dealing the last cards of those facing up.

The first card dealt each player faced down. Showing, Geronimo had an ace of hearts and the eight and ten of clubs. Jed's hand displayed a queen of spades, a small diamond, and a five of hearts. Geronimo's last card was a jack of clubs. Jed dealt himself a queen of hearts.

"A pair showing," Diamond breathed. "Unless Geronimo's hole card is an ace —"

Chuckling as he looked at his hidden card, the Apache counted out a handful of small pebbles and placed them on the ground. Jed studied his hole card, counted out an equal number of pebbles, and added ten.

Geronimo put in ten more. Frowning slightly, he added five. Jed met the raise. Geronimo placed an ace of diamonds beside the ace of hearts. Jed couldn't restrain a wince. "You win," he said. He swallowed but even so his voice came out high and breathless. "We're tied, two and two."

Free said this in Apache. Most of the Apaches shouted their glee, but some, apparently those who'd bet on Jed, looked disgruntled. Geronimo grinned. Free reported his boast. "He say he win. Small yellow hair make great Apache warrior."

Jed's hands fumbled, dropped some cards as he tried to shuffle. He picked them up, managed the shuffle, offered them to Geronimo for cutting.

First card down. Seven of clubs for the chief. King of hearts for Jed. Jack of diamonds, ace of clubs; nine of spades, six of diamonds;

queen of clubs, ten of hearts. "Ace-king high," murmured Diamond. "Jed's got him beat on the board, so it's his bet. That damned hole card —"

Jed shoved all his pebbles into the middle. Geronimo matched them. Not even waiting for Jed to show his hole card, the chief held up a jack of spades. White-lipped, Jed turned over a seven of clubs.

In the presence of his enemies, he looked even younger than he was, a fair-haired child with blue eyes amid these dusky, formidable warriors. Katie wanted to run to him, fold him protectively in her arms, but she knew he wouldn't want that. This couldn't be happening, she told herself dazedly. It couldn't be that her brother had gambled away his freedom — more than that, his very identity!

"You've won," he told the preening victor. "I — I will stay with you. But let the girl and the others go back. The horses I won from Juh, I'll give them to you." He looked appealingly toward Katie. "Can't I?"

Choked by a hard, tight knot, Katie nodded, trying not to break down before these enemies, trying not to disgrace her brother.

Geronimo refused before Free had even finished translating. "Maybe trade girl one day for captured warriors," the scout explained.

Corrigan said, "On behalf of the girl's

father, I can offer a hundred head of cattle delivered at the border if you'll release the children."

Interest gleamed in Geronimo's eyes. "Two hundred head — fat cattle!" he bargained.

"One hundred and fifty."

The chieftain laughed. "Two hundred and fifty."

The lieutenant kept an expressionless face. "Two hundred."

Geronimo spoke further. "He say bring cattle here. If Apache meet at border, maybe trap."

"And maybe there'll be a trap for men who bring cattle here," returned the officer. "There'd be nothing to prevent their murder while the Apaches scoot into the Sierra with the cattle and prisoners."

Geronimo glared at Corrigan and burst into invective. "Chief no trust you," Free said. "White men lie, always lie. He go to border for cattle, maybe soldiers hiding. Kill Apaches or drive back to reservation." With a glance of malice that prickled Katie's scalp, the Indian said something more.

Free stiffened. Reluctantly, he turned to Corrigan. "You kill kinsman. You die. Because you brave, come of own will, not torture. Others" — the scout touched himself and gestured at the rest of their party. "We captives."

He gave Katie a pitying look. "You young, strong, make good wife." He glanced from Griffin to Diamond to Nacho. "Us men, maybe sell to Mexicans to sell back to whites. Maybe kill."

The warriors who surrounded them swiftly took the soldiers' sidearms, Diamond's revolver, long knives from Nacho and Free, and even pocketknives. They also took Diamond's watch and ring. Saddles were tossed off their horses, and their belongings, especially the rifles and carbines, were eagerly inspected and appropriated. The horses were turned loose with the well-guarded Apache animals and herd stolen from the Pitchfork, which grazed along the base of the mountains.

Hallie broke loose from Katie, scrubbed at her tears, and ran to Jed, who sat hunched by the fire. Going down on her knees, the girl put her arms around him. "Jed," she pleaded, "don't feel bad. You — you were so brave to come down here all alone! Brave and smart and — and well, just wonderful!"

Disengaging himself, he got to his feet and pulled her up. "I didn't get you loose," he said miserably. He looked at Katie and Diamond, Nacho and the soldiers. "All I did was get folks in trouble." His face twisted as he faced Corrigan. "Lieutenant, sir, maybe they won't kill you. Maybe —"

561

Corrigan shrugged. "I'm a soldier, Jed. It's not a profession one chooses if a long safe life is a consideration."

"But —"

"None of us had to come down here," the officer said. His eyes, so like Diamond's, met the gambler's. "Sir, if we're allowed the opportunity, I would like to talk with you."

Diamond's face softened, grew young, eager, hopeful. "Lieutenant, I want that more than I've ever wanted anything." He looked around at the Apaches, who were still diverted with the contents of saddlebags and ration bags and with cantle rolls and other gear. "I guess they aren't going to tie us up or use us for entertainment. Since we're on foot, unarmed and without supplies, they know we couldn't get far if we did escape."

Turning to Jed, he took the boy's shoulders in his hands and smiled down at him. "Jed, anyone bright enough to figure out your scheme to gamble for Hallie and the Steel Dusts is going to think of some way, sooner or late, to get away from the Apaches, especially now you have your big sister to help. I'm proud of you, son. I believe in you."

"Oh, Uncle Jack!" Jed buried his face against the gambler's chest. "I — I'm sorry you came down here after me, but I'm glad, too!" He gazed up, blinking at tears, and managed a grin. "But we will get away. All of us! We'll go fishing again and have lessons and — and —"

Diamond cast Katie a teasing smile. "Sure we will. And, my lad, I'll finish your education in games of chance so that next time you get a deck changed on you, you won't be at a loss."

Free strolled up, chewing on a hunk of meat. Griffin, following his example, accepted a chunk one of the warriors carved off and tossed to him as one might feed a dog.

"Better eat," Free advised. He didn't seem particularly worried. He and Nacho could survive barehanded in this wilderness. If they lived, they'd eventually escape.

Steeled for torture or abuse, Katie gradually decided that Geronimo's grace to Corrigan extended to the rest of them. The lieutenant and Diamond had been given meat and were sitting to themselves. They were ringed by Apaches coming and going, but no one molested them.

Here, at the end of the world and the end of the son's life, he and his father would finally know each other. Katie couldn't hold back her tears, but she hid them in her brother's yellow hair as she hugged and kissed him.

"At least, we're together," she said, and took Hallie's hand. "Let's get something to eat. And then, Hallie, let's try to do something with your hair."

XXII

The meat was almost certainly from a horse. Remembering Red Rover, Katie gagged as she tried to chew it, but she knew she had to keep up her strength, so she somehow got down a few bites, washing them down with good water from the abundant spring. Free was chatting amicably with some of the warriors while Griffin settled down with Katie's group.

Wiping her hands on Nacho's old trousers, she sat on the ground between Jed and Hallie and tried, with her fingers, to work out some of the snarled tangles.

Hallie whimpered. "I wish we had a brush!"

"It wouldn't help much till we get some of these matted places taken care of," Katie said. *"Do* try not to jerk, Hallie! I'm being as careful as I can."

"I will make a comb," said Nacho. He went off and after a little while, returned with a bunch of very stiff grass that he had tied securely at one end with a narrow strip of cloth, probably ripped from his shirttail.

This helped tremendously. Though the combing hurt, it also seemed to comfort Hallie. Sometimes weeping, she told about her terror at being captured and how cold and awful the three nights had been.

"Geronimo gave me a dirty old blanket," she said. "But I was still about to *freeze!* I was so scared I think I'd have shivered all night even if they'd plain buried me with covers! Every time we stopped, I was afraid they were going to do something terrible, but they never hit me or anything like that. We just rode till I'd have fallen out of the saddle if they hadn't tied me on." She burrowed between Katie's arm and bosom. "I know it's wicked, but I'm so glad you're here!" she said in a muffled voice. "When I saw Jed ride in, I — I can't tell you how happy I was just to see someone I knew, someone who cared about me. I'd been so nasty to him that Jed should've been glad the Apaches stole me. But Miss MacLeod, you're going to hate me when I tell you why Papa was away, why he went to Tombstone —"

Hallie broke into wrenching sobs. Katie smoothed her hair, held her as she would have Melissa or Rosie. Courts and law, Tombstone itself, seemed unreal and far away from these unknown and trackless wildlands where they could all perish at a momentary whim of their captors.

"I know why your father went to town, Hallie. It doesn't matter now. What counts is that we're all together and can help each other. And please call me Katie."

Hallie sighed, body relaxing. "I wish you were my sister. I — I never told anyone but Chapita, but I was real jealous when I saw you and Melissa and Jed at the Fourth of July. You had each other and a sweet little baby at home. It didn't seem fair that I didn't have even one brother or sister."

"You've got your father. He loves you a lot."

"Yes, but I can't play with him."

The thought startled Katie into a chuckle. "No, I suppose you can't, though you *could* play checkers or dominos."

"Or poker," offered Jed.

"Jed!" Katie scolded, saw his grin, and knew he was trying to cheer them up. His smile faded, and he stared at Diamond and Corrigan. "Maybe Uncle Jack can think of some way to keep the Apaches from killing the lieutenant. I didn't know they knew each other."

Jed and the others would have to be told Diamond's secret, but Katie couldn't explain right then without breaking down. She avoided her brother's puzzled eyes by concentrating on Hallie's curls. "They met a long time ago," she said, struggling to keep her voice steady. "They have a lot to talk about."

Hallie snuggled even closer. "Can I sleep with you tonight, Katie?"

"Of course." They'd all been wearing jackets and the Apaches hadn't taken these away, though they hadn't given back any of the rain gear or blankets. "We'll probably all snuggle up close tonight to keep warm."

"Mickey'll wheedle us a few blankets," Griffin said. "It's not too bad out of the wind. We'll manage. Just wish they hadn't taken my chewing tobacco."

"When did you find out I was gone?" Jed asked and added hopefully, "Are there a whole bunch of soldiers or cowboys on our trail?"

Katie answered his questions while she worked on Hallie's hair. Some snarls were so tightly meshed that the comb broke them off, but much of the red-brown hair was smooth enough to look like burnished copper where firelight struck it. "I wish you had your harp," Hallie said drowsily. "I wish you could sing."

Katie started to say that she couldn't but checked herself. Why not? It would lift their spirits, and so long as it didn't anger the Apaches, it might have the useful effect of baffling them. "Why don't we all sing? Do you have a favorite, Sergeant Griffin?"

"Oh, for a cavalryman, it'd have to be 'The Girl I Left Behind Me.' That's a good, lively tune, one of Custer's favorites, they say."

After what happened to Custer five years ago, Katie wasn't sure the song was a good omen, but she said, "We don't know all the words, Sergeant, but you start, and we'll join in when we can."

With a chuckle, Griffin said, "Lord love you, miss! You don't want to learn some of the verses. But there's a few decent." He had a surprisingly pleasant tenor and sang the lilting, spirited verses while the others joined in the chorus. He next suggested "Across the Wide Missouri." He knew different words from those Katie and Jed had learned, but they still could sing with him most of the time.

For seven long years, I courted Nancy,
Hi, hi, the rollin' river —
She would not have me for her lover,
So away, we're bound away, across the wide
    Missouri.

Because I was a cavalry soldier,
Hi, hi, the rollin' river —
Drinkin' rum and a-chawin' tobaccy,
So away, we're bound away, across the
    wide Missouri.

The Apaches watched them curiously but let them alone. It was probably the first time they had ever heard prisoners sing. They seemed amused at the effrontery rather than inclined to squelch it. It wasn't the time for

568

mournful songs, but for lively marching tunes or funny ones like "Sweet Betsy from Pike," "Hog Drovers," and "Turkey in the Straw."

Hallie, still snuggled close to Katie but relaxed enough to pipe in when she knew the words, said, "The only song Papa knows is 'The Old Chisholm Trail.' Could we sing that?"

"We probably don't know all the verses," said Katie. "But you can teach us."

Color glowing in her cheeks, Hallie sat up straight and launched into the trials of a cowboy driving cattle north to the railroad. It was full of grumbling and good-natured profanity, but Katie was startled at the vim with which Hallie delivered the cowboy's concluding remarks to his boss:

I'll sell my horse, I'll sell my saddle!
You can go to hell with your longhorn cattle!

Come a ti-yi yippee, yippee yea, yippee yea,
Come a ti-yi yippee, yippee yea.

"That's a good song, Hallie," approved Jed. "You sure know a lot of verses I never heard before."

"Papa sings it all the time," Hallie said modestly. "That's why I know it." With her hair fairly well untangled and tied loosely back with a string Katie had found in Nacho's pocket, she looked more herself. "You — you have a real nice voice, Jed." Her smile faded as she looked past him to the Apaches, and her mouth quivered as she buried her face against Katie. "I — I almost forgot where we are!" she wailed.

"We're together," Katie soothed. "Besides, your papa or the army will figure out some way to get us back." *Bill would — if he knew, if he were alive —*

Mickey Free strode over with several blankets. "Juh say stop howl like coyote. Sleep."

At least they'd have a little covering from the wind that grew ever more piercing. The blankets smelled, but no one was inclined to quibble. Nacho and Griffin used rocks to gouge out a depression in a small slope, and they all helped twist off grass to spread for a thin mattress.

"You settle down on one of the blankets with the young 'uns, ma'am," said the sergeant. "Nacho and me'll tuck in on either side."

He worked off his high boots. The others took off their footgear and belts but otherwise lay down clothed, even keeping on their hats. Back against Jed's, Katie shifted around till she found a tolerable way to cradle Hallie's head against her shoulder. Nacho lay down on the other side of the child, while Griffin tossed him one end of the blanket, held to the other, and arranged himself by Jed.

"Snug as bugs in a rug," he said. "Speakin' of bugs, I sure hope these blankets got tossed on anthills lately to clean out the graybacks."

On the occasions when a wayfaring minister or stranger had stayed overnight in the Mac-Leod cabin and left crawling little mementoes, Mama had said, "It's no disgrace to get lice. It is to keep them." Then there had been hair combing and washing with a strong gentian solution, bedding and clothing washed and aired, furniture and floors scrubbed — war to the knife till the creatures were routed.

It could have been imagination, but Katie felt as if something were already crawling on her neck and something else journeyed along her leg. Real or imagined, she had to endure it. They were packed too tightly to move without disturbing the others and tearing the blanket loose from its human moorings. They were reasonably warm and must be grateful for that.

Opening her eyes, Katie saw that Diamond and his son were still together, still conversing. Tears blurred her vision. A sorrowful way for them to be reconciled, but given the stubborn pride of the both of them, would they otherwise ever have listened, spoken what was in their hearts?

Katie felt that she should keep awake, hold vigil with the young officer on this last night even though he wouldn't know it. In a way, Geronimo was being merciful. Corrigan hadn't been tortured, and no one had interrupted these hours with his father. Katie prayed for him, entreating either a miracle to save him or, if that could not be, a swift death.

Already breathing heavily, Hallie whimpered. "It's all right," Katie murmured, "We're with you, honey."

Strange. If by wishing it, she could be away from here, safely at home, she wouldn't have done it unless Hallie could be there, too. Sometime, surely, they'd get away, be ransomed or rescued. Till then, it was up to Katie to hearten the children, keep them remembering who they were. They would sing — yes, they would; even without the harp, they would sing.

Thinking of the highland harp brought Mary MacLeod to mind, and her sweet singing. *I'm sorry I had to leave Melissa and Rosie, Mother, but I had to come to Jed. If you can, help them.*

As she fell into slumber, Katie heard the harp and that lullaby Mary had crooned so often to the other children. Could it be that at last she sang it for Katie? *"Oh, I searched the hill from side to side, from side to side and down to the stream; I searched the hill from end to end. I did not find my* cubhrachan."

There in the Mexican mountains with Apaches all around, Katie suddenly knew that her mother loved her, always had, in spite of the shame and grief and loveless marriage she had caused.

Mother must have loved my real father, Katie thought. I'm going to believe that he loved her — that he died or there was some reason he couldn't marry her. Deeper and deeper, as that beloved voice lingered in her mind, Katie sank into soft warm darkness.

The warmth didn't last. Katie's side next to the grass-covered ground stayed fairly comfortable, but the one covered only by clothing and the thin blanket got so cold that she gradually roused and lay awake, longing to turn over. She couldn't without disrupting the precarious sleeping arrangement and wished desperately for morning till she remembered Corrigan must die then.

Opening her eyes, she saw that he and Diamond still sat by embers that quickened to flame when the wind stirred them. By this fugitive glimmer, several warriors, evidently guards, amused themselves with Griffin's cards, softly chuckling and exclaiming.

Wasn't there some way to at least put off Corrigan's execution, delay it till he might have a chance to escape? Katie racked her brain but she could think of nothing. Cramped, cold, yet dreading the dawn, Katie lapsed into a stupor.

She was jarred from this uneasy rest by a barking voice and sharp pain in her thigh. A pock-marked, thickset warrior was kicking them. Bending, he jerked off the blanket.

Griffin sat up, swearing under his breath, and pulled on his boots. Knuckling his eyes, Jed tumbled over and tugged on the scuffed, scarred boots he usually kept so proudly polished. Hallie, still more asleep than not, clung tighter to Katie, trying to recover snugness lost when Nacho got up and the blanket vanished.

Groggily sitting up with the child still in her arms, Katie blinked as reality flooded back. A wide fan of pearl gray softened the darkness of the eastern sky. Diamond and the lieutenant still sat where Katie had last seen them. They must not have even tried to sleep. All the Apaches were on their feet, though, peering toward the northwest, talking excitedly.

The horses neighed restlessly, cantering up and down but unable to elude their herders. A rumbling like distant thunder gradually grew louder. As night waned, a far-off cloud obscured the plain south of the San Luis Mountains.

"Big herd," Nacho said.

Geronimo and the other leaders scanned the billowing dust. They glanced toward the prisoners, seemed to argue. Katie couldn't breathe. It was as if she drew mud into her lungs rather than air.

Had Beau or Larrimore decided to move a ransom herd south rather than wait for notice? Or was it rustlers with a herd stolen from across the border? "Get on your shoes, Hallie," Katie said, hastening to slip on her own and button them.

"Is — is it Papa?" Hallie whispered.

"I don't know, dear. Let's hope so."

Mickey Free translated a shouted order from Geronimo. "Try run, get shot. Stay one place." He called Corrigan and Diamond, who slowly rose and joined the others.

The Apaches were arming, most with rifles. Four ranged themselves around the prisoners. Geronimo paused to speak to the warrior nearest Corrigan. This Apache playfully jammed the barrel of his Springfield against the officer's midriff and said something his companions roared at. Katie was glad Free didn't explain.

Holding tight to Katie, Hallie gazed up with fear-widened green eyes. "Are — are they going to kill us?"

"Of course not," Katie said more boldly

575

than she felt. She was sickly positive that if whoever was raising that dust didn't succeed quickly in placating the Apaches, no prisoner would be left alive.

The herd was close enough for her to see cattle, a mass of them, advancing ahead of the dust. The shouts that carried to the spring were in English. Katie released a long-held breath. At least the men urging the cattle this way weren't Mexican thieves. Keeping Hallie consolingly close, Katie strained to see. Through the haze, she saw horsemen but couldn't tell who they were, couldn't even be sure of the color of their mounts.

But — wasn't that a *gray* one?

Her heart stopped, then plunged crazily. "There is Slim Jones," said Nacho. "I see his big red moustache. On the other side, that is Hi Phillips, I think." He sucked in his breath. "Katie! Is that not —"

Katie's heart swelled, overflowed with glowing, radiant light. "Bill! It — it's really Bill!"

Riders started the cattle milling, turned them so they went around in a great sprawling circle that shrouded them in dust. Bill rode forward, flourishing his white hat on a yucca stalk, the other hand raised to show that he held no weapon, not that it could have availed with seventy-odd Apache rifles centered on him.

As gaily confident as if he were approaching a dance, Bill reined up. His gaze swept past the warriors, fixed on Katie. A real smile broke over the reckless one. He dipped his hat in a salute before facing back to the chiefs.

Sweeping a hand toward the cattle, he pointed next at the captives, indicated that if they went *there* — indicating the San Luis — the herd would come *here*.

The chiefs consulted. Potbellied Juh yelled at the prisoners. Free went to stand beside Geronimo, who rasped a brief question. "How many cow?" the scout queried.

"Three hundred head."

How wonderful to hear Bill's voice! Katie could still scarcely believe her eyes. It was as if she had needed and wanted him so badly that she'd created a phantom. But he looked solid, and his deep tones reverberated through her.

With a buzz of eagerness, the chiefs again talked among themselves. This was ransom beyond anything they could have dreamed of, winter food and many hides for all their people in the Sierra.

"What's all the palaver about?" demanded Bill. "That's a lot of cows for three kids and five men."

After listening to another round of discussion, Free said, "How know soldiers not behind you, attack when captives gone?"

"I have eight men," returned Bill. "No soldiers, no one else. If the Apaches don't trust me, they can leave a bunch to guard us and the captives till the rest can get a day or two ahead with the cattle. We'll hand over our guns if the chiefs give their word that we'll get them back and can go home in a day or two."

The Apaches listened to this with evident surprise and gratification. They talked it over for a time, and then Geronimo gave a short answer to the scout.

"Chiefs believe you. They take cattle, you take captives. You go home." Free stopped. When he went on, his voice sounded rusty. "All but Lieutenant Corrigan. He kill kin of Geronimo. He die."

Bill's smile vanished. There was taut silence. After a moment, he said, "I will bring another hundred head of cattle for the lieutenant."

The scout turned hopefully to the chiefs. They argued hotly over the offer. Geronimo's voice kept rising. At last, Juh and the others were still, and Free passed on Geronimo's growled response.

"He say no. Not for two, three hundred cows. Lieutenant die."

Corrigan stepped forward. "You've done all you can, sir. I beg you not to say more and

578

possibly anger these savages into slaughtering everyone. If the children go free, I die content."

Diamond moved past his son. At a motion from Geronimo, the guards permitted it. Somehow, in spite of two days' hard riding and being up all night, the gambler still looked almost impeccable and his step was light as a young man's. He spoke softly to Free, so softly that no one who understood English could hear.

The scout's single black eye glittered. He asked something. Diamond replied. As Free explained to the Apaches, Geronimo, frowning in turn from Corrigan to Diamond, asked several questions, which Free relayed to the gambler.

Geronimo mulled over the answers. Finally he responded in a way that made Diamond smile. He shook hands with his son, said a few words. It looked as if he had started back to the prisoners when he halted and faced around.

Gaze fixed on Diamond, Katie hadn't seen Geronimo bring up his rifle and aim. The bullet struck Diamond in the chest, knocked him backward. With a cry, the lieutenant sprang for the chief, but Mickey Free grappled him long enough for Juh to club the officer with the butt of his rifle.

Katie and Jed ran past the guards, who didn't try to stop them. "Uncle Jack!" Jed gripped Diamond's shoulders. "Oh, Uncle Jack —"

Diamond tried to speak. Blood frothed from his mouth and nose. He raised one slender hand to Jed's curls, ruffled them and smiled. The hand went limp, fell to the earth. For a moment longer, Katie thought Diamond knew her, was trying to speak with his eyes. Then something went out of those eyes. They only stared unseeingly.

"He can't be dead!" Jed wailed.

Calling the name of his friend and teacher, he tried to lift him, but the body was too heavy. The wound in the chest wasn't big, but the ground was blood-soaked on either side; Diamond's back must have a big hole blown out of it.

Hallie ran to Jed and knelt beside him, putting her arm around him, hugging him close. When they saw nothing could be done for Diamond, Free, Griffin, and Nacho went to the lieutenant. Numbed, unable to move, Katie stayed on her knees.

Warm, strong hands closed on her shoulders. "Katie." Bill raised her to her feet, walked her toward the closest rocky hillock, where they were out of sight and earshot of the others. "Oh, Katie, darlin'!" He held her against him, face bent to her hair. "I don't know why Jack made the swap, but it was what he wanted."

Katie sobbed out the story. "But you!" she breathed, touching his cheek, even in her shocked grief full of thankfulness. "You — the Earps claimed they killed you!"

He grinned. "Kind of mistaken, weren't they?"

"But — but what —"

"Some of my friends and I did have a little shoot-out with the Earps at Iron Spring in the Whetstones. One of the men with me was killed. His face was pretty messed up, but he had black curly hair." He shrugged. "Maybe the Earps really thought it was me. We buried the man after they rode off. Struck me it was a fine time to bury Bill Radnor, too. Start over."

"And you let me worry and — and —" Katie tried to twist free, but he held her even closer.

"There was a reason, honey."

"What?"

"You're only seventeen."

"What does that have to do with it?"

He sighed. "Quite a lot. You've changed my thinkin', Katie. Things I used to do for fun aren't fun anymore. I want" — he hesitated. His sun-washed gray-blue eyes caressed her in a way that made her heart stop, turn over, and then pound furiously. "What I thought was that if I could start over — go straight and keep out of trouble for three or four years, then I could be pretty sure of going on that way for good. And if I was sure of that — well, then, I'd come back and see you."

"*See* me!"

He blushed. "Uh, yeah."

"And all that time, you were just going to let me think you were dead? Why, I — I could almost strangle you myself, Bill Radnor!"

He said doggedly, "Thinkin' I was dead would've made you more likely to find some young fella nearer your age, someone who didn't have blood on his hands. You deserve that, Katie. You still do."

Her heart sank. "What — what are you going to do?"

"Honey, I'm going away. In fact, I'd be in California now if I hadn't run into Slim Jones and heard about the raids and your gallivanting down here." He gave her a little, loving shake. "Don't you have any sense?"

Ignoring that, she pleaded, "Why can't you just settle down on your ranch and stay here?"

He shook his head. "Wouldn't work, honey girl. I've got too many enemies who'd want to hang my hide up to dry if they thought

I'd got religion and lost my touch with a six-gun. That's another thing. You've got your ranch started. It's your dream. You sure have earned it. But, Katie, I can't live here, not ever."

Convulsing inwardly, she had to admit it was true. In Cochise County, in all this border country, he would always be Lord Bill Radnor who lived by the gun. She thought of Home Mountain, her brother and sisters, fleet Steel Dusts and gentle Guernseys, all beloved, all worked for with her heart and mind and body, the sum of her whole existence.

Except for this man. Except for the harp. She could take that with her. The words of the song that voiced her love for Bill came to her lips. *"I would go, I would go with you . . . I would go between you and the crag. I would go between you and the wind. I would go between you and death —"*

"Hush, Katie!" His eyes were tormented, yet a fierce joy blazed in their depths. "I'm not worth that."

"I love you."

"Then I'm blessed. Those are the words and your sweet voice I'll hear in the darkness."

"When Rosie's older — when Melissa's grown up —"

He touched his finger to her lips. "I won't take promises from you, darlin'. When we hit the Animas Valley, I'm going one way and you're heading home."

She clutched at what he'd said. "But in four years? Maybe three? Please, Bill, please come back!"

"If I'm alive. If I've kept out of trouble. If I think I could even start to make up to you for all you'd be losing —"

She brought down his head and kissed him, wouldn't let him evade her mouth. He swept her close. She felt the length of his body, the sweetness of his mouth. No matter that he wouldn't let her pledge him in words. She pledged him with her body and all her heart and soul. If he didn't come back, she would have no other man. With a shuddering breath, he stepped away, dropped a kiss on her forehead, and led her back to their friends.

Some Apaches were already mounted and collecting the cattle, while Bill's men sat their saddles well to one side. Geronimo and the chiefs had walked out to examine this amazing ransom. Free and Griffin were helping Corrigan to his feet.

The lieutenant stumbled to his father's body. Dropping beside Jed and Hallie, he took them both in his arms. His shoulders heaved, but after a while he let the children go, reached out to close Diamond's eyes.

"I want to bury my father in our own country," he said.

Free nodded. "Chiefs leave your horses, saddles. Diamond's too — gift for son. Apache keep weapons, cartridges, supplies."

Bill helped the soldiers wrap Diamond in one of Bill's blankets, then tie him across Raven's saddle when Nacho led the horse to them. The herders had obligingly cut out the Steel Dust mares, Shiloh, and the other horses belonging to Katie's group. As quickly as their saddles could be located in the jumble of gear and tossed on their mounts, those who were left of the rescue party and Hallie and Jed rode out of the camp and away from the dust churned up by the departing herd.

No one looked back.

It was noon when they buried John Diamond on a slope overlooking the Animas Valley and the blue range far away where he had found death, but his son, too. Bill and his men helped mound rocks, and Corrigan, with a knife borrowed from Bill, made a sturdy cross of peeled branches. On it he carved:

JOHN TREVATHAN
Beloved Father of James Corrigan
1832–1881

So John Diamond, gambler, was buried under his true name, mourned by his son and friends. Jed sobbed against Katie, who was crying, too, and didn't try to stop. Diamond had been to her a dear and faithful friend. She would always miss him but was unspeakably grateful that he died reconciled with his son.

When the cross was firmly embedded among rocks too heavy to be washed away by torrential rains, the lieutenant looked helplessly at Katie. "Do you know some words? Some scripture?"

All she could think of were the Lord's Prayer and the phrases she'd spoken over her parents. Swallowing, she bowed her head. "In my Father's house are many mansions: if it were not so, I would have told you. I go to prepare a place for you." She had to stop, take several deep breaths before she could begin the prayer. Bill and several of the cowboys joined in along with Corrigan, Nacho, and Jed.

"Can't we sing him a song?" asked Jed, rubbing his eyes against his sleeve. "He sure liked 'Loch Lomond.' "

With that old Highland song of a soul traveling the spirit road home, they said farewell to John Diamond. Bill helped Katie up on Chili, whom she was riding now while leading Tom's pinto. Poor Chili, to lose two colts

— perhaps Larrimore would lend them a stallion —

Katie's thought skittered like storm-driven leaves. She couldn't bear to think why Bill was looking up at her like this, why his men, waving and calling good-byes were already looping away.

"Bill — oh, Bill, please —"

He gripped her hands till they hurt. "Katie, listen to me, darlin'. I'd do anything in the world you wanted — except stay. Won't a day pass, probably not even an hour, when I won't think about you, try to imagine what you're doin'."

"You — you promised to come back!"

"I will, if I'm alive and can make myself into a halfway decent man. But, honey, if you meet some nice young guy, don't fret about me. Do what will make you happy and I'll be happy, too."

"I won't —" she cried. He brushed his fingers against her lips.

"No promises, sweetheart, except this from me. It's no promise, just a fact. I'll always love you."

He kissed her hand and strode to Shadow. Mounted, he chuckled. "That three hundred head of cattle wear the Pitchfork brand. I didn't have time to find them somewhere else. Reckon Ed won't kick about that and you've heard the last of his tryin' to get appointed your guardian. He'd be ashamed to pull that now, and even if he wasn't, folks wouldn't let him get away with it. Give Rosie and Melissa a kiss for me."

"Bill! Bill, take Shiloh! We were going to give him to you in the spring when he could carry you a while." Katie turned to Jed. "Weren't we?"

"Yes," Jed nodded. "We all want to. Take him, Bill."

"You keep him for me," Bill said. "That would be as big a favor as givin' him to me in the first place."

He waved a last time, looking the way he had when Katie had first seen him in the desert. He had saved them then, and now he had again. Katie couldn't bear to watch him out of sight.

I will go, I will go with you, she vowed to him. Gazing at the cross among the rocks, she thought, *I never will forget you, John. Jed won't. And neither, now, will your son.*

Reining the mare northward, she started for Home Mountain.

XXIII

Ginger danced along the crest trail, one ear forward, one pricked back to hear Katie's softest word. The golden sorrel was Chili's foal by Lightning, the Steel Dust stallion Ed Larrimore had insisted on giving the MacLeods when they'd accept no payment for going after Hallie. Even now, four years later, Katie smiled wryly to remember how their little party had met him as they rode out of Skeleton Canyon — him and an assorted army of miners and cowboys.

Holding his daughter close, he'd looked at Katie and cleared his throat several times before he growled, "There's no way I can ever thank you. I've acted like a low-down sneakin' polecat. Don't have the gall to ask you to forgive me, but — well, I hope you know you'll have no more trouble with me."

He'd turned red when he heard three hundred Pitchfork cattle had been bartered for the captives, but after a moment, he swallowed and shrugged. "I'd give every cow, every horse I've got, for Hallie." He shook Jed's hand. "Son, I sure hope you'll come to work for me when you're a tad older. You'll be the kind of man I'd trust with anything."

Jed had gone to work at the Pitchfork last year when he turned fourteen. Hallie worshipped him. It was pretty clear that he'd one day run the Pitchfork, so it was a good thing that Tom Buford had fit in so well at Home Mountain. There were thirty cows in the dairy herd, and every few weeks someone drove to Willcox with pounds of the pale golden thistle-patterned butter, fresh milk and buttermilk, all packed in salt to keep fresh, and in season, vegetables and fruit. Bill's gift apple and pear trees had flourished, shading the yard between house and shed, and the orchard planted in the spring of 'eighty-two was starting to bear its first plums, peaches, and apples.

Nacho's stone house stood where his old tent had. Katie had been glad when he decided to build it; it meant he felt at home now and would never leave.

Tom and Melissa had been married that spring on Melissa's seventeenth birthday and were expecting a baby early in the new year. It was true they were young, but it was clear there'd never be anyone else for either of them. Rosie was as elated as the expectant mother and disciplined her almost five-year-old fingers to sew tiny garments.

"I know I'm the baby's aunt," she said solemnly. "But I feel like she's my sister." With her curly dark hair and deep brown eyes, Rosie looked the way Mary MacLeod must have as a child. She climbed now into Katie's lap and hugged her. "It's the way you and M'liss are my big sisters, Katie, but like mamas, too. I *can* be an aunt and a sister, can't I?"

"I don't see why not, honey." Katie gave this small sister a kiss and chuckled. "The main thing is to love and take care of her and help her grow up."

"Like you did M'liss and Jed and me?"

Those eyes so like her mother's gazed trustingly into Katie's. In a strange, wonderful, healing way, through Rosie, Katie felt she had a second chance to know her mother, though never, after that night in the Mexican mountains, had Katie doubted that Mary loved her.

Kissing Rosie, Katie thought back, sighed, and laughed. "I had to grow up, too, Rosie. I guess you could say we all helped each other do that — and we had a lot of help from our friends." Rosie couldn't remember one of the best, the man whose mound and cross faced the broad plain and far-off mountains of Mexico.

He had a namesake now, John Trevathan Corrigan, not quite two years old. James Corrigan had called on Katie several times, once to report that he'd taken Private Harris's things to his sister, once when on a scouting expedition into Mexico with General Crook. The lieutenant had invited her to a dance at Fort Bowie — he'd arranged for her to stay with a fellow officer's family — but Katie had declined, though making it clear that, as a friend, he was always welcome at Home Mountain. A year later, she had gone to his wedding just before Captain and Mrs. Corrigan were assigned to Fort Sill in Indian Territory. They had promised that when Johnny was old enough, he could, if he wanted to, spend his summers at Home Mountain.

Thinking of the baby M'liss and Tom would have, Katie allowed herself to daydream a bit. Wouldn't it be nice if the child was a girl and she and Johnny —

Maundering on like an aged spinster! At almost twenty-one, Katie sometimes felt like one. Bill had been gone nearly four years. Not a word from him or about him. In the second year, she'd started watching the horizon. In the third, she'd tried to look as pretty as she could even when doing messy chores, just in case he rode up. As this fourth year wore on, she began to fear he wasn't coming at all.

He might be dead. He might love someone else, though she refused to consider that horrid possibility for more than the briefest moment. Or, heaven forbid, perhaps he'd lapsed back into his old ways. Once Tom and Melissa were married, Katie would have gone looking for him if she'd had the faintest glimmering of where he was, but he could have been anywhere from Mexico to Alaska. When the Galeyville smelter burned in 'eighty-three, the mine had closed and the town was now abandoned except for a few old prospectors. Bride had gone to Leadville, Colorado, to open a fancy restaurant with her savings. Conquering any hurt she felt that Katie knew Bill was alive when he hadn't let her, Bride, know it, Bride had promised to watch out for him and write Katie if she heard about a man of his description.

Bride's first letter said she was marrying Liam Schaughnessy, her former boarder. He and his brother Pat had struck a rich vein of silver on their claim and were wealthy men. The next letter sent a daguerreotype of twin babies, Melissa Rose and Mary Katharine, the Mary being after Bride's mother. Bride wrote every few months, but there'd been no mention of Bill.

Tombstone hadn't vanished like Galeyville, but when declining profits led to a cut in wages from four to three dollars a day, miners went on strike and the Hudson bank closed. Troops from Fort Huachuca were called in to keep order, and Cornish pumps were installed to get rid of the water flooding the tunnels, but the glory days were gone. Only a few thousand people remained in what had been the largest, most prosperous town in Arizona Territory. Katie didn't want to see the place as it was now; in fact, she'd never gone back after that magic birthday, though she'd been invited often to perform. It would hurt too much to visit the places that she'd been with Bill. The family did its shopping in Willcox, and several times a year Katie played at the Norton Opera House or in Colonel Hooker's big adobe non-denominational church.

So much had happened, so much had changed, that it made Katie feel that twenty years had passed instead of four. The Earps had stood trial in November of 'eighty-one but had been acquitted, to the anger of those who called the killing of the MacLowerys and Billy Clanton the same as murder. In March of 'eighty-two, Morgan Earp was shot from cover. His brothers killed the three suspects. Rather than stand trial, they and Holliday rode out of town, Cochise County, and the Territory.

The rustlers had also vanished. Johnny Ringo was buried down in the valley below. He'd been found shot to death under a giant oak in July of 'eighty-two. Officially, it was ruled suicide, but many thought it murder.

Geronimo with his followers had repeatedly broken off the reservation, leaving a trail of death and destruction all the way to the Sierra Madre, where he then preyed on Mexicans. There could be no peace and security on either side of the border till he was dead or captured, but so far he had eluded both U.S. and Mexican troops.

Ginger had reached the end of the mountain, the ridge from which Bill had shown Katie what had become her world. Slipping down from the saddle, Katie fed the mare an apple and took a juicy, tartly sweet bite as she surveyed Home Mountain Ranch.

The cattle grazed nearer the buildings, but the horses, eighteen of them, with the summer's foals, were on the other side of the creek among the scattered oaks, burnished shades of copper, red-gold, and mahogany. Colonel Hooker and Ed Larrimore vied in buying as many as she'd sell and took them three and four at a time so they'd stay with companions, but it was a wrench to part with them. Two fillies and a male colt of Shiloh's siring raced across the slopes, so entrancing that it took a moment for Katie to rouse to the sound of approaching hoofs.

Heart thudding, she grabbed the Winchester from its scabbard and moved behind a ledge. The hoofs crunched just around the bend. Katie looped Ginger's bridle around her arm and raised the rifle. Into her sights, mounted on Shiloh, came Bill.

Was she dreaming? Had she wanted him so much that she'd summoned up his image? He was on the ground in a twinkling, laughing as he took the rifle and slid it into the sheath. "So that's the greeting you give me, Katie MacLeod!"

She ran into his arms. He was real, he was here, his mouth was warm and hard, melting her into him so that his heart seemed to beat within her body. "Oh, Katie, Katie," he murmured at last, smoothing her hair, caressing her face and throat, gazing at her as if to fill his eyes. "You were a rose just budding when I left. Now the petals are open. Lordy, are you beautiful!"

"If that's a fancy way of saying I'm an old maid, it's your own fault," she said, laughing, crying. "What took you so long?"

"Oh, I've been to Alaska and just about every place west of here, honey. Had to save up honest money for us — and I've done that." He took her face between his hands and turned it up to him. "Katie, are you sure? When I stopped at the house, the kids seemed to think you'd be glad to see me — just think, Melissa almost a mama — but maybe they don't know how you really feel." He nodded down at the ranch, the orchard, fields, cattle, and horses. "It's your dream, Katie, why you came all the way from Texas. I know how you love the young 'uns and your Steel Dusts, even the doggoned cows. Are you sure you can leave it?"

With pride and a sense of rending loss, Katie looked down at what she'd helped to build, at the place filled with all the happenings of the last five years. Home Mountain, oh, Home Mountain!

"I'll always love it," she told Bill. "Just as I'll love Jed and M'liss and Rosie and Tom and Nacho. But they can do very well without me now. In fact, I'm beginning to feel a little in the way." She laughed shakily and said the old words. *"I would go, I would go with you — "*

When that kiss finally ended, Bill said huskily, "Anyhow, darlin', it won't be across that Irish Sea. I've got us a place in southern Colorado about as close as I figgered was safe. You can visit the kids and Rosie can come stay with us sometimes, and those little nieces and nephews we're goin' to have. And it's only fair, like M'liss and Tom said when they made me ride Shiloh up to fetch you, that you take some of the Steel Dusts with you. What I have goin' is a horse ranch, so they'd fit right in. Shucks, we can even herd three or four Guernseys up there if you want."

And she could take the harp. Katie touched his face, letting her fingertips smooth the crinkly lines at the corners of his eyes, the deeper ones graven at mouth and nose. "You were thinking about me," she said. "Even if it did take you too long to come back! Let me tell you this, Bill Radnor! You're never getting out of my sight again unless I know exactly where you're going and how soon you'll be home!"

He grinned. "You already sound like a wife. Let's go make you one so I can get some sweetness along with my scoldin'. I brought a preacher out from Willcox with me so's we could get married in front of your family. Tom's rode over to the Pitchfork to get Jed — Hallie, too, if she wants to come. Won't hurt if Ed knows I'm alive, even if the last cows I ever stole were three hundred head of his."

"You've thought of everything," Katie said, cheek against his heart. "But Bill, this place up here is special, where you brought me to pick out our land. I've come here all these years to remember that, feel close to you. Could we — do you think — after we're married, could we come back up here?"

His startled look changed to one of delight. "Why not, my darlin'? I've got a bedroll and there's grass under that big pine. Guess no one will blame us much for sneakin' off from the party."

Meeting his kiss, Katie thought this was the finest wedding day and bridal bed, above the world and under the sun, that anyone could have.

Author's Note

This story began to form when Peggy Bass told us about the girlhood of her great-aunt whose mother brought her fatherless children to Whitetail Canyon and made a ranch-home there at the turn of the century. As I tried out and discarded various ideas, I decided to bring a family of orphans into this region back in the dramatic year of 1881. My Katie is solely born of my imagination, but it was Peggy's stories of another indomitable Katie that struck a spark in my mind.

The location of Home Mountain Ranch came from a hike along the ridge from where all the canyon, flanking mountains and plain, stretched out like a huge relief map. Though I have lived in the Chiricahuas for nine years, I hadn't before found a story to place here. Now it began to come together. Years ago, Arch Steele, a noted newspaper correspondent, was leaving the region and gave me a treasure box of material he'd amassed on the area when he'd planned to write a book about it. I saved it, not peeking, till Katie's adventures began to form in my mind. Arch's collection furnished much useful information, and I am in his debt.

This book is a mixture of careful research and free-wheeling rearrangement of same. Was I to leave out my favorite (indeed, *only* admired) general of the Indian-fighting army because Crook, in 1881, was with the Department of the Platte? He did return in 1882 to Arizona. Tom Horn was at this time not a scout and perhaps not even a packer but was a companion of Seiber and Free. Crook's views on how to deal with the Apaches are almost verbatim quotes from his letters.

Bill Radnor is based on Curly Bill Brocius, who did many of the things attributed to my Radnor — collected taxes with Breakenridge, voted San Simon's barnyard critters, rode two hundred miles shot through the hips, championed a widow, and so on. By all accounts, he was a reckless, generous, fun-loving person, though he was also a rustler and killed men. Wyatt Earp claims to have killed him (but in March of 1882, not late October of 1881 as I have it in this book), but did not produce a body when he tried to claim the reward. Several people who knew Bill claim to have seen him after his alleged death, and I'd like to think he did go to Montana, or Mexico, as the legends run, marry, and live out his life as an honest family man.

The Reed cabin, built in 1879, is a few miles up the canyon from my house, the dwelling of the director of the Southwest Research Station of the Museum of Natural History. I have an account of Stephen Reed written by his descendant, Walter Reed, which tells of this period in these mountains. Galeyville is gone, but some of its buildings had a second life in Paradise, the mining town that sprang up a few miles away in 1902, and some of *those* buildings are reincarnated in Portal, where I get my mail.

For the flavor of the times from a cowboy's view, I benefited from *Around Western Campfires* by Joseph Axford (Tucson: University of Arizona Press, 1969). *Arizona Nights* by Stewart Edward White (New York: Grosset and Dunlap, 1907) has the most pungent, genuinely funny, and unrestrained frontier language I've encountered. It's good that a new edition of this delightful book is now available from Rio Grande Press in Glorieta, New Mexico. For horse facts and lore, I referred to *The Horse of the Americas* by Robert M. Denhardt (Norman: University of Oklahoma Press, 1975) and *Fabulous Quarter Horse: Steel Dust* by Wayne Gard (New York: Duell, Sloan and Pearce, 1958). Frontier ministers receive a lively salute in Ross Phares's *Bible in Pocket, Gun in Hand* (Lincoln: University of Nebraska Press, 1971). There's also considerable about them in *Saloons of the Old West* by Richard

Erdoes (New York: Knopf, 1979). *Black Powder and Hand Steel* by Otis E. Young, Jr. (Norman: University of Oklahoma Press, 1976) tells much about miners as well as their work. Their food and life in the camps are described in *Bacon, Beans, and Galantines* by Joseph R. Conlin (Reno: University of Nevada Press, 1968). *Folksongs and Folklore of South Uist* by Margaret Shaw (Aberdeen: Aberdeen University Press, 1986) has a wealth of Hebridean traditions and songs. *Billy King's Tombstone* by C. L. Sonnichsen (Tucson: University of Arizona Press, 1972) is a fascinating look at life north of Allen Street. It has the only understandable account of jerk-line drivers I've ever found. *Helldorado* by William M. Breakenridge (Glorieta: Rio Grande Press, 1970) has much about Galeyville, Curly Bill, and the turbulent era during which he was deputy sheriff. *Tombstone* by Walter Noble Burns (Garden City: Doubleday, 1929) also has tales of the outlaws and Galeyville. Descendants of some of Burns's informants say he tailored the facts a bit, but this is still a colorful picture of Cochise County in its heyday.

For cavalry equipment and uniforms, I'm indebted to Randy Steffen's monumental *The Horse Soldier*, volume III (Norman: University of Oklahoma Press, 1978). *Mickey Free: Manhunter* by A. Kinney Griffith (Caldwell:

Caxton, 1969), makes fascinating reading. The author, who knew the old scout and did exhaustive research, differs considerably from most authorities in his depiction of the man. I've followed his description. For details of the amazing foray led by an ancient warrior, I followed on *Nana's Raid* by Steven H. Lekson (El Paso: Texas Western Press, 1987).

To detail Katie's journey into Mexico, I've drawn on the many times I've hiked Skeleton Canyon and two accounts of Chief Loco's flight to Mexico in the spring of 1882. The Apache point of view is given by Jason Betzinez in *I Fought with Geronimo* (New York: Bonanza Books, 1959). The cavalry's pursuit led by General George Forsyth almost led to an international incident, but it was let pass because a "hot pursuit" agreement had almost been completed. *General Crook and the Sierra Madre Adventure* by Dan S. Thrapp (Norman: University of Oklahoma Press, 1972) describes this escapade. Other useful works were Donald E. Worcester's *The Apaches* (Norman: University of Oklahoma Press, 1979); *Western Apache Raiding and Warfare*, notes by Grenville Goodwin, edited by Keith H. Basso (Tucson: University of Arizona Press, 1971); and *Apaches: A History and Culture Portrait* by James L. Haley (Garden City: Doubleday, 1981).

Firsthand experience has taught me something about native foods. I've also drawn on Carolyn Niethammer's invaluable *American Indian Food and Lore* (New York: MacMillan, 1974) and on *By The Prophet of the Earth: Ethnobotany of the Pima,* by L. S. M. Curtin (Tucson: University of Arizona Press, 1984).

I found helpful background at the Arizona Pioneer Historical Society Library in Tucson, and Myrtle Kraft of the Portal Library and the Cochise County Library staff were most obliging in locating books I needed. Reference librarian Kimberly Holman also helped track down some details about Tombstone.

Alden Hayes, who is writing an anecdotal history of the Cave Creek region, most kindly read the manuscript. From his experience as a rancher, archaeologist, and long-time student of the Chiricahuas, he advised on every aspect of the story, and though I didn't follow all of his suggestions, the book is infinitely more accurate because of him. He must not, however, be blamed for any of my mistakes.

My good neighbor, Dr. Sally Hoyt Spofford, read the book for birds and natural history. Her husband, Dr. Walter Spofford, advised on firearms. Dr. Don Worcester, who raises Arabian horses, helped me with some fine points on horses. My husband, Bob Morse, also checked for natural history and general plausibility. The comments of all these experts have enriched my story, and Katie and I thank them!

I would also thank my capable editors, Hope Dellon, Carolyn Marino, and Karen Trimble. And appreciation is always due Claire Smith, my agent and my friend.

Cave Creek Canyon
The Chiricahua Mountains
February 27, 1990